SHOOTOUT ALONG THE RIO GRANDE

Heart racing, Jeff jumped his sorrel horse into the water. Then he paused, for he heard a roar of fury from Booth. The cowboy aimed and fired his rifle. Freed rocked back in the saddle and grabbed his left arm. Booth spurred toward Freed's men, firing his rifle again.

"Kelly," Jeff shouted. "They'll kill you!"

It was futile. Perhaps Booth did not hear him, or perhaps he chose not to. Rage had pushed judgment aside.

Jeff saw a flash from among the horsemen and heard the shot. Booth's horse seemed to stop in midstride, then went down heavily.

Jeff turned in Booth's direction and held his body tense, expecting another shot from among Freed's men. . . .

Also by Elmer Kelton

SLAUGHTER
HONOR AT DAYBREAK
THE DAY THE COWBOYS QUIT
THE TIME IT NEVER RAINED
THE GOOD OLD BOYS
THE WOLF AND THE BUFFALO
STAND PROUD
DARK THICKET
THE MAN WHO RODE MIDNIGHT
BOWIE'S MINE
JOE PEPPER
MANHUNTERS
EYES OF THE HAWK
MASSACRE AT GOLIAD
LONG WAY TO TEXAS
LLANO RIVER
HANGING JUDGE
HORSEHEAD CROSSING
AFTER THE BUGLES
WAGONTONGUE

THE FAR CANYON

ELMER KELTON

BANTAM BOOKS
NEW YORK · TORONTO · LONDON · SYDNEY · AUCKLAND

All of the characters in this book are fictitious,
and any resemblance to actual persons, living or
dead, is purely coincidental.

This edition contains the complete text
of the original hardcover edition.
NOT ONE WORD HAS BEEN OMITTED.

THE FAR CANYON

A Bantam Book / published in association
with Doubleday

PUBLISHING HISTORY
Doubleday edition published August 1994
Bantam edition / November 1995

ISBN 0-553-57259-8

Published simultaneously in the United States and Canada

Bantam Books are published by Bantam Books, a division of
Bantam Doubleday Dell Publishing Group, Inc. Its trademark,
consisting of the words "Bantam Books" and the portrayal of a
rooster, is Registered in U.S. Patent and Trademark Office and in
other countries. Marca Registrada. Bantam Books, 1540 Broadway,
New York, New York 10036.

PRINTED IN THE UNITED STATES OF AMERICA

OPM   0 9 8 7 6 5 4 3 2 1

*This novel is dedicated to our daughter Kathy,
our sons Gary and Steve, and their families.*

THE FAR
CANYON

ONE

Texas high plains, June 1874.

Crow Feather vaguely remembered that he had been shot.

He awakened to the buzzing of flies and a tickling sensation as they landed to feed on the raw wound where the bullet had struck him. He had no notion of time, no idea how long he had lain in the cool, shallow waters of the creek. He could open his eyes only a little against the blinding glare of a late-afternoon sun. The trees along the bank were but a blur, swaying in one direction and then in another. Moving his hand to where a fire blazed in his side, he felt the soothing flow of water over it. Or was it blood? He tried to raise the hand and see, but he could not bring it up so far.

Fleeting fragments of memory teased him. He could not be certain what was real and what was dream, or perhaps not a dream at all but a vision. If it was a true vision, it might be brought by the bear, the guardian spirit which had shown him the path he should travel as a Comanche warrior. He thought once that he saw his two wives standing over him. He called their names, White Deer first, then Rabbit. Giving him no answer, they turned and climbed up away from the creek, beckoning him to follow. He could not bring his body to move. They were gone, and he knew they had been an illusion.

It came to him that he had taken a bullet from a wagon camp, from the hunters of buffalo. He remembered that he had ridden with a war party which had charged recklessly down upon the *teibos*, the hair-faces. The others had expected an easy victory. They would not listen to his warning that the signs had turned against them. The medicine of the great buffalo-killing rifles had been stronger than their own. The warriors with him had gone down. Only he had remained a-horseback, with a burning hole torn in his side.

He had a vague recollection that it was not a man who had fired the shot. In the moment before the flash and the searing blow, he had seen a woman holding the rifle . . . a white woman with long dark hair in which the sun had cast a tinge of red. Almost never had he seen a woman with the buffalo wagons. And a woman with red hair! Who would have believed such a thing?

Now Man Who Stole The Mules was dead. All of the raiding party were dead except Crow Feather. That his frightened horse had carried him this far and had dropped him in the water was probably the work of the bear spirit.

He wondered that the white men had not followed and killed him. He wondered also that he had not drowned. Either he had fallen on his back or he had managed to turn over so that his face was out of the water; he could not remember. He tried again to open his eyes, but the sun was too bright. Or was it the sun? Could it be that he was dead like the others, that the light was meant to guide him toward the spirit land from which no one ever returned except in the form of a ghost?

Years ago, as a youth seeking to cross over into manhood through a grueling vision quest, Crow Feather had seen the apparition of a great bear in the ordeal's fourth and final dark night. The bear had imparted to him its wisdom and its strength. He called now to the bear for guidance, but he received no answer. Many times of late he had called to the bear. It had not heard or, if it heard, had not chosen to respond. He had been tortured by a fear that he had offended the bear spirit and turned it against him. A warrior who lost his medicine was a forlorn soul wandering in darkness, naked and without defense against whatever evil wind might search him out.

He managed to open his eyes a little, to try and see clearly the branches of a tree extending out over the creek above him. Turning his head, he strangled as water rushed into his mouth, his nostrils. It came to him that he must somehow work his way up and out from here. He called again to the bear for help. Somehow he found strength to pull himself up onto the side that was not wounded and began inching his way from the water.

The flies troubled him, settling in the wound and on its edges, some biting the raw flesh. His feet still in the water, he scooped up a handful of mud and pressed it against the place where the bullet had struck. The contact sent him into spasms of blinding pain, for the impact of the bullet had broken some of his ribs. The bullet had driven through the flint-hard bullhide shield he had held against his body, and through the shield's heavy padding of buffalo hair. In the past that shield had turned away other bullets, and arrows flung against him by the blood-enemy Apache. But in those fights an approving bear spirit had wrapped its protective powers around him like a blanket. That protection seemed now to have deserted him.

Perhaps not altogether. He found a second hole, this one in his back, where the bullet had gone out. At least it was not still in his body, festering, working its black powers against him. Probably the shield had stolen much of its force. His ribs had deflected the partially spent slug from his vitals. He packed mud against this wound also, that the flies would not find it. At every movement he clenched his teeth and forced down a cry that struggled for release. A warrior's pride did not easily permit such a breach of stoicism. Even if no one else could hear, *he* would know.

He felt himself passing in and out of consciousness. At times he thought he heard White Deer calling. Then he would realize she was far away, in the camp where the rest of the band awaited the return of its warriors. He wondered, when he was rational, why he had not also heard Rabbit in his dreams. She was the youngest of the two sisters he had married, the most pleasant to his eyes. But White Deer was the more serious of the pair, the one he could depend upon to see that his lodge was properly raised, that the meat he brought was preserved for the lean times, that the children were watched over. She was the one he had married first, the one who sat beside him in the lodge. It was fitting that her voice be the one he heard.

He fell easily into a dream. He was on his favorite horse, leading other hunters in a surround, plunging his arrows between the ribs of buffalo forced to run in an ever-tightening circle. Somewhere beyond sight, the women and the children and the old men waited to commence the joyous skinning and cutting of meat. This was a good hunt, and many buffalo fell to the young men's arrows, the thrust of their lances.

Then, so suddenly he gasped in surprise, there were no buffalo, none that were alive. He found himself riding among their whitening bones, nostrils offended by the sharp odor of rotting flesh. Anger stirred like spoiled meat trying to fight its way up from his stomach. This was the work of the *teibo* hide hunters, the white men who came down from the north with their rifles and their knives and their wagons. They took the skins, leaving most of the meat for the wolves and the flies and the maggots. They were dark-spirited people who had no respect for the Comanche or their cattle, who gave no thought to the children and the women and the old left hungry. It was the warriors' duty to kill as many of these invaders as they could reach and drive the others back to wherever the steel rails of the iron horse had come from.

As his periods of consciousness lengthened, Crow Feather remembered that he had been part of a huge expedition which had sought days ago to overwhelm a new wagon village the hair-faces had built just north of the Canadian River. The raiders had been mostly Comanche, but Kiowa had ridden with them, and Cheyenne. Boldly they had charged against the white-man houses with the rising sun at their backs, expecting to catch their prey asleep. But their medicine had failed them. The white men's great shoot-today-kill-tomorrow rifles slaughtered many and drove the rest reeling back in confusion and dismay.

Bristling for vengeance, Crow Feather had ridden away with one of many small war parties which splintered off, determined to visit punishment upon scattered hunting camps wherever they might find them. But they had found one too many. Now he lay in the water and mud, too weak from loss of blood to bring himself to his feet. He would die here and be meat for the wolves, and his wives would never know where he had fallen.

He slept, or lost consciousness again; he could not discern which. He dreamed of the last fight, of the woman with the red in her hair who had brought him to this.

He became aware, somehow, of men's voices, speaking in low tones. He brought his eyes partway open and saw two men leaning over him, feathers tied in their braided black hair, their faces painted with the colors of war. His heart gave a small leap. Blinking to clear his vision, he saw that these were not enemies. They were warriors of the People, Comanche like himself. But he did not know them. The faces were not of his band.

One of the men passed his shield to the other and knelt. "We feared you were dead. Can you move, brother?"

With difficulty Crow Feather found voice. "I cannot bring my feet beneath me."

He felt hands washing away the mud he had daubed on the wound. Gritting his teeth against the pain, he thought the ragged edges of the broken ribs must be punching against his vitals.

The one who examined him said, "We have wounded of our own, and we have buried several dead. This has not been a good day."

The man who held two shields declared, "But we

have damaged the white men. They are loading their wagons and leaving."

Crow Feather found consciousness elusive. He was too confused to absorb all they were telling him. "The *teibos* . . . they are going?" It seemed too much to hope for.

"They are moving toward the wagon village where we fought the big battle."

"But we did not win that fight."

"They are frightened like rabbits. We think they will soon leave the wagon village also and go north to where they came from."

For a moment Crow Feather entertained a fantasy about catching the hunters at the wagon village and annihilating them. But he knew it was a futile thought. If the great gathering of warriors had been unable to defeat a handful forted up behind the walls, what chance would they have to overcome a far larger number? But he took some comfort in the knowledge that the invaders were withdrawing from the People's land.

The warriors who had found him had several extra horses taken from hide hunters. Two of the men made a travois of poles from the creek-bank timber and tied it to a tractable dun-colored animal with saddle marks on its back. Gently as they could, they carried Crow Feather up from the water. The movement racked him with pain, but he saw that he was not alone. Two other men were being dragged on similar travois behind horses. The white men's rifles had exacted a heavy toll. Crow Feather was placed upon blankets tied across the two poles.

"We have far to travel," said the one he had first seen. "It will not be easy for you."

Not since the *teibos* had invaded the People's land had anything been easy for Crow Feather. He had to suppress a cry as the dun began to move and the ends of the poles bumped across the uneven ground. He wondered if he would survive to see the sun go down. The agony drove him out of consciousness, into a half-real world where nothing was quite as he had known it. He saw the woman with red hair again, firing the shot that would bring him down. She was much closer this time. He could see her face more clearly than before. He would remember that face for however long the spirits allowed him to live.

He saw White Deer wandering around the white-man houses where they had fought and lost the great battle. She was calling, but he had no voice to answer. He saw Rabbit lying still as death, eyes lifeless and sunken, face haggard and without color. He reached to touch her, but she was gone. Where she had lain, he saw the decaying remains of a buffalo, stripped of its shaggy robe. He saw white men departing with their hide-laden wagons, signaling to him that they would be back.

Anguished, Crow Feather decided this was a true vision. The white man was going, but he would not stay away. He would return to despoil the grand, infinite prairieland of Crow Feather's people.

Out of his tormented dream came an idea that would evolve into fixation. The woman with the red hair had been some kind of spirit, or a messenger from the spirits. She might have been sent to do him evil, or she might have saved his life. Had she not wounded him and turned him back, he would have been cut to pieces by the other guns.

Perhaps someday he would meet her again and determine whether she was evil or good. If evil, he could kill her as she had tried to kill him. If good, that would mean the bear spirit smiled upon him after all.

Two

Kansas plains, August 1874.

Lying belly-down in the brittle, summer-dried grass, Jeff Layne wiped his sleeve against gritty perspiration that tried to roll into his eye. He sighted along the barrel of his saddle gun as a small band of antelope advanced by short stages, yielding one moment to apprehension, the next to curiosity. A little to his right, a steel ramrod stood with one end pushed a few inches into the ground. Tied to the upper end, a white handkerchief lifted and fell with the vagaries of the prairie wind.

Flagging of antelope was an old ruse the white man had learned from the Indian, who took advantage of the pronghorns' natural inquisitiveness about the new or unusual to draw them within arrow range. The animals approached in a ragged single file, large brown eyes alert, ears nervously poked forward. A dominant old doe was their leader, but Jeff aligned his sights on a young female in good flesh. Either she was barren or had lost her baby so that her body no longer suffered the stress of producing milk.

He expelled a breath, then squeezed the trigger. The stock shoved hard against his shoulder as the doe went down kicking. Through the black smoke he watched the rest of the antelope break and run, white rumps bobbing

as they fled. They circled in single file, cutting in behind
him at long range. He arose stiffly, for he had lain too long
waiting for the antelope to come close. He pressed a hand
against the hip where his strained position had caused a
ten-year-old war wound to throb. He had always suspected a fragment remained there from the Union bullet
that had taken him out of the war.

He limped to the fallen doe and cut her throat to
hasten the end of her pain as well as to drain blood from
the carcass. "Sorry, girl," he said, wiping the razor-sharp
blade on her hide, then on his britches, "but the camp can
use fresh meat."

It had been a long time since he had taken any pleasure in killing, but it did not trouble his conscience when
there was need for food. He retrieved his ramrod and
handkerchief and reloaded the rifle. It had been a while
since Indian trouble had been reported this near to Dodge
City, but long experience made him careful. He took a
sweeping look across the open plain. He lacked only a
little now in reaching forty. He had every intention of
making it there, and then some.

It pleased him that his tall sorrel horse remained
ground-hitched some distance back. It had shied a bit at
the gunshot, but it had made no move to run away. He
had bought the animal in Dodge a few days ago to replace
a favorite lost on the buffalo range far to the south. The
seller had given him all the assurances he thought Jeff
might want to hear, but Jeff classed a horse trader's word
only marginally higher than that of politicians. It was not
so much that they lied outright; it was just that they often
left out important elements of the truth. He deplored the
vice, but recognized it as a fact of life.

Gutting the doe, he watched the wagon leave the
Dodge City–Wichita trail and bump across the prairie
toward him, its hoops bare like ribs in a buffalo skeleton.
A man and a woman shared the seat, and a horseman rode
alongside, his considerable bulk slumped comfortably in
the saddle. Two more horses trailed, halter ropes tied to
the wagon.

Watching the young couple, Jeff forced down a rising envy, which he considered a futile and draining weakness. Nigel and Arletta Smithwick sat so close together that there would have been room for Jeff to join them on the seat, or perhaps even fat Cap Doolittle. Scarcely more than a week had passed since the two had taken their wedding vows before Parson Parkhill in Dodge.

Though they considered Jeff their best friend, even he would admit that they were an oddly matched pair. Smithwick no longer looked the educated Englishman that he was. His skin had become deeply tanned, and he wore the same plain store-shelf clothing as most other men in the buffalo-hunting camps. Nevertheless, he betrayed his background the moment he spoke. He talked as if he were reading out of the dusty, leather-bound books from which he had acquired most of his early assumptions about life. A year on the frontier had turned many of those assumptions upside down.

Arletta, by contrast, was an untutored Ohio farm girl, her only schooling a harsh and demanding outdoor existence which had given her a strong grip on reality. Her language was ungrammatical but usually went to the point like an arrow centering a target. Though she read slowly and poorly, she had a natural aptitude with figures. She could do sums in her head faster than most merchants and hide buyers could work them on paper. Not often had she been bested in a trade.

Whatever their cultural dissimilarities, the Smithwicks had one vital element in common, a fierce attraction one for the other. So long as they shared that, Jeff would not give a Confederate dollar for the differences.

Cap Doolittle spurred his horse up ahead of the wagon, dismounting slowly and with care for bones that had supported too much weight for too long. Like Jeff, he had left Texas years earlier as a drover, helping push someone else's Longhorn cattle northward up the trail to the shining new rails in Kansas. Where Jeff had capitalized on his proficiency with a rifle to become a professional hunter, Cap had become a camp cook.

He spat a string of tobacco juice, then rubbed a sleeve across a generous moustache the color of rusted metal with a mottling of gray. "Close as they got, you could've shot half the bunch."

"One ought to carry us to Wichita. Any more than that would be a loss in this heat." Jeff had shot thousands of buffalo for nothing more than the hides, worth just two or three dollars apiece at the railroad in Dodge. The waste, the uncountable tons of good meat left to rot on the prairie, had gradually soured him on the business. Now he was on his way back to his boyhood home in Texas, putting the years of slaughter behind him.

Some might argue that game was plentiful on the prairie and a little waste did not matter, but Cap nodded a solemn agreement. He was of a frugal nature himself, saving his money for the important things in life, like good biscuits, good whiskey and a friendly game of poker. "If it ain't enough, you can always shoot another. I've rarely seen you miss."

"Cartridges cost money. I'm keepin' mine to buy cattle with."

"Speakin' of waste, it's a pity we've got to go so many days out of our way, takin' the Wichita road. I wish we could travel south down along the Texas caprock. Prettiest country I ever saw."

"That would be a *real* waste . . . of our hair."

The shortest way to Texas would be from Dodge due south across the staked plain, but that was too dangerous. The butchery of the buffalo herds had stirred the Indians into full-scale war. Only a few weeks had passed since a desperate battle at the Adobe Walls trading post had shed much Comanche, Cheyenne and Kiowa blood. The fight had been followed by vengeful Indian raids on scattered skinning camps. The hide men had abandoned the hunt and rushed back to Kansas, seeking sanctuary. They waited impatiently in Dodge, demanding a military campaign against the hostiles so they might venture again toward the southern buffalo grazing grounds.

Instead of dropping directly across the Cimarron and

into the Comanche fury, Jeff and his party were traveling in an easterly direction. He intended to strike the Chisholm Trail, which in recent years had brought tens of thousands of Texas cattle up through generally peaceful Indian Territory to railroad shipping points at Ellsworth, Newton and, more recently, Wichita. Jeff originally had come up that trail with a group of cowboys and a herd. For years afterward, he had been part of one hunting outfit or another made up of several wagons, shooters and skinners. It felt strange traveling with only three companions.

Nigel Smithwick reined the mule team to a stop near the fallen antelope. The Englishman climbed down over the wagon wheel to inspect the kill. "A rare good shot, I must say. You placed it squarely in the neck."

By Jeff's standards it had been no challenge. He had brought down more buffalo than he cared to acknowledge, at many times the range. Smithwick could have done it with equal ease. A sport shooter in England, he had demonstrated deadly accuracy with a buffalo rifle.

Jeff saw nothing remarkable about a sophisticated Englishman mixing with rough-hewn hunters and skinners on the buffalo range. He had encountered several. They shared what most people regarded as the far reaches of civilization with Irishmen, Germans, Swedes and others who had come seeking a new and better life than they had left in the old country.

He wondered how many actually found it, for this was a long way from the Garden of Eden. Out here, the forbidden fruit had been buffalo hides.

The flat skyline wriggled like a snake in the afternoon's dry heat. By instinct rather than design, Jeff gave it another moment's study. The trail was well traveled, so he had no particular reason to expect trouble, but caution had become second nature. Hide buyers often walked the streets of Dodge unharmed though they carried thousands of dollars in their pockets and even ventured into the hunting camps with bundles of greenbacks. On the other hand, men had been killed in Dodge's dark corners and on the buffalo range for the price of a jug of whiskey.

Arletta seemed to read his mind. They were carrying the money from the sale of several wagonloads of hides and the disposal of a hunting outfit. From the wagon seat she said, "Ain't nothin' back yonder, Jeff. Me and Nigel, we been watchin'."

Jeff's spirits lifted as he looked at her. Many might not regard the young woman as a striking beauty, but to Jeff she was handsome enough, slender, with a hint of red in her hair when she took off her bonnet and the sun struck it right. She had a way of smiling that could warm the heart of a statue on a courthouse square. She wore a bright-colored calico dress a hide buyer's wife had made for her in Dodge, and an eye-shading slat bonnet of the same material. Though dusty from travel, it was a welcome change from the drab gray work dresses he had seen her wear in the hide camps. He hoped she would not revert to the accustomed colorless, shapeless style once the new wore off her marriage—if indeed it ever did. So far as he could see, the flame had not so much as flickered yet.

It would be a mistake for anyone to judge from her appearance that she could not take care of herself. When her father died at Cheyenne hands, she had taken charge of his hide wagons and had bossed a shooting and skinning crew. After the Adobe Walls fight she had helped stand off an attack upon her wagons. Jeff had not been there, but he had been told that she had fired the final shot and turned back the last Indian.

Smithwick picked up the antelope carcass and placed it atop the tarpaulin that covered a cargo of supplies, bedding and a rolled-up tent. One of the tied horses smelled the fresh blood and pulled back hard against its thick halter rope. Smithwick spoke softly and patted the animal on the neck to calm it.

Jeff said to Cap, "English ought to've been born in Texas, the easy way he's got with horses."

"He has the makin's. We'll turn him into a sure-enough Texan."

As the wagon moved on, a wheel dropped into a hole, giving the two riders a jolt. Arletta exclaimed with surprise and delight as she fell against her husband. Smithwick grabbed her, laughing. "Whoa, girl!" He held her considerably longer than was necessary to restore her balance.

Cap drew his black horse up beside Jeff's sorrel. "She says they been watchin', but them two ain't seen nothin' all day except one another. They're itchin' for night so they can raise their tent."

"You jealous, Cap?"

"Hell, ain't you?"

"A little, maybe. But it'll pass." Jeff turned involuntarily, looking behind him toward Dodge City with a fleeting feeling of emptiness. He had hoped to be taking a woman of his own back to Texas, but she had not waited. Charity had simply gone, and had left no message. That, he supposed, was message enough.

Twice in his life he had made up his mind to marry, and twice he had been dealt a busted flush, while this Englishman from the other side of the world had lucked into a winning hand. Jeff could not begrudge him. He just wished Fate would grant her favors a little more evenly. She could kiss one man with a woman's tenderness and kick the next man in the belly.

Cap said, "At least you've had good luck with horses."

Jeff leaned forward and rubbed his hand along the sorrel's neck. He had had no occasion to test the animal for speed, but the long legs hinted that it was there. He liked the easy way the gelding responded to the rein, even to a gentle shift in the rider's weight from one side to the other.

"Has he got a name?" he had asked the trader in Dodge.

"No name, just a price. Pay the price and you can call him what you want to."

The sorrel had stocking feet all around. Jeff remembered an old saying that four stocking feet were not a favorable omen. But the horse was young—his teeth marked him a four-year-old—and his alert eyes indicated intelligence. Jeff had decided to defy superstition by calling attention to the stocking feet. He named the animal Socks.

Cap said, "He'll make a good cow horse when you get that ranch you been wantin' so long."

"I don't know if he's ever seen a cow. He'll have a right smart to learn."

"So will we, I expect. We been gone from South Texas a long time. Probably been a lot of changes."

"I hope so. Things wasn't good when we left." A reconstruction government, backed by federal troops, had jailed ex-Confederates on the flimsiest of pretexts, confiscated property of the disenfranchised and occasionally loosed a corrupt state police to murder when other tactics did not produce. But Jeff had heard that Texans had recovered their voting privileges, and most of the carpetbag regime had recently been booted out of office. It was about time, lest they prize up the whole state and haul it back to Yankeeland.

He yawned. "I ain't slept good the last few nights. I keep wakin' up, wishin' I was already home."

Cap removed his hat and wiped perspiration from his face onto his sleeve. "There's a lot of miles ahead of us yet." A glistening drop of sweat still clung to one ragged end of his heavy moustache. "Reckon there's any chance you can buy back the place they taken from you and your daddy?"

Remembrance brought Jeff a stab of pain. "The thought of it has kept me goin' for years."

A while before sundown they came to a brush-lined creek Jeff remembered. He had once managed to hold a stand of buffalo a mile or so south of this trail. Forty-two had fallen to his Sharps Big Fifty before the rest broke into a run. He had gloried in his marksmanship at the time, but the memory had turned from cream to clabber as he witnessed the extermination of most of the Kansas buffalo herd. Whitened skeletons lay scattered all over these prairies, awaiting the attention of the bone gatherers. They would write the final pitiable chapter for herds once so immense that they had sometimes blackened the range.

He said to Smithwick, "English, let's turn and go upstream to where there's some firewood left." So many travelers had camped at the crossing that they had burned up all the nearby timber. Charred remnants of old campfires lined both sides of the creek.

Smithwick replied, "We have traveled far today. The mules are beginning to lag a bit." He and his wife exchanged smiles that said the mules were not their first consideration.

Jeff pointed the wagon across the creek. He saw no trace of a cloud, but it had always been his practice to cross a creek before camping. That way an unexpected rise in the night would not strand him on the wrong side until the water ran down. He and Cap led the horses and mules to drink while English dug a fire pit and kindled a blaze with dead wood from a thin stand of timber along the creek. Arletta drove a long iron rod into the ground at each end of the pit and ran a third rod through rings at the tops. When the blaze died down a bit she suspended a coffeepot and a bucket of beans she had slow-cooked through the night before.

She called, "Cap, you want to whip up a mess of biscuits?" She was careful to make it sound like an invitation, not an expectation.

"I'd be tickled, hon. Soon's we get the stock watered and hobbled." Though cooking had become Cap's profession—it was easier than working cattle—he was relinquishing that chore to Arletta for the duration of this trip. Except the biscuits. He prided himself on his Dutch-oven sourdough biscuits. Cap was a few years older than Jeff and fifty pounds heavier. He took willingly to suggestions but never to orders. In the Confederate army a decade earlier his officers had regarded him with the same favor they would accord a boil on the backside.

Supper done, Smithwick helped his wife wash the pots and pans and tin plates. Jeff and Cap held on to their coffee cups, carrying them to the edge of the creek. There, in the dusk, they squatted and stared down into the clear, slow-running water.

Cap said, "You know what this reminds me of? One of those canyons where we hunted buffalo last winter. Creek looked somethin' like this one. Damn, but that was a pretty country."

Jeff smiled to the remembered scene, far to the south on the Texas plains. It *had* been a beautiful place, a grassy valley with high canyon walls providing winter shelter to several thousand buffalo. His and other hunting parties had camped there until almost the last of the shaggies had fallen to the roar of the big rifles.

Cap said, "We talked about what a great place it'd be for cattle. As long as I've known you, you've wanted land of your own. Now, *there* would be a place for a man to build him a ranch."

Jeff had awakened in the middle of the night sometimes, remembering the strong call of that canyon and the long valley beyond. "Someday, maybe. Right now the Comanches hold the deed. Anyway, we're goin' to *South* Texas. We're goin' home."

"It *was* home. I wonder if it still is."

Smithwick and Arletta retired to their pyramid-shaped tent, lighting a lantern inside. Cap remarked, "I was wonderin' how long they could wait." He kept staring in their direction.

Jeff remembered Charity. And he remembered another woman in South Texas. Years ago she had kissed him goodbye as he rode away to fight for the Confederacy. She had promised to wait forever, if it took that long. But forever had been much shorter than expected. Within six months of his leaving she had married someone else.

He turned back toward the creek so he did not have to look at the tent. "It's hell to be a bachelor."

Arletta suspended the lantern from a hook in the tent's center pole. As she turned, she found herself in her husband's arms. She warmed quickly to the embrace but said,

"We'd ought to wait till the light's out. What'll Jeff and Cap be thinkin'?"

"The flap opens to the south. They can't see in."

"They can see our shadows on the canvas."

"They are men of the world. They understand how we feel about one another."

"But they *are* men. Some things ain't for the whole world to be watchin'." Withdrawing from his arms, she opened the lid of a small wooden trunk and brought out a book. "I was hopin' you'd teach me some more readin' tonight." She gently touched the palm of her hand against the side of his face. "Just for a little while." She left a promise unspoken but understood.

"You have a deucedly strong yearning for learning." But he smiled, for it pleased him as much to teach as it pleased her to improve herself. As a girl, she had had little opportunity for schooling. Work had begun before daylight on the family's rocky-soil farm, and it had gone on long after the candles were lighted at night. Her mother had died when Arletta was yet small. Her father had been unsuccessful as a farmer. Reluctantly he had given up his land to try freighting, at which he was even less successful. Ultimately, Arletta had gone with him and his wagons to the buffalo range, where he had fared marginally better until a Cheyenne arrow had put him in an unmarked grave.

Arletta had been left the burden of what everyone else considered to be a man's job, managing a hunting outfit. She had never been self-conscious about her lack of education until chance had brought a tired and footsore Nigel Smithwick limping to her father's wagons. Before, she had been content to take care of the camp, to cook and occasionally to shoot when the need arose. But Nigel's diction, his knowledge of the world, had given her a hunger to know more, to read and to learn. He had become her inspiration, her teacher and finally her husband.

Now, in partnership with Jeff Layne, they were on their way to southern Texas. What that region was like and what they were to do there she had only the vaguest notion. She had seen part of the Texas high plains, but the place to which they journeyed now was hundreds of miles farther south. Jeff had his mind set on acquiring land and taking up cattle ranching, an idea which intrigued Nigel though he knew not the first thing about it.

Arletta instinctively trusted the Texan. He reminded her of her older brothers who had marched off to fight for the Union and had never come home. She had confidence too in her husband, who had proven his adaptability on the buffalo range. If he had learned about buffalo, he could learn about cattle. Nigel Smithwick was at one and the same time a student and a teacher. He was learning the ways of the American West even as he taught her the magic that was to be found in books, transporting her to lands and ways she had never even dreamed of.

She seated herself upon a stool and handed Nigel a speller he had bought for her in Dodge City. "Call out the words to me. Let's see if I can spell them." She felt confident, for she had studied the pages until she could see them with her eyes closed.

He pulled another stool up next to her own. *"Aardvark."*

She raised her eyebrows. "That's not in the book. What's an aardvark, anyway?"

"A small animal in Africa."

"I ain't ever goin' to Africa. I'm doin' mighty well just to go to Texas. Ask me about somethin' I'm apt to see there."

Smithwick chuckled. "Cap says we will encounter armadillos. Spell *armadillo.*"

"That's not in the book either, but I'll try. A-r-m-o-d-i-l-l-a."

"That's close enough. I'm not sure how to spell it myself. I have never seen an armadillo." He put his arm around her waist. "Why this great hurry to learn so much, so quickly?"

"Because you know so much, and I don't want you feelin' ashamed of me. If any of your folks was to ever hear the way I talk, and see how slow I read . . ."

"Some of the most disagreeable people I ever knew could read and speak far better than I. My family would love you for what is in your heart. They would not ask if you can spell *armadillo*."

"Just the same, I wouldn't want our young'uns someday bein' ashamed of an ignorant mama. Now, read me some words out of that book."

Only once did he have to correct her, for putting a second *e* in *cashier*. "You're doing splendidly. You should soon be able to read *Oliver Twist* for yourself."

"You've already read that one to me. When we get to Wichita I wish you'd look for some more books that I can be studyin' on."

"Most women would want ribbons and bows, and perhaps a fancy hat."

"I'll have little use for ribbons where we're goin'. But I can read books anyplace. If you'd married a woman who'd been to school you wouldn't have to be playin' teacher. I hope you don't run out of patience with me."

"I'll never run out of patience with you. I'll teach you all I know, and wish I could teach you more."

She took the speller from his hands and closed it, putting it back into the little trunk. She turned, smiling. "With the whole wide world for you to travel in, how come you landed right where my daddy's wagons were at?"

"An angel must have been sitting on my shoulder."

"Or on mine." She blew out the lantern and took him into her arms.

THREE

An increase in traffic told Jeff they were approaching Wichita. They met two immigrant wagons drawn by draft horses and laden with household goods and farm implements. Two milk cows and a bull trailed docilely on ropes tied behind the wagons. Jeff would have been content to let the travelers go by with a simple "Howdy," but Arletta had not seen another woman since they had left Dodge. She bade her husband to stop the mules so she could exchange pleasantries with the two farmers' wives.

Jeff and Cap dismounted to let their horses rest. Jeff rolled a cigarette while one of the farmers—they appeared to be father and son—lighted a pipe. Two small boys in knee-length canvas pants spotted a rabbit. Along with their spotted dog, they went chasing after it in the dry grass. Jeff smiled at their haircuts, remembering his own at their age. Their hair was trimmed in bowl fashion, long on top, short on the sides. Smithwick walked over to join Jeff and Cap, giving the farmers a genial nod but saying nothing. Jeff guessed he did not care to explain where he had come from, and why. It was the first question most people asked him as soon as they heard him speak.

Jeff jerked his thumb in the direction of Wichita. "How far on into town?"

"Couple hours." The older farmer eyed the Smithwicks' wagon with curiosity. "I don't see no plow."

"Wasn't figurin' on needin' one. But I see you've got two."

"We're lookin' for a likely place to unhitch and set down. You see any promisin' farmin' country back the way you come?"

It was too late in the year to be planting a crop except perhaps some winter wheat, but Jeff guessed these folks would probably break the ground and raise a sod house before cold weather set in. They would be ready to plant corn or whatever come spring. "I'd say most of it shows prospects. But if I was you I wouldn't want to settle too far from town. Not all the Indians have gone south."

"Me and Son, we figured we'd spend the winter gatherin' up buffalo bones. They'll keep us in groceries till we can make us a crop."

The final indignity to the buffalo, Jeff thought darkly. But he held no blame for the farmer. If there was blame, a share of it was his own. "I don't reckon that can do any harm now."

The immigrant said he and his family were from Illinois, looking to make a new beginning where there were no limitations to a working man's growth. "Land's got too high back there, and money's tight. Wasn't no chance for Son to start, so me and Sara decided to sell out and come with Son and his family to where there's plenty of new ground for all of us. I take it you ain't a farmer."

"We're bound for Texas. We're figurin' to raise cattle."

"Texas must be an unholy place, judgin' by them cowboys we come across in Wichita. Hell-raisin'est bunch of heathens . . . scared the young'uns half to death. 'Y gonnies, they even scared me, a little."

"It's a long trail up from Texas. Most any horse'll pitch and play when you turn him out after he's been shut up for a spell. The boys are all right once you get them away from town."

"Maybe so, but the Book says a man is supposed to earn his bread by the sweat of his brow, which means plowin' and plantin' and makin' the earth provide. It don't say nothin' about chasin' cattle around the countryside and whoopin' and hollerin' like heathen Indians."

There had been sweat enough in the cowboy trade, Jeff remembered, but he saw no reason to argue the point with a stranger he would never see again. "I reckon we all fall short in the eyes of the Lord."

"That we do. But I expect there'll be more farmers in Heaven than cowboys."

Jeff winked at Cap. "I'm in no hurry to go find out."

Farther on, Jeff could see the line of trees that marked the Arkansas River. Nearby, a large herd was held loosely on the dry summer grass. The sight sent his spirits soaring. He turned toward Cap. "Did you ever see anything prettier?"

"Not in many a year. You reckon they're up from Texas?"

The cattle had the rangy Longhorn look Jeff knew so well. "Where else?" The sight carried him back to his growing-up time and to his days as a drover, helping bring a herd up the trail to Abilene when it was the first Kansas railhead town. That trail had been fenced off as farmers had plowed up the grassland. Ellsworth, farther west, had briefly succeeded Abilene before it too turned from the cowman to the plowman. Newton had in turn supplanted Ellsworth. Jeff wondered how long it would be before Wichita went the same way. Not long, if the farmers he had just met on the trail were any indication.

In a country where the soil was as deep and rich as in most of the Kansas he had seen, it was a foregone conclusion that the cattleman would enjoy a far shorter reign than the Indian and the buffalo had. The plow almost always took precedence over the cow if the land was arable. The only question was time. Jeff did not debate the rightness or wrongness of it; he accepted what was patently fact.

The steers were well scattered, half a dozen horsemen deployed far apart, giving them plenty of room to graze near the river. They were quiet, for steer herds were not given to the bawling and general unrest common to a gathering of cows and calves. There were no anxious mothers searching for strayed offspring and no hungry young clamoring for milk.

Cap's eyes sparkled with delight. "Takes me home, it does. Makes me wonder how come I stayed so long up here where a man can get frostbite at night and sunburn in the daytime. A healin' sight, it is." He pushed ahead of Jeff in his eagerness, his large belly bouncing as he spurred up to the nearest horseman. "Where you from, cowboy?"

The rider was a youth of eighteen or nineteen, more fuzz than whiskers on his sun-darkened face. The brim of his tipped-back hat was warped out of shape by exposure to wind and sun and rain and to other rigors of three months on the trail. His shirt sleeves were worn through at the elbows. His britches were crudely patched at the knees, the work of a man who had scant experience with or interest in needle and thread. Looking little different from so many buffalo skinners Jeff had seen on the plains, he was obviously no stranger to poverty. But to tell him so might precipitate a fight. The man on horseback, though he had not a dime in his pocket, was inclined to look down on the richest banker in town if that banker was afoot.

"From Karnes County, Texas, and proud to say so."

Cap slapped his thick leg. "Well, I'll swun. I'm from Karnes County too, down by Helena. By God, ain't this somethin', two old Karnes County boys all the way up here in Kansas!" It had been a long time since Cap had been a boy, but at this moment he had a boy's enthusiasm. He grabbed the outstretched hand and shook it with a vigor that made the youngster's hat fall off. "I want you to meet Jeff Layne. He comes from a little farther south, nearer to the Rio Grande." He pronounced it *Rye-o.*

The cowboy acknowledged the introduction. "I'm Davy Osborne. Boss is over in town tryin' to get these steers sold. Market's gone to hell. Says we ought to've been here a month ago."

Jeff recalled from his own experience that the first herds to reach the railroad each season usually fetched the best prices. As the supply of cattle increased, prices invariably took a whipping. In war, the victory normally went to the side that had the most artillery, and here the buyers held the guns.

The young cowboy said, "Be glad when we can leave this damn-yankee country."

Jeff smiled at Cap. That had been his own first reaction a few years ago, until he had found that the percentage of kindly and honest versus the soreheads and swindlers was about the same as among the folks he had known at home. But old antagonisms from the war died hard. They were bequeathed from Jeff's generation, which had fought it, to the one coming into maturity after it was over. He wondered how many more generations would inherit them before the taint would finally be bred out of American blood. "Maybe Cap or me knows your boss. Who is he?"

Davy Osborne leaned back in the saddle, bracing his arms against the horn. "Name's Freed."

Jeff felt a chill. "Freed? Not *Vesper* Freed?"

"That's him. You know him?"

Jeff looked away, sourness creeping into his voice. "Used to."

"Ought to be back before long. If you'd like to wait, the chuck wagon's down yonderway. Bet Mr. Freed'll be real glad to see you."

"I doubt it." Jeff jerked his head without looking at Cap. "We'd best be movin' if we're to make Wichita by daylight."

Disappointment thinned Cap's voice, for he would have preferred to stay and visit. He ranked friendly talk right up there with good food and strong whiskey. "Whatever you say."

Jeff glanced back to be sure the Smithwicks and their wagon were following. He rode with his gaze fixed on the trail ahead, stomach roiling with an old, remembered anger.

Cap waited awhile before breaking the silence. "You looked like a kid who just lost his candy when he mentioned Vesper Freed."

"I had cause."

"Want to talk about it?"

"I'd as soon not."

"Then you don't have to." Cap waited a minute. "He must've done you a bad turn some time or another."

"Every chance he got."

"You don't have to talk about him if you don't want to." Cap fretted for a hundred yards. "Like what, for instance?"

"We were kids together. He lived up the road a ways. We used to fight almost every time we met."

"Whupped you, did he?"

"He'd win one scrap, and I'd whip him the next."

"Best friends I ever had, I fought with them before we decided to shake hands."

"Vesper never was one for shakin' hands. Just his fists, and usually in somebody's face. After the war started I joined the army. They tried to conscript Vesper, but he left the country. After the war he turned scalywag and sided with the bluecoats. It was him that sicced the carpetbaggers onto our old home place and caused Dad to lose it."

"Then it don't seem likely you'll want to shake hands now."

"Maybe when hell freezes over."

At the edge of town the trail led by a wooden sign:

EVERYTHING GOES IN WICHITA. LEAVE YOUR REVOLVERS
AT POLICE HEADQUARTERS, AND GET A CHECK. CARRYING
CONCEALED WEAPONS STRICTLY FORBIDDEN.

Cap snorted. "First they tell you that everything goes, then they tell you to check your guns. Sounds like they don't want any outsider defendin' himself."

"If a man stays clear of the wrong places he don't have to defend himself."

They rode through the saloon and red-light district west of the toll bridge. Jeff glanced back uneasily at Arletta but knew she was not likely to be flustered by

anything she might see here. She had seen aplenty of it in
Dodge and other towns where her father's travels had
taken her. Jeff paid the toll for the outfit to cross. From
where he sat, looking eastward along Douglas Avenue, he
thought Wichita resembled Abilene as he had first seen it,
though it was larger. Most of the buildings were of lumber. Only a few were of brick or stone, indicating that
most residents had reservations about the town's future.
But in Jeff's experience the average railroad boomtown
enjoyed an initial flush of high prosperity, then settled
down to a slower though more secure role as a supply and
shipping point for a growing farming clientele. The element that thrived on quick and easy money moved on,
usually westward, leaving a community that was more sta-
ble, if a great deal duller.

Wichita was anything but dull. In late afternoon,
heavy horse and wagon traffic moved in its dirt streets.
Cowboys, freshly relieved of herd duty, ambled up and
down its wooden sidewalks, most in groups of three to
half a dozen, as if sticking together for mutual protection
against the unknown. Some still wore the bedraggled
working outfits with all their marks of the trail. Others
sported new clothes bought from the shelves of the New
York Store, trying to achieve the height of fashion. But
clothes could not change their walk or the weathered look
of their faces. They were mostly white, though scattered
among them were brown faces and black. Merchants and
saloon keepers were moderately tolerant about skin color
so long as the southern cowboys had money in their pockets.

Jeff saw two hotels ahead, the Douglas Avenue House
and, on the other side, the Texas House. He chose the
Texas House because of its name. Pulling back beside the
wagon, he said to Arletta and English, "Bet you-all would
appreciate a real room for the night. It's apt to be your last
one for a while. Me and Cap, we'll camp with the wagon."

Arletta protested that she was used to the tent. "A
room is liable to cost us two . . . maybe even three dollars." But her voice betrayed her wish.

Smithwick said, "Jeff, you've made a sterling suggestion." He placed his hand beneath his wife's chin. "A soft bed, and a genuine roof over your head instead of canvas. Don't you think that is worth a couple of dollars?"

"We could buy books with that much money, or enough food to last us most of a week." Still, her pleased smile showed that the resistance was of form rather than substance. She slipped her arm beneath her husband's, glorying in the prospect of a little luxury, perhaps even a bath down the hall.

Jeff said to her, "We'll bring the wagon back in the mornin' and pick up whatever supplies you think we'll need to get us past the Red River. Till then, me and Cap will leave you two alone."

Smithwick grinned. "You are a gentleman, sir, and a scholar."

Cap dismounted and tied his horse behind the tailgate. He watched until the couple had disappeared into the hotel's small lobby, arm in arm, then climbed stiffly up into the wagon. "Like you said, it's hell to be a bachelor."

Jeff placed their money bag in a bank safe so he would not have to lie awake all night worrying about somebody stealing it. He led the wagon to a campground at the edge of town where some of the cow outfits were temporarily headquartered. There, Cap was much in his element, among his own kind. He eagerly visited nearby wagons, telling lies and being lied to, while Jeff fed grain to the horses and mules, hobbled and staked them. There was no grass. Too many outfits had camped here since the first herds had begun arriving in the late spring.

Cap returned, finally. He lifted a shovel from its place on the side board of the wagon. "Reckon I'd better dig us a fire pit if I'm goin' to get some supper started." He hesitated, waiting for the reply he seemed to sense was coming.

"Let's don't mess with cookin' tonight. We'll do like the rich folks and eat supper in an honest-to-God restaurant."

Cap had operated a hole-in-the-wall cafe himself for a

while in Dodge City, until boredom in the confinement of
four walls had driven him to accept a cooking job for a
hide-hunting company. He dropped the shovel as if the
handle had turned hot. "Suits me. Looks like with all these
cattle a man ought to get himself a decent slab of beefsteak."

That sounded good to Jeff. He had eaten a lot of
buffalo meat, antelope and venison, but little beef, in recent years. He had resolved to have aplenty of it when he
got back to Texas. Searching for a likely place to eat, he
and Cap were distracted awhile listening to a brass band
playing on a platform in front of a saloon. The street and
sidewalk traffic had increased heavily since dusk, and
Wichita was considerably noisier than Dodge City had
been.

Cap said, "I hope their cemetery is a long ways out.
This racket would disturb the dead."

They had left their pistols at police headquarters as
the sign directed, but half the men on the street carried
guns. A wide gap existed between regulation and enforce-
ment.

They found a restaurant, and when the food arrived,
Cap attacked his steak and potatoes with gusto. "I can tell
by the taste of it, this steer was raised on salt grass and
prickly pear, and slaked its thirst in the San Antonio
River." He ate so much that Jeff began to fear for his old
friend's welfare. Cap at last loosened his belt and contentedly rubbed his large belly. "Now for a quart or two of
Kentucky's finest to ease the digestion. What do you say?"

It had crossed Jeff's mind that Charity might have
come to Wichita. For a moment he considered making a
search. But if she had wanted him to find her she would
have left word. He forced aside a sense of loss. "Maybe
just one."

Slowly nursing his second drink, Jeff rocked his chair back
on its hind legs and watched Cap dancing with a tall,
gaunt, overpainted and overpowdered woman to the lively
if discordant music of a fiddle and a banjo. There could

hardly have been more contrast between the fat old cowboy and his long-legged partner, who appeared to be at least two or three inches taller than he was. She wore a purple dress with old sweat stains under the arms and missing a few of its original tassels. He wondered idly if Cap intended to take her upstairs.

He wouldn't. But Cap's standards for pleasure were simple and easily met.

The hall was plain and utilitarian, no great expense invested in its decoration. Like Cap, most of its customers were not demanding. The bar was doing a splendid business with cowboys and railroad workers and laboring men of the town. Jeff had seen a couple of fancier places farther up the street, but he felt more at home in this crowd. The whiskey was passable enough and the price not exorbitant. When he tired of watching the dancers on the rough pine floor he shifted his attention to poker players hunched over round tables which took up at least a third of the room. It was easy to tell the cowboys from the professionals, not only by their clothing but by the stacks of coins and greenbacks in front of them. With every hand played, the money seemed to move inexorably from the cowboys to the other side of the table.

A lot of the Texans would return home as broke as when they had left. *They ought to know better,* he thought, then remembered that he had done the same on his first trip north. Book-learning was all right as far as it went, but much of it was easily forgotten. Experience taught lessons that lasted a lifetime.

Watching the players, Jeff became aware of someone standing in front of his small table, staring at him. "Jeff Layne! Or am I drunk?"

Jeff knew the brusque voice before he looked up at the face. His muscles stiffened, and he let the front legs of the chair drop to the floor with a hard thump. It was a moment before he brought himself to answer. "If you're drunk, Vesper, I wouldn't be surprised a bit."

"What the hell are you doin' here?" The question was voiced like a demand, an assertion of a right to know.

Jeff warmed to an old resentment. "I'm free-born and a long ways past twenty-one. I've got a right to be anywhere I please."

"I can see that you still hold on to old grudges."

"I doubt that you've buried yours either." Vesper Freed had his arm around a girl who appeared to be in her early twenties, shorter and prettier and considerably better rounded out than the one Cap danced with. "Are you still a married man, Vesper?"

Freed dug a silver dollar from his pocket and handed it to the girl. "Go over to the bar and get yourself somethin' to drink, honey. I want to talk to my old friend a few minutes."

She fingered the dollar as if it were a diamond. "Don't you be too long, sugar." She weaved her way through the dancing couples toward the bar.

Vesper pulled a chair from beneath a vacant table. "Any objections if I set myself down?"

"Do what you want to. You always did, or tried to." Jeff studied the face he had attempted over the years to shove back into a dark corner of his mind. It was harderbitten than he remembered, and considerably older, as was his own. Vesper Freed's eyes had smoldered with perpetual antagonism from the time they had first met as boys. He had seemed to blame society at large for having been born poor. He had lashed out with hostility against everyone around him, though all had been as poor as himself. He had lorded it over those he had felt were weaker and had put up a blustering stance against those who were not.

He was no longer poor, but the eyes had not lost the burning malice Jeff remembered of old.

Vesper made no effort at reconciliation, and Jeff courted none. Vesper's voice was cold. "It still sticks in your craw, don't it? She married me instead of you, and you ain't ever got over it."

"I got over Eva a long time ago. But I never forgot that you helped those carpetbaggers steal Dad's home place."

"You was gone all the time, workin', and your daddy

was too old to take proper care of things. It was a hard-scrabble place any way you look at it. I don't see that you-all lost very much." Vesper's eyes narrowed. "Where *is* your old daddy? You know the law's still got paper out on him down there."

"That was partly your doin'. But you can't hurt him anymore. He's dead."

"Sure enough?" Vesper studied Jeff as looking for sign of a lie. He seemed to satisfy himself. "I'll tell the authorities when I get home, so they can take him off of the books. I don't want them wastin' my tax money huntin' for a dead man." Exhibiting no sympathy or regret, he looked toward the bar. Resentment flashed as he saw that the girl was talking to a cowboy, and Jeff thought for a moment that he might go to pull her away. But Vesper gave him a hard stare instead. "It's just as well that you're up here in Kansas. There's people down yonder that still don't think kindly of anybody named Layne."

"The only one I know of goes by the name of Vesper Freed." Jeff allowed himself a grim smile. "I'm fixin' to disappoint the hell out of you. I'm on my way home."

Freed digested that information with a ridging of his square jaw. "You'll find it's changed a lot from what it used to be."

From boyhood, Jeff had looked upon that belligerent jaw as an inviting target for his fist. He resisted the temptation. "I'm countin' on that."

Freed leaned forward, his chin jutting out. "Down there a lot of people look on me as the *jefe*. I say *frog*, and they jump."

"I never jumped for you before. I ain't fixin' to jump for you now."

Jeff met his challenging gaze until Freed blinked. Freed pushed back the chair. "Well, don't you let me catch you messin' around with anything that's mine. That includes Eva." He started to leave but turned back. "You ever get married?"

"Never did."

"You don't know what a favor I done you, takin' Eva.

That woman's colder than a catfish. Only good thing I ever got out of her was a son. He's eleven now and growin' like a bull calf."

"Congratulations."

"At least there'll be another generation of Freeds. Looks like the Layne line has about petered out."

Freed strode to the bar and roughly pulled the girl away from her conversation with the cowboy. Jeff would have left the hall, but Freed left it first, his arm locked possessively around the girl's waist. Jeff had a taste in his mouth as if something had crawled into it and died. He poured his glass full and downed the whiskey in a long double swallow.

Cap materialized from somewhere, alone. Jeff poured a drink for him. "Where'd your dancin' partner go?"

"Went off with some railroad man. It's just as well. Them raw bones of hers have bruised me in a dozen places." Cap nodded toward the door. "Who was your friend?"

"Vesper Freed."

"I guessed as much. I didn't see you-all smoke a peace pipe."

Jeff shook his head. "He takes a lot of the pleasure out of goin' home."

"You ain't changin' your mind?"

"No. Come hell, high water or Vesper Freed, we're headed for South Texas."

He had become vaguely aware of rising dissatisfaction at a nearby poker table. Four cowboys had slowly been transferring their trail earnings to a weepy-eyed gambler who wore a black coat, despite the summer night's heat. The man's face had the pallor of one who spent his time in lamplighted saloons and seldom lingered long in the sunshine. A cowboy who appeared to be in his early to mid twenties was down almost to the last of his roll. Jeff had been thinking it was a good thing the Texan had bought himself a new set of clothes before he sat down at the table, because it did not appear he would have enough left to buy a pair of socks.

The gambler took a handkerchief from his coat pocket and wiped his eyes, then his nose. As he started to put the handkerchief back into the pocket, the cowboy grabbed his arm. "No you don't! I seen you palm that card!"

He twisted the gambler's wrist, and a card fell free of the handkerchief. "Jim, look in his pocket."

Another player reached into the gambler's coat and withdrew the ace of clubs. "Looky there, would you? He was fixin' to make a switch."

The cowboy's face flushed red as he grabbed the gambler by the collar and gave him a hard shaking. "You been cheatin' us ever since we sat down. We're takin' our money back. Get it, boys."

Jeff saw murderous intent in the gambler's eyes and muttered to Cap, "We'd better move. It's always a by-stander that gets killed."

He had barely pushed to his feet when he saw the gambler's hand dip beneath the table. The cowboy took a step backward and drew a pistol from his waistband. It roared half a second before the gambler's little palm gun, which put a bullet into the top of the table and scattered the cards. The gambler dropped his Derringer and fell back, his chair clattering to the floor. He cried out, gripping his thigh with both hands. Blood seeped between his fingers.

Sucking a sharp breath between his teeth, the gambler glared up at the angry cowboy who towered over him. "You son of a bitch, look what you've done! You've shot me in the leg!"

"I aimed higher. I never was much good with a pistol."

Jeff knelt to pick up the palm gun. He doubted the gambler would try to use it again, the shape he was in, but he saw no point in taking the chance. The barrel was hot against his fingers.

The players counted out their individual shares of the

money on the table and handed the rest to the cowboy. He said, "Part of it was his to start with. I ought to have about seventy dollars comin'."

Nobody moved to count the money, so Jeff took it upon himself. He put seventy dollars into the cowboy's left hand and pitched the remainder onto the table. "If I was you, I'd be seein' how fast my horse can run, and I wouldn't wait long about it."

The cowboy started to shove the pistol back into his waistband but flinched from the barrel's heat and kept it in his hand. "Looks like I'm already too late."

A heavyset man had rushed through the door, a badge on his sweat-streaked shirt and a derby hat on his head. Several bystanders pointed him toward the cowboy.

Cap grumbled, "Why can't people mind their own business?"

The lawman drew a short-barreled pistol and advanced. "Put that six-shooter down, cowboy."

The Texan laid his weapon on the table amid the cards and spilled whiskey, the splinters and the gambler's money.

The gambler still sat on the floor, gripping his bleeding thigh. He had lost what little color had been in his pale face. "Look at me, Marshal. Son of a bitch shot me. I'm bleedin' to death."

The lawman betrayed no discernible sympathy for either party. "It's a long ways from the heart. You better get some friends to take you to the doctor . . . if you've got any friends." He turned to the cowboy. "You know there's a city ordinance against packing iron. Now you've gone and shot a man."

"He was cheatin' us, Marshal."

"Hell, they all do that. You ought to've shot him in the hands so he couldn't manipulate the cards anymore. As it is, he'll get well and go on cheatin' other people. But not you. You'll be in jail."

Jeff put in, "That tinhorn drew his gun first. This boy fired in self-defense. A bunch of us saw it." He glanced at Cap, who nodded affirmation.

"If he hadn't been carrying that six-shooter in violation of the statutes, it wouldn't have happened at all. I'll swear, between gamblers and cowboys, a man can't close his eyes around here." The lawman gave Jeff and Cap a severe study. "You two can come down to the court in the morning and swear an affydavit. Might help shorten this boy's sentence. Depends on how the judge feels."

The Texan asked, "How does the judge feel about cowboys?"

The lawman sniffed. "He don't think much of them. They do cause him a lot of work."

The cowboy gave Jeff a wan look. "Thanks anyway, friend."

Jeff asked, "What's your name, so we can tell the judge who we're talkin' about?"

"Booth. Kelly Booth."

The wrinkles deepened in the lawman's face. "Booth? That name'll go against you. The judge has got a picture of Abraham Lincoln hanging on his wall."

The name triggered an old memory for Jeff. "There used to be a man down in South Texas by the name of Hunter Booth. You any kin to him?"

Reluctantly the cowboy answered, "Some."

The marshal said, "Come on, Booth. We got a room waiting for you at Wichita Town's own special cowboy hotel." He marched the young man ahead of him and out the door.

Jeff watched, shaking his head. "Hunter Booth. I'd almost forgotten the name."

The gambler still lay where he had fallen. Nobody had offered to help him. Jeff took off his neckerchief. "Here, wrap this real tight around your leg. It'll slow the bleedin'."

The music had stopped at the sound of the shots. It resumed, and couples made their way back onto the dancing section of the floor. Card games started again.

Cap asked, "Who the hell was Hunter Booth?"

"A man who considered himself a natural-born hell-raiser, till he ran into a feller who really was." Jeff sipped his drink and found it tasted sour. "Don't you think we've had about enough fun for one night?"

"It's kind of run out the thin end, all right."

They set off down the sidewalk in the direction of camp. The image of Vesper Freed came back to Jeff, and he gritted his teeth. "There's probably two thousand people in town tonight. How come I had to run into *him*?"

FOUR

Arletta Smithwick stood beside the wagon, which was pulled up parallel to a splintered loading dock at the side door of a long, white-painted frame general store. She kept a mental tally as a clerk and his helper loaded barrels and boxes into the wagon bed. She was not so much concerned that they might cheat her as that they might simply overlook something she and the others would need on the long trail south. Her husband was inside, totting up the bill with the owner and dickering over each item's price to keep the total as low as possible.

She doubted that the merchant stood much of a chance. Nigel Smithwick had a gift with the language and its persuasive powers. By the time he got through outtalking the merchant, the poor man would not know north from south, up from down. She smiled, picturing his discomfort.

Jeff Layne had left this chore to her and Nigel. He and Cap had felt obliged to go to court and testify on behalf of some Texas cowboy who had gotten himself into a shooting difficulty last night. She knew little about cowboys, but she supposed they were much like the buffalo hunters and skinners she *had* come to know in recent years. After long weeks and sometimes months out on the prairies, these had tended to cut loose the wolves when they got to town. They indulged themselves recklessly in whiskey, gambling and sporting women. Having lost her mother at an early age, she had grown up among men. She had no illusions about them; at least she hoped not.

The clerk rubbed his smudged hands on a canvas apron that might have been white a week or two ago. "That's the last of it, ma'am. Wouldn't you like to come back inside, into the shade?"

"Thanks, but I'd as soon wait here till my husband gets finished. Wouldn't want the mules strayin' off with our wagon."

"As you wish." The clerk pulled a tarpaulin over the load, though the sky showed no sign of a raincloud. "We've served dozens of these cattle outfits returning to Texas, but I can't remember any of them having a woman along. Are you not apprehensive?"

"I have my husband with me, and two of the best friends we've got in the world. There won't nothin' happen to me."

"You'll likely encounter a lot of cowboys coming up the trail. They are a wild and lawless lot."

Jeff and Cap were cowboys, or at least had been in the distant past. Outwardly, they sometimes looked rough, even barbaric, but they were as civilized as anyone she knew other than her husband. "I've spent years around buffalo skinners, and there never was a one of them hurt me. I doubt as I'll need to worry about cowboys."

"I would not want to take *my* wife on such a journey, in a wagon."

"I been livin' out of a wagon since I was half grown. It's when I get under a roof that I feel out of place."

Indeed, though she had always looked forward to visiting a settlement—Dodge City, for example—she was never at ease there. After a couple of days she would be looking forward to the open prairie more than she had looked forward to town. It was quieter there, and not overrun with people. She did not know how many lived in Wichita, maybe a thousand or two. It had seemed to her last night that every one of them was on the street at one time, bustling around as if they all had to be somewhere else and were already half an hour late. It was quieter now in the relative cool of the morning, but she suspected they would be out again by afternoon and night. She had as soon be on the trail before that.

She heard a shout and turned toward the street. She saw a young man running hard alongside the general store. Thirty yards behind him, a heavyset, middle-aged man rounded the corner and came pounding after him, his face red with exertion and mottled with sweat. She saw a badge on the pursuer's shirt.

Startled, the two mules jerked their heads up as the young man ran past them. They surged forward, pulling the wagon a short distance before Arletta grabbed the lines and stopped them. "Whoa! Whoa there!"

The young man touched his fingers to his broad-brimmed hat but did not slow any that she could see. "Sorry, ma'am," he shouted, and disappeared around the corner of the building. His hat and high-topped, high-heeled boots were like those she had seen on many cowboys here in Wichita.

The lawman wheezed and puffed as he passed. Arletta wondered if he had another hundred yards left in him.

She talked quietly to the mules, patting the more skittish of the pair on the neck. "Be gentle now. Be gentle."

In a few moments she heard heavy boots pounding across the floor inside. The same cowboy popped out the side door and onto the loading platform. Looking back over his shoulder, he jumped to the ground. He gave her a quick glance, put a finger to his lips in a signal for silence and disappeared beneath the dock.

She heard other hurried footsteps. The lawman appeared in the doorway, sweat dripping from his face. He was heaving for breath as his gaze quickly searched the space between the buildings. He looked down at Arletta, his mouth hanging open as he struggled for air. "Did you . . . did you see . . . where'd he go?"

The store owner and Nigel and the clerk all came out onto the dock, staring in curiosity.

Later Arletta would wonder why, but before she had

time for reasoning it out, she pointed toward the rear of the next building. "Yonder."

Shaking his head in frustration, the lawman used the steps to descend, and he trotted halfheartedly in the direction she had pointed. Nigel turned to the merchant. "Now, what in the deuce do you suppose that was all about?"

"Some cowboy having a little trouble with the law. It happens from the time the first herd gets here in the spring until the last one is shipped in the fall. Now I fear we'll have to add those figures again. I lost my place."

The three men turned back into the store. Arletta waited until she saw no one, then peered under the dock. The cowboy crouched on his heels in a dark corner. She asked, "Did you rob a bank, or kill somebody?"

"No, ma'am. All I done was shoot a damned gambler . . . pardon me, I mean a gambler . . . in the leg. It ain't like he was goin' to die or nothin'."

"That sheriff or whatever he is, he's liable to be back in a minute."

"You goin' to tell him where I'm at?"

"No, but he's liable to look anyway. Get up into the wagon, under the tarp."

He gave her a doubting glance as he came out into the sunlight, but he quickly climbed up into the wagon bed and burrowed under the tarp. She tucked it down within the side boards.

His voice was a little muffled. "How come you doin' this for me, ma'am?"

"I don't know. Just seems like the Christian thing, somehow." Indeed, now that she had done it, she wondered what had come over her. The best she could guess was that the young man had an honest-looking face, and the lawman hadn't appeared to be putting his whole heart into the chase. Shooting a gambler in the leg didn't seem all that serious an offense. Most of them deserved a lot worse.

"What do we do next?" came the voice, barely above a whisper.

"Lay there and be quiet. I see that sheriff comin' back."

"He's just a deputy city marshal."

"Whatever he is, he looks madder than a scalded cat. No tellin' what he'd do if he was to find you now."

The lawman leaned against the wagon's tailgate and breathed hard. He removed his derby hat and wiped his arm across his face. The sleeve came away half soaked. "I swear . . . that boy must . . . must have jackrabbit blood in him."

Arletta feared she heard the faint sound of suppressed laughter from under the tarp and hoped it was only her imagination. "Maybe you ought to go inside yonder and set down in the shade for a spell."

The deputy slowly regained his breath. "A *long* spell. I ain't anxious to go back . . . and listen to the judge raise h— cain with me. He had just sentenced that boy to six months in jail."

"Six months, just for . . ." Arletta caught herself. "For doin' what?"

"For springing a leak in a gambler's leg, something I'd like to've done myself. Me, I'd as soon give the boy a medal. But the judge says we can't have citizens taking the law into their own hands."

"Sometimes that's the only way to have any law."

"I ain't the judge. The boy has got his horse and saddle down at the wagon yard. He ain't likely to leave town without them. Like as not I'll get him when he tries to pick them up." The deputy regained enough strength to climb the steps and pass through the store's side door.

Arletta walked around the wagon and leaned over the side board. "You heard that, I suppose?"

"I sure did. I can't leave town without my horse."

Nigel Smithwick stepped out onto the dock, holding a package wrapped in brown paper. He was smiling. "The merchant's father immigrated from England when he was a boy. I persuaded him to give us a discount."

"That's nice." Arletta glanced at the open door. "Is the deputy sittin' down in yonder?"

"He is exhausted. I think he is not likely to move for a while. Why do you ask?"

"Then we've got time. Climb into the wagon and let's go."

She flipped the reins and clucked the mules into movement. She turned them to the right at the street corner.

Sitting beside her, Nigel unwrapped the package and revealed half a dozen books. "I have a surprise for you."

She chuckled. "I've got one for you, too." She pulled the mules to a stop in front of a large livery barn. She turned and looked back at the canvas. "We're at the wagon yard. You'd best jump out."

The tarp moved. As Smithwick stared in amazement, the cowboy climbed down.

Arletta said, "If I was you I'd pay my feed bill and get out of town before that deputy feels rested enough to come huntin' for you."

The cowboy looked up at Smithwick. "Is this good lady your wife?"

Smithwick was still taken aback. "That she is."

"If I was in your place, I'd bow my head six times a day and give thanks to the Lord." He turned to Arletta. "Much obliged, ma'am. I hope I can do *you* a favor someday." He tipped his hat and trotted through the big door of the livery barn.

Smithwick turned to his wife, his mouth hanging open. "I suppose you know you have made yourself an accessory after the fact."

She smiled. "Ain't it a shame, though!"

It was the custom for trail herds traveling north to move slowly, allowing the steers to graze their way along and pick up weight, or at least to lose as little as possible. As the season wore on, the trail widened, drovers seeking fresh grass not already pounded into the ground.

When the wagon cleared the southern limits of Wichita, Jeff Layne pointed a southerly direction a little west of the beaten pathway to avoid breathing the dust of northbound herds, yet near enough that he and Cap could visit with the drovers if the notion struck them.

The two were riding a little ahead, so Arletta felt no restraint against putting her arm around her husband and leaning to him, inviting a reassuring kiss. She was not sure he quite sympathized with her helping the cowboy escape. Jeff had said nothing one way or the other, though Cap had taken considerable satisfaction in it. He saw it as justice served, not justice evaded.

Cap had spat a long stream of tobacco juice before serving up his studied opinion. "The judge used to be a Yankee army officer, so he's got a prejudice against southern men. Didn't seem to be much love lost between him and the deputy, either. I doubt as that John Law'll miss any sleep over losin' his prisoner." He had shifted his weight, making his large belly press against the saddle horn. "Anybody as fat as him ought to have a settin'-down job anyway."

Nigel Smithwick was more dubious. "What your cowboy did to that gambler may indicate a violent pattern of behavior. How do we know what he may have done elsewhere?"

Arletta had said, "He had a good face."

"Many a man with a pleasant face has been sentenced to hang at Old Bailey, and with good reason."

Now, not receiving the kiss she had invited, she gave her husband one instead. He reacted with mild surprise. "What was that for?"

"For free. I wanted to see if you were still mad at me."

"When was I ever angry with you?"

"A while ago, after you saw what I'd done."

"I was not angry. Surprised, of course, and perhaps apprehensive about possible consequences." He put his arm around her. "I can't conceive of anything you might ever do that would make me angry with you." He kissed her, a hint of a smile in his eyes. "You liked his face, did you?"

"I thought it looked honest."

"And perhaps handsome as well?"

"Not as handsome as yours."

He gave her a little squeeze. "Had you been born in England they might have found a place for you in the diplomatic service."

Delayed in leaving town, they were able to put in only half a day of travel before Jeff spurred toward the river to look for a suitable camping place. They had passed four herds traveling in the opposite direction. Dust hovered over the steers like a persistent choking cloud, so Arletta was glad Jeff had the foresight to guide them west of the main trail, upwind. Though she had witnessed massive movements of buffalo, she had never seen so many cattle bunched in single herds. Jeff said most ranged between a thousand and two thousand head. Any fewer were difficult to justify in terms of the expense involved in walking them so far. More than two thousand were difficult to handle and strung out too much on the day's march. Larger herds were usually separated into two or more units for easier control.

The route carried the wagon past a couple of newly established farms, the sod freshly turned and maturing its first crops of corn and livestock feed. The heads of corn were large and filling out well.

"You watch," Jeff had said. "If it rains right, new soil'll make a bumper crop the first year or two. Word'll spread that this is the bonanza land. Then this cattle trail will be closed off like the one to Abilene."

Cap said, "Maybe the herds'll shift west. If Dodge City can put up with the stink of buffalo hides it ought to put up with Texas cattle. Most folks'll stand for anything that fetches money enough."

"For some things, money just isn't enough."

Arletta assumed he was speaking of the buffalo-hide trade. But Cap asked, "You mean like doin' business with Vesper Freed?"

"That's one of them. There'll be snow twelve inches deep on the Fourth of July before *I'll* do it."

Who, she wondered, was Vesper Freed? She had not

heard Jeff mention any such person, but he tended to keep his problems and concerns to himself, nursing them in secret. From others she was aware, for example, that he had been serious about a woman in Dodge City, but he had not talked to Arletta about her. All she knew for certain was that when Jeff had returned from the buffalo range the last time, the woman was gone. Arletta had sensed his pain, but he had shown no inclination to share it with anyone except perhaps Cap. He and Cap talked alike and thought alike.

If Jeff could be more open, perhaps she and Nigel could help. She supposed he felt that to open up his feelings would mean a loss of privacy, a compromise of dignity. She had observed the same trait in other men. She sensed that even Nigel withheld things about his life in England. He had locked some unhappy memories within, giving her no opportunity to help him lift their burden.

Jeff returned after a time, pointing toward the river. "I've found a place that ain't tromped to death. It's a ways from where they're beddin' down the next herd for the night."

The river at this point angled southward and a little east, down toward Indian Territory. When Nigel stopped the team, Arletta descended over the wagon wheel and walked the short distance to the river. She was gratified to see that the water appeared clear. Too often she had had to let mud settle to the bottom of a bucket and then pour off the semiclear water from the top before she could make coffee. Cap claimed that a little hoof-stirring improved the flavor, but he had been known to stretch facts in the interest of a good story.

Cap mixed up a batch of biscuits and put them in a blackened Dutch oven while Arletta began the rest of the cooking for supper. They had bought a hindquarter of beef in Wichita—as much as she had figured they could eat before it spoiled on the trail—and she was slicing steaks with a sharp butcher knife when she heard Cap say, "Looky comin' yonder."

Turning, she saw a man walking down the river, leading a dun horse that appeared to be limping a bit.

Cap said, "Jeff, ain't that . . ."

"Looks to me like. I thought he'd be halfway to Indian Territory by now."

Arletta recognized the young cowboy whose escape she had aided. She was gratified that he appeared to have gotten away clean.

Nigel dropped an armload of dry firewood on the ground. "You cast your bread upon the waters, Arletta, but it did not float very far."

"Far enough. I don't see no deputy chasin' him."

The cowboy grinned as he approached. "I thought I recognized you folks when you passed, but I laid low behind the riverbank, just in case." He gave Jeff and Cap a quizzical look, then shifted his attention to Arletta and Nigel. "I had no idea the four of you was together."

Jeff studied the dun horse. "Looks like he went lame on you."

"Throwed a shoe. That stableman was goin' to shoe him fresh, but I got out of town in a little of a hurry." He smiled at Arletta. "Thanks to this good lady and her husband."

He had a blanket roll tied behind the cantle. Arletta said, "At least you had time to gather up your possibles."

"Everything but my six-shooter. It's still in the marshal's office. I reckon that's my gift to Wichita Town."

Jeff's voice carried a faint hint of rebuke. "That pistol was what got you in trouble, that and your temper. You're better off without any iron on you."

"It was a gambler's cheatin' ways that got me in trouble. I never was one to stand by suckin' my thumb while somebody ran a whizzer on me." He looked hungrily at the Dutch ovens and the coffeepot, but he did not ask.

Too proud to act the beggar, Arletta thought. She liked that. "There'll be aplenty if you'd like to share supper with us." She did not ask the men's approval. The thought never occurred to her.

The cowboy nodded his appreciation. "I'd be obliged. It's been a long day."

Arletta suggested, "Why don't you unsaddle and stake your horse with the others? You can fix that shoe after supper."

"You-all make a body feel welcome. There's some that wouldn't, especially if they knew I'd just shown my shirttail to the law. But six months in that jailhouse . . . it'd be the dead of winter before I could start home. The thought of all that snow . . ." He slipped the saddle from the dun horse and eased it to the ground. He led the animal to where the others were staked on long ropes so they could graze.

Jeff watched him guardedly. "He *seems* all right."

Cap said, "I'm glad we spoke up for him. Us Texas boys have got to stick together."

Nigel warned, "An alliance with the wrong person could put you in the dock yourselves."

Arletta wondered at Jeff's and her husband's reservations. "I still think he's got an honest face. Anybody know what his name is?"

Jeff replied, "Kelly Booth." Speaking the name seemed to bother him a little.

Arletta asked, "What've you got against him?"

"Nothin' against *him*, exactly, but there used to be a Hunter Booth down home when I was seventeen-eighteen years old. This feller is some kind of kin to him."

Smithwick asked, "Was this Hunter Booth a bad sort?"

"He wanted to be."

Smithwick touched his wife's arm. "I hope you won't have reason to regret your generous ways."

"Parson Parkhill said be kind to every passin' stranger, for you never know when you might be helpin' an angel, unaware."

Jeff said, "They called Hunter Booth other things, but nobody ever said he was an angel."

Returning to the wagon, Kelly Booth poured a cup of coffee to sip while he waited for supper. Arletta felt complimented when he cradled the cup in his hands and showed pleasure with brown eyes soft as new leather.

At length Booth asked, "Where are you folks headed?"

Jeff said, "South Texas."

"Me too. Came up here with a trail herd from San Antonio. Boss hasn't sold his cattle yet, and I couldn't afford to wait for him."

"Kind of risky, ridin' south all by yourself."

"The reservation Indians are mostly tame if you don't do somethin' to stir them up. And those that ain't, they respect a Texas man who acts like he knows how to use a gun."

"You don't have a gun."

"You've got me on that. I may wait here for some cattle outfit on its way home and see if I can ride with them."

Arletta waited for Jeff to make the suggestion. When he held silent, she said, "I don't see why Mr. Booth couldn't join up with us. He could help with the camp work."

Jeff appeared slightly displeased, which surprised her. Then he softened. "I guess it makes sense. Four men would look stronger than three." He glanced at Cap and Nigel. "We've got Arletta to watch out for. What do you-all think?"

Cap said, "We both seen what happened between him and that gambler, and he didn't lie none in court."

Arletta felt Nigel's eyes appraising her and sensed his uncertainty. He said, "I will abide by the majority decision."

She offered, "Four men won't be no harder to feed than three."

Jeff still appeared to have reservations, but he nodded at Booth. "Looks like you're with us."

Booth turned his smile to Arletta. "I promise, I'll tote my share of the load and then some."

Later, lying on their bedroll in the tent, Nigel leaned

on his right elbow. She pressed her right hand against his left, which lay warm upon her breast. "Thanks, Nigel."

"For what?"

"For the books you bought me."

"Oh. I thought you were talking about my accepting Booth. I hope we did the right thing. Every time I look at him, I seem to find him looking at you."

"He's just grateful, that's all, for me hidin' him out."

"I hope that's the extent of it."

She felt a pleasant arousal at the thought that her husband might be jealous. She drew herself closer, resting her head on his right arm. "There's only one man for me, and I've already got him." She pulled him down across her body and kissed him. "What would it take for me to show you?"

"I am sure you will find a way."

FIVE

If Kelly Booth had a lazy bone in his body, Jeff saw no sign of it. The cowboy pitched in quickly at each evening stop, staking horses, digging a fire pit and dragging up wood for Arletta. He seemed to warm himself in Arletta's smile of appreciation.

All his life Jeff had found that he was drawn to some people upon their first meeting. Others he had to get to know. Some he disliked from the beginning, and that feeling rarely changed. The more he saw of Booth, the more he felt that his original favorable judgment in the saloon had been correct. But he was still nagged by two principal reservations: the memory of Hunter Booth and the evidence he had seen of Kelly Booth's quick temper.

Cap Doolittle watched Booth chopping wood for the campfire. No one had asked the cowboy to do it, but he had taken it upon himself. Cap told Jeff, "I like that boy."

"You don't really know him. The reason you like him is that he comes from Texas."

"Hell, ain't that enough?"

"It wouldn't be in Vesper Freed's case."

"Well, every place has got to have a few sons of bitches to make you appreciate the good folks."

It wasn't quite enough for Jeff, at least not enough to allay all his reservations. There was a third: Nigel Smithwick. Clearly, English was less than convinced. He stayed closer to Arletta than before, if that was possible.

He reminded Jeff of the few wealthy men he had known. Instead of being warmly content with their good fortune, they spent much of their time worrying about the possibility of losing it.

Jeff felt that English was in no such danger with Arletta. That she adored her husband was obvious in the way her eyes lighted when she looked at him. Nights, they would sit in their tent, lantern light casting their shadows against the canvas as they huddled, reading together the books English had bought for her. Sometimes Jeff could hear her voice as she laboriously picked her way through a passage of Dickens.

He told Cap, "English is a good teacher. She's readin' faster and easier day by day."

Cap agreed but saw little reason for all her work. "What has a woman got to learn so much for? It don't make her a better cook, or help her with the washin' and sewin'. And someday when she's got a passel of young'uns it won't help her wipe their runny noses."

Kelly Booth put in, "Learnin' is good for its own self, man or woman. I had a little schoolin', off and on. Maybe it don't make me any better hand with cows and horses or a hammer and saw, but I've read some books. Made me feel good, knowin' I could. If I don't do nothin' but work cows the rest of my life, I'm glad I had that learnin'."

Jeff nodded assent. "Arletta's seen a lot of hard times, and there's every chance she'll see some more. If it pleasures her to bury herself in a book and get away from them now and again, then I say it's a blessin' to her."

Cap was unpersuaded. "It's apt to teach her about a lot of things she'll never have, and make her discontented with what she *has* got."

"Her daddy said the same thing when English first started teachin' her. Arletta's a stronger woman than that."

Booth said, "There's nothin' too good for a woman like her."

Jeff saw a wish in Booth's eyes that made him vaguely

uneasy. "We'd best check the stock, then crawl into the soogans. We've got a long ways to go."

Most of the Indians Jeff had seen in recent years had been hostile. Though reason told him those he would encounter in the Territory should be peaceable, an old reflex made him reach down for the saddle gun when he saw half a dozen of them bob up a-horseback over a low hill to the east, survey the wagon, then surge down toward it.

He remembered that Kelly Booth had no gun, and he recalled the cowboy's poor marksmanship with a pistol. He drew his horse up beside Booth's and handed the cowboy his saddle gun. "Don't make any threatenin' moves with it."

"They're just comin' to see what they can bum off of the outfit. They visit the trail herds and ask for a beef or two as a toll. Generally there ain't any trouble unless some hotheaded cowboy starts it."

"I saw a hotheaded cowboy in Wichita a few nights ago."

"I had cause then. But I ain't lookin' to fight any half-starved Indians with holes in their britches."

Jeff rode out to meet them. He intended, if he could, to keep them at some distance from the wagon lest they swarm upon it and take everything. Cap and Booth spurred up to flank him. He raised his hand in a gesture of peace but warily judged how quickly he could draw his pistol if necessary.

He thought these were probably Cheyennes, but he was not sure. They were dressed in a mixture of white-man clothing and traditional buckskin. The leader's gaunt and wrinkled face was shaded by a flat-brimmed black hat with an eagle feather in its band. As the old man rose up from his rawhide saddle to respond to the peace sign, Jeff saw that he had cut the bottom out of his heavy jeans, leaving his rear covered only by a wide red breechclout. It was not an uncommon compromise between the old and the new among reservation Indians.

Jeff hoped one of them might speak a little English,

for he knew not a word of Cheyenne, and he had never
learned much of sign talk. Most of his contact with Indians had been over a gun barrel.

Cap said, "Whatever we give them, they'll tell all the
others. We'll have Indians beggin' us all the way to Red
River."

"Better than havin' them *fight* us all the way. I asked
Arletta to take on some extra coffee and sugar and to-
bacco. I figured we'd be called on as we go through the
Territory."

None of the Indians spoke English, or at least none
gave any such indication. Jeff remembered that along the
Texas-Mexico border many Mexican people concealed
their knowledge of English for self-protection. It was easier to plead ignorance of the language than to argue a
point with intolerant gringos.

The leader of the Indians made motions toward his
mouth and his stomach that were as clear as any words he
could have spoken. He brought out a crude pipe and
pointed to its empty bowl.

Booth suggested, "Indians like sugar. Give them a few
pounds and they'll go away happy."

"All right. Would you mind goin' to the wagon and
askin' Arletta to put some sugar in a bag? And sack up
some tobacco. Show them we're friendly, and maybe
they'll stay friendly too."

Booth turned to comply. The Indian leader looked at
the two horses tied behind the wagon for English and
Arletta. His eyes showed his appreciation, and his motions
made it clear that he would not be unwilling to accept one
or both as a gift. Jeff pointed at the couple on the wagon,
then at the horses and tried to decline the request in the
friendliest possible manner.

The Indian nodded solemnly, accepting the situation.
Jeff surmised that he subscribed to an old adage: he who
does not ask is not likely to receive.

The younger Indians began talking among themselves, motioning toward the wagon. Arletta was doling a

liberal ration of sugar out of a barrel and into a canvas sack. Suddenly four of the men put their horses into a trot, passing by Jeff and Cap before Jeff could even turn his sorrel around. He shouted, "Arletta . . . English . . . you-all watch out!"

He thought the Indians meant to swarm over the wagon and take everything they wanted. Nigel Smithwick quickly brought up a rifle from beneath the seat but was careful not to point it at anyone. Booth took a protective stance beside Arletta. He held Jeff's saddle gun slackly at his side. The Indians made no move to climb onto the wagon. Spurring toward them, Jeff realized they were concentrating their attention on Arletta.

Though she must have felt apprehensive, she managed a calm outward appearance, even a tentative smile. She tied a string around the top of the sack and extended it toward the young Indian nearest to her. She handed another sack to a second man. "Tobacco. You know, smoke?" She mimed the puffing of a cigar or pipe.

Jeff said, "I don't think they mean you any harm. They're just not used to seein' a woman on this trail."

The leader had ridden up beside Jeff and stared at Arletta. His hand signs asked if she were for sale or trade. But his thin smile showed that he knew better; he was enjoying a little joke.

English let the tension go out of his shoulders. "Tell him, Jeff, that she is a terrible cook and has a frightful temper. It is better for him that he take the sugar and tobacco."

Arletta elbowed him in the ribs and made a mock gesture of outrage.

One of the younger Indians evidently understood English, because he translated, and the others laughed. So did the old man, who then spoke to the young ones. They withdrew from the wagon. He said something that Jeff assumed was thanks and turned his horse around.

He stopped after riding a few yards. He came back, untying a flat leather bag tied to his saddle. He withdrew a

small deerskin pouch and handed it to Arletta. Solemnly
he said something which neither she nor anyone around
her understood.

Surprised, she opened the pouch and took out a light-
colored stone roughly the size and shape of a hen's egg.
She puzzled over it until Cap exclaimed, "By God, it's a
madstone."

"Madstone?" She rubbed it uncertainly.

"I was bit one time by a hydrophoby skunk. They put
a madstone on the bite and drawed out the poison."

Smithwick smiled. "I always thought you might be a
bit mad."

Cap ignored the remark. "I been lookin' for a stone
like that ever since. They come out of a deer's stomach,
maybe one in a hundred or a thousand."

Arletta thanked the old Indian pleasantly, and he
turned away. Shortly the six disappeared eastward over
the little hill in the direction of a dust cloud stirred by a
herd of cattle.

Arletta examined the stone, in reality a calcified
hairball which resulted from a deer's licking itself over a
period of years. She offered it to Cap. "Since you've been
lookin' for one, it's yours."

"No, hon, the old chief wanted you to have it. He was
right taken with you or he wouldn't've offered you such a
gift. You might hunt from here to Texas and not find another one like it."

"But I didn't do anything except give them a little
stuff."

"That and a smile. It was the smile done it. You
throwed your bread on the waters and it came back multi-
plied. Every time I ever throwed *my* bread on the waters it
just sank."

Kelly Booth climbed down from the wagon and
handed the saddle gun back to Jeff. "That madstone was
the best he had to give. Poor devils. We took away everything they had and turned them into beggars."

"Not all of them. If you went west out onto the plains

you'd find aplenty that'll still fight you till hell freezes over, then come at you on the ice."

The first time Jeff noticed the horsemen and wagons behind him they were more than a mile away. The next time he looked they had closed the distance by half. "Kelly, it don't seem likely the Wichita law would've trailed you this far. But it might be just as well if you got under the tarp and out of sight."

"It'd be awful hot under there."

"Not as hot as it might be out here."

"I'll take my chances. If it was the law, why would they bring two wagons?"

"Suit yourself."

Cap shifted his bulk around in the saddle for a look. " 'Pears like a Texas outfit on its way home, and anxious to get there. But they'll have their horses wore down to the hocks before they get to the Red River. Bunch of kids, like as not."

It defied good judgment to travel at such a rate for any length of time. But a lot of outfits were made up of very young men—boys, actually. Jeff had seen trail herds bossed by youths no older than twenty or twenty-one, the hands all in their teens, working for an owner who did not accompany the drive. "They'll learn fast if they have to walk and lead their horses for a couple of days."

As the procession neared, Smithwick drew the wagon team to a stop. Jeff reined around to greet the oncoming company. He heard Booth groan, "Aw hell!"

Jeff squinted, trying to bring the faces into focus. One came clear, and he joined Booth in a growl. "Vesper Freed."

Freed raised his hand as a signal for a halt. Jeff counted eight riders with him. Two wagons trailed, one a chuck wagon, the other a hoodlum wagon, carrying bedrolls and miscellaneous equipment.

Freed's voice was coarse. "Well, Jeff, I'd hoped you might change your mind about goin' back to Texas."

"You ought to know me better than that. In kind of a hurry, ain't you?"

"Had a little trouble yesterday. We need to get the river between us and the Territory as quick as we can."

Trouble. Even as a boy, Vesper Freed had been a schoolyard bully, drawing trouble like a lightning rod. If it did not come of its own will, he sought it out.

Freed's eyes narrowed as they found Kelly Booth. "I know you. Name's Booth, ain't it?"

"Kelly Booth. Yes, you know me. And I know you." His dour expression made it clear that their acquaintance-ship had not been pleasant. That automatically elevated Booth's status in Jeff's estimation.

Jeff was reluctant to ask, but he felt he should. Freed's troubles had a way of drawing in those around him, willing or not. "What have you done, Vesper?"

"Shot me a damned Indian. Thievin' red heathens came up a-beggin', and I told them they couldn't have anything. One of them jumped into the chuck wagon and was goin' to take what he wanted anyway. So I shot him."

"Dead?"

"As dead as he'll ever be."

Jeff felt a little sick. He had killed Indians himself to save his life, but not to avoid giving them a small handout. He looked for the young cowboy he and Cap had met on the river before they had reached Wichita. Shamefaced, Davy Osborne cut his gaze to the ground the moment their eyes met.

"Damn it, Vesper, these Indians are hungry."

"Let the government feed them; it ain't my place to do it."

"But it's their land we're crossin'. Looks like they're due somethin' from us."

"*I* didn't give them any land. It was them softheaded politicians in Washington. This is a white man's country. We fought for it."

Jeff gave full rein to his sarcasm. "As I remember, when the real fightin' was bein' done, you ran off to stay out of it."

"That was white man against white man. It was a stupid war."

"I can't argue with you about that. But we thought we were doin' right at the time."

"And lost everything down to your shirt. But I didn't." Freed nodded toward Booth. "What's this man doin' with you?"

"Goin' to Texas."

"Well, you keep him away from me and what's mine. I'll shoot him the way I shot that Indian, and never look back."

Jeff saw Freed's contempt mirrored in Booth's eyes. "Seems to me you're lookin' back right now, the rate you're travelin'. Indians've got you scared, haven't they?"

Freed snorted. "We could whip a hundred of them red devils and never break a sweat. One taste of lead and they'd run like scalded dogs. They did yesterday."

Jeff thought, *You'd sing a different song if you'd been at Adobe Walls.*

Freed said, "But I figure they went cryin' to the army. It costs too much to have trouble with the soldiers." He gave Jeff a severe study. "I don't want any with you, either. Texas is a big country. When you get there, find yourself a place that won't be crowdin' *me.*"

"I'll crowd you if I feel like it. And I may feel like it."

"If the army comes askin', tell them you ain't seen me."

"I don't lie even for my friends, and you're not one of my friends."

Freed muttered under his breath and gave an arm-swinging signal to the men behind him. The big rowels of his Mexican spurs jingled as he touched them roughly to his horse's ribs. The horse lunged forward in response to the pain. Jeff did a quick study of the cowboys' faces as they swept past him. He saw not a single Mexican among them. Most of the outfits from deep South Texas brought at least some Mexican hands.

Davy Osborne hung back as if he wanted to say

something, perhaps make some explanation. But he gave up and followed the others without speaking a word.

Arletta looked distressed. "Did I hear right, that he killed an Indian?"

"So he said."

"I wonder if it might've been one of those that came a-visitin' us. There wasn't no harm in them."

Worry began stirring in Jeff. "We'd best keep our eyes open. To the Indians, one white man looks pretty much like another. If they can't catch Vesper, they may settle for whoever comes handy."

Cap pointed to a rising of dust. "There's a cattle outfit yonder. They'd ought to be warned."

Cap liked to visit the Texas hands anyway. "Go ahead. You can catch up to us in your own good time."

As Cap angled southeastward, Jeff motioned for Nigel Smithwick to set the wagon in motion. He noticed that Kelly Booth drew his horse up close to it, looking with concern in Arletta's direction. He pulled in beside Booth.

"I gather there's been trouble between you and Vesper Freed."

Booth's jaw clenched. "He shot me."

Arletta looked down at the cowboy, her eyes widening. "Why'd he do that?"

"He was runnin' some friends of mine off of their land. I tried to help them."

Arletta's eyes softened with sympathy.

Jeff said, "You seem to've survived it in good shape."

Booth touched his left side. "Bullet just took a little bite from one of my ribs. His carpetbag partners throwed me in jail for a couple of months."

"And your friends?"

"Scattered. Some are in Mexico. Freed is runnin' cattle on the land that used to be theirs."

"Your friends, I take it they were Mexicans?"

Booth went defensive. "Their name was Ramírez. You see somethin' wrong with that?" Some old Texians would. They remembered the Alamo, and Goliad.

"No, we had Mexican neighbors, me and Dad. Most of them were good people. A few weren't worth killin'. About like the average run of folks all around."

"I was a lost, hungry kid. If it hadn't've been for old Santiago Ramírez I might've starved to death, or got shot stealin' somethin' to eat."

Jeff tried to remember. It had been a long time, and Ramírez was a common name. "Can't say that I knew him. The folks that lived close to us were named Sánchez and Ortiz and Rojas. They'd been on the same places for generations. For all I know, they're still there."

"Not if Vesper Freed wanted their land."

Jeff rode awhile in silence, wondering. "Do you always go lookin' for trouble?"

"No, but I don't run away from it."

"From what I remember about Hunter Booth, folks said he *did* go huntin' for it. Then he found too much and couldn't get away."

Booth's face darkened. He slowed his horse so that he dropped back behind the wagon, out of Arletta's hearing. "Hunter Booth was my daddy."

"I sort of figured that."

"As a young'un he was the runt in the family. My uncles was always whuppin' up on him. Time he was grown, though, he got to be the biggest, and he whupped up on all of *them*. He got it in his head that he had to prove he was the toughest everywhere he went. He was always lookin' for somebody to fight."

"He fought once with my daddy, and lost."

"When he did lose now and again, it made him worse the next time. I was just a button when he got into his last fight. He saw that he had picked on the wrong man. He tried to back away, but it was too late. Feller pumped three bullets into him while my daddy begged him to stop."

Booth rode along looking at the ground. "There wasn't a dozen people came to his funeral. My mama had died when I was little. I didn't have any idea whichaway to turn. Day after the funeral, old Santiago came by the cemetery and found me just sittin' there. He already had all the family he could feed, but he took me home with him."

"So that's why you fought for him against Vesper Freed."

"Wouldn't you?"

"I'd hope so. But I'd hope I did it out of gratitude to Ramírez, not just tryin' to make up for my daddy's shortcomin's."

Booth's face reddened. "You think that was the reason?"

"I can't say. I didn't know you then. I'm not sure I know you now."

Jeff and the other men took turns standing guard that night in case Indians showed up seeking vengeance. None did. About the middle of the morning, however, the army caught up. A patrol of fifteen or so blue-clad cavalrymen galloped in from behind, led by a sun-punished first lieutenant whose trimmed moustache was coated by dust. Jeff thought some of the gray was probably permanent. Two Indians accompanied the troopers. One was the older of the group who had visited their wagon. Jeff recognized the flat-brimmed black hat, the wrinkled face.

He did not have to signal Smithwick to stop. The team came to a halt as the soldiers swept past in a semicircle, surrounding it. The lieutenant appeared surprised by Arletta's presence. He touched his gloved fingers to the brim of a dusty hat. "Ma'am." He turned to Jeff. "I assume you are in charge of this company."

Jeff wondered how he assumed that when Cap, Booth and Nigel Smithwick were all with him. "As much as anybody is, I reckon."

The lieutenant signaled for the two Indians to come forward. To the younger he said, "Ask him if these are the ones."

Jeff sensed what the question was about. The older

Indian clearly recognized everyone present. Though the words he spoke were unintelligible to Jeff, it was evident that the elder was declaring this party innocent.

The younger Indian spoke. "He says these people give sugar. Give tobacco. Good friends."

The lieutenant relaxed somewhat. "On the day before yesterday a wagon party like yours shot down an Indian in cold blood. We have been trailing them. They must certainly have passed you."

Freed's trail was still plain, so a lie would have been wasted even if Jeff had considered one. "Yes, an outfit passed us yesterday in a right smart of a hurry."

Booth said, "You'll have to ride fast to catch up with them this side of the Red River, Captain. The man you're lookin' for is Vesper Freed."

Jeff had not intended to volunteer Freed's name. Though it had been more than ten years since the end of the war, the Confederate in him still shrank a little from a blue uniform.

The lieutenant took a small notebook from his pocket. "Would you spell that, please?"

Jeff let Booth do the talking. He said nothing when Booth misspelled the name with an *i*. Booth offered a brief physical description. "You'd be doin' me a big favor, Captain, if you'd shoot him in the side."

The lieutenant was intrigued. "Why in the side?"

"Because that's where he shot me once. I'd like him to know how it feels."

The lieutenant cracked the smallest of smiles. "I'll take it under consideration. Should it come to that, I may let the Indians do it. That would serve justice." He turned to Arletta. "My apologies, ma'am, if our manner caused you any apprehension."

"I hope you catch him."

The officer glanced at Booth. "And I thank you, sir, for the promotion, but I am only a lieutenant."

"If you catch Freed, maybe you'll make captain."

Watching the troopers move on in a brisk trot, Cap

declared, "They'll play hell. Freed'll be washin' his feet on
the Texas side of the Red and laughin' at them."

Booth said, "I had half a notion to ride with them and
make sure they catch up."

Jeff asked, "Why didn't you?"

Booth glanced at Arletta, who was in deep but quiet
conversation with her husband on the wagon seat. "We'll
still be in Indian Territory for a ways. I might be needed
here."

They were half a day short of the Red River when they
met the cavalry patrol riding northward, the horses tired
and holding to a walk, the soldiers' shoulders slumped in
weariness. The two Indians were solemn.

The officer gratefully accepted Arletta's suggestion
that she fix something for the company to eat. She said, "A
trail outfit gave us a forequarter of beef. And there's a pot
of beans I cooked all last night. They'll heat while I'm
fixin' the rest of it. Looks to me like you men stand in need
of some nourishment."

The lieutenant swung down stiffly from his horse and
loosened the girth to let the animal breathe easier. "We
never got close enough even to smell Freed's dust. I had no
authority to pursue him into Texas. I doubt that the civil
authorities there would have any interest in bringing him
to justice for killing an Indian. They're doing it themselves
at any opportunity."

Jeff sympathized. "If it's any comfort, a man like Vesper Freed generally brings about his own punishment
sooner or later. He'll bully the wrong man or break one
law too many."

"I suppose I am too impatient. I dislike seeing justice
deferred."

Arletta said, "Every man must stand before St. Peter
one day and answer for his sins."

Booth spat. "I hope I get an excuse to rush up that
meetin'."

Jeff gave his attention to the two weary Indians. He
did not remember that he had ever studied any this closely

before. He saw despair in the older one's eyes, and he found himself sharing some of the man's pain. He remembered the times he had shot at Indians, and had been shot at *by* Indians.

He hoped it would never come to that again.

SIX

Crow Feather watched in helpless sorrow as the shaman Comes Down From The Mountain sprinkled his magical powders over Rabbit's fever-wracked body and resumed a long series of chants calling upon the spirits to drive out the evil force that had invaded her. Rabbit's girl baby whimpered until White Deer opened the front of her deerskin dress and brought the infant to her breast. White Deer was having to nurse two now, her own and that of her sister, for Rabbit's milk might carry the sickness to her newborn, if indeed she had any milk to give.

Crow Feather's side still ached when he exerted himself. The broken ribs had not completed their healing. He could mount a horse only with difficulty and pain. He had remained several weeks with the band whose warriors had found him lying wounded in the creek, for the bullet hole had turned angry and blue, and the ribs had been in no rush to knit. For a time it had appeared he would not live to return to his own.

Both of his wives had been with child when he left for the attack on the white-man trading post. In his absence White Deer had given birth first and with no particular difficulty. But Rabbit's pregnancy had taken a terrible turn. She had been only intermittently conscious since her baby had been born. Now he despaired, for it appeared the shaman's efforts would be in vain.

Crow Feather blamed himself. Though he did not know when or how, he felt that he must have offended the bear spirit that had watched over him since the vision quest of his youth. That was the only explanation he could see for the many things gone wrong for him since the white hunters had invaded the People's land: the buffalo slaughtered in numbers unimaginable simply to steal their hairy hides, the defeat before the walls at the white-man houses, the loss of Crow Feather's war party, his own wounding . . . and now this, the illness that seemed about to take his younger wife. The bear must be angry indeed.

After his return to his own village, finding Rabbit in such a deplorable condition, he had gone off to himself to seek a new vision, to try to summon up the bear spirit and determine what was wrong, to learn what he might do for penance that his medicine be restored. But the bear had never come. Crow Feather had found no vision that gave him hope. One dream had kept recurring, and he hoped it was *not* a vision. In it, he wandered in darkness, unable to find his wives and his children though he could hear them crying. And, very briefly, he glimpsed the woman who had red hair.

From outside, the cool morning air brought him the sounds of the band breaking camp. They were dismantling their tepees, packing their horses, loading their travois for the long trip to the customary winter encampment in the great canyon whose high walls would shield them from bitter north winds, whose broad valley would provide grass for their horse herds until spring returned. Because of his wound he had been unable to accompany the other men as they conducted their buffalo hunt. It had been a tolerable success, and they had encountered no white hide men. Many believed they had driven the *teibos* out forever, but Crow Feather doubted that. He remembered too well his dream in which the white men came back stronger and more numerous than before. The dream had been too real to be lightly put aside.

Comes Down From The Mountain had stood the vigil

with Crow Feather and White Deer all night, chanting periodically, saying the words of magic passed from one generation of shamans to the next. They had been handed down for longer than any man could know, perhaps from the time the buffalo had first ventured out of their hiding place in the earth and had spread across the plains with their mission to feed and clothe the chosen ones. Sweat dripped from his face as he bent over Rabbit and shook a rawhide rattle with the short black switch of a buffalo's tail attached. From the hollow look in his eyes, Crow Feather sensed that Comes Down had almost given up hope. But he would not lend voice to that fear lest some beneficent spirit be offended by his lack of faith.

The old man glanced at White Deer, nursing another woman's child while her own lay sleeping in a willow cradle nearby. Outside the tepee, Crow Feather's two older children would be watching the preparations the rest of the band was making for the move. Little Squirrel was old enough to understand the crisis taking place inside, but the girl—Rabbit's daughter—was not. She had asked several times when her mother was going to get up and hold her in her lap as she had always done before.

Comes Down turned back to Crow Feather, his face grave. "Whatever dark spirit has captured her, its medicine is too strong for mine. When we reach the canyon I will find a more powerful shaman for her."

Crow Feather's throat felt swollen. "We cannot take her to the canyon, not until she is stronger."

"Unless you take her to a better shaman she will die. Look, the light is gone from her eyes."

Rabbit's dark eyes were half open, but they did not see.

Crow Feather had wrestled with this dilemma most of the night. Moving her now would kill her. Yet Comes Down From The Mountain was right. She needed stronger spiritual help than he could provide.

"Could you not go to the canyon and send a shaman back to us?" Crow Feather asked.

"She may not live to see him."

Crow Feather looked at White Deer, asking her silently, receiving the answer from her eyes. Her sister was not to be moved.

"That will be for the spirits to say."

Comes Down accepted the judgment. His eyes revealed the thought behind them: it probably would make little difference either way. He said he was going to take a sweat bath and purify himself, then come back for one more attempt to draw the darkness from Rabbit before he joined the rest of the band in their migration. He passed out of the tepee.

Another man entered. Goes His Own Way paused just inside the flap, then circled around the fire pit as a guest customarily did upon entering a neighbor's lodge. He looked at Rabbit, then at White Deer before turning his gaze to Crow Feather. There was no need to ask questions. He said, "If you like, my family and I will stay."

Goes was younger than Crow Feather, but he was an able hunter, a fierce companion in battle, a friend to ride with and to trust.

Crow Feather demurred. "The others will need your good counsel. We will follow when we can."

"There is talk of pony soldiers. It might be dangerous for you to stay here alone."

"And if *you* stayed, would two of us make a difference against the soldiers? No, you go. You will be needed."

"Then we shall leave you more meat." Goes had been generous after the buffalo hunt, as had others in the band. The People did not permit the injured, the widowed or the old to starve so long as there was food enough for all. Generosity was prized, while the greedy person's path was narrow and lonely, strewn with sharp stones.

Such a one was Finds The Good Water, who during Crow Feather's long absence had proposed marriage to White Deer on the supposition that her husband had died at the white man's hand. White Deer had met the proposal with contempt. Finds The Good Water had left no meat at

Crow Feather's lodge after the buffalo running. Even if he had, White Deer would have fed it to the dogs.

Goes had but one wife to feed, whereas Finds The Good Water already had two. If Goes had had *six* wives, he would still have been generous to his friends.

Goes gave Rabbit a final sad look. "We will save a proper place for your lodge." He bade Crow Feather and White Deer goodbye and departed as he had come.

Rabbit's baby had fallen asleep at White Deer's breast. White Deer arose to lay the infant girl in a new willow cradle next to her own baby boy. Whether Rabbit lived or died, White Deer would mother this new child as if it had come from her womb rather than her sister's. Before Rabbit fell ill it would have been difficult for a stranger to determine which of the two older children belonged to which mother. Each woman had treated the other's child with the same gentleness she gave her own. In theory, that was the way of the Comanche, though it was not so in all families.

Before the sun was halfway across the sky, Crow Feather and his family were alone. The rest of the band had disappeared toward the southeast, where broad, deep canyons slashed across the broken edge of the open plains. Crow Feather walked out beyond his lodge. His son, Little Squirrel, followed a couple of steps behind him. Silently they surveyed what a few hours ago had been a busy camp, strung broadly along the banks of a meandering creek. Now only bare, foot-packed rings showed where the tepees had stood, black fire pits dead and cold where the centers had been. A miscellany of discarded trash lay scattered about . . . worn-out moccasins, pieces of leather string, a remnant of dry hide. Two abandoned dogs quarreled over buffalo bones, leavings of some family's feast.

Little Squirrel's own dog, a foolish beast, had followed along with the rest of those belonging to the band. It was probably more fortunate than these two, however. They would fall prey to prowling wolves, more than likely, for their fighting spirit would be no match for the fangs of the first foraging pack which passed this way.

Only four horses remained. They were staked along the creek on rawhide ropes so they would not follow the others toward the new encampment. One was for Crow Feather, two mares for the women and their travois. Squirrel's pony was the fourth.

The boy was uneasy. For all of his six summers he had been used to large numbers of people around him. Never had he been left with only his immediate family. Crow Feather knew the prairie must look huge and empty to him in this unaccustomed solitude. He said, "Sometimes it is good to be alone, away from chattering voices. It is good because you can listen to the earth. It speaks too, in its own way."

A raven circled overhead, making its cawing noise, then flew downstream. Squirrel asked, "How do you know what it is saying?"

"You do not, always. But if it wants you to know, you *will* know."

"How long must we stay here? When will we go to the others?"

"Only the spirits know. They have not told me."

In those brief periods when she was lucid, Rabbit clung to her new baby as tenaciously as she clung to life. Crow Feather would see the light come into her eyes and feel a resurgence of hope, only to lose it when her eyes closed and she fell back into the unforgiving arms of the fever. Long days passed, and long nights. Geese flew over on their way south, and Crow Feather knew it would not be long before the first winter storm howled down from the cold, blue north. Though the days were warm, the mornings were increasingly brisk, and winds whistled as they tugged at the tepee's smoke flap.

Days, when he felt he had to leave the lodge for a while, he would grit his teeth against the pain and mount his horse for a short ride, surveying the plains around the campsite. He kept remembering what Goes His Own Way had said: there had been talk of pony soldiers.

And one day he saw them, a blue-clad patrol scouting for sign. Drawing back into timber along the creek, he counted three times four. Heart thumping, he hurried back to his lodge. Once he had had a good rifle, taken from a luckless buffalo hunter, but he had lost it. Now he had only his bow and his arrows, made new since his wounding. Against so many he would have little chance. But he would stand as long as he could, defending his family.

The soldiers never came. They veered away without riding in sight of the tepee. Crow Feather shared the relief he saw in White Deer's face, but he knew their situation was precarious. Next time the pony soldiers might come close enough to see.

That night the spirits took Rabbit away. Crow Feather had dozed, sitting up against his backrest. He awakened suddenly to White Deer's keening. His sits-beside-me wife knelt by her lifeless sister and rocked back and forth, singing a death chant. Crow Feather looked with grief at the now peaceful face of his younger wife, then at the four sleeping children. He walked out into the darkness and shouted to the bear.

It was not Comanche custom to remain long in the presence of the dead, or in a place where death had occurred. Days ago Crow Feather had found a small rock outcropping along the creek, a suitable place to bury Rabbit. He took her there and left her, along with her personal possessions. It seemed appropriate that Rabbit's mare had disappeared. She had somehow loosed her tether and strayed away. Crow Feather wanted to think that Rabbit had taken her.

With nothing to hold them here but memories, he and White Deer and the children set out southeastward in a cold rain to join the rest of the band in the winter encampment. They had only his horse, White Deer's mare and Squirrel's pony.

They crossed a set of fresh horse tracks, fixed deeply into the mud. Crow Feather tried not to let concern show in his face, for White Deer and the children had trouble enough, and grief enough. The horses had worn iron on their hooves. Either some fortunate warriors had stolen them from white men or, more likely, they were being ridden by white men.

Pony soldiers! He was almost certain of it.

He saw through White Deer's silence that she sensed it too, though she would not speak of it and alarm the children.

He pointed toward a break in the gently rolling plain. "There you will find water, and timber to conceal yourselves. Go, while I see what may be ahead of us."

It bothered him that the travois made such deep impressions in the mud. Pony soldiers might overlook horse tracks or assume them to be made by other soldiers, but travois tracks would be unmistakable. He had worried that the cold rain might sicken the children, particularly the two infants. Now he hoped the rain would continue, to wash away the telltale sign.

He rode a long time along the trail of the cavalry, climbing painfully down from the horse when he approached any sort of rise in the prairie so he would present less of a silhouette to sharp-eyed soldiers. He came in sight, finally, of a place the soldiers had chosen to camp for the night, on a tiny creek that afforded little timber, poor cover and no grass for their horses. He watched as they attempted to start a fire. The dead wood was too wet to accept flame easily, and the rain quickly drowned out any fire the soldiers managed to light.

He made a grim smile and hoped they spent a miserable night. Returning to his family, he found that White Deer had set up a makeshift tent with some of the lodge skins to shelter them from the rain. She had managed to make a fire, but like the soldiers, they spent a miserable night.

The rain halted before daybreak. Walking out to look around, Crow Feather was pleased to see that the travois tracks had dissolved, for the most part. But any movement now would create new ones, and there would be no rain to carry them away. He told White Deer they had better remain where they were until the ground dried, and until he felt confident no pony soldiers were around. The tent would have to suffice, for a tepee would stand too tall against the creek bank's low timber, easy for white men's eyes to see.

She had managed to keep the babies dry and reasonably warm. He marveled that she provided milk enough for both. Rabbit's older daughter sobbed and asked several times why they had left her mother, and when they would return to get her. Squirrel was dispirited, but accepted without complaint. Already, Crow Feather thought, he was acquiring the spiritual strength he would need as he grew into a warrior's place.

He did not ride out for three days, lest muddy horse tracks betray the little camp. But idleness and uncertainty about what might be happening elsewhere made him fretful. When he thought the ground was firm enough, he ventured forth. He saw more sign of shod horses, crisscrossing the prairie. The soldiers were like wolves, prowling in all directions. To move his family toward the winter encampment now would be hazardous, the risk of discovery high.

He was about to turn back when he detected movement on the horizon. Breath short, he dismounted quickly and led the horse into a shallow depression where he might not easily be seen. In his anxiety he forgot his sore ribs.

The dark objects proved to be horsemen. For a time he feared they were soldiers, but as they drew nearer he realized they were of the People. The passing of anxiety brought a renewal of pain from his ribs, but he swung up onto the dun's back and set the animal into a long trot.

The men were Comanche, six of them, but their faces were not familiar. He raised his hand in greeting as they halted and waited for him. "I thought everyone would be at the encampment now. Are you looking for the pony soldiers?"

The reply came from a warrior whose deeply lined face told of many summers and many cold winters. A scar across his cheekbone told of a long-ago battle. "The pony soldiers are looking for *us*. Not many of us escaped the encampment with our horses."

"Escaped?" Crow Feather's jaw dropped.

"The soldiers are all around us, like hornets. They found the canyon and surprised us just as the sun came up. They stampeded most of the horses and overran the encampment. They burned the lodges and destroyed everything. Our people are scattered everywhere."

Crow Feather could only stare at him in disbelief. The winter encampment had always been huge. With so many warriors to protect it, how could the soldiers have accomplished such a thing?

"We were asleep, most of us. It was done before we could make ourselves ready. Only a few of us managed to hold on to our horses and get away."

"What of your families?"

The warrior gave him a look of despair. "We do not know. They fled like quail along the canyon bottom and up the walls. They have no food and no blankets. They did not carry anything with them when they ran. It was a terrible thing."

"What will they do?"

"They have little choice. Many have begun walking toward the reservation. Those who have not already started will have to go or starve. The soldiers are herding them like cattle."

"How many were killed?"

"I do not know. Not many, I think. The soldiers were upon us so quickly . . . there was little time to fight."

Crow Feather slumped, his stomach in turmoil. It was almost beyond his imagination that such a thing could happen. The pony soldiers had never seemed difficult to whip, or at least to delay so that they were thwarted in whatever they intended to do. "You say they stampeded the horses. It has never been hard to steal horses from the soldiers. We could get them back."

"Not unless you can make dead horses rise up and

walk. The bluecoats threw our horses together and slaughtered them. We will never ride them again."

A heavy sadness settled over Crow Feather. These men had been driven away from their families. They were fugitives in their own land. Had it not been for Rabbit's illness, his own family would have been in the encampment, and they might be lost to him now as these men's families were lost.

The warrior asked, "How is it that you were here, and not in the camp with the rest of us?"

Crow Feather avoided using Rabbit's name, for one did not speak the name of the dead. "The one who was sick has died. The rest of us were on our way to the encampment when we stopped because of the soldiers."

"It is useless to go there now. For the sake of your family, it would be best that you take them to the reservation. There, at least, they will have food and shelter."

The thought made Crow Feather's stomach crawl. "No! The soldiers have no right to drive us away from our land."

"We are men, and we intend to stay free. But for the women and children, it is best they go for the winter. Perhaps in the spring, when the cold is past, we will find a way to free them."

The reservation . . . Crow Feather had heard much about it, none of it to his liking. There a man was little more than a prisoner, treated like a white man's dog, forced to beg inferior men for his food and his blankets and his shelter. He had no intention of being a prisoner. He had no intention of seeing White Deer and the children become prisoners. Free they were, and free they would remain.

When he declared as much, the warrior said, "You will have to hide them well and be vigilant. The soldiers are trying to find all of us who remain free."

Crow Feather clenched his teeth. "I know a canyon where there are many places to hide. The soldiers will not find us."

The warriors wished him well and rode away. Crow

Feather watched them so long as they were in sight. He saw one turn back, leaving the others. The call of his family was too strong; he was traveling toward the reservation. The others rode on. Crow Feather wondered how long they would hold out before they too decided to turn eastward and yield up their freedom.

At least he had his family with him.

He rode back in the direction he had come from. If he could take his family to his canyon they should be safe until the spirits found a way to release the People from bondage. The spirits had given this land to the Comanche. Surely they would see that the Comanche found a way to keep it.

His ribs started to ache so much that he had to dismount as carefully as he could and walk the last part of the way, leading the dun. The pain made him think of the woman with red hair. He had not told White Deer about her. It was bad enough that he had been brought down by a *teibo* bullet. That it had been fired by a woman was not a thing a warrior would willingly admit . . . unless the woman were truly a spirit, as he suspected. Who had ever seen a real woman with red hair?

Perhaps, if his guardian bear relented, he might someday find the woman. Perhaps then the pain would go away.

SEVEN

Those who lived on the Nueces River pronounced it *New Aces*. Lipan Apaches still challenged newly arriving settlers at the river's beginnings atop a vast limestone plateau and in the ragged green-cedar hills far west of San Antonio. For more than three hundred miles the Nueces snaked crookedly southeastward down the broken edge of the plateau, through the chaparral and across the coastal plain to spill itself into the Gulf of Mexico at the old Texian port of Corpus Christi. Since the revolution against Mexico the region between the Nueces and the Rio Grande, known as the Nueces Strip, had remained in bloody contention. It was held by Texas but claimed by Mexico on grounds that *Presidente* Santa Anna had had no legal right to sign it away. Merciless with the lives of others but a coward when it came to his own, he had accepted all of Sam Houston's surrender terms after his ignominious defeat at San Jacinto.

Into this strip far below San Antonio the Layne family had moved from Alabama when Jeff was a boy, in the days of the Texas republic. They had coaxed crops from a reluctant soil more prone to drought than to rain and raised a few cattle in the heavy brush and on sparse grasslands that disappointed more often than pleased. Despite the hardships, they had endured until war between North and South had impoverished Texas and split the family asunder. Their holdings, meager though they were, had been coveted by opportunists who sought to reap where they had not sown. Blood had been spilled, and old Elijah Layne had fled from a vindictive carpetbag regime that denied justice to those who had supported the Confederacy.

Now a freed electorate had swept the oppressive postwar government from power, and Jeff was returning to this land of his roots. It should be a peaceful land now, and he had seen violence enough. But nagging concerns began to plague him after the party crossed the Red River on its southward journey. Stopping for supplies in the trailside town of Fort Worth, he saw not one face that he remembered. Just a village before, it had spread out like a growth of weeds and had become a town in the years since he had last passed through as a drover with a northbound herd. It was busier, noisier, not unlike Wichita or Dodge City. It seemed that instead of leaving those places behind, he had brought them with him.

On the night they spent there, two men quarreled over a card game, and one of them died in the sawdust on a saloon floor. Jeff was not there, but he heard the shooting and knew what it meant. It took him back to the war, back to the buffalo range, to his several fights with Indians. He had hoped to put all that kind of trouble behind him. This was not the tiny, peaceful Fort Worth he had seen before.

Cap Doolittle put into words the concern Jeff felt. "We been gone a long time. Down home, we ain't apt to find things the way we want to remember them either."

Jeff tried to portray more confidence than he felt. "We couldn't expect everything to stand still just because we weren't here. We can get used to it."

"I wouldn't want to take an oath on it. The more I see here, the better I like the plains."

San Antonio reinforced Jeff's feeling of stepping into a new and strange land. New buildings, new faces, new voices he heard on its dirt streets made him feel less at home than he had hoped. He had accepted change in places farther north, places he had entered as a stranger and for which he felt no ties to what they had been before. Here the changes were discomforting. They gave him a sense of old ties severed, old memories violated.

Granted, some of the landmarks appeared the same. The San Antonio River snaked lazily through the ancient town, unchanged except that its muddied waters were used to carry away much of the refuse from the homes and businesses which squatted beside it. Jeff recognized the strong Mexican flavor of the old stone, adobe and picket houses, and the German influence in such sturdy prewar structures as the Menger Hotel. The Alamo stood as he remembered it.

Nigel Smithwick said, "Even in England, we heard of the Alamo."

Arletta studied the battle-scarred building with awe. "That's where they all died a-fightin', to the last man?"

Jeff had grown up with the legend. Even now he felt a cold shiver as he looked at the battered stone walls that originally had been part of a Spanish mission. "Near two hundred of them. But they held Santy Anna back for two weeks while Sam Houston built up his forces."

Someone had built a roof over the ruined shell of the church. It was being used as a warehouse. To Jeff that seemed a sacrilege, for its floors had been soaked with the blood of men who had given all there was to give.

Cap muttered, "Ain't there no end to what people'll do for money? Probably all them damnyankees that came after the war."

"We can't blame the Yankees for everything. There's a new generation of Texans who don't appreciate what's been paid to give them what they've got."

To Arletta and Nigel the town was quaint, its ethnic mixture of Mexican and American, German and Czech, Polish and Irish and Alsatian making it more exotic than either had ever experienced. They strode off arm in arm to absorb its unusual sights, its sounds, its smells of Mexican spices and European cooking.

Kelly Booth stared after the couple, wishing to go with them but knowing they wanted to be alone.

Jeff pointed. "Yonder's a good saloon that used to offer honest whiskey."

The walls were decorated with horns from Texas steers, from Mexican fighting bulls and whitetail bucks. In between were a pair of colorful serapes and a Mexican sombrero with fancy stitching. But Jeff saw no Mexicans. He guessed they were probably not allowed. Old racial antagonisms still ran strong, nearly forty years after the Texas revolution.

He was relieved to find the bartender's face familiar, though he could not have called the man's name for a hundred dollars. He ordered three glasses and a bottle.

Cap bellied up to the bar, and an ample belly it was. He slapped a big, freckled hand down upon the surface. "We been on a long trail, and we've built up a thirst that'd bring a mule to its knees."

The bartender was used to cowboys returning from the cattle drives, dried out and desperate for refreshment. He was also used to seeing a percentage of them too broke to pay for their liquor. He waited until Jeff placed the money on the bar before he brought out the bourbon. "I don't know what this would do for a mule, but I've seen it bring some cowboys back to life."

The three men were into their second round when a deep voice demanded, "Wouldn't you be Jefferson Layne?"

Feeling defensive, Jeff was slow to turn. The last time someone had called his name like that he had stared into the hostile face of Vesper Freed in Wichita. But in this rancher's aging face he found friendliness, a welcome familiarity.

"Press Anthony?"

"The same. Damn it, Jeff, I like to've not knowed you. You've got some older since last time I seen you." He grinned, a gold tooth catching the light. It was the only thing about him that bespoke any degree of prosperity; his range clothes were dusty, the shirt cuffs raveled from wear. His high-topped boots were run over at the heels.

His sweat-stained hat looked as if it had barely survived a stampede.

"I'd have to say the same about you." The two men gripped arms in the *abrazo* style of southern Texas. Anthony had been a friend of Jeff's father. In those happier times he had appeared somewhat younger than Elijah Layne, but now he seemed to have caught up, his hair completely gray. He was lank, even skinny, the lines of a harsh life carved deeply into his face. He was a man who spent his time outdoors, exposed to the punishing Texas sun, the drying, biting wind. "I didn't expect to see any of you Laynes back in these parts ever again. Where's your old daddy?"

"He died. Up on the plains." It still brought Jeff pain to speak of his father.

"Too bad. I hated the way those damned carpetbaggers and scalywags hounded him out of this country."

"He always wanted to come back, but he knew he couldn't." Jeff introduced Anthony to Cap and Booth. Anthony's eyes brightened in recognition. "Booth, seems to me like I've seen you with old Santiago Ramírez and his boys. And didn't you have a run-in once with Vesper Freed?"

"I did."

"Wisht you'd killed the son of a bitch. But his carpet-bag friends would've hung you, so it's better you didn't. Somebody will, one of these days."

Jeff said, "Vesper passed us on the trail, comin' south."

Anthony gave Jeff a dark study. "Are you figurin' on goin' back to Piedras?"

"It's my home."

"*Was.* You'll have a hard time stayin' out of Vesper's way there now. What you plannin' on doin'?"

"What I always wanted to do, get me some land of my own. Raise cattle."

"It's too late in the season to start a herd up the trail to Kansas, so prices are cheaper than they was in the spring. I'm startin' to buy steers to throw onto my country for the winter. They'll go north when the grass rises again."

"Steers are just for the short term. I'm more interested in buildin' a cow herd."

"I know where there's cows to be had. I'll introduce you around when you're ready to buy. But where'll you put them?"

"I'm thinkin' I might find some grass for lease." In the back of his mind, unspoken, was a hope that somehow he could reacquire the old family home place. It would not be large enough for much of a cow operation, but he would like to have it for remembrance.

"I'd feel better if you'd settle somewhere besides Piedras, but I can understand the way you look at it."

"That's the country I know best."

"*Used* to know. Things've changed. All the carpet-baggers and scalywags ain't left. And there's bandits that come across the river from Mexico to take everything that ain't lashed down with rawhide and stood guard over. I'm afraid you may not like the country much anymore."

Jeff grimaced. Was there no place a man could go to get away from violence? "I've at least got to see it. Then I'll decide if I want to stay."

Anthony's own ranch lay twenty or so miles west of Piedras, a land of mesquite and prickly pear and chaparral within less than a day's ride of the Rio Grande. "Come see me when you're ready. I'll help you find some cows and some country to run them on." His face furrowed deeply. "But I feel like I ought to warn you. You may not want to stay long." He raised his glass. "Here's to Elijah Layne, a damned good man who just wanted to be left alone. God rest him in peace."

In contrast to Fort Worth and San Antonio, Piedras seemed to have shrunk. Its dirt streets were as quiet as if everybody had gone to a funeral. Like San Antonio, it had been a Mexican village since before the revolution, and despite much *Americano* infusion it still retained the Mexican atmosphere—stone and adobe houses, brush *jacales* for the poorest of the poor. A significant percentage of these dwellings seemed to have been abandoned, however.

Unless Jeff had miscalculated, this was Saturday. In earlier times, a Saturday afternoon would have guaranteed a goodly amount of horse, wagon and foot traffic around the courthouse square. He saw only two horsemen and a Mexican ox cart now as he rode along the dusty, rutted street, Booth on his right-hand side, the Smithwicks following with the wagon.

Cap had taken a different fork in the road to visit his old home in Karnes County. He had promised to come to Piedras in two or three weeks, once he had said his howdies to all his kith and kin. He had looked forward to seeing them, but he said one should take his relatives in moderation, as he should take his whiskey.

Jeff had thought Booth too might take his leave, for Piedras had been less than hospitable to him in the past. But the cowboy had said, "Winter's comin' on before long, and I probably won't get steady work till spring. If you can find any use for me, I'd be tickled to stay with you."

Arletta pitched in, "You'll be needin' some experienced help, Jeff. Nigel here, he's got it all to learn when it comes to cattle."

Booth gave Arletta an appreciative glance. Jeff could not tell from English's expression if he agreed with his wife. In any case, he made no comment.

Jeff said, "I don't know that we can pay much for your help till we get some cows. But we'd feed you and find you a place to roll out your blankets." Though he had not seen Booth work with cattle, the cowboy's willingness to carry his load and more in camp indicated that he would be a good hand. Jeff's principal concern remained Booth's streak of recklessness, a tendency toward quick flashes of temper. That, he supposed, was his heritage from a wayward, confrontational father.

"Fair enough," Booth responded. "I don't fancy sittin' out the winter in town, countin' off the days in some leaky *jacal*. Besides, if you have any trouble with Freed . . ."

"Why should I have trouble with Freed?"

"It's plain enough that you've got no use for one another." Booth pointed toward the stone courthouse and a small but formidable-looking stone jail that stood beside it. "Yonder's where I spent time starin' out between the bars for the trouble *I* had with him."

"They tell me his friends don't run the courthouse anymore."

"He's gotten big enough that maybe he don't need friends in the courthouse. Sheriff Golightly would like to hang a charge around his neck, but he ain't been able to."

"Golightly? Would that be Morris Golightly?"

"That's him. Used to be a Ranger before the war. Soon's the Confederates got their vote back they elected him sheriff. Got themselves a decent judge too, for a change. But they can't undo everything the carpetbaggers did. They can't take back everything that was stolen."

Jeff could see the wagon yard beyond the courthouse. Every town of any consequence had a wagon yard where visitors in from the country could put up their mounts or teams and, if they couldn't or wouldn't pay for a hotel room, could sleep on a cot under the roof of a barn or shed. "I remember Golightly as a fair man. I'll go have a talk with him soon's we get camped."

The courthouse was two stories high but relatively small, reflecting the county's limited financial resources at the time it was built, before the war. Most of the population had been small farmers and ranchers, far more Mexican than *Americano,* hard put to pay even the modest taxes levied against their lands. Like the Laynes, they had lived with a wolf at the back door, or at least at the back gate. From the half-deserted look of the place now, it was even worse off than before.

A small hand-painted sign extended at a right angle from a door frame on the first floor. In letters that started large and squeezed up toward the end, it proclaimed SHERIFF. A tall, chunky, gray-haired man sat hunched at a

rolltop desk, laboriously scrawling out a letter with a
metal pen that scratched in protest against the paper.

"Sheriff Golightly?"

The man turned, peering over a pair of reading glasses
perched halfway down a prominent nose. "I'm him. Somethin' I can do for you?"

"I'm Jeff Layne. Remember me?"

The sheriff quickly removed the glasses, as if ashamed
to be caught wearing them. He arose from a rawhide-
covered chair that had sagged under his weight. Despite
his years, he had a grip like a blacksmith's vise. "I
wouldn't have knowed without you told me. Last time I
seen you was when you went off to war. You had barely
learned how to shave your face."

"I've shaved it many a time since."

"Ain't we all? It's good to have a Layne back in this
country. Sorry about your daddy."

"You already know?"

"Vesper Freed came in to see me the day he got back
from Kansas."

"In a hurry, wasn't he?"

"He wanted to know if there was any charges hangin'
over *you*. I told him there wasn't. You had already left
with a herd of cattle when your daddy got into his shootin'
scrape with them land grabbers."

"He sure didn't want me to come back."

"As I remember, you two commenced tanglin' when
you were kids in school. Seems to me like you both
courted the same girl, too."

"Eva. But he's the one who married her, so I don't see
that he's got anything to be concerned about there."

"From what I hear, the only thing holdin' the marriage together is a piece of paper and that boy they've got.
Vesper may be afraid you'll bust his family in two."

"I haven't seen Eva in fifteen-sixteen years. I'm not in
the business of bustin' up marriages."

"Vesper doesn't know that." The sheriff pulled a pint
whiskey bottle from a desk drawer. Jeff took a small
drink. Golightly then turned it up for a long swallow.

"With the help of the courthouse gang and the scalywag
state police, Vesper took over a lot of land durin' reconstruction. They'd raise taxes to where folks couldn't pay,
then he'd take their places for a few cents on the dollar.
When he couldn't buy them out, he got the state police to
help him run them out. That was the meanest, worst cor-
rupted bunch of skunks that ever smelled up Texas."

"I can remember when the Freeds were as poor as us
Laynes. Maybe poorer. It was always a mystery where
Vesper got his first money."

Golightly made a grunt that seemed to come from
deep inside. "You recall, don't you, when Old Man Freed
was killed?"

"Mexican outlaws, was the way I heard it."

"Vesper was just a button, fourteen-fifteen years old.
Him and the old man was out gatherin' their little shirttail
bunch of scrub cattle when the border-jumpers took after
them. The old man made Vesper take his horse because it
was faster, so Vesper managed to outrun them. They
caught the old man. He didn't have anything worth
stealin' except a slow horse, so they throwed a rope
around his neck and drug him to death in the brush.

"Vesper declared war on the whole Mexican race.
There was first one and then another of them found dead,
and nobody knew for sure who killed them. When he was
barely grown he dropped out of sight for a while. We kept
hearin' stories out of Mexico about some gringo bandit
robbin' banks and merchants and such, and leavin' a trail
of dead Mexicans behind him. We never did know for sure
it was Vesper, but when he finally showed up again he had
half a wagonload of Mexican silver."

Jeff remembered. "Me and Dad, we talked about
that."

"Pretty soon after he married Eva he disappeared
again, just ahead of the conscription officers. We always
figured he went to California or someplace out West.
Wasn't likely he went to Mexico, because they'd've stood
him against the wall. After the war he came back and dug
up his silver from wherever he had buried it. Fell right in

with the carpetbag government. Started takin' over land, especially from the Mexicans. He purely hates the sight of a Mexican."

"I don't suppose he mentioned to you that he killed a friendly Indian on his way back from Wichita? He got across the Red River just a little ahead of the army."

Golightly scowled. "He forgot to tell me about that. I wish he'd done it on this side of the river."

"Can't you arrest him anyway?"

"The state of Texas ain't goin' to extradite anybody for killin' an Indian. I'll have to wait for him to step over the line here at home."

Jeff began to fidget in his chair. "Sheriff, that old home place of ours . . . do you know who owns it now?"

Golightly appeared pained at the question. "After all the trouble died down, it went like so many other places did around here. Vesper got it."

Jeff had half expected that answer, but it hit him like a blow to the stomach. Of all the people he could think of, Vesper Freed was the last he would want to see owning the old Layne place. "You reckon there's anything I can do to get it back, any legal knots that Vesper didn't tie up good and tight?"

"There's been others tried. As corrupt as the reconstruction was, whatever they did was legal at the time. They wrote their own laws." He reached out to lay a heavy hand on Jeff's shoulder. "Be honest with yourself. That wasn't much of a place. Soil poor, and thinner than paper. There's good land to be had all over Texas, better than yours ever was."

Jeff squeezed his hands together, his right thumb digging a deep hole into his left palm. "I can't argue with you about that. But do you think there'd be any harm in me just goin' by and takin' a look at the old place? My mother's buried there, you know, and a baby sister."

"I'd be glad to ride out with you, just to be sure there won't be any trouble."

"Thanks, but I'd rather go by myself. There's too many memories . . ."

"All right. But don't start anything with Vesper or let him start anything with you. Bad as I'd like to put him away, I wouldn't want it to be for killin' you."

The wagon yard owner had already heard from Arletta and English the plans for going into the cattle business. When Jeff returned from the courthouse, the man said, "I don't suppose you'd like to go into the wagon yard business instead? I'd let you have this place worth the money."

Jeff had seen at first glance that the barn and corrals had been neglected. Gates sagged, and some fences leaned in one direction or another. Several broken boards needed replacing in the sides of the barn, from which much of the original red paint had long since peeled away. Only a few horses stood in the corrals. "Doesn't look like the trade has been too lively."

"It takes people to make for good business, lots of people. Too many around here was squeezed out while the thieves ran the courthouse." He spat tobacco at a chicken that pecked amid old horse droppings. "You bein' a Layne, you'd know about that."

"I would, for a fact."

"One big rancher or farmer just don't spend as much as a bunch of little ones. The bigger they get, the tighter they hold on to their money."

Jeff had no interest in going into the wagon yard business. He nodded toward the tent Arletta and English had set up to assure their privacy. It seemed incongruous beneath the protective roof of a shed. "I saw several vacant houses in town. Reckon there'd be one available for those folks till we get settled someplace?"

"I've got just the one. Belonged to my partner before he sold out to me and moved to San Antonio." The livery-man winced. "Only smart thing I ever seen him do."

The house was of frame construction, a contrast to the many neighboring Mexican adobe and stone buildings. It had a barn out in back. Jeff told Booth, "The barn'll do for me and you to sleep in. We wouldn't want to crowd the newlyweds."

Booth agreed. "Arletta deserves to live in a real house instead of a tent."

Jeff had no argument with that, but he was a little troubled over the forceful way Booth said it, as if he had a proprietary interest in her welfare.

The liveryman volunteered that the house had some leaks in the roof. He offered its use free of charge if Jeff and English and Booth would replace the bad shingles and do a little other repair work to keep the place livable until he could find a buyer for it. That suited Jeff's sense of constructive frugality.

Booth confided that he had spent a couple of winters carpentering when he could not find a riding job. Growing up in a privileged family, Nigel Smithwick had little experience with hammer and saw, but he had shown himself to be a willing learner at other phases of manual labor. He exhibited no reservations about this one.

When Jeff had everybody suitably settled to the tasks at hand, he decided it was time to ride out and look at whatever remained of the home place. He regarded the visit with a mixture of anticipation and dread—anticipation for the memories it would bring back, dread over the fact that the place was in the hands of someone who would probably do whatever he felt necessary to see that it never again belonged to a Layne.

Booth and Nigel Smithwick were apprehensive. Booth asked, "Don't you think we'd ought to go with you, in case you run into somebody?"

Jeff knew who Booth's *somebody* was. "Sheriff Golightly asked me the same thing. I'm not takin' a gun with me, so I don't see how I can get into any trouble."

Smithwick said, "I wish you would reconsider. Without you, Arletta and I would be lost here."

"Nothin's fixin' to happen to me."

Arletta brought Jeff some bread and meat in a sack. "We wouldn't want to see you get hungry." A hint of tears showed in her eyes before she looked away from him. "I reckon I can understand how you feel about seein' the place where you growed up. I used to wish sometimes I could go back to the farm where we lived in Ohio. Then I'd get to thinkin' how much it had probably changed, and about my family bein' dead. Goin' there would just open up a lot of old wounds that was a long time healin'.'' She looked back at him, the tears more than a hint. "I hope it won't turn out that way for you."

"If I don't go see, I'll always wonder."

The old farm was twelve miles from Piedras. Jeff held the sorrel Socks to a modest trot, choking down a strong urge to push him into a lope and get there quicker. He did not want to abuse the horse. He had gone all these years without seeing the home place; he could endure a little longer.

His heartbeat quickened as the old wagon road made familiar turns and he saw an open flat where he used to hunt quail on a neighbor's land, dividing his kill with the landowner to keep his welcome warm. He stopped a few minutes on a narrow creek where he had often sunk a hook, usually catching more sleep than fish. Just out of sight, over a low ridge to the north, lay the old Freed family farm. Folks said Vesper had torn down the small shack where he had spent a resentful boyhood. He had built a large frame house with gables and steamboat gingerbread trim in an effort to overwhelm the grating memories of early poverty. Jeff had no wish to see it.

He came finally to the rise that would carry him within sight of the old Layne house. He could no longer resist. He touched spurs to Socks and set him into a lope.

He drew up on the reins before he had gone twenty yards down the slope. Disappointment struck him hard, like an unexpected fist. The adobe house was gone. The yard fence was gone. Even the barn and corrals were missing. It was as if a tornado had stripped the place naked.

He blinked hard, not quite believing. He set the horse to moving again, this time in a walk, delaying the inevitable. For a moment he entertained a wild thought that he had taken a wrong turn on the wagon road, that he had come to the wrong place. But that was a foolish notion. He knew the road too well; he could have followed it in the pitch black of a cloudy night. He *had*, many a time.

He saw one familiar landmark, a chinaberry tree in what had been the front yard. He had climbed it often as a barefoot boy. He had fallen from it once and cracked a bone in his arm. The tree had grown since he had last seen it, but there was no mistaking its shape.

The only remaining sign of the house was a crumbling outline of its former dimensions. The adobe walls had been dismantled and the blocks taken away except for the bottom course. A pile of stones marked what was left of the chimney. Some shattered bluish glass lay on the ground, remnant of a windowpane. Every vestige of lumber from roof and doors had been burned or carried off. Behind the house, a deteriorating stone fence marked the place where his mother and father had kept a garden. The ground had grown up in weeds. Several young mesquites stood waist high, their stems about as big around as one of his fingers.

"My God!" he declared aloud to himself. "It's like us Laynes never existed."

He angered at the thought that this had probably been Vesper Freed's reasoning. His feelings against the Laynes—Jeff in particular—had led him to remove all possible trace of the lives they had lived here.

He thought of the family cemetery, out on a gentle hill a quarter mile west of the house. *Surely even Vesper wouldn't be so low and mean* . . .

He spurred the sorrel to a long trot, slowing once he saw the waist-high rock fence. That, at least, had not been disturbed. Neglect had allowed weeds to take the small plot, but otherwise it had escaped the indignities suffered by the house and the barn. He dismounted and dropped the reins. Socks would stand as if he were tied. Some previous owner had trained him well.

The little wooden gate sagged but was barrier enough to prevent cattle from entering. Jeff swung it outward on its dried leather hinges. He knelt before a rough stone slab and pulled up enough summer-dried weeds to reveal his mother's name. He rubbed an accumulation of dirt away from the carved letters and removed his hat.

"Mama, it's just as well that you went when you did. You missed a lot of things you wouldn't've wanted to see."

He glanced at the spot that had been left for his father, beside his mother. Elijah Layne would never rest here. He lay in an unmarked grave far to the north, on the Comanche-dominated buffalo range. There was not a chance in a thousand that Jeff could ever find the exact place again. "I'll have a stone put here with his name on it. That's the best I can do."

He pulled the rest of the weeds from his mother's grave, then did the same where a baby sister lay beside her, opposite the spot intended for Elijah. His throat tight, he turned again and looked down the hill to where the house had been. He felt empty.

He squeezed the hat between his hands. "Goodbye, Mama." He walked out and carefully closed the gate. He would send somebody to clean the cemetery and put in a new and stronger gate, an iron one next time. He was not sure he would come back himself. He was not sure he would ever want to.

In obliterating the old place, Freed had cut Jeff's roots out from under him. It was not home anymore. He sensed that it never could be again. He doubted that he could ever feel totally at home anywhere around here.

He paused just a moment at the site of the house, then pushed onto the trail toward town. He had gone but a short way when he saw three horses at the top of the slope. Two men sat in their saddles, and one stood on the ground. His heart took a small jump. He wondered if he had been wise in not bringing a gun. Then he recognized the men, and the tension drained away.

They waited for him, Sheriff Golightly standing beside his horse, Nigel Smithwick and Kelly Booth sitting on theirs. Booth had one leg hooked casually across his saddle horn.

The sheriff spoke first. "We didn't want to disturb

your privacy, but we thought it might be smart to keep an eye on you."

English seemed to expect rebuke, and he tried to head it off. "Kelly and I went to the sheriff. We were concerned that you might find yourself at a disadvantage, being unarmed."

They meant well. That they had worried about him made Jeff lean toward gratitude rather than resentment. "I didn't see a soul. Anyway, Vesper wouldn't shoot an unarmed man."

English said, "Have you forgotten that poor Indian?"

The sheriff said, "There's another consideration. These bandits that come over from Mexico, they'd kill for that sorrel of yours."

"Bandits?" Jeff remembered that Press Anthony had spoken of them.

"It goes both ways. There's some Texas boys who don't see nothin' wrong with raidin' over into Mexico. I figure Vesper has done it. And there are Mexicans who take it as their patriotic duty to raise hell on this side of the Rio Grande. Sometimes it looks like an even swap. Unless you get caught in the middle."

Jeff chewed thoughtfully on his lip. "That could make it risky to set up ranchin' here, couldn't it?"

"You could move farther west along the Nueces and get away from the bandits. But there you'd never know when the Apaches might ride down from the hills and come callin' on you. If I was considerin' ranchin' I'd go north, toward the plains. There's a whole empire of unclaimed range up yonder."

English declared, "And more than a sufficiency of Comanche Indians."

"Not for long. Word is that the army is movin' from all directions to drive them to the reservation. Mackenzie's regiment marched north from Fort Clark to be part of the campaign. If I was a Comanche and saw Mackenzie comin', I'd hightail it quick. That is one tough Yankee."

The buffalo hunters' complaints must have caught Washington's attention, Jeff thought. The hide men around Dodge City were probably chomping at the bit, waiting for the army to declare victory so they could resume the slaughter. They were welcome to his part of it. He had taken his last buffalo hide. But the thought of all that open range up there intrigued him. Without the Indians standing in the way . . .

The sheriff said, "It may tickle you to know that these bandits seem to have a special grudge against Vesper Freed. They've hit him the hardest of anybody."

"I'm not surprised. He's made a lot of enemies."

The sheriff shifted his gaze to Booth. "As I recall, you spent some time in the Piedras jail for tryin' to stand in Vesper's way."

A remembered anger flared in Booth's eyes. "It wouldn't've happened if you'd been the sheriff then."

"They throwed me out of office for bein' Confederate. I had about as much authority as a jackrabbit in a coyote den."

Jeff perceived that the buggy's occupants were a woman and a boy before he and the others met it in the wagon road. A horseman rode alongside. Jeff saw him draw a rifle from its scabbard beneath his leg and lay it across his lap, moving around to the left-hand side of the buggy so the muzzle would point away from the woman.

The sheriff squinted, trying for recognition. "Jeff, I believe you'll know the lady."

Eva Freed wore a duster and had a broad-brimmed man-style hat pulled down over her eyes. Saying something to the boy who sat beside her, she sawed on the reins. The black buggy horse stopped. She spoke to the horseman, who slipped the rifle back into its scabbard. Jeff recognized the young cowboy Davy Osborne.

Eva smiled self-consciously, but the smile did not successfully cover the rush of emotion in her face. "Hello, Jeff." She stared at him as if he were an apparition. "Vesper told me you were back in the country."

Jeff's throat tightened, making it difficult to speak. Fifteen years fell away, and in his mind's eye he saw the girl who had promised to wait for him when he marched off to join the glorious fight, which was not supposed to last more than three months. Her promise to wait had lasted six.

The face was much as he had remembered it, but it was no longer a girl's; it was that of a mature woman. Her voice had deepened. Her gray eyes showed creases at the corners, and a sadness that hinted of internal scars.

"Eva." His voice sounded unnatural to him. "I hadn't figured I'd see you."

"You've been out to visit your old place?"

"What's left of it."

"It must've been a disappointment to you. I'm sorry." She turned to the boy beside her. He appeared to be eleven or twelve. "This is my son Daniel. Daniel, Mr. Layne."

Daniel's eyes were unfriendly. So was his voice. "Daddy told me about you."

"I'm sure he did." Jeff wanted to say, *Don't believe everything he says,* but a boy at this age was supposed to revere his father. There would be time enough in the future for the alienation that so often arose between generations. Though Jeff had loved his own father, there had been occasions when they had disagreed almost to the point of violence.

Eva tried to introduce Jeff to the young horseman. Jeff explained that they had met weeks before, near Wichita. Osborne nodded, ill at ease. "Howdy again, Mr. Layne."

Eva said, "Vesper won't allow me to go to town, even, without a bodyguard. He's afraid of bandits."

"From what the sheriff tells me, he's got reason." He did not want to talk about bandits. "You look fine, Eva. Time ain't done you any harm that I can tell."

"*You've* changed. I don't see anything left of the young man who went off to war."

That young man had disappeared during the hardships and horrors of nearly four years' campaigning, had suffered through the long healing process after taking a bullet in his hip, had tasted bitter disappointment upon finding that the girl he had intended to marry had accepted someone for whom he had no use. Whatever remained had ground itself away during the hard years on the cattle trail and the buffalo range. He could have told her all that, but he said only, "It was a long time ago."

"Now that you're here, do you plan to stay?"

He started to tell her he doubted it. Changes had been so drastic that this no longer was home. But she would probably pass the information on to her husband. He did not want to give Vesper that much satisfaction. "We haven't decided, my partners and me."

"I wish you'd come out to the house sometime. We'd have a lot to talk about."

Jeff saw no welcome in the boy's eyes. They were very much the eyes of the Vesper Freed he had fought so often on the school grounds, and wherever else they met. "I don't know as it'd be a good idea. I doubt that Vesper would like it."

"He wouldn't. But I feel that I owe you some explanations."

"You don't owe me a thing." He touched the brim of his hat. "It's been good to see you." He set the sorrel to moving. He heard the creak of the buggy wheels and tried not to look back, but he had to. He saw that she had turned in the buggy seat, still watching him. All the old emotion, the old sense of loss, welled up in him again.

The other three horsemen spread out on either side. Nigel Smithwick said, "A splendid-looking woman." Jeff had told the Smithwicks very little about Eva. They knew only that a girl had disappointed him years ago. English was sensitive enough, however, to grasp that Eva was the one.

Jeff said, "She made her choice a long time ago." He tried to put down anew the disappointment he thought he had buried in the distant past. "I wonder what Arletta's fixin' for supper."

EIGHT

Arletta Smithwick had a book propped on the kitchen table in front of her while she peeled the skin from a potato. She spoke some of the words in a low voice, trying to remember how Nigel had told her they were supposed to be pronounced. Though her husband had assured her she was making good progress at learning proper English, she fretted that she could not always understand the reasoning. Two words might be spelled almost alike, yet be pronounced differently. What was the use in studying rules if the rules were so often ignored?

And her husband, educated in England, pronounced certain words in a way that set him apart from the men around him. His diction might serve very well if he were still in England, but he was in Texas now, and it was likely that in Texas he would stay. If she followed his example, would she not find herself a misfit here, just as Nigel still was in some respects?

She wondered if she might already be something of a misfit. Most of the women she encountered in Piedras were Mexican and spoke little or no English. She was having problem enough learning what her husband regarded as the proper use of her own language; she could hardly find time to learn Spanish as well. And the climate: even in September the days were still hot and humid. She found herself perspiring from the time she left bed each morning until long after the sun went down. Jeff said it was because of moisture drifting in from the Gulf of Mexico. Sometimes the nights cooled to a comfortable level, sometimes they did not. She had never encountered this difficulty on the high plains.

Kelly Booth came through the open kitchen door, carrying an armload of wood chopped to the right length for the big iron cook stove. The wood box was already full, so some of the sticks rolled off and clattered upon the floor despite his best effort to stack them neatly.

She said, "I didn't really need any more yet."

"You can never have enough wood. I just wanted to be sure you didn't have to go out and chop any of it yourself."

She sensed that Booth simply sought an excuse to come into the house where she was, if only for a minute or two. While his attention pleasantly fed whatever female vanity she harbored, it troubled her that he might become too serious. Booth needed to find some other young woman upon whom to concentrate his yearnings. Arletta's exposure to the folks of Piedras had been too limited for her to seek out anyone she thought might serve that purpose. Some things a man was supposed to do for himself anyway.

She asked, "Any sign of Nigel and Jeff?"

"Not yet. It's a good ways out to the ranch where Press Anthony was takin' them."

"You know this country. Would that be the kind of place they've been lookin' for?"

"I worked once for Old Man Jones that owns it. Nice old feller. Carpetbag taxes made him sell off all the cattle he could gather, but he managed to hang on to the land in spite of Vesper Freed."

"Freed won't be pleased if Jeff takes a lease on it."

Booth grinned wickedly. "No, he won't." He took out a pocketknife, wiped a blade against his trouser leg and began to peel a potato. Arletta doubted that the trousers were any cleaner than the knife, but frying in hot

grease ought to kill anything that might have been trans-
ferred.

She cut her potato into thin slices. "Jeff hasn't talked
much since he ran into Mrs. Freed. What did you think of
her?"

"She's fair-lookin', for an older woman."

"Older? She can't be more than in her middle to late
thirties."

"To me, that's an older woman."

Booth was still in his early to mid twenties, the best
Arletta could judge. "I don't see how she could've turned
her back on a good man like Jeff and married the likes of
Vesper Freed."

"Sheriff Golightly says she had her reasons. Most
people just figured she married him because he had some
money."

"She ought to've had her hair pulled out for what she
done . . ." She caught herself, knowing Nigel would have
corrected her. "*Did* to Jeff."

"How come you're so concerned about Jeff?"

"I had some brothers that didn't come back from the
war. Jeff's sort of taken their place, the best anybody
could." She stopped peeling the potato. "*You* remind me
of my youngest brother, a little."

"Brother?"

She knew that was not what he wanted to hear. "He
was too young for the war, but he rode off west to look
for his fortune. Me and Papa never heard from him again.
I daydream sometimes that he'll come ridin' up one day
with his saddle bags full of money, rich as Croesus. But I
know he's probably dead. Else we'd've heard somethin'."

"I guess it don't hurt to dream, long as you don't put
all your hopes into it. I've done it myself, now and again."
He gave her a glance, then quickly looked away as their
eyes met. "That English, he treats you all right, don't he?"

Arletta suspected she knew what he really wanted to
ask. She tried to find the right words. "I love him. He's the
best thing that ever happened to me."

He peeled another potato, wasting nearly half of it. "Just as long as you're happy."

"I am."

He wiped the blade on his trousers again and walked outside.

Up north on the buffalo range she had often been aware of men in camp following her with their eyes, but she had known it was not so much personal as simply that she was the only woman around. With Booth, she suspected it was more than that. She did not know what she could do about it.

She heard hoofbeats outside, and the jingle of spurs. Her heart warmed at the thought of Nigel's return. She quickly set aside the potato-peeling task, wiped her hands on her cotton apron and hurried to the door.

Instead of Nigel, she saw Cap Doolittle standing there with Booth. Cap turned toward her, his big moustache lifting in a broad smile. "My, hon, but ain't you a sight for eyes that ain't seen nothin' pretty since I left you!"

He didn't appear to have shaved in days, and his shirttail hung out, its edges frazzled.

"Well, *you're* a sight too. Thought you was goin' to visit your kinfolks longer than this."

"Two days was like two weeks. Kinfolks! A man don't have no choice; he's born with them. But at least he's free to pick his friends."

"Nigel and Jeff ought to be in directly. I'll be gettin' supper started. I expect you're hungry."

"I could eat a boar hog, tusks and all." He turned with Booth, leading his horse toward the barn. Arletta watched him, glad he was back. Despite his jovial air, Cap Doolittle could turn dead serious in an instant when the need arose. He could stand like a rock against whatever came at him.

She turned toward the stove to stir up the coals and kindle a fire for supper. She felt suddenly queasy, the room unsteady before her eyes. She braced herself against the wood box until the moment passed. It was not the first time.

She thought she knew what the trouble was, if *trouble* was the right word for it. She was overdue for her monthly period.

Wouldn't Nigel bust his buttons if he knew! But she would not tell him, not until she was sure. She did not want him disappointed if the signs turned out to be wrong. She smiled to herself, picturing his reaction.

She heard a knock on the door frame. It was not like Jeff or Booth to knock. They just walked in, unless it was after bedtime and the lamp was out. She turned and caught a sharp breath.

Vesper Freed stood on the tiny front porch, his hand poised to knock again. "I'm lookin' for Jeff Layne." His voice was stern, almost accusatory, as if he thought she might be hiding him somewhere.

"He ain't . . . isn't here. He went out in the country."

A boy sat on a horse and held the reins to the one Freed had been riding. She guessed this was the Freeds' son.

She had not invited Freed in, and he made no move to come in on his own. "You're that Englishman's wife, ain't you?"

"I'm Mrs. Nigel Smithwick."

"You don't sound English to me." Before she could think of a reply, he continued, "I got a message for Jeff. You tell him I warned him not to mess with anything that's mine."

She felt defensive. "I don't know that he has."

"He was out to the place that used to belong to his family. It belongs to me now, and he's not welcome. And he talked to my wife and boy on the road. If he does it again he'll find more trouble than he knows what to do with."

Her anger began rising. "As to him runnin' into your wife, that was pure accident. And as to him visitin' the place where he lived when he was a boy, I don't see how you could deny him that much."

"What's mine is mine. I don't want him or anybody else messin' with it."

She put her hands on her hips. "You must live a miserable life, Mr. Freed."

His eyes narrowed. "What do you mean?"

"From what I hear, you don't like anybody much. I don't think you even like yourself."

He stared so hard that she felt he was looking through her. "You're wrong. There's one person I care the whole world about." He nodded toward his son.

"If you cared as much as you say, you wouldn't bring that boy with you on a visit like this, and let him hear you talk like you just did."

Color spread in Freed's face. She suspected that had she been a man she would have a fight on her hands. "He's old enough to learn the way the world works."

"You, sir, are a damned poor teacher!"

The fierceness subsided in his face. "You speak right out, don't you?"

"I generally say what I'm thinkin'."

"That's better than just turnin' the silence on a man and freezin' him with your eyes."

She discerned pain in his expression. She sensed that he had endured a lot of the silence of which he spoke. For a moment she could almost feel sorry for him. "I'll tell Jeff what you said. But I reckon he'll do whatever he feels like. He don't take kindly to orders, and neither do I."

Freed nodded stiffly. "I expect your Englishman has got his hands full, all right. Tell him he's a lucky man." He turned back toward the horse his son held for him just as Kelly Booth and Cap came around the corner from the barn.

Booth demanded, "What're you doin' here, Freed?" His right hand was on his hip, where he wore a six-shooter each time he rode out.

Arletta's heart quickened before she saw that Booth was unarmed. He had evidently left his pistol in the barn. *That's the Lord's blessing,* she thought.

Freed said, "I came to deliver a message. I delivered

it." His gaze went back to Arletta. "You tell Jeff." He took the reins from his son and swung onto his horse. He gave Arletta another moment's appraisal, then rode away, the boy spurring to catch up.

Booth moved quickly onto the porch. "If he did anything to upset you, Arletta, just tell me. I'll go catch him."

"He did nothin'. He came to see Jeff, not me."

Booth knotted his fists. "He ever bothers you, you let me know. That'll be the last time."

Cap looked at Booth and blinked. Arletta saw a light of understanding come into his eyes.

When Jeff and Nigel failed to show up at the usual suppertime, she fed Cap and Booth. Cap stuffed himself as if he had not eaten during the whole time he had been away. She was going to have to peel a couple more potatoes for the other two. Just at dusk she heard horses and went to the bedroom window that faced the barn. She saw Jeff and Nigel greeting Cap as if he had been gone for a month.

Put those three together—and add Kelly Booth—and Vesper Freed could raise all the hell he wanted to; it wouldn't make a particle of difference, she thought proudly.

Nigel came into the house a little ahead of Jeff. She suspected Jeff delayed on purpose to let them have their private moment first. Nigel crushed her in his arms. "I must say, my lady, that I have missed you terribly."

"You've only been gone since daylight."

"Each hour was like a week." He turned to look at the stove but did not take his arm from around her waist. "And what delights are you offering me tonight?"

"If you mean for supper, beefsteak. That's the only thing around here that's cheap and plentiful."

"Supper was what I had in mind. For now." He studied her intently. "Are you feeling all right? I see a slight flush in your face."

She wondered if he could guess the truth. "It's this heat. I'm not used to it yet."

"That will pass. Autumn is upon us, and winter is not far away."

Nigel took his arm from Arletta's waist as Jeff's footsteps sounded on the porch. Jeff washed his face in a pan outside and was still drying his hands on a cotton towel when he stepped into the kitchen. "Sorry to be late, but we had a right smart of business to talk about. We took a winter's grass lease on the Jones ranch."

"Just for the winter?"

"Come spring we'll probably take our cattle and leave here."

"But this is your home country."

"It used to be." Jeff turned to Cap and Booth as they walked in. "You-all ready to do some real cowboyin'?"

Booth grinned at Cap. "Rarin' to go."

"Jones says there's maybe a hundred or two wild cattle out in the brush that he never was able to gather. They're ours, as many as we can catch and keep ahold of. Every cow we can take means one less we have to buy. Every steer or bull we get we can sell to a trail driver in the spring and buy a cow."

Arletta had seldom seen him so exuberant. She decided to wait until later to tell him what Vesper Freed had said. She did not want to shatter the mood that had him stepping so high.

She said, "It's easy to stand here in the kitchen and talk about catchin' those cattle. It's liable to be some dangerous when you actually go to do it."

"We've all done it before."

"Nigel hasn't. I wouldn't want you goin' and gettin' him killed."

Smithwick protested, "I learned to survive the buffalo range. I should be able to survive the cattle range."

She felt the stirring in her stomach again and hoped it did not show in her face. "I just wouldn't want you takin' chances."

Jeff promised, "We'll look out for him. Anyway, we won't start the roughest work just yet. We need to buy us some gentle cows to put out there and help hold the wild ones. And some oxen we can neck the *ladinos* to and make them settle down."

She had only the vaguest idea what he was talking about. She wondered what a *ladino* was, but she would not ask and show her ignorance. She would listen and figure it out sooner or later in the context of the men's conversation.

While Jeff and Nigel dug hungrily into their supper, Cap poured coffee from his cup into a saucer and blew across it to cool it down. He stared so intently at Arletta that she became uneasy. After supper she began washing the dishes in a pan. To her surprise, Cap picked up a cotton towel and began drying them. He never had done it before. She had to stop once when queasiness came over her.

He said, "You ain't told English yet, have you?"

"Told him what?"

"Look, hon, I been around longer than these other fellers, even Jeff. I can see it in your eyes. You're in a family way."

"I ain't . . . I'm not sure yet."

"It's true. It's as plain as if it was wrote on a chalkboard in a schoolhouse. And don't you be worryin' about English. We'll watch out for him. We won't let you become a widow before he becomes a papa."

She let a plate slip back into the pan of soapy dishwater as she turned to the old cowboy. "How long has it been since a woman has kissed you?"

"Not countin' kinfolks? A way too long."

She put her wet hands against his cheeks and kissed him hard.

Surprised and delighted, he rubbed his big knuckles across his moustache. "That was worth the long ride back . . . even if it does taste a little like soap."

Nigel reentered the house. Cap stood grinning at him a moment before slapping a big hand against the Englishman's shoulder. "Good night, *papacito*."

Nigel blinked in confusion. He picked up the lamp

and followed Arletta into the small bedroom. "If I didn't know better, I would think Cap was drunk."

"Only on coffee."

Nigel removed his boots, then his shirt and trousers. He turned down the patchwork quilt as Arletta slipped a cotton gown over her head and entered the bed from her side of it. He asked, "What was that word Cap called me?"

"*Papacito*. I think it's Mexican."

Nigel turned down the wick, then blew out the lamp. A rising moon reflected enough light through the window that she could watch him as he crawled into bed beside her. "Peculiar-sounding word. What do you suppose it means?"

"Little daddy, I think. Little father."

Nigel was silent a moment, then reached for the lamp. He jerked his hand back in surprise from its hot glass chimney and blew on his fingers, uttering a few words he had not taught her but that she knew well enough. He got up and found his trousers where he had laid them across a chair, fumbling in his pocket and striking a match. He held its flame close enough so he could study her face in its flickering light.

"Am I to take that as meaning . . ."

"Cap said it shows in my eyes."

"I don't see anything."

"You're fixin' to *feel* somethin' if you don't blow out that match."

It burned his fingers. He blew out the flame and returned the room to near darkness. "But we have not been married all that long. How the deuce do you suppose it happened?"

Laughing, she reached for him. "Come back to bed. Maybe I can explain it to you."

NINE

Old Santiago Ramírez spoke but little English. Riding with him and his son Vicente, Jeff struggled to regain the rudimentary border Spanish he had learned as a boy but had not used in years. There had been a time when he could speak and understand the essentials of it without having to pause and translate it mentally word for word.

It had been Kelly Booth's suggestion that he hire Santiago and Vicente. Santiago had been the only person who paid notice to a young boy sitting forlorn and hungry in the Piedras cemetery where his hapless father had been buried the day before. He had taken Booth home to a little shirttail piece of land inherited from Ramírez forebears who had acquired it when Texas and Mexico still belonged to Spain. From him and from his sons Booth had learned the working techniques of the brush-country vaquero. Now Santiago was more or less a pensioner on the Press Anthony ranch and a couple of other ranches. He did odd jobs wherever they turned up so he could earn food, a cot to sleep on and a few dollars a month for his simple needs, mostly tobacco and *pulque*.

Jeff recalled having seen him in the past, though he had never actually known him. Santiago seemed smaller than Jeff remembered him, his scarred brown fingers curling with arthritis. He could no longer handle a rawhide *reata* with the ease of long ago, nor was he the wiry *jinete* of old, able to keep his seat aboard the roughest bronc until it surrendered to his mastery. A bullet had taken his right leg at the knee when Vesper Freed and the state police had forcibly taken over the Ramírez land several years ago. That was the fight which had wounded Kelly Booth and put him in jail.

Santiago wore a wooden peg carved from mesquite. It fitted into a special leather loop he had added above his stirrup. Despite his infirmities, Santiago had forgotten little or nothing. The tricks of the vaquero trade that he could no longer do for himself he could teach to younger men. He could still look at a cow or a horse and describe what they were about to do before they themselves had decided.

Santiago's landless sons were scattered as working cowboys on other men's ranches between the Nueces and the Rio Grande. The oldest had taken refuge in Mexico after killing one of the enforcers who had come with Vesper Freed to take over the Ramírez property. Booth told Jeff privately that Manuel Ramírez rode with the *bandidos* who crossed the river periodically to prey upon the herds of Freed and other gringos. Santiago never mentioned it, and for all the cows west of Piedras Jeff would not have asked him.

Jeff was pleased over the instinctive cow sense shown by the sorrel horse Socks, but he borrowed one of Press Anthony's better-trained mounts for the specialized job of cutting cattle from a herd. He had bought three hundred cows from a rancher named Hawkins with a provision for a twenty percent cut, meaning he could reject one out of five from those offered. This would allow him to leave the oldest and plainest-looking. The younger the cow the easier she would adapt to a new range, and the more productive years she still had ahead of her.

Cutting was a slow and deliberate process, for most of the cows had calves at side, and the calves were thrown in with the deal. He had to be careful that when he rejected a cow he cut out the right calf with her. Many were large enough to thrive on their own, but he did not want to wean any younger ones accidentally. When he spotted a cow he wanted to reject, he took his time until her bawling summoned a calf to her side. Few cows willingly accepted any calf but their own at their udders.

Sitting hunched on a horse at the edge of the herd, Santiago had the look of an Indian about him, a very old Indian. Though his black eyes appeared half asleep, they were anything but. He pointed a gnarled finger. In Spanish he said, "Jeff, that cow, she of the twisted horn and the eye of a devil . . . she will run away as soon as you do not watch her. She will be back here in her *querencia* before the sun is up tomorrow."

Jeff was glad Booth had recommended Santiago and that the old man seemed to have taken an instinctive liking to him. Santiago had a rare understanding of animals; it was as if he could read their minds. Once he had called attention to it, Jeff could see the look of the devil in the brindle cow. Rings around the bases of her sharp-pointed horns indicated years of experience. Her wily ancestors had roamed the chaparral and isolated *mogotes* for generations, hiding from or fighting off whatever sought them, human or predatory animal. She had joined the gather because of the cow's natural instinct for the herd, but as soon as she perceived that she was being driven from her home range she would bolt for freedom, along with the spring-born spotted calf that stayed close at her side. Kelly Booth might take pleasure in dropping a rawhide rope around her horns and throwing her back on her haunches, but that treatment would not tame her. It would only make her wilder.

Jeff had a certain admiration for the *ladinos*. Outlaws, most people called such cattle, but they were outlaws only in the sight of those who wished to possess them. In their stern resistance to capture they were being true to their natures, to the wild freedom which was their heritage. He remembered some that would stop running and sull when escape proved impossible. They would lie down and die on the spot rather than submit.

In that respect, they reminded him of the Comanche

and Kiowa and Cheyenne warriors he had seen give up
their lives hurling themselves against the stern defenses of
Adobe Walls rather than yield the buffalo range to the
white man.

In the end, Indian and *ladino* alike would lose, over-
whelmed by the numbers, the skills, the technologies of
those who came to dispossess them. But Jeff could admire
their will, the courage that kept them fighting, even as he
lent his own strength to bring them to heel. He looked at
Santiago, whose leathery, nut-brown face bespoke the
strong blood of Mexican Indians, perhaps of Monte-
zuma's own people. It occurred to him that a strain of
ladino was in Santiago and his kin. If indeed one of Santiago's sons rode with the *bandidos,* he would only be
answering the call of his blood. In his heritage was a resistance to tyranny that had emboldened so many of his people to respond with arms to the *grito,* Padre Miguel
Hidalgo y Costilla's defiant call for freedom from Spain.
Many died, but the *grito* echoed on until Mexican independence was won.

Jeff eased the brindle cow and her calf from the herd.
Two hundred yards out, Hawkins's teenage son Teddy
held the cut, the rejected cattle, to prevent their mixing
back in with the main herd. The cow trotted toward them,
then realized they were under restraint. She gave a haughty
snort and broke into a hock-rattling run, skirting past
them and heading for a distant thicket. Her calf raced behind her with its tail curled over its back. The Hawkins
boy started after them but quickly realized the futility of a
chase. As soon as the main herd was set to moving, the cut
would be released anyway.

Santiago watched the cow and calf all the way to the
thicket, a thin smile lifting the corners of his mouth. He
gloried in their wildness.

Nigel Smithwick sat on his horse at the edge of the
main herd, stationing himself between two experienced
Mexican cowboys, one of them Santiago's son Vicente.
English asked questions when he felt it necessary, but
mostly he watched, then emulated the actions of the other

men. He was a fast learner, Jeff had noted with satisfaction. However, it could take years of observation to develop an instinct for what cattle were likely to do next. In most cases, the best cowboys were born to the trade or came into it young enough that they grew up with it and could act by reflex. Such a one was Kelly Booth, who sat on the opposite side of the gather from Smithwick. Like Santiago, he appeared half asleep, slouched in the saddle. But the least tremor in the herd would bring an immediate response from him.

A mile away, Cap Doolittle was camped with a chuck wagon beside a set of corrals, cooking dinner for the hands. Over her protests, Jeff and Smithwick had elected to leave Arletta in town, where she had the convenience of a solid roof over her head. It was not that this region was subject to excessive rainfall. It had rained relatively little in or around Piedras since Jeff had returned from the buffalo range. Had the Jones ranch not been almost totally ungrazed for a couple of years, building up a good stand of grass, the cows Jeff was buying might face a hard winter.

Vesper Freed's cattle had been drawn to the fresh feed. Jones suspected that Freed or his hands had purposely pushed a lot of them onto it. But the rancher had vigilantly patroled the fringes of his unfenced range, throwing the strays back onto Freed's own overgrazed land. Jones blamed Freed for his having to sell off his own cattle to pay taxes. He would burn in hell before he would let Freed's cattle have free use of his grass.

Jeff found a cow that he guessed to be fifteen years old, maybe twenty. Given any kind of chance, Longhorns had a long life expectancy. He had seen cows known to be twenty or older, trailed every spring by a new calf. This one was sided by a cream-colored heifer he guessed to weigh two hundred fifty or three hundred pounds. He would have liked to keep the calf, but the cow was too old. A cold winter on the Texas plains would probably kill her if the long walk up there did not. He eased her to the edge of the herd. Some of the nearby cows ambled along with her. At the critical moment Smithwick's horse moved forward, cutting in behind the old cow and her calf, stopping the others from leaving the herd.

Jeff said, "Good move, English. We'll make a cowboy out of you yet." He watched the pair start toward the cut as Hawkins's son circled way around to pick them up.

"It was the horse. He moved on his own." Smithwick was riding a black borrowed from rancher Hawkins. Jeff decided to try to buy the animal. It could be a good teacher for English.

When the cutting was finished, Jeff rode out to where Hawkins squatted in the shadow of his horse. Hawkins stood up and declared ruefully, "You didn't forget much durin' the years you were out of Texas." He nodded toward the animals in the cut. "There's not a one of them out there worth five dollars."

"What Elijah Layne has taught you, you don't forget." Jeff pointed in the direction of the corrals. "We'll brand them before we put them on the trail to the Jones place." That way, if any followed their homing instincts and drifted back, Hawkins would know whose they were. But Jeff thought it likely that most would stay, for the grass on the Jones ranch was better than here. He and the hands would turn them loose on the creek and keep riding the outer perimeter until the cattle became accustomed to their new range.

"What're you goin' to brand them?"

"I got a blacksmith in Piedras to make up some irons for a TE Connected. That's *T* for Texas, *E* for England. Half the outfit belongs to the Smithwicks."

They strung the cattle out, moving them in a walk. Jeff watched for any that looked as if they might make a break. One did, followed closely by her calf. Vicente Ramírez spurred his horse up beside her, grabbed her long tail, wrapped the switch end of it around his saddle horn and turned away. The cow went rolling. Wobbly, she rose to her feet hind end first, shaking her head in anger at the man and horse. Mucus streamed from her nose. But just when it appeared she would charge, Vicente pushed his horse toward her and gave a shout. Losing courage, she

turned and trotted back toward the herd. The calf circled
around the horseman and joined her.

Kelly Booth looked disappointed. He had his rope
down and a loop made, but Vicente had thwarted his opportunity to use it. "The next one is mine," he yelled in
Spanish.

He did not get an excuse until the cattle approached
the corrals, made of heavy mesquite limbs wedged hori-
zontally between pairs of posts and tied in place with
strips of rawhide dried hard as iron. The cattle associated
the pens with past episodes of pain and stress, so several
broke away. All were brought back, well chastened and at
least temporarily reformed.

Smithwick made several casts with his loop but
caught nothing in it except a couple of catclaw bushes.
Santiago rode over beside him. Jeff could not hear the
words, and he doubted that Smithwick understood many
of them, but by hand motions the old Mexican demonstrated the way to hold the rope and give it a couple of
swings overhead to open the loop before the throw. English would have to endure a lot of tiresome practice to
gain any proficiency. Jeff had seen men born to the trade
who could not catch anything except the wind.

As the riders pushed the cattle through the open gate
and into a large corral, Smithwick pulled the black horse
in beside Jeff. "I fear it is my lot to be a bookkeeper for
this partnership. I shall never become a cowboy."

"Bookkeepers get paid better anyway."

Hawkins had furnished a fat beef for the chuck
wagon, so Cap had cooked as much as he thought the men
could eat. It was a mixed bunch, part gringo, part Mexican. Santiago took his tin plate and sat down on the
wagon tongue beside Smithwick, anchoring the peg leg
firmly in the sand. Though given to long silences, the old
man was uncharacteristically talkative today. Jeff smiled,
watching Smithwick nod as if he understood everything
Santiago was saying.

After dinner the crew settled down to the branding.
While irons heated in a fire of dry mesquite, Booth and

one of the vaqueros roped the cows one by one, Booth taking the head, the Mexican the heels, and stretching the animals on the ground. The TE was burned into their hides, on the left hip adjacent to Hawkins's original brand. Most of the calves were roped around the neck. It was the job of the flankers to throw the jumping, kicking, bawling critters down. Many an anxious mother followed her captured offspring to the flankers, and a few had to be fought off as they lowered their horns and attempted a rescue.

Late in the afternoon, with much of the task still left, Hawkins came running toward Jeff, his face anxious. "We've got company comin'. Everybody better grab a gun!" Most had shucked their weapons for the work, hanging pistols and belts on fence posts and saddle horns.

Jeff saw more than a dozen horsemen emerge from a thicket half a mile away.

"*Bandidos,*" Hawkins said. "I'd bet my shirt on it." His anxiety was infectious.

Jeff's pulse quickened. He guessed that the riders had seen the dust from the corrals and had heard the cattle bawling. They probably figured this herd was theirs for the taking. They appeared to outnumber Jeff and Hawkins's slim crew by almost two to one.

Hawkins looked around for his teenage son. "Teddy, I want you out of this. Grab your horse and hightail it for home."

When the boy protested, his father grabbed him by the collar and gave him a hard push toward his horse. "I said go!" Hawkins watched apprehensively until he saw that the youngster was well on his way. Only then did he turn back grimly to Jeff. "They're not takin' this herd without a fight. I've worked too hard . . ."

"They're my cattle now. If you want to follow your boy and take your vaqueros with you, I'll understand."

"You ain't paid me yet. And if they was to kill you, where would I be?" Hawkins and Jeff fetched the rifles from their saddle scabbards. The cowboys spread themselves along the inside of the pen. They had one strong advantage, the protective cover of the heavy mesquite branches that made up the corral fence. On both sides of him, Jeff heard gun hammers click back.

Santiago watched keenly as the riders fanned out to make their approach. At length he said in Spanish, "Do not anyone fire. This is a time to talk." He opened the gate and hobbled out alone, his body jolted a little by each step he took with his wooden leg.

Jeff shouted, "Santiago, come back. They'll kill you!"

The old vaquero gave little sign that he had heard, beyond a motion of his hand that signaled everyone else to stay put. In short, awkward steps he continued walking toward the riders. They halted, all except one. Santiago stopped. The lone rider reached him, dismounted and gripped the old man's arms in the Mexican *abrazo*.

Jeff and Hawkins glanced at one another in surprise.

Santiago talked for a minute, then turned. He began walking back toward the corral, the bandit beside him, leading his horse. Before the man was near enough for a clear look at his face, Jeff knew who he had to be. Vicente climbed over the fence and ran toward him.

Kelly Booth shouted, "Don't anybody shoot," repeating in Spanish. He nodded for Jeff to accompany him. "We'll leave our guns behind." Jeff handed his rifle to Smithwick and walked through the gate with Booth, closing it behind him so the cattle would not break out and run. He moved twenty or thirty yards and stopped, letting the bandit and Santiago and Vicente come to him.

Family resemblance made it obvious that the bandit was one of Santiago's sons. Booth extended his hand. *"Qué tal, Manuel?"*

Manuel Ramírez reached out to Booth and hugged him. But he had a hardness in his eyes, a look that said *danger*. Santiago introduced him. "Manuel," Jeff said, feeling wary.

"Layne. Jeff Layne." Manuel pronounced it more like *Cheff*, as did Santiago. "I remember your papa. He hired me when I needed work. He fed me well."

"He was a kind man. He would be disappointed to see you in such company."

"Much has been taken from us. We take back what we can. My father tells me these are your cattle."

"They are."

"Then we have no interest in them. We thought they might be of the Vesper Freed. It is justice that we take his. He has stolen so much from the poor people."

Jeff had read stories about Robin Hood, taking from the rich to give to the poor. He doubted that all the poor who had lost property to Freed would share in the proceeds of these raids. But it did not seem good politics to bring up the subject at this time and place.

Santiago leaned upon his son for balance and drew a TE Connected in the sand with the end of the peg leg. "This is the brand on Jeff's cattle. You would do your father a kindness to pass that word." He traced an H Bar beside the TE. "The Mr. Hawkins, he is an honorable man too."

Manuel nodded assent and gave Jeff a long study. "Of course we are not the only ones who ride this way. It would be well for you to remain watchful."

That came natural to Jeff. He had spent years hunting in hostile Indian country. "But how will I know if it is your group or another? By the time I find I am mistaken, I may be dead."

"I will pass the word. That is all I can do. My father tells me you have had trouble with the Freed."

"We are not friends."

"Then you will not mind that we relieve the Freed of property. He has so much. It is best that you see little and say less."

"I have seen nothing here today. And I will remind all the cowboys that they have seen nothing."

Manuel made a thin smile. It seemed an effort, as if it were something he rarely did. "May you become rich and fat. And may I become even richer and fatter."

Jeff turned back to allow Booth and the father and sons to talk without concern about an outsider. Smithwick

met him at the gate, his eyes asking. Jeff said simply,
"Family reunion."

"I assume we are not to have a fight with the bandits."

"Not these, not today." Jeff signaled for the rest of
the men to gather around him. First in English, then in
Spanish, he said, "We ain't seen anybody. Let's go back to
the brandin'."

After a time Manuel rejoined the riders, and they
withdrew into the brush. Booth and Santiago and Vicente
returned to the corral. The younger men resumed their
work, Booth roping, Vicente helping hold down the
stretched animals while they were branded. With his mes-
quite-limb leg Santiago rescued an iron that slipped too far
into the fire as the burning wood collapsed in a shower of
red coals.

Jeff said, "You know what Freed or any of the other
ranchers will do to Manuel if they ever catch him."

"He is a grown man. He has given me grandchildren.
It is for him to decide what he must do." But Jeff could see
a touch of fear in the old black eyes, and perhaps even a
tear. If asked, Santiago would say the tear was caused by
the smoke. Jeff would not ask.

Hawkins's son Teddy returned shortly after the riders
disappeared. He had not gone all the way home as ordered. Hawkins reprimanded him for disobedience, but
Jeff saw pride in the rancher's eyes as the boy went back to
work.

It was near dark when the branding was finished. Jeff
was tempted to leave the cattle in the corrals overnight,
but they were used to freedom and nervous about the con-
straint of the fences. During the night the least provoca-
tion might set them into a run. By sheer force of numbers
and the power of blind panic they would break down the
brush fence, probably crippling or killing some of themselves. If they were to stampede, he had rather it happen in
the open where they were less likely to be hurt. With luck
and a little hazing they might even run in the direction of
the Jones ranch.

The cowboys drifted the cattle to a nearby water hole to let them slake their thirst, then backed off a little to allow them room to graze and bed down. It took some time for the cows and calves to pair up and quit bawling. Afterward, an uneasy quiet came over the herd. Hawkins and his son withdrew, though the two Hawkins vaqueros would stay and help drive the cattle off the ranch. Jeff set up a rotation plan for night herding, two men at a time to ride slow semicircles, meet one another and turn back.

"Sing to them, boys."

It was not that music meant anything in itself, but it let the animals know where the men were so they would be less likely to spook when they heard an unexpected noise or suddenly saw a rider pass by.

Smithwick said, "They are probably accustomed to hearing Spanish. I wonder how they will react to my accent?"

"It never seemed to bother Arletta."

"I have never tried to sing to her."

"Then just talk to them, low and easy."

Jeff had given himself a night guard tour in the first hours after midnight. He tried to sleep beforehand but could not. He could hear a distant Mexican song repeated over and over. The vaquero seemed to know only the one. From farther away he could hear the yipping of coyotes communicating with one another or perhaps simply talking to the moon. He hoped they did not move closer to a herd already much too restless. Some of the cows had never bedded down.

He kept thinking of Manuel Ramírez and the bandits, and wondering how many other raider organizations there must be who would not know Jeff from Vesper Freed, or care.

Disillusionment with his home country had caused Jeff to think often in recent days of a canyon on the plains, far to the north, where he had camped for several weeks and brought down many buffalo. He had thought then, and still thought now, that it should be a fine place to raise cattle.

He tried to estimate how many miles it must be to the canyon, at least four hundred, perhaps closer to five. At ten miles a day, which he could not count on without the devil's own luck, the trip would require six weeks, perhaps eight. And what of the Indians? Sheriff Golightly had said the army was in the midst of a campaign to push them to the reservation, but Jeff had seen the army at work in Kansas. All too often the only Indians it saw were those who chose to be seen. It seemed possible that he might be obliged to remain here in the Nueces Strip, adjacent to Vesper Freed's range, much longer than he might want. The thought was not conducive to sleep.

He did not know what caused the herd to stampede. Riding slowly beyond its outer edge, humming a wordless tune he had picked up during a quiet night in a Dodge City saloon, he heard nothing in particular. It could have been no more than one cow stumbling over another in her restless wandering, or a calf hooked away after seeking milk from the wrong udder. Whatever it was, a ripple went through the herd. The cattle jumped to their feet and began to run. Jeff spurred the sorrel and pushed to get near the lead.

There would be no stopping the stampede in its first minutes. Brush crackled and snapped as cattle plunged headlong through it, unmindful of obstacles. In their fright they would as readily run over a man or a horse. Jeff's immediate intention was to stay up with them and press toward the leaders, hoping that as they began to weary and their first blind fear subsided, he might be able to turn them and start them to milling. He could only trust that the rest of the crew at the chuck wagon had heard the racket and were pushing to catch up.

The cattle began to string out, the slower ones unable to match the pace of the leaders. Calves in particular were dropping back. Jeff could feel sweat breaking out on the sorrel's hide, though he could not see it. The big horse had a hardy constitution, however. It seemed to have lost none of its speed.

He had only a vague sense of the distance he had traveled, probably a mile or a mile and a half. He could tell that the leaders were slowing. Some cows were stopping, bawling for calves lost behind them. On the opposite side he saw the dim form of another rider, the Hawkins vaquero who had shared his guard tour. Jeff managed to move ahead of the leaders and switch over to join the cowboy. "Let's try to turn them," he shouted.

He had experienced several wild stampedes driving Longhorns up the trail to Kansas. It seemed to him that cattle milled most easily toward the right, in a clockwise direction. He began pressing the leaders, shouting, slapping his coiled rawhide rope against his chaps-protected leg and, when he could, in their faces. Gradually they yielded, turning slowly, painfully, until he had them running back in the direction from which they had come. Those behind followed the changing course.

In a little while the leaders had circled around and were mixing with the calves and slower cows that had fallen back into the drags. He could hear the other cowboys now, shouting, pressing the cattle into a tight mill. In the moonlight they were only vague shapes, and he was unable to make an accurate count of the men even if he could have seen them all. He hoped none had suffered a fall, racing through the darkness.

The momentum ran out. Many of the cattle continued to walk, but they did it in a circle around the outer rim of the herd. The noise was deafening as most of three hundred cows began bawling for their calves, left behind in the panic of the run. Calves responded in various degrees of desperation.

It would take the rest of the night for most of them to become properly paired. All the cowboys could do was hold them and let them take care of the rest for themselves. Every cow knew the voice of her own calf, and every calf the sound of its dam. In due course they would find one another.

He rode around the herd, counting cowboys. He was short two: Smithwick and Kelly Booth. When he asked the vaqueros, none of them knew. They had been too busy to see what, if anything, had happened to the gringos.

Jeff set out on the back trail, worriedly calling their names. As he rode, he kept passing calves that had fallen out of the run and were trotting now to catch up, bawling for their mothers. He wondered if anyone could hear him over the racket. Finally he heard Booth's voice: "We're comin'. Better slow than not at all."

He perceived that Booth's horse was carrying double. Smithwick rode behind the cantle, holding on to Booth and looking shaky. His shirt was ripped, one sleeve hanging off his arm. Booth said, "His horse stumbled."

Smithwick's voice trembled as he slid to the ground. "Kelly saved my life. I would have been trampled had he not heard me shout. He turned back to grab me and pull me up."

Booth did not meet Jeff's eye. He turned his head away. "Anybody would've done the same."

Jeff wondered. Instead of the pride he should be taking in what he had done, Booth looked almost ashamed.

Smithwick insisted, "He makes light of it, but it was no small thing."

Jeff's heart was beating rapidly. He had not realized until now how deep his fear had gone. "I was already askin' myself how I'd tell Arletta if I found you tromped to death. Damn it, English, don't ever do anything like that to me again."

"I didn't do it to you. I did it to me. And I do not relish the thought of doing it a second time, ever."

"You probably will, if you stay with the cowboy life very long. A man in this business isn't considered full grown till he's eaten his peck of dirt and had his face stomped into the ground half a dozen times. You've barely started."

Booth seemed eager to get away. "I'll see if I can find his horse." Then he was gone.

Jeff removed his left boot from his stirrup, a silent invitation for Smithwick to swing up behind him. The Englishman did it with some difficulty, for he was still shaking and weak. He said, "I have had my reservations about Kelly, but from now on he can have anything of mine that he ever wants."

What he really wants, Jeff thought, *you won't want to give him.*

TEN

The Jones ranch had a raw-looking one-room rock house Jones and his wife had lived in during their early years before they had put together money enough to build a larger home up the slope, farther from the barn and corrals, the noise, the smell and the flies. As Cap put it, the place was not big enough to cuss a cat in, but Jeff was not surprised when Arletta insisted that she and English move into it. At least it allowed her to spend nights with her husband rather than be alone in the rented house in town.

The thick walls, plastered inside, afforded comfortable insulation against the chill as winter tentatively sought its way through South Texas toward the Rio Grande. It would never be so cold here as on the high plains, but the north wind could occasionally cut like a knife nevertheless. She cooked for herself and English on a stone hearth. In town she had had an iron stove, but she insisted that using the hearth was no inconvenience. In recent years she had cooked most of her meals over an open pit outdoors. Here, at least, she had the protection of walls and a roof.

Jeff was beginning to sense a subtle change in her, something he could not quite put a name to. One evening he was eating supper with Booth, the two Ramírezes and a couple of other vaqueros in a picket bunkhouse the rancher had built for his hands. Jones had no need for hired help now, for he had no cattle to tend. Cap leaned against the doorjamb, holding a cup of coffee as he watched them eat what he had cooked. He tried to rub dried biscuit dough from his left hand onto a dingy white apron that sagged beneath his large belly.

Jeff asked, "Cap, you notice somethin' different lately about Arletta?"

Cap's eyes took on a gleeful gleam. "I wondered how long it'd take you to see it. She ain't told anybody but English."

"Told him what?"

"That he's goin' to be a daddy. You-all been payin' too much attention to your cows and not enough to Arletta."

Kelly Booth's jaw dropped. "You sayin' she's *preñada*? How in the world . . . ?"

"How? I'll tell you someday when you're old enough."

Booth looked as if his best horse had died. He sat staring at the food on his plate for a minute or two, then got up and left it uneaten. Without a word he passed by Cap and walked out into the dusk.

Jeff said, "Now, what do you suppose is the matter with him?"

"I got to tell you about that too?"

"I guess not. I think I began to see it the first night or two out of Wichita. I can only guess what he was hopin', but this slams the door on it."

"Want me to go talk to him?"

"I'll do it. I've been down that road a couple of times myself. But I'm goin' to finish my supper first."

Taking two cups of coffee, his and Booth's, he went outside. He found Booth seated on a crude bench beside the bunkhouse, staring toward the stone house Arletta shared with Smithwick. Jeff handed him one of the cups. "Your supper's gettin' cold."

"Lost my appetite."

"Lost somethin' else too, I think. But you had no reason to've expected otherwise. She was already a married woman when you met her. A happily married woman."

Booth seemed surprised. "I didn't know it showed."

"It did."

Booth sipped disconsolately at the coffee and stared at the ground awhile. "I been carryin' a load on my conscience ever since that stampede. I thought I could handle it all by myself, but now I've got to tell you."

Jeff's eyebrows lifted.

Booth said, "I saw English's horse go down and tried for a minute to pretend that I didn't. I had a wild notion that if he wasn't around, maybe Arletta would turn to me."

Jeff spilled a little of his coffee. Gravely, he digested the full dimensions of that revelation. "But you went back and got him."

"Only after I had wrestled with the devil. He sure didn't want me to go."

"You went, though. That's what counts."

"It wouldn't've counted for much if those cattle had tromped him before I got back."

"Maybe the devil wasn't the only one ridin' on your shoulders that night."

"I'm afraid I scared off the angels a long time ago."

"Not all of them. Looks like they haven't given up on you."

"But I wanted him dead. Thought I did, anyway."

Jeff seated himself on the bench beside Booth and drank most of the coffee from his cup. "I felt the same way once. Eva Freed . . . she was Eva Holloway then . . . her and me, we had us an understandin' when I went off to war. I'd been gone maybe six months when she married Vesper. It hurt real bad at first, and then I got mad. I took it in my head I was goin' to desert the army, come back here without anybody seein' me and ambush him. There wouldn't nobody but me know what had happened."

"Damned pity you didn't do it."

"I started, but I hadn't gone a mile before I ran into a bunch of Yankees tryin' to work around behind us for a surprise. They shot the horse out from under me. I hid in some undergrowth till the sound of the shootin' brought a bunch of our boys to rescue me. Nobody ever guessed what I was fixin' to do. They treated me like a hero for spoilin' the enemies' plan."

"You never tried again?"

"Them Yankees put the fear of God into me. I figured He sent them to stop me. Maybe He did and maybe He didn't, but I never let myself get tempted like that again."

"When I think that I could've left that baby without a daddy . . . I've got a lot to make up to her for, her and him both. I don't know if I can ever bring myself to tell them."

"I don't see the need. They're both grateful for what you did. I'd just leave it that way."

"But I still owe them, and I've always been one to pay my debts."

The winter work was light. It consisted largely of riding the perimeters of the Jones ranch to keep the TE herd from straying beyond its limits and encroaching on other ranches' feed. That required considerable attention at first because of the Longhorn's instinct to return to where it had been raised. But good grass soon won out over the call of *querencia*. Another chore was to check daily for any cattle that might have become mired in a bog. Rain had been scarce, so the few water holes had shrunk, and the approaches to them could be treacherous.

Jeff and Smithwick were working together to bring a cow up out of the mud when they became aware of dust in the distance. The north wind brought the sound of bawling cattle. A herd was crossing the Jones range. Jeff did not have to puzzle long.

"*Bandidos*. Looks to me like they're bringin' cattle to this water hole."

"Our cattle, do you suppose?"

"I hope not, but I don't think it'd be smart for us two to hang around and ask them. Let's get this old sister out on dry ground and head for that thicket yonder."

Gratitude was not in a range cow's nature. Once freed of the muddy trap that had held her, she made a furious run first at Jeff's horse, then at Smithwick's. Weakened by her imprisonment, she went to her knees. Trembling, she remained that way a minute, slinging her head in challenge.

Smithwick remarked, "Her attitude reminds me a bit of Vesper Freed. She would gladly gore us both."

She pushed to her feet and made a wobbly retreat toward the thicket. Smithwick tossed a rock in her direction to help her along. "I don't know if I will enjoy her company there."

"Had you rather enjoy the company of those bandits?" Jeff put the sorrel into a trot. He looked over his shoulder at the herd, perhaps half a mile away.

Entering the thicket, he could hear the muddy cow moving on, the brush crackling as she pushed through. Most of the mesquite and catclaw was not tall enough to conceal a man on horseback, so he dismounted.

Smithwick followed his example. "You know, of course, that if they see our tracks they may come looking for us."

"In that case we'll find out just how fast these horses can run. The last thing I want is a shootin' scrape with a bunch of *bandidos*."

"It's a good thing Cap is not with us. There is not a horse on the place that could carry his weight and win a race. But I wish Booth were here."

Smithwick and Arletta had both invested a lot of faith in Kelly Booth since the stampede. Jeff was glad Booth had not told them the straight of it. "I'm glad Booth's someplace else. He'd be inclined to meet them and fight. We'd lose, like as not."

The bandits brought fifty or sixty cattle to the half-dry water hole, which would be a lot drier by the time all the animals had drunk their fill. The distance was too great for Jeff to read the brands, but he was fairly sure he recognized one of the riders. "The one on the brown horse yonder, I believe that's Santiago's son Manuel."

Relief swept into Smithwick's face. "He promised not to steal any of *our* cattle."

"They're probably Vesper's."

"I don't suppose you are planning to do anything about it."

"Not one damned thing."

Jeff reasoned that Manuel would do him no harm if he were to show himself now, but some of the other dozen or so riders might shoot first and ask Manuel later. He and Smithwick remained in the thicket. As the cattle finished watering, the horsemen pushed them southward at a stiff pace no trail herd could have sustained for long. The bandits wanted to reach the Rio Grande as quickly as they could. It would be tough on cattle, horses and men, but they would have time for rest on the other side.

Manuel made a wide circle, pausing a moment to stare at the ground. He had seen the horse tracks. He looked toward the thicket but made no further move in that direction.

Smithwick said, "Perhaps we should go out and talk to him. He might have a message for old Santiago."

"I'd imagine they've got ways of passin' messages without me and you gettin' mixed up in it. What we don't know, we won't have to lie about."

They had been back at the ranch headquarters only a few minutes when Smithwick called Jeff's attention to half a dozen riders coming toward them in a long trot. Jeff soured, recognizing Vesper Freed out in front. As the group reached the corral Freed sought out Jeff with his eyes. "I've come to ask you for your help."

"The hell you say! The last message I got from you was to stay away from you and what's yours."

"Bandits have run off with a bunch of my cattle. We're tryin' to catch them on this side of the river."

Jeff placed his hands on his hips. "You might do it if you ride hard enough. But they've got you outnumbered by two to one."

Freed's eyes widened. "You've seen them?"

"Me and English, we watched them from a thicket.

There's a good dozen of them, at least. I don't think you want to stick your head in that bear's mouth."

"It'd lower the odds if you was to ride with us, you and however many men you've got."

"I can't think of one good reason I'd want to do that." Jeff studied Freed's cowboys. He recognized Davy Osborne, who looked apprehensive. And he saw someone else: Freed's son Daniel. "You're not takin' that boy of yours along, are you? You'd stand a good chance of gettin' him killed."

"He was with me when we came across the tracks. Anyway, he's old enough to learn that a man takes care of himself and what's his. Else people will be runnin' over him as long as he lives."

"Does his mother know where he's at, and what you're gettin' him into?"

"She's got no say in this. I'll not have her makin' a sissy out of him. I'm teachin' him to be a man."

"You're teachin' him to be a fool." Jeff walked out among the riders and grasped Daniel's reins just below the bits. "Son, you better stay here with us."

The boy's blue eyes were defiant. "I'm goin' with my daddy."

Jeff turned to Freed. "He'd better stay if you don't want him killed. I'll tell you again: there's too many bandits for this bunch to whip."

He could see the doubt in Freed's eyes, the conflict between anxiety for his son and a desire to toughen him. After a minute Freed turned to the boy. "You'll stay here, Danny."

Daniel protested vigorously but to no avail. Freed said, "Jeff, I've never asked any favors of you or given you any. But I'd take it as a favor if you'd see that he doesn't follow after us. See that he gets home."

"I can promise you that. But I'll do you another favor and tell you one more time: don't go on a fool's mission. Those bandits'll chop you into little pieces." He looked at Davy Osborne, who seemed in a struggle to keep his fear under control. "Davy, if you were ever tempted to quit your job, this would sure be the time."

The young cowboy stared at the horn of his saddle. "I reckon I'll stay with Mr. Freed."

Grittily, Freed declared, "We'll save my cattle. And I'll bring back a string of bandits' ears and hang them on the courthouse door."

Jeff held on to Daniel's reins as the boy dourly watched Freed and the rest of his men ride off southward. Daniel cursed him in language that would have befitted a muleskinner. He spurred his horse in an effort to break Jeff's hold. The horse surged forward, but Jeff kept a strong grip. The mount almost ran over him as it whirled around. Daniel was catapulted from the saddle, landing on his shoulder.

"You hurt, boy?"

The boy would rather have taken a whipping with a wet rope than to admit it, even if he was. "I'm all right, but you won't be if you don't let me go with my daddy."

He pushed to his feet and reached for a saddle gun in its scabbard. Jeff quickly turned the horse away from him and took possession of the rifle. He emptied its cartridges onto the ground and placed the weapon back in its scabbard. "I told your daddy I'd see that you get home. It's time we started."

Smithwick asked, "Do you want me to go with you?"

"Arletta's probably fixin' supper for you. I think I can handle this young outlaw by myself." He tried to smile at Daniel, but the boy's belligerent stare was like a bucket of cold water thrown in his face. He looked very much like Vesper Freed as Jeff had known him in their school days. This young apple had fallen close to the tree. "Mount up, young'un, and let's be goin'."

Jeff knew he would face a long ride home in the darkness and the night cold, but he did not want to be responsible for this boy any longer than necessary. Daniel sulked the whole way, speaking not a word even when Jeff tried to draw him out with innocent questions about his schooling, about his mother and father.

Dusk had enveloped them by the time they rode up to the Freed ranch house. It was two stories tall, of frame construction and painted white. As Jeff had heard, it was resplendent in gingerbread trim. It was a far cry from the simple cabin in which Vesper Freed had spent his boyhood.

"Looks like your daddy has provided real good for you-all."

Daniel made no reply. An elderly man limped around the corner of the house. By the hunched-over look of him Jeff assumed him to be an old cowboy, too stove-up for horseback work anymore and consigned instead to menial chores around the headquarters. Daniel dismounted and silently handed the man his reins, then stomped up the front steps and disappeared into the house. The old-timer looked quizzically at Jeff.

Jeff asked, "Is he always like this?"

"He's like a headstrong colt. His mother pulls him north and his father pulls him south. He plays one against the other."

The image of Vesper Freed at that age, Jeff thought.

He saw the outline of a woman just inside the doorway. Eva Freed stepped onto the porch, her solemn gaze on Jeff. "It *is* you. When Daniel told me, I could hardly believe it. I never thought you would come to this place."

Jeff stepped down from the horse and removed his hat. "I promised his daddy." In truth, he had been thinking of Eva's feelings in this matter, not Vesper's.

Eva moved out to the edge of the porch. She still retained much of the beauty he remembered from school days, though now it was the beauty of a mature woman moving toward middle age. The sight of her brought old memories rushing back, with all their pleasures and all their pain.

She said, "I thank you for bringing Daniel home. Was he telling me true? Is Vesper really chasing after bandits with only five or six men?"

"Just four. Vesper makes five."

Eva brought a hand to her mouth and looked back

over her shoulder at the front door where her son had gone. "My God. He could've gotten Daniel killed."

"Him and all the rest. I tried to argue Vesper out of it, but he had his mind set on killin' bandits."

"There's no reaching him when he goes into one of his cold rages. It's like he's gone crazy. He won't stop till he's seen something smashed or somebody killed."

"I hope you won't get upset over me sayin' this, but that boy of yours favors him in a lot more than looks. Time he's grown, he'll be just like Vesper."

He saw despair in her eyes. "I've tried to turn him in another direction. But lately he doesn't pay much more attention to me than his father does."

Whatever old anger Jeff might have harbored against her had dissolved into compassion. "I wish there was somethin' I could do, but . . ." He was convinced that only two things would ever change Vesper: a funeral and a good deep burying. He turned to his horse, catching the reins up short and lifting his foot toward the stirrup.

Eva said, "You're facing a long ride home in the dark. Let me fix you some supper first."

He lowered his foot to the ground and hesitated. "I'd like to. But there's no tellin' what Vesper might think, or do."

"I got over being afraid of him a long time ago."

"Maybe you shouldn't have. If I was you, I *would* be afraid of him." He swung into the saddle, determined to ride away before he gave in to temptation. He knew if he stayed he would probably still be here when Vesper got home. He turned once after he had ridden fifty yards or so. She was still standing on the porch, watching him.

For a nickel he would have turned back then and there. But nobody was around to offer him a nickel.

Dawn's early pink light brought Vesper Freed and three men riding up from the south. The droop of their shoulders spoke of misery and defeat. The hindmost rider led a horse with a body tied across the saddle, face down. As they came close enough for Jeff to see them clearly, he looked for Davy Osborne but did not find him. He knew who was on that last horse. Sadness touched him, then gave way to silent anger against Freed. He forced down a strong wish to shout *I told you!*

Freed made no explanation. None was necessary; it was obvious he had overtaken the bandits and evident how the fight had come out. "I got two men wounded here. They need doctorin', and it's a long ways to Piedras."

A cowboy was slumped forward, his shirt red with blood. One of his sleeves had been torn away for a make-shift bandage. He appeared only half conscious.

"We'll do what we can." Smithwick was hurrying up from the rock house. Cap and Booth and two vaqueros helped the wounded men down. They had to carry the hardest hit into the bunkhouse. Jeff asked, "What about Davy Osborne?"

Freed looked back at the body. "There's nothin' left for him but the buryin'."

"He's probably got family someplace."

"I never asked him, and I don't remember him sayin'. Just a kid run away from home, I always figured."

"His folks'll never quit wonderin' what became of him."

"There ain't nothin' I can do about that. I got troubles enough of my own." Freed scowled. "Funny thing to me: I got close enough to see the brands on them cattle before we had to back away. I didn't see nobody's but mine. I didn't see no TEs at all."

Jeff's temper flared. "Are you sayin' I'm in league with the bandits?"

"I ain't sayin' that. But if it turned out to be true, I wouldn't be surprised no hell of a lot." One of the vaqueros stepped out of the bunkhouse and trotted off toward the Smithwicks'. Freed's eyes narrowed. "Ain't that one of old Santiago's sons?"

"Vicente."

Freed's voice went raw with his anger. "You can tell him I just seen his brother. Real close."

"Sure enough?"

"If my pistol hadn't snapped on a bad cartridge there'd be one less Ramírez in the world. Next time I'll finish the job."

"Next time you'd better take more than four men with you. You'd better have a small army."

"I will." Freed's eyes narrowed as he watched Vicente coming back carrying some cloth and a bottle. "And you tell Vicente and Santiago and any others in that family that if ever I catch a Ramírez on my land—any Ramírez—I'll kill him too dead to bury."

Freed mounted his horse and rode off alone toward his own ranch, leaving his men for others to take care of. He left even Davy Osborne behind.

Arletta came up from the rock house, carrying more cloth for bandages. "Vicente told me there's men up here need doctorin'."

"They're in the bunkhouse. All except Vesper Freed. The doctorin' *he* needs, you couldn't give him. I don't know that anybody can."

ELEVEN

———————

Crow Feather disliked traveling at night. Dark spirits stalked about, seeking hapless victims for their witchcraft. Times, he could hear their voices on the chilling wind. But as he moved his family eastward toward his chosen canyon those spirits seemed less a threat than the soldier patrols crisscrossing the open prairie, searching for scattered Comanches and Kiowas who still resisted a move to the reservation. A couple of times Crow Feather had heard distant rifle shots. He was convinced they were fired by soldiers. Perhaps they hunted for meat, or perhaps they were shooting at resistant remnants of the People. He looked to his little family and shivered.

The trouble had all begun with the buffalo skinners, he thought. Until they came, soldiers had seldom crossed these plains. They had little reason. This country was not meant for white people, and none so far had tried to settle here. Moreover, on vast stretches of it water was hard to find unless one knew where to look. Thirsty soldiers had sometimes ridden as near a watering place as Crow Feather's bow could fling an arrow, yet they never found it. So white men had largely shunned these plains until the madness had come over them about the buffalo hides. What they were to do with so many skins he could not begin to understand. Cheyennes had told Crow Feather the *teibos* sometimes went crazy over a yellow dust found in mountains far to the north. They were a strange people, greedy and wicked. Surely the spirits must sooner or later take notice and punish them, driving them from this land.

Repeatedly, Crow Feather had called upon his guide, the bear, to invoke the aid of other benevolent spirits and bring down calamity upon the white hunters and the soldiers. But for some time now the bear had given no sign that he heard. The way of the spirits was mysterious. They could bless a man with all manner of good things, then sweep them away with the swiftness of the devil wind that occasionally twisted across the prairie, ripping up and destroying whatever its anger touched.

Crow Feather had decided to abandon the travois and carry only what could be packed on the horses. Soldiers might overlook horse tracks, but they were not likely to miss the twin drag marks of a heavily laden travois. Crow Feather led his horse, which carried a few tepee skins and his parfleche. White Deer followed in his track, leading her mare laden with other belongings and the two babies, securely tied in their cradleboards. Little Squirrel brought up the rear, leading the pony that carried his younger sister. She no longer cried for her mother, but she looked back often, as if she still expected Rabbit to catch up.

Moving at night improved their chance of reaching the canyon without the soldiers finding them, but it offered hazards of its own besides the threat of adverse spirits roaming the darkness. Crow Feather occasionally stumbled across obstacles he had not seen: the edge of a buffalo wallow, a rock hidden by tall grass, the steep bank of a dry creek bed. At least he did not have to worry about rattlesnakes. Colder weather had driven them into their underground shelters to hibernate until spring warmth would bring them out again. They were, he had always thought, agents of the malevolent spirits that constantly sought to trap the unwary.

With each dawn he would seek a sheltered place for his family to spend the day, a place not easily seen should soldiers pass nearby. Once, they had to content themselves with a buffalo wallow, the only depression they could find as a hiding place. Far better was a creek bottom with its fringe of low timber. While the family rested, Crow Feather would ride out in a long circle to hunt for meat and watch for soldiers. He managed once to stalk a deer until he was close enough to bring it down with an arrow. He wished for a rifle but knew that even if he had one it would be dangerous to fire it; the sound might bring soldiers.

The only buffalo he saw were dead, their skinned carcasses rotting as he had seen them so many times before, in reality and in dark visions. He had heard tales of times when warriors on a raid would become hungry enough to chase away the wolves and coyotes and eat spoiled meat from a decaying carcass. Usually they fell ill, and the unlucky ones died. He had never known such desperation. He hoped he never would, nor any of his family. If they ate sparingly they could make the deer last them as far as the canyon. Surely he would find game enough there. It was one place from which he had never come away without fresh meat. He could only hope the *teibos* had not yet killed all the buffalo.

White Deer voiced no complaint, though the strain showed in her face. She had chopped her hair short and slashed her arms over the loss of her sister. Crow Feather shared her pain, but he could not allow grief to stand in the way of what he must do to bring the rest of his family to safety. Not in days had he seen sign of another Comanche or even a rope-haired Kiowa. For all he knew, he and his might be the only ones left, the last holdouts against exile to the reservation about which he had heard so many dreadful accounts.

He located a spring where he had camped more than once while scouting for buffalo. Actually, it was little more than a seep that fed into a creek. Its yield of water was so small that the creek never flowed much farther than a dove might soar on its short wings. But it provided water enough for a circle of small trees. Tracks of many animals were pressed in its mud—wolves, rabbits, antelope. Bitterness soured his stomach as he realized there were no buffalo tracks. The hide hunters had been thorough in their work.

White Deer kindled a small fire that would give off but little smoke. She sharpened a thin limb and used it as a spit to roast some of the venison. "How many more nights must we travel? The children do not sleep well in the daytime."

He held up two fingers, then three. He was not sure. An accurate feel for the pace of travel was difficult when one moved in darkness. "I do not hear them complain."

"But they become tired and cross. They could easily sicken when the wind blows cold."

"It is better for them here than on the reservation. They say many children die there." He looked at the newest baby, the one to whom Rabbit had given life shortly before yielding up her own. White Deer was nourishing it the best she could, sharing the milk that should have been for her child alone. "At least we are free."

Free in the sense that they had not been caught. But they were not free to travel at will, wherever and whenever it suited them as the People had done since before the times of his great-grandfathers. He had a sense of their being stalked like animals, fugitives in their own land. In that respect, they were already prisoners of the bluecoats.

The steep creek bank provided shelter against the biting north wind. White Deer erected a small, rude tent with the lodgeskins they had managed to carry, then nursed the two babies. After eating a little venison, Crow Feather prepared to scout the area around them for sign of soldiers or any of the People who might still be at large. Little Squirrel said, "*Powva*, let me go with you. I have good eyes."

"But you have a slow pony. You must stay and keep watch. You must be the man here."

It was not the People's way for a boy so young to argue with his father, and Squirrel did not. Gravely he accepted the responsibility his father imposed upon him, though he was yet too young to be either a warrior or a hunter should evil befall his father. Crow Feather knew he must take no risks that were not absolutely necessary.

Without him his family might not survive the winter that already chilled them with its cold breath.

He tried to ride only where grass or hard ground would hide his tracks. He had been told that the soldiers were not good at following an obscure trail. Sometimes, however, they used the cannibal Tonkawas to do the tracking for them, or the dark-faced Seminole-Negro scouts. It was said they could trail like a dog.

He had traveled much of his planned circle when several blue-clad cavalrymen suddenly popped out of a dry creek bed. They and Crow Feather saw each other at the same instant. His heart made a tremor in surprise. His immediate instinct was to whirl around and set his horse into a hard run northward to decoy them away from his family.

Dust puffed ahead of him where a bullet plowed into the ground. An instant later he heard the rifle. He knew they intended to kill him if they could not catch him. He knew too that the soldiers' horses were fed grain that kept them strong, whereas his had subsisted of late only on winter-dry grass. Another bullet droned past him. It seemed to lend strength and determination to his horse. Crow Feather dropped down into a depression which would hide him a few moments. He reined the horse to the right, toward a slight rise. Perhaps he could pass around the base of it before the soldiers saw him again.

They were too close. They fired at him before he could gain that momentary cover. Their marksmanship was poor, for they were trying to shoot from the backs of running horses. Should one have the presence of mind to dismount and take steady aim, Crow Feather knew he would be an excellent target.

He began to gain, widening the distance. The soldiers fired occasionally, but the shots fell short or struck to one side. Possibly their horses were not so strong as he thought. Or perhaps they feared he was not alone, that he might be leading them into an ambush.

He wished that were so.

An old warrior who had confronted soldiers several

times had once told him to be wary always of the Rangers, for they were like angry badgers that kept charging into the fight no matter how bloodied they became. But he had said the soldiers could be killed with a stick.

Crow Feather doubted it was that easy, for had the soldiers not fallen upon the People's grand winter encampment and put it to rout?

He could sense the horse wearying beneath him when he chanced upon a dry creek bed that carried water only after a rain. Its banks were not deep, but they might hide him for a few precious moments. The creek bed followed a crooked course that swung in a generally southeastward direction. He followed it, looking back over his shoulder. He could not see the soldiers, but it was unlikely they had given up the chase. They had simply fallen behind. Shortly, he left the dry water course and cut back to the south, making a wide circle that carried him around behind the soldiers. They would probably expect him to remain ahead of them. He hoped they would not be looking for him to their rear.

He came after a while to the trail the soldiers had made after they took up the chase. He paused to look back and saw nothing. He set his horse into a southerly direction, riding in the soldiers' tracks. Even if they managed to follow him this far, he thought it unlikely that they would notice one set of hoofprints headed south when all the others were pointed north. He had seen hunted animals use the same ruse, circling and doubling back upon their own trail. Poor was the person who could not or would not learn from the creatures around him.

The plains' apparent flatness was deceptive. Like the coyote, the land could play trickster. It rose and fell more than a casual observer might realize. A herd of buffalo could be concealed in its gentle depressions, unseen until a hunter was almost among them. The Comanche and his allies had long ago learned to take advantage of the plains' illusions to shake off pursuit. To the untrained who did not know the country well, the quarry could be in plain sight, then seemingly disappear like smoke before one's eyes.

He thought he had probably seen the last of the soldiers, unless . . . He had not been able to see them clearly enough to determine whether they might be accompanied by Tonkawa or Seminole scouts. Those would be difficult to fool for long. He dared not go back immediately to his family.

Dismounting to let the horse rest, he climbed up a small knoll afoot. He crouched to provide as little silhouette as possible. A long, careful study of the horizon revealed no movement anywhere. He had probably eluded pursuit, but he could not be certain. He seated himself in the grass to wait. He could see for a considerable distance, yet he was unlikely to be spotted by the soldiers unless they had the strongest of medicine.

He had time to dwell sadly upon all he had lost . . . Rabbit, the normal association with his own people, his freedom to travel where he wanted without concern. He let his mind run free, and a grief he had tried not to reveal to White Deer and the children welled up like a storm from deep within. He shouted aloud in his frustration and pain. He called to the bear to show him the way, if there *was* a better way. He slumped, weary of body and soul, and waited to see if some answer came.

It did not. The only sound came from the hostile north wind that pinched his face and stiffened his hands with cold.

He wished he knew what penance the bear might demand to put him back in its good graces. If the bear or some other benevolent spirit would not give him a sign, he would have to rely on his own judgment. That judgment told him to get his family beneath the protective walls of the canyon as quickly as he could.

He waited until dusk to return to the spring where he had left White Deer and the children. He saw nothing of them at first. Fear grabbed at his throat. The soldiers might have found them! Then his wife appeared from the scrub timber where she had hidden the children, the mare and the pony. A pent-up breath sighed between his teeth. The relief that came into her face told him of the anxiety she had suffered while he was gone. Her voice quivered. "I feared the soldiers had found you."

"They did. But my horse was faster than theirs."

"Soldiers passed this way too. I think they were looking for water, but they did not notice the spring."

If that was so, Crow Feather thought, the soldiers had learned little about these plains. The timber around this seep, scant though it was, should have told them they could find water here. But he was grateful for their ignorance. Had they come, it was unlikely White Deer could have hidden four children and two horses.

He wondered. Would the soldiers have taken them prisoner, or would they have killed them? A woman and four children would have been a burden, a burden five bullets would easily eliminate. Cheyennes had told him about a soldier massacre of their families far to the north many years ago. No mercy had been shown even to the littlest among them.

Squirrel said proudly, "I saw the soldiers first."

White Deer nodded assent. "He stayed up there where he could watch. He did as you told him. He was the man in the camp."

Crow Feather put his arm around his son's thin shoulders. "You will become a good warrior when you have enough years."

White Deer frowned. "Will there be any place for warriors by then? The white men are as many as the gnats. There may be no war trail, and no buffalo."

"There will always be a place for warriors. Now, let us eat a little, then leave this place. The next soldiers who come may have better eyes."

He called upon his sense of direction and a knowledge of the stars to point their way. One of the babies whimpered a little. Hungry perhaps. He wondered if White Deer still had milk enough for both. The traveling had weakened her. Some of the strength which should have gone into producing milk had gone instead into the long, tiring nighttime walk.

Had it not been for his horse he might have fallen over the edge and into the canyon. He was walking ahead, leading the animal, when it snorted and jerked back on the rawhide rein. A small black cloud had moved across the moon and left him almost blind. He had known he must be approaching the canyon, but he had not realized how near he really was. As the cloud moved aside he could see the chasm just another step or two ahead.

He called to White Deer to stop. He paused to pat the horse on the neck, a reward for its timely warning. "We have found it. We must wait for the sun to show us a way down."

He greeted the sun's rising with a prayer of gratitude at the canyon's rim. As dawn's rosy light began creeping across the canyon floor, he looked down into the chasm, seeking a familiar landmark. A buck deer watered in a narrow creek that snaked its tree-lined path down the length of the gash as far as Crow Feather could see. His gaze lighted upon a distant formation that stood alone, well apart from the steep wall. A rock cap at its top had sheltered the red clay beneath and slowed its erosion under the periodic onslaughts of hard rain. He remembered it by its shape. It reminded him of a standing woman, wrapped in a blanket the color of rust.

He pointed northward. "Ahead of us is a trail the buffalo follow to go down into the canyon." Years ago he had seated himself at the head of that trail for the four days and nights of his first vision quest. It was there that the bear spirit had come to him on the final night. He had long wondered why it had been the bear instead of the buffalo, but one accepted whatever came and did not question the spirits aloud.

The trail was narrow in places, and steep. Dried droppings and remnants of tracks told him that buffalo had recently descended into the sheltering canyon, their instincts bringing them away from the bitter winds that would sweep the open plains throughout the cold moons to come. This canyon had been a winter home to the bison, probably ever since they had first emerged from their hole in the ground to populate the earth. He had often heard the old storytellers describe the creation of the world and the People and the buffalo.

Down the canyon he saw a few black shapes, their heads down as they grazed the cured grass. The white hunters had not yet killed them all. "We will find our place, then I will bring fresh meat." The venison was gone. They had consumed the last of it yesterday.

It was evident that hunters had been in this canyon, for buffalo bones littered its floor. Wherever an animal had died, the grass was taller, the soil fed by whatever decaying flesh the wolves and the coyotes and the buzzards had not taken. The state of the skeletons indicated that the killing had been done some time ago, probably last winter. The surviving buffalo seemed oblivious to the meaning of the bones. They nosed among them for the sweeter grass.

The canyon was narrow at its upper end but gradually widened to the south. Crow Feather's goal was a small header that cut back into the wall. He remembered a tiny spring which trickled a constant stream of water about as wide as two of his fingers. There he once had killed a deer that sought refuge in the timber clustered around the spring. The header was barely noticeable from the canyon floor. Its dense growth of trees and low brush should shield a small tepee from any but the most observant.

The place was so well hidden that he almost passed it by without seeing it. He took that as a good omen. If he knew about it and nearly missed it anyway, it should fool any soldiers who might happen upon the canyon and search it. He led his family up into the small side canyon, into the timber, all the way to the sheer cliff where the spring formed a small pool of clear water. He looked upward. The wall towered over him, the caprock extending outward a little from the top so that anyone standing on the rim above could not see what lay directly beneath.

"This is a good place to put up a small tepee," he told White Deer. "Here we will have water, and we will have meat. We will stay until the hunters have finished and the soldiers are gone. The People cannot be held forever on the reservation. We will be waiting here when they come back."

White Deer had never questioned his judgment. She clutched his arm. "Yes, this will be a good place to wait."

He slept peacefully that night, except for one dream which awakened him in a cold sweat. He dreamed of the spirit woman with red hair.

TWELVE

Jeff Layne sat on a rough bench against the rough picket wall of the bunkhouse in late afternoon, letting the warmth of the autumn sun draw away a chill that had penetrated to the bone during the day's long ride. He smiled, watching Nigel Smithwick practice with a Mexican rawhide *reata*, tossing loop after loop at an upturned wooden bucket. Now and then the loop would settle over the target, but usually it fell to one side or the other.

Cap came out wiping his flour-covered hands on a dingy cloth apron tied around his waist. He had been preparing supper for the hands, for Jeff had decided Arletta should be relieved of that chore. He seated himself beside Jeff and began idly whittling a small piece of wood into something that faintly resembled a horse. It was going to be a toy for Arletta's son. He had never questioned that the baby might not be a boy. Neither had anyone else, except perhaps Arletta.

"Reckon English'll ever learn how to use a rope?" Jeff asked.

"Give him time. You growed up holdin' one in your hand. English growed up holdin' a teacup."

Old Santiago Ramírez hobbled out to Smithwick on his wooden leg and took the *reata* in his hand. Talking in a soft Spanish, he demonstrated how to make a loop and how to hold it, how to swing it overhead and cast it at the bucket. He made a perfect catch and handed the lariat back to Smithwick. Smithwick tried to emulate Santiago's moves, asking him in English if each step was correct.

Jeff thought it unlikely that either man understood half what the other said. Their best communication was through a makeshift sign language. He looked up at Santiago's son Vicente. "Maybe you'd better go interpret for them."

Vicente made no reply but simply walked out to stand beside his father. He was not given to conversation. Jeff had first thought it was because he felt uncertain about his use of English, but after a time he had realized Vicente spoke very little in Spanish either. Santiago's advice to Smithwick was long and detailed. Vicente's translation was brief and to the point, ten or fifteen words to Santiago's hundred.

Arletta came up from the little rock house to watch her husband. She smiled with approval as he settled a loop over the bucket. Then she laughed as he tried again and missed. Her stomach was beginning to expand a little. There could be no doubt that she was, as Cap had put it, in a family way. Jeff did not think he had ever seen her glow as she did now.

He thought again, as he had so often, how lucky Smithwick's life had been. And he felt a vague emptiness in his own.

Cap commented, "It might be just as well if English never learns too much about the rope. Catchin' is the easy part. Sometimes it's turnin' them loose that divides the men from the boys. You ever rope a badger?"

"I've tried. Never caught one, though."

"They'll come up the rope to meet you. Ain't nothin' scarier than seein' a mad badger come chargin' at you with his teeth primed for raw meat."

Jeff's attention went to a rising of dust. A dozen or so riders were approaching from the direction of Vesper Freed's place. "Speakin' of mad badgers, could that be Vesper comin' yonder?"

The horsemen moved at a brisk pace. There was a chance, though a slim one, that they could be Mexican raiders. The outlaws had been giving Freed a lot of trouble, but they had left the TE cattle alone. Jeff figured he had old Santiago's influence to thank for that.

Cap squinted, his face crinkling with disapproval. "It's Vesper, and he ain't comin' here to dance."

The Smithwicks moved up close to Jeff and Cap. Santiago and Vicente followed, their faces solemn. Kelly Booth poked his head out of the barn, where he had been patching a broken bridle. He came out holding a rifle and positioned himself beside the two Ramírezes.

Freed's face was flushed with belligerent purpose as he brought his horse to a dusty stop a few feet from Jeff and the others. Jeff did not mean it, but courtesy demanded that he say, "Get down and rest yourself." He knew Freed would not accept the invitation, so the offer carried no risk. He was a little surprised when Vesper nodded at Arletta and touched his fingers to his hat brim. "Ma'am." He had never seen Vesper play the gentleman.

Vesper turned his attention to Jeff. "They've done it again. Sons of bitches hit my place this mornin' and ran off close to two hundred head. Wounded one of my cowhands, too."

Again, courtesy demanded that Jeff say, "Sorry to hear it." He was not, really, except about the cowhand. "Hurt him bad?"

"Bad enough that he won't be able to work for a while. I had to let him go."

That, Jeff thought, was no surprise, coming from Vesper.

Freed said, "I'm givin' you a chance to show that you're not in cahoots with them outlaws. Ride with us."

Jeff wondered that the back-door accusation provoked him more to disgust than to anger. It was about what he would have expected.

Freed said, "I've got guns enough this time to give them a good whuppin'. All we got to do is catch up with them."

Jeff was disappointed to see that Vesper had brought his son Daniel again. He wondered if Eva knew, and if she had tried to stop him. "The bandits ain't bothered us. That might change if we rode with you." He studied the riders on either side of Freed, giving special attention to the boy. "I don't see Sheriff Golightly or any of his deputies."

"The sheriff! It'd tickle him if them bandits cleaned me plumb out." Freed's poisonous gaze fixed itself on Santiago and Vicente. "Maybe it ain't just luck that they don't bother you. Looks to me like you've made a pact with the devil."

"No, but I don't go out of my way to aggravate him."

Freed pointed to Santiago. "Bet you a thousand dollars that old scoundrel is a spy for that outlaw boy of his. I got a notion to stretch a rope with him."

Kelly Booth stepped protectively in front of Santiago and Vicente. He held the rifle across his arm in a way that gave Freed a good look at its muzzle. "Just try. I'll give your brisket an airin'."

Freed's gaze touched a moment upon the weapon, then went to Booth's face. "Still hangin' with them Mexicans, are you? You're liable to hang with them off of a rope."

Booth's grip tightened on the rifle. "They took me in when I was a lost kid grabbin' for help. I didn't see no gringos rushin' to do it. Especially no Freeds."

Freed dismissed him with an impatient shake of his head and turned back to Jeff. "Since you ain't with me, you're against me, like every damned Mexican from here to the river."

Jeff knew Freed was baiting him. He kept his voice under control. "It'll be dark in a little while. How do you figure to trail them at night?"

"They're makin' a beeline for the river. As long as we hold to their direction we ought to come up on them whether we can see their tracks or not." Freed jerked a thumb toward Santiago. "You tell that old chili-belly that I'll get his son Manuel. I'll hang his carcass on my barn door like a coyote hide."

Santiago's English might be limited, but the hatred in

his eyes showed he understood enough. He clenched his
arthritic hands into fists as Freed pulled on his reins and
turned his horse half around.

Jeff said, "If it comes to a fight, that boy of yours
could get hurt."

"He's old enough to learn to take care of what's his. I
wasn't much older than him when I shot my first Mexican."

"Leave him. I'll see that he gets home to his mother."

Freed's eyes blistered Jeff. "That'd suit you just great,
me handin' you an excuse to go see her. But I ain't givin'
either one of you that satisfaction." He jerked his head as
a signal and led his men southward.

Kelly Booth moved up beside Jeff. "He's got murder
in his eyes. It'll go hard with any Mexican he comes
across, bandit or not. I'm trailin' along to see that he
doesn't kill somebody out of spite."

"He'll shoot you sure as hell."

"Not if I shoot him first."

The grim determination in Booth's eyes left Jeff no
acceptable choice. "Bad as I hate to ride with Vesper, I
can't let you go alone. English, I'd like you to hightail it to
Piedras and fetch the sheriff. Kelly, maybe you and me
together can keep Vesper from doin' anything drastic."

"Even if we have to shoot him?" That would clearly
be Booth's first choice.

Cap declared, "I'm goin' too." Jeff had known he
would. He had not felt it necessary to ask him.

Socks had not been ridden today, so the horse was
fresh. Hurriedly Jeff saddled the sorrel and fetched his
coat, for the evening would soon turn cold. The sun was a
vague silver light behind a line of blue wintry clouds low
on the western horizon. If this had been the high plains,
Jeff would have predicted snow.

Cap and Booth were quickly ready. Vicente gave Santiago a boost to swing up stiffly onto his own horse. The
old man anchored his wooden leg with the leather strap
above his stirrup.

Jeff did not like the shape of things. "Santiago, you

and Vicente had better stay here. Vesper's liable to shoot you and claim he mistook you for bandits."

Vicente spoke for his father. "My brother may need our help."

"That would make outlaws of you too."

Vicente glanced at his father. "What more could they take from us? The Freed already has our land."

"He has not taken your lives."

"My father would say he has taken those too. The land was our life."

Anything they did to help Manuel would compromise Jeff's neutrality, but he saw no gain in further argument. They were going, regardless. "The two of you stay close to me, then, and as far from Vesper as you can."

Cap came out of the bunkhouse with a sack. "Got some grub here for us. Freed and his bunch can go hungry for all I give a damn."

Smithwick and Arletta hugged each other, then Smithwick set out toward Piedras. He turned once to wave at his wife, and she waved back.

Cap observed him with doubt. "Time the sheriff catches up, anything that's goin' to happen will be over with."

"He can press charges, if any are needed," Jeff said. "In case of real trouble I'd rather English was someplace else." Arletta stood alone in the open yard, watching her husband disappear into the distance. "For her sake. And the young'un's." He touched spurs to the sorrel.

Just at dusk they caught up to Freed's riders, who had angled eastward to regain the trail of the cattle. There had been no practical way for the raiders to hide their tracks. They were depending upon speed to get them safely across the river. Freed turned in the saddle, his eyes suspicious. "I figured you was sidin' with them bandits."

"We're not sidin' with anybody. We've come to make sure you don't hurt anybody that's innocent."

"From here to the river, there ain't nobody innocent." Freed glared at Santiago and Vicente. "You keep them out of my way or the world'll be two Mexicans short."

"I've sent for the sheriff too."

"You've got a damned long nose, and a bad habit of pokin' it into my business." Freed spurred on.

The moon rose full and bright enough that the cattle tracks were often visible. The best Jeff could guess, it was past midnight when they led up to a small adobe house and a set of brush corrals. Freed fired his pistol into the air. "Ochoa! Felipe Ochoa! You hustle yourself out here, *pronto*!"

In the house a baby began to cry. The door opened, and a man stepped out in underwear and trousers, his feet bare. "*Quién es? Qué pasó?*"

Freed pushed his horse up almost to the door. "You know damned well what's *pasoed*. A bunch of cow thieves watered stolen stock at your tank. My stock. And it ain't the first time."

"*No entiendo.*" Ochoa was saying he did not understand.

"The hell you don't *entiendo*. I'd ought to shoot you right where you stand." Freed leveled his pistol at the man's face.

Jeff put spurs to the sorrel, pushing between Freed and the Mexican. "Pull that trigger and I'll see you tried for murder."

Vesper cursed him roundly. "We've got to teach these damned chilis a lesson. This ain't none of your business."

"Murder is everybody's business."

"He helped them. He let them water the cattle here."

"I don't see how he could've stopped it, one man against so many."

"He didn't *want* to stop it."

That was probably true, Jeff thought, but he said, "You don't know that for sure. A man is innocent unless you can prove him guilty."

"He's a Mexican. They're all in league against me." Freed still held the pistol. His men began crowding closely, but Jeff concentrated his attention on Freed. "Put that six-shooter away. You're not killin' anybody here."

"He's got it comin'. They all do." But Freed looked

past Jeff, and he wavered. From the corner of his eye Jeff saw Kelly Booth moving in beside him, his rifle pointed at Freed. Booth said nothing. The cocked rifle spoke for him. For emphasis Cap Doolittle drew up on the other side.

Reluctantly Freed slipped the pistol back into its holster on his hip. "Damn all of you! Damn you all to hell!" He turned his horse away and set out southward on the trail left by the cattle.

Jeff expelled a breath he had held too long. His lungs ached.

Booth put the rifle back into the scabbard beneath his leg. "You've just got to know how to reason with him, that's all."

They rode through the night without catching up to the stolen herd or reaching the river. As a false dawn began to break through the darkness, a grumbling among his men forced Freed to make a breakfast-fixing stop near another small adobe house. They drew water from a dug well so they could boil coffee. The owner wisely stayed inside, not showing himself and risking Freed's wrath. To be certain Freed did not decide to go in after him, Kelly Booth stationed himself near the front door, the rifle in his hands. Cap carried him a cup of coffee and a cold biscuit. "I'll fix you a little bacon soon's I can get a fire started."

Vicente told Jeff, "The man who lives here is a cousin to me, but it is better the Freed does not know." He and Santiago put their horses into a corral behind the house and went inside.

The boy Daniel looked weary. Jeff offered him some cold bread and fresh bacon, but the youngster refused. "I'll eat what my daddy eats."

At least he had learned loyalty, Jeff thought. That was a point in his favor. But it was reckless of Vesper to put him at risk on a mission like this, where at best he was more likely to witness vengeance than justice. If Eva had not known before, she would have realized by nightfall where he had gone. Jeff could imagine the fear that had probably kept her up all night, walking the floor of that big house. She would be standing at the window or the front door now, waiting, steeling herself for the worst.

Freed paced back and forth while men and horses rested. Finally he shouted impatiently for his men to get back in the saddle.

Santiago came out of the house alone. Stiffly he mounted his horse and slipped his wooden leg into the loop that held it steady. Pulling up close to Jeff, he spoke in a voice hardly more than a whisper. "My nephew says it is only a little while since Manuel and the others left this place. They move the cattle slow now. They think they are safe."

"How far to the river?"

"Far enough."

Jeff gritted his teeth. His sympathies were with Manuel. All night he had hoped the raiders and the cattle would be safely across before Freed's riders reached the Rio Grande. That hope dimmed now, for it appeared that Manuel had grown complacent. "I don't know anything we can do to warn him."

"It is being done."

Jeff realized that Vicente had not come out of the house with his father.

Santiago said, "My nephew gave Vicente a fresh horse. He went out the back and into the brush, *por allá*, so no one would see."

Jeff saw laughter in Kelly Booth's eyes. Booth had stood guard at the front door so neither Freed nor any of his men would enter. He must have known what was happening. Cap had been too busy fixing the coffee and the bacon to notice. Had he known, the triumph in his face might have given the show away. Cap had never been a good poker player.

Jeff's spirits began to rise.

Freed eyed Jeff's group belligerently. He stiffened as realization struck him. "You're short a man."

Jeff said nothing, neither admission nor denial.

"Son of a bitch!" Freed whipped his horse south in a

long lope. His men strung out behind him, spurring to catch up.

The sign was very fresh as they neared the river. Droppings steamed in the sharp morning air. Jeff's mouth was dry with anxiety as he began to hear cattle bawling, men hollering.

Freed shouted, "They're puttin' them into the river. Come on, boys. We've got them if we hurry!" The tiring horses had forced him to slow his pace the last miles, but now he pushed hard again, mercilessly digging spurs into his heavily sweating mount.

Jeff glanced at Cap and Booth and Santiago. "We want no part of a gunfight."

Booth demanded, "Then what did you come for?"

"Like you said, Vesper was in a mood to've killed somebody at those *ranchitos*. You saw his face."

Cap pointed. "There ain't goin' to be no gunfight, not unless Vesper is crazy enough to try to swim the river."

The raiders had crossed over with most of the cattle, leaving a dozen or so that probably had resisted entering the water. In their rush the Mexicans had given up these rather than risk losing the herd. The cattle were still in plain sight, drifting southward on the Mexico side. The raiders had turned to stand their horses in a ragged line, presenting a silent challenge to Freed and the men who rode with him. Jeff counted ten. Manuel and Vicente were side by side in the center of the group.

Old Santiago smiled with pride and victory.

Freed pushed his horse into the river. "Come on! We got them outnumbered." His men balked at following. He turned on them fiercely. "What's the matter with you? This is our chance to clean out the whole damned nest."

He remained by himself in the water. Jeff said solemnly, "Take another count, and think what a target you'd make in the middle of the river. They wouldn't let a one of you reach the far side."

"You're cowards!" Freed shrilled at his men. "If you don't come with me you're fired, every goddamned one of you!"

A Freed rider said defensively, "Layne's right. They'd pick us off one at a time while we're tryin' to swim. There ain't no job worth committin' suicide over."

Freed drew his rifle from its scabbard and pointed it toward the raiders. His horse fidgeted, anticipating the shot, so that Freed's aim was spoiled. The bullet harmlessly kicked up a spray of water. Freed cursed and returned to dry ground. His angry gaze touched on Santiago, then on Jeff. "I hope you're satisfied. We'd've caught them if you hadn't sent that old heathen's boy ahead."

"I didn't send him. He went on his own."

Freed seemed not to hear. "I won't soon be forgettin' this." He looked at Santiago again. "You tell that old man it's open season on his boys. I'm offerin' five hundred dollars to whoever kills one of them. A thousand dollars for both."

Santiago's face darkened. He needed no one to translate for him.

Freed appeared to take satisfaction from the old man's obvious distress. "Nobody can ever say I didn't give fair warnin'." He turned his horse and headed northward, his son at his side. His men began to straggle after him, uncertain whether they still had jobs.

Jeff turned his attention back across the river to Manuel and Vicente. He spoke grimly to Santiago. "You understood what Freed said?"

"I understood."

"Then you know Vicente can't come back now. He's outlawed like Manuel."

Santiago gave his thin shoulders a shrug. "We have nothing left to keep us on this side anymore. I go now to join my sons." He extended his twisted, bony hand.

Jeff took it, feeling sorrow for the old man. "I owe you and Vicente some wages. Can I send them somewhere?"

"They would amount to little. When the English and his woman have their son, buy him some little gift and say it comes from the family of Ramírez. And if there is any money left, buy yourself a bottle of tequila and drink it on some bad day when you need a bit of cheer."

Santiago shook with Cap and Booth, then set his horse into the river.

He was halfway across, the horse swimming, when a rifle's sharp report made Jeff flinch. The old man snapped forward over the horse's neck, then slid from the saddle. His body hung limply down the mount's side, his wooden leg held by the rawhide loop which served in lieu of a stirrup. The frightened animal plunged wildly, swinging Santiago back and forth like a rag doll.

Heart racing, Jeff jumped his sorrel horse into the water. Then he paused, for he heard a roar of fury from Booth. The cowboy aimed and fired his rifle. Freed rocked back in the saddle and grabbed his left arm. Booth spurred toward Freed's men, firing his rifle again.

"Kelly!" Jeff shouted. "Come back. They'll kill you!"

It was futile. Perhaps Booth did not hear him, or perhaps he chose not to. It would be nearly impossible for him to hit anyone from the back of a running horse, but rage had pushed judgment aside.

Jeff saw a flash from among the horsemen and heard the shot. Booth's horse seemed to stop in midstride, then went down heavily.

From the other side, Jeff saw that Manuel and Vicente were in the river, pushing toward Santiago. Some of the raiders followed after them.

Momentarily he was torn between trying to help Santiago and rushing to where Booth lay pinned beneath his horse, which threshed in the agony of its dying. He saw that the two brothers had reached their father, so he turned in Booth's direction. He held his body tense, half expecting another shot from among Freed's men. It did not come. They were riding away.

Cap reached Booth first. The dying horse was still trying to arise on its forelegs, then falling back on Booth. Cap grabbed the saddle horn as the horse struggled to get up. His excitement gave him strength to hold the animal long enough for Booth to crawl free. The cowboy clutched desperately at his leg.

Cap probably had no idea how loudly he shouted. "Good God, boy, you tryin' to get yourself killed? You ain't got a lick of good sense!"

Booth gripped his leg with both hands. Angrily Cap declared, "Damned wonder if it ain't broke in twelve places."

"He killed my horse. Son of a bitch killed my horse!"

"To hell with the horse. Let's see about your leg." Cap felt of it with his big hands, and none too gently.

Booth flinched. The trouser leg was ripped all the way to the knee. He pushed Cap's hands aside and rubbed the limb with more caution than Cap had shown. "I don't think it's broke. But I lost enough hide to make a pair of boots."

Jeff's initial fear gave way, and he caught some of Cap's impatience. "What were you thinkin' of, chargin' at that bunch?"

"I was thinkin' of Freed, damn him, shootin' that old man. For spite, that's what it was, pure spite. But I think I winged him. I seen him twist around like he was hit."

Cap agreed. "Damned pity you didn't hit him in the heart, but you ain't that good a shot. It's not no bigger than a walnut."

Jeff said, "Are you sure it was Vesper shot Santiago? Did you see him? Could've been one of the others."

"Wouldn't make no difference. They all belong to Freed."

Jeff thought of the boy Daniel and the shock he would have suffered seeing his father killed before his eyes. It was bad enough seeing him wounded, even if the wound was slight. He watched Freed and his riders moving away, well out of rifle range. "A killin' is easier to talk about than to live with. You-all stay here. I'm goin' over to see about Santiago."

Even before he finished crossing the river, he knew by the attitudes of the Ramírez brothers and the other riders that Santiago was dead. The old man lay motionless in the sand. Some of the bandits stood around him with hats in their hands. Jeff dismounted as soon as he reached dry ground, leading the sorrel horse. He asked no questions. There was no need.

Bitterly Manuel said, "The Freed robbed him of his land. Now he has robbed him of his life."

Jeff knew that nothing he said could mitigate the grief.

Vicente's voice was strained. "Why did Papa ride out into the river?"

"He said he was fixin' to join his sons. He had no reason left for stayin' on the other side."

Vicente clenched his fists. "The Freed is a dead man. I will follow after him and kill him myself."

Manuel caught his brother's sleeve and held it. "No, not now. It is better that he live, for a while."

"First he took our land. Now he has taken our father."

"You would kill him much too quickly. You would not give him time to feel the pain."

Vicente stared at his brother, not comprehending.

Manuel's eyes were cold. "We will kill him many times, a little today, a little tomorrow. It was for greed that he stole our land. The best punishment for a greedy man is to take away what he owns. He will die a little each time we take a piece of what is his."

Jeff had seen tiny heel flies drive a large bull crazy. "Don't underestimate him. You'll get no mercy if he catches you."

The two brothers exchanged glances. Manuel said, "We will not be caught." He turned his gaze to the other side of the river. "What of the Booth? Is he shot?"

"Just skinned and bruised. He's lost his horse."

Manuel unsaddled his own. "It is too far for him to walk or to ride double. Give him this one." He seemed to read the doubt in Jeff's eyes. "It is not stolen. Many of these others once belonged to the Freed, but not this one."

"Thanks." Jeff knelt beside Santiago. "And what about him? Are you goin' to bury him in Mexico?"

The two brothers looked at one another. Manuel said, "Can we ask of you a favor?"

"Anything I can do."

"Generations of our family are buried on the land that the Freed took from us. Our father should be buried there, beside our mother."

Jeff could envision Freed's indignation. The thought pleased him. "I'll see to it."

Manuel signaled to a man who held the reins of Santiago's horse. He untied a slicker from behind the cantle of his own saddle that lay on the ground. Reverently the two brothers wrapped the slicker around their father, hoisted the body up over the saddle and tied it securely.

Jeff studied the faces—particularly the eyes—of the other men. He saw several that made him cringe. He could believe that some were like Manuel Ramírez, convinced they were extracting just payment for past wrongs. But he sensed that others were simply criminals, seizing upon an easy excuse for their thievery. If they had not had this one they would have found another or would have plundered without an excuse. The same was true of Texans who raided south of the river. They rationalized their crimes on the grounds of patriotism, but they gladly kept the spoils.

Vicente took the reins and led Santiago's horse into the river. Jeff shook Manuel's hand, then led the horse Manuel had given up for Booth.

By the time they reached the other side Booth was trying to walk, but he limped heavily. "It'll take a better man than Vesper Freed to kill me."

Jeff shook his head. "No it won't. I don't know how bad you hurt Vesper, but you can bet it wasn't bad enough to drain the venom out of him. He'll be comin' for you or sendin' some of his men. He'll see to it that you're outlawed."

"Maybe next time I'll get a better shot."

"Or maybe *they* will. I hate to lose your help, but I think you'd better make yourself scarce."

Booth looked at Cap, who gravely nodded agreement. "He's talkin' sense. You heard Freed offer five hundred dollars a head for Vicente and Manuel. He'll add you to that list."

Tight-lipped, Booth laid a hand upon the body lashed to the saddle. "He was a good old man. There ain't many would've picked up a scared and hungry gringo kid like he did and take care of him till he could take care of himself." He rubbed a hand across his face. "You-all bury him right. There ought to be a priest."

"We'll do the best we can."

Booth faced Jeff and Cap. "We'll see one another again. It may be in heaven, or it may be in hell."

Cap said, "We've already come as close to hell as I ever want to get."

Jeff gripped the saddle horn tightly. "There's some hard-lookin' *hombres* in that crowd across the river. I wish you boys and Manuel would associate with better company."

Booth's voice was stern. "Right now, hard *hombres* are the kind of company we're lookin' for."

Cap saddled the led horse and helped Booth climb up painfully. Jeff watched Booth and Vicente cross the river, his fists clenching and loosening without his willing it.

Cap muttered something under his breath, then mounted. He reached down for the reins to the one on which Santiago was tied. "We truly goin' to bury him on Vesper's place?"

"He belongs there amongst his own."

"Vesper's liable to raise hell."

"Anything wrong with that?"

"Not one blessed thing."

Jeff wished he had that bottle of tequila Santiago had spoken of. This was as bad a day as he had seen in a long time.

THIRTEEN

Arletta had slept little, worrying about those who had ridden away after Vesper Freed and his men. She had little fear for her husband. Nigel had gone to Piedras to fetch the sheriff, so he should be safe enough. But she felt concern for Jeff and Cap, Booth and the Ramírezes. With the exception of Cap, all had a history of difficulty with Freed. Booth's and the Ramírezes' had been violent. She suspected it would take little to provoke violence again.

She had clung to a thin hope that Nigel and the sheriff might come by, but she had known it was more likely they would cut across to intercept the trail of the cattle, hoping to catch up before Freed and the others reached the river. She had sat in an uncomfortable straight-backed chair much of the night, waiting. Eventually she had given up and gone to bed, but sleep had eluded her except for brief stretches in which dreams of a violent nature prevented her from receiving any rest. Her stomach turned over several times, a product of both her pregnancy and her anxiety.

She prepared breakfast but was able to eat only a little of it. She went about her housecleaning chores with little heart for them and found herself sweeping out the kitchen a second time without having intended to. She walked outside often to look southward in the direction the men had taken. Through a thin blanket of gray clouds,

the cold round ball of the winter sun indicated it was past
noon when she finally saw them, close to a dozen men on
horseback. They were too far away to identify. She assumed they included her husband, Jeff and the others. Relieved, she poked at the coals in the fireplace and added
wood, hanging a coffeepot from the iron rail that extended
across the hearth.

The sharp sound of horses' hooves in the yard
brought her to the doorway of the little rock house,
searching eagerly for Nigel, then feeling her spirits sag. She
saw only Freed and his men, and the boy named Daniel.
Freed was slumped as if in pain. She realized with a start
that the left sleeve of his coat was bloody and torn. It
bulged from a crude bandage wrapped around the arm.

She walked out into the yard, stopping in front of
Freed's horse. She asked with some fear, "Where's my husband, and the rest of them?"

Freed made no attempt to answer. His face was much
paler than she remembered it.

One of the horsemen said, "Mr. Freed's lost a right
smart of blood, ma'am. Reckon you can see your way
clear to help him?"

She nodded, though her question remained unan-
swered. "Bring him into the house. Bring that boy, too.
He's blue from cold." She did not relish the thought of so
many men crowding into her small house, especially men
potentially hostile to her own, so she did not invite the
rest.

She held the door while one of the cowhands assisted
Freed. The boy followed closely. He did not speak, but his
worried eyes remained on his father. He was trembling a
little, from fear or cold or perhaps both. Arletta told him
to go to the fire and warm himself, then pointed the cowboy toward the chair in which she had spent much of a
restless night. "Set Mr. Freed down there and let's see
what I can do about that arm."

She had helped doctor bullet wounds and had set broken bones on the buffalo range, so she was hardly a nov-
ice. Still, she always had to brace herself. She and the

cowboy removed Freed's coat, sliding the bullet-torn sleeve gingerly down the man's arm. Blood had dried and hardened in a large circle around a ragged hole. She found that the sleeve of the shirt had been cut away crudely with a knife and had been wrapped around the wounded arm.

"A pity his shirt wasn't cleaner," Arletta said.

"We made do with what we had."

The dried blood clung to the wound, making it difficult to remove the cloth without causing pain. She guessed Freed deserved it, but she had to feel pity for him nevertheless. The bullet had torn through the muscle but appeared to have missed the bone by little more than the thickness of a silver coin. She tossed the sleeve into the fireplace. "Who did this to him?"

"Feller named Booth."

The news gave her a jolt, and a renewed rising of fear. "What happened to Booth? What about my husband and the others?"

"Booth got his horse shot out from under him is all. And there was a Mexican hit, the old man Ramírez. The way things looked, I suspect he's dead. We never crossed over to see."

Arletta felt queasy. "You didn't tell me about my husband."

"The Englishman? We met him and the sheriff a ways north of the river. Everything was over with by then. We didn't visit with them but a minute, and then they went on."

Her relief was only partial. She would not be at ease until she saw them all: Nigel and Jeff, Cap and Booth, and knew they were all right.

The boy had come away from the fireplace and was watching his father apprehensively. She said, "Your daddy'll be all right, Daniel, if he don't take blood poisonin'. You better go back and get warm. There's some biscuits on the table, and some bacon I didn't eat for breakfast." The boy wolfed them down as if he were starved.

She gave Freed an accusing stare. "You ought to be

ashamed, takin' a boy with you when you knew you were liable to wind up in a shootin' scrape. His mother must be beside herself, worryin'."

Freed tried to look her in the eyes but could not hold against her sternness. "About *him*, maybe. I doubt that she gives a damn what's happened to me."

She washed around the wound with hot water and a cloth, then brought out a bottle of alcohol. "This is goin' to burn somethin' fierce." She started pouring with a touch of malice, but her mood quickly shifted to sympathy as she saw him struggle to suppress a cry. Stiffening, he managed to make no sound except a hissing between his clenched teeth.

"I'm sorry," she said.

"I know." His voice was thin and edged with pain. He sat stoically as she wrapped a clean bandage around the arm.

"This ought to get you home. Then you'd better have your wife take a look at it."

"I wouldn't ask her to do anything for me."

"You'd better go to a doctor, then. I once saw a littler wound than this one turn green and kill a buffalo skinner."

"Your menfolks'd probably throw a party if I was to die."

"I wouldn't. I don't know what-all you've done, but I wouldn't wish anything that bad off onto you. And I'd hate to see that boy lose his daddy . . . even if his daddy does take him into things a boy oughtn't to be any part of."

"It's the best schoolin' I can give him. You got to learn to be harder than anybody around you if you want to have anything in this world. Else they'll run over you and take it all away."

"Like you've done to others I've heard about?"

"They'd've done it to me if they'd had the chance."

"You've got a poor view of the world, Mr. Freed."

"Grow up as poor as I did and that's the view you get."

"I growed up poor too. From the time I was able to use a needle and thread, I was sewin' patches on top of patches. But my old daddy never took from anybody else so we could have more."

"Like as not, they was takin' from *him*. There's two kinds of people in the world: them that takes and them that gets taken from. I got almighty tired of seein' first one and then another take from us . . . bandits, merchants, banks, courts . . . and my old daddy not knowin' what to do about it. So I made up my mind to ride the other horse awhile and see how it felt. I'll tell you, lady, it felt damned good!"

"So you're tryin' to teach your son to be just like you."

"It's better to hold the whip by the handle than to be on the other end of it."

"Maybe I feel a little sorry for you, Mr. Freed, and maybe I don't. But I do feel sorry for your boy."

Freed pushed shakily to his feet, reaching out with his right hand to grab the back of the chair and steady himself. When he felt secure, he took a couple of steps toward the door. His son rushed to his side. The cowboy set down a cup from which he had drained the last drop of coffee and moved to support Freed.

Freed gave Arletta a long moment's study. "You're a good-hearted woman, Mrs. Smithwick, and I'm obliged to you. Maybe if I'd met somebody like you when I was younger . . ." He seemed to be trying to finish the statement but did not. He turned toward the door. "I'd as soon be gone before your bunch gets here. There's been shootin' enough for one day."

She followed them as far as the door. She felt a twinge of conscience for letting the rest of the men wait out in the cold. Had circumstances been different she would have invited all of them in, regardless of the crowding, and made coffee enough to go around. She noted how the boy Daniel stuck close to his father, his anxiety evident. No man could be *all* bad, she thought, and raise a son who cared about him that much.

She decided it would not do to express such a view around Jeff, though, and certainly not around Kelly Booth.

Watching the men ride northward, she realized she had not heard the boy speak a word, not even a *thank you* for the food and the fire. She had seen gratitude in his eyes, but she had not heard it spoken. Probably he was not used to hearing his father speak it.

She cleaned up the wash pan she had used in cleansing Freed's wound, and she pitched a damp scrap of blood-streaked cloth into the fire, where it steamed awhile before it dried enough to burn. She kept going to the door, looking for her own menfolks. When they came, finally, she realized there were only four . . . Nigel, Jeff and Cap. The fourth was the sheriff; she remembered him from town. Santiago and Vicente Ramírez were not among them, nor was Kelly Booth.

Nigel stepped down from his horse, and she moved quickly into his arms. After a long embrace, she said, "You're missin' some men, looks like."

A grim expression on his face, Jeff pointed his thumb toward the horse Cap was leading. She realized that the slicker-wrapped bundle tied across its saddle was a body.

"Santiago?" she asked hoarsely.

Nigel nodded.

"Where are Booth and Vicente?"

"They both crossed the river. They will not be among us anymore."

The news about Booth only deepened the sadness she felt about Santiago. She was going to miss that cowboy, miss him a lot. She faltered a little in speaking. "Who shot Santiago?"

Jeff spoke up. "Vesper Freed, or maybe one of his men. Tracks show that they came by here. How long they been gone?"

"An hour or so, maybe. He was wounded, you know."

Cap said, "Kelly Booth done that. It was bad, I hope."

"His left arm. Bullet missed the bone. I expect his arm'll be some stiff from now on."

Jeff studied her with a sudden intensity. "You sound as though you had a close look at him."

She reacted defensively against a perceived rebuke. "I cleaned the wound and put a new bandage on it. I'd do the same for any human."

"Vesper Freed ain't human." Jeff looked back at Santiago, his face dark.

Nigel's arm tightened around her waist. "You acted properly, dear. Jeff is a little overwrought. He has lost a friend today. Three, when you consider Kelly and Vicente."

Jeff's voice calmed. "I didn't aim to criticize you, Arletta. You just answered your true nature, and a good nature it is. I'd like to think I might've found it in me to've done the same, but I probably wouldn't." He stepped down stiffly from his horse and turned toward Santiago. "It's too late for us to take him to his restin' place today. Anyway, we'll need to get the priest from town."

The heavyset lawman said, "I'll fetch him out tomorrow to the old Ramírez place."

Jeff made an effort at smiling, but it died a-borning. "That'd be kind of you."

"I'll want to be there anyway to be sure you don't have any trouble with Vesper Freed. There's already one man dead. I wouldn't want his buryin' to get somebody else killed."

Jeff pointed his chin toward the picket bunkhouse. "We'll put him there for the night and take turns settin' up with him."

As Cap led the burdened horse, Arletta turned back into her husband's arms. "I'm glad you weren't there when it happened."

"I wish I had been. Sheriff Golightly might have been able to prevent it."

"Why didn't he arrest Freed?"

"He said there would not have been case enough to take to court. The raiders had just crossed the river with stolen cattle that belonged to him, and Santiago was on his way to join them. He was, you might say, an accessory after the fact. At least, that is the way a court would probably see it. And Freed did not escape punishment entirely. Kelly's bullet through his arm was his retribution."

They watched Cap and the sheriff dismount at the bunkhouse and lift Santiago from the horse. Nigel said, "One violent act begets another. Violence sometimes carries its own punishment."

"How much will it take before everybody has had enough?"

"I wish I knew. I only wish for a short winter and an early spring."

"What does that mean?"

"Because the sheriff says the army has been successful against the Comanches. In the spring Jeff intends for us to go back north. Then we can leave all this trouble behind."

She wished they could leave tomorrow. But she wondered how much good it would do, even if it were possible. "Been many a time in my life that I thought I'd left trouble behind. But I'd look back, and there it was, followin' after me like some sheep-killin' dog."

Arletta insisted there would be no harm in her riding horseback, but Nigel Smithwick would not hear of it, nor would Jeff and Cap. Jeff said, "It might be safer if you didn't go at all. There could be trouble if Vesper finds out we're fixin' to bury Santiago on his land."

"The way Mr. Freed looked when he left here yesterday, he's feelin' too low to be causin' any trouble. That arm is probably painin' him so that he won't even leave his house."

She had found long ago that if she looked and sounded determined enough, the men usually backed off. They knew she would not give up until she had gotten her way, and they chose not to put themselves through the aggravation of an argument they were predestined to lose. Jeff said, "If you don't mind ridin' on the wagon with Santiago . . ."

She had seen death on the buffalo range, enough that she did not shrink from the sight of it. "The poor man deserves all the company he can get before he goes into the ground."

The wagon seat had a good set of springs, but Nigel added a blanket and a pillow as a precaution. "You may not mind a bit of jostling, but that is my heir you are carrying."

Jeff had only a vague idea how to find the old Ramírez place, so he and Cap started early. One balanced a pick across his saddle, the other a shovel. The air carried a chill, but yesterday's clouds were gone, and the morning sun promised a warmer day.

Arletta prepared some food to carry beneath the wagon seat. This errand was likely to require the full day, and there was no reason they should go hungry. They would probably not return before night, probably long after dark.

Nigel drove the wagon, Arletta seated close beside him. After several miles they came upon Jeff at a fork in the road. He sat on a black horse. He had let the sorrel rest at home. Jeff pointed. "We found the family cemetery down thisaway. Cap's diggin' a grave."

Arletta could not quite conjure up a mental picture of Cap working with either shovel or pick. His large stomach would always be in the way.

Nigel asked, "Any sign of trouble?"

Jeff seemed to try to avoid Arletta's eyes. "A couple of Vesper's hands rode up as we started diggin'. They went back toward Vesper's house. He hasn't showed up yet, so I don't know if he intends to give us a fight or not."

"What about the sheriff and the padre?"

"That's probably them comin' yonder."

Turning, Arletta saw a buggy with two people in it. But instead of two men, the passengers were a woman and the boy Daniel. Arletta caught in Jeff's face a look of surprise that turned to pleasure before he forced himself to cover it. She heard him say, almost under his breath, "Eva."

She saw that a buckboard followed a short distance behind the buggy. That would be the sheriff and the priest from town.

Arletta had not seen Eva Freed before, though she knew this was the woman who was supposed to have waited for Jeff to come home from the war and had not. She had not expected to like her, but she saw nothing to dislike in Eva Freed's face. She guessed the woman to be in her middle to late thirties. Her hair was dark, a few streaks of gray beginning to show. It was her eyes that took Arletta's attention. They were gray, and they were sad. It was not the transient sadness that comes from a passing event like attending a funeral, but a deep and permanent one that comes from living day after day, year after year, with a heavy burden. Yet in the set of her jaw Arletta thought she sensed an inner strength. Whatever her burden, she had managed to carry it.

Jeff removed his hat, and Nigel followed his example. Jeff said, "Eva, you're the last person I expected to see here today. I didn't figure you ever knew Santiago."

"I didn't. But I felt I had a responsibility."

"Because of what Vesper did to him?"

"It wasn't Vesper who fired the shot; it was one of the hands. He figured Vesper would want him to."

"Either way, it's Vesper's doin'. But why'd you bring the boy?"

"Because there's something cold and final about a funeral, and a graveyard. His father gave him a taste of violence yesterday. I want him to know what the aftermath feels like."

The boy was looking at Arletta. Though he did not acknowledge her directly, Arletta thought she saw gratitude in Daniel's eyes. It was probably contrary to his father's teachings—or at least the boy's interpretation of his father's teachings—to express gratitude in words.

Jeff introduced the women to each other. Arletta could not reach Eva's hand without dismounting from the wagon, so she settled for a nod of acknowledgment. Eva's smile was pleasant, if small and tentative.

Jeff said, "You met Arletta's husband once before, out on the road by my old place. He's Nigel Smithwick."

Arletta told herself it was probably imagination, but she thought she saw a flicker of relief in Eva's face. She wondered. Could Eva have thought that Arletta and Jeff were . . . No, that was too farfetched a notion. But it was interesting to toy with.

The sheriff pulled up in his buckboard. A brown-skinned priest sat beside him. Golightly introduced him as Father Valentín. Eva seemed to know him well. Arletta had encountered many Protestant ministers like Parson Parkhill up north, but she had had little contact with priests. Father Valentín's collar and his vestments seemed strange and otherworldly to her. She knew little of Catholicism except that its God was the same one the Protestant ministers talked about. She had wondered sometimes why there had to be so many different churches when they all had the same deity. The outdoor life she had led had given her only an occasional chance to see the inside of *any* church, so she assumed there must be a lot she did not know.

Sheriff Golightly said to Eva, "I hope Vesper's not figurin' to cause any trouble over this buryin'."

"He's too sick to give anybody much trouble today. A couple of our cowboys came in and told him that Jeff and his friend were digging a grave. I could tell he didn't like it much, but he just said, 'At least I'll always know where that old man is. He can't cause us any more trouble.'"

Jeff said, "That old man is liable to cause Vesper a *lot* more trouble. Come on. I left Cap doin' the diggin'. I expect he'll be lookin' for some help."

Arletta was relieved that there was to be no difficulty. There probably would have been were Vesper not suffering too much from the wound Booth had inflicted upon him.

Booth. She had mixed feelings about the cowboy. In a way she was relieved that he was no longer there to be following her with his gaze, making her uncomfortable because she could read the wanting in his eyes and knew

no way—certainly no way she would regard as acceptable
—to relieve what was ailing him. Even to acknowledge the
reality to herself seemed somehow unfaithful to Nigel. On
the other hand she could not help worrying about what
was to become of him. Sheriff Golightly had said nothing
in her hearing, but the guarded few things she had picked
up from Nigel and Jeff and Cap indicated that the lawman
now had to regard Booth as subject to arrest should their
trails cross. Right or wrong, Kelly Booth had made himself
an outlaw.

She found the little cemetery a lonely and forbidding
place, sadly neglected since Freed had acquired the land.
The withered stems of wildflowers, left here long ago,
drooped from glass bottles and jars set beside wooden
crosses of varying ages and degrees of weathering. The
only protection from wandering animals was a stone fence
less than three feet high. Some of the stones had been
knocked down by cattle that had stretched their necks to
reach the tall grass within the enclosure. She picked up the
fallen stones and placed them back on top.

At a distance of perhaps two hundred yards she could
see the remnants of what had once been an adobe house.
She assumed Freed had razed it as he had razed the Layne
home place, trying to eliminate as much trace as possible
of its previous owners.

She did not understand much of the ceremony. Father
Valentín gave most of it in Spanish or Latin—she could
not tell the difference. She watched him and bowed her
head when he bowed his.

She thought it a poor funeral in that none of Santiago's family was here, just the priest and seven others to
say goodbye. She wished Vicente could have been present,
and his brother Manuel. And Booth, for in a sense he was
a foster son. But she supposed they were here in spirit.
And wherever Santiago was now, he probably knew. At
least that fitted the teachings she had learned from Parson
Parkhill and others.

She knew the service was over when the men lowered
the plain wooden box into the ground, and each took his

turn dropping a shovelful of earth in atop it. The sheriff and Father Valentín said their goodbyes, climbed into the buckboard and set off on the road toward town. Jeff took the shovel and began filling the grave.

Arletta saw a movement at the edge of a thicket. Two men led horses out of the brush, mounted and rode toward the little cemetery. As they came closer she recognized Vicente. She assumed the taller man beside him was his brother Manuel. Jeff stopped his shoveling and wiped a sleeve across his sweaty face as he watched the two riders approach.

Silently the brothers dismounted and came to the edge of the grave. They looked down into it, hats in their hands.

Jeff said, "I'm sorry you came too late for the service."

Vicente nodded back toward the thicket. "We watched. We waited for the *cherife* to go." He reached for Jeff's shovel. "This is for us to do, my brother and me."

Jeff looked worriedly toward the Freed house, which lay out of sight a couple of miles away. It would not do for any of the Freed riders to show up while the Ramírez brothers were here. He turned his eyes to Eva. She shook her head as if to say in silence that she would not interfere.

There was the boy, of course. He stared intently at the two Mexican brothers. It was obvious he knew who they were, but he could do nothing until his mother took him home. She appeared in no hurry to leave. Arletta sensed that she would give the brothers plenty of time to disappear.

Jeff asked, "Where's Kelly Booth? Why didn't he come with you?"

Manuel and Vicente studied one another a moment before Vicente answered. "He has other business. He pays his respects to our father in another way."

Jeff looked disturbed. "What kind of business?"

"It is not for us to say."

Arletta could read all kinds of worry in Jeff's face, and that worry was contagious. Given his reckless nature, there was no way to predict what dangerous course

Booth's quest for vengeance might take. But there seemed nothing anyone here could do either to help him or to stop him.

Jeff said, "He's got his heart in the right place, but sometimes I don't know where his head is at."

Eva reflected Jeff's worry. "What do you think he might do?"

"There's no tellin'. He was mighty upset over Santiago. But maybe he'll cool down after a few days. I wish you'd tell Vesper to give him time and let him find his way."

"Vesper doesn't listen to me. He doesn't listen to anybody."

"Him and Kelly, they ought to go into partnership. They'd make a good pair."

The impatience in his voice aroused a spark in the boy Daniel. "You're talkin' about my daddy."

Jeff stared at the boy. Arletta wondered what must be running through his mind. Had Eva married Jeff, as originally planned, this boy might be Jeff's son, not Freed's. Or could it be . . . Arletta dismissed the notion. Daniel had Vesper Freed's eyes and many of his features. She saw nothing of Jeff in him. *A pity,* she thought. *He could do with some of Jeff's qualities.*

At least the boy had spunk, speaking up for his father in a crowd clearly antagonistic. He asked his mother, "When're we goin' home? I don't like it here."

"In a·while. A little while." Arletta knew she was waiting to give the Ramírez brothers a long head start toward the river in case any of the Freed hands were sent after them. She wondered if there might be another reason, if Eva might be stalling to remain near Jeff as long as she could. The thought appealed to Arletta's romantic nature.

Jeff and Cap spelled Vicente and Manuel at intervals to hasten completion of the job. When it was done, finally, and the grave neatly mounded over, Jeff told the brothers, "I hope you'll be headin' south. *Way* south."

Vicente nodded. "We go now. We must meet the Booth."

Arletta knew Jeff wanted to ask again where Booth was, but he caught himself. "Tell him I said he'd best lay low and forget about doin' anything to Vesper."

Manuel was staring toward the north. Vicente turned, a hint of a smile lifting the corners of his mouth. "I think he has done it already."

Daniel shouted and pointed. "Mama, that smoke! Looks like it's comin' from home!"

Rising against a cloudless winter sky, the smoke was light-colored, ranging from silvery to soft brown, like grass fires Arletta had seen on the buffalo range. Eva Freed's eyes were wide with anxiety as she hurried her son toward their buggy.

Jeff said something under his breath. "Kelly Booth! I believe the boy has gone out of his head." He turned to Eva. "Me and Cap'll ride ahead of you and throw the gates open. We'll see if there's anything we can do to help."

Nigel said, "Arletta and I will follow."

"No, we'll travel fast, and it'll be too rough a ride for Arletta. You-all go on home. Don't look for us till you see us comin'." He gave the Ramírez brothers an accusatory glance. Neither betrayed any reaction.

Nigel retrieved the pick and shovel, placing them in the back of the wagon as Arletta watched Jeff and Cap spur away ahead of Eva's buggy. She said, "Maybe we ought to go anyway. Maybe we could be some help."

"Whatever Kelly set afire, it would be in ashes before we could get there. Jeff was right. We have to consider your condition."

"My condition is just fine. I'm a long way from havin' that baby yet." But she knew Nigel was correct. It was unlikely they could contribute enough to justify even a minor gamble. She hoped the smoke did not come from Eva's house. Regardless of whatever punishments Vesper Freed deserved, Arletta had decided she liked Eva. She would not like to see her lose her home.

She shifted her concern to Booth. "What do you suppose they might do to Kelly?"

"Nothing, unless they catch him. And that, I would wager, is highly unlikely."

As they drove away she looked back at the lonely little cemetery and its fresh mound of earth. It seemed even more dark and forbidding than when she had first come.

Nigel drove slowly, mindful to avoid bumps as much as the uneven ground would allow. They reached the ranch headquarters at dusk. She saw three horses in front of the bunkhouse. She recognized the two the Ramírez brothers had been riding. She exchanged glances with Nigel, who nodded agreement with her unspoken thought and drove the wagon up close to the bunkhouse door. The two brothers stood beside their horses. They nodded but said nothing.

Kelly Booth limped out carrying his thin bedroll and a small bag of belongings. He smiled at Arletta.

She demanded, "Kelly, what did you do?"

"Just came by to get what belongs to me. It ain't much. One thing this country is short of is rich cowboys."

"You know that's not what I mean. I hope you didn't burn that poor woman out of her home."

Booth tied his blankets behind the cantle of his saddle. He hung the drawstring of the bag over the horn. "I thought about it, but the house was too much in the open. So I settled for his barn and his haystack. They was closer to the thicket."

"And what do you think you've accomplished?"

"I served notice that it's pay-up time. Me and Manuel and Vicente, we've got more in store for him."

"And he'll have somethin' in store for you too. Jail if you're lucky. A bullet if your luck runs out."

"I'm on good speakin' terms with Lady Luck. She won't let me be caught by the likes of Vesper Freed." Booth turned to Nigel. "English, I hope you know what a great hand Lady Luck dealt you. You take good care of her."

"I will. You keep yourself in good health. The farther from here, the healthier you will be."

"Don't fret yourself about me. I ain't ever goin' to

die. I'll live to be a hundred and turn into an old gray mule."

He waved and was gone, the Ramírez brothers following him southward.

Nigel said, "A hundred? He'll be lucky to live another month if he doesn't stay on the other side of the river."

Arletta felt a pang of grief, though Kelly Booth was still very much alive. "I don't believe he'll do that."

"You *know* he won't."

FOURTEEN

Crow Feather saw soldiers only once during the winter. He had tied his horse in a fringe of creek bank timber and was stalking a deer when he heard the hoofbeats, a jingling he could not identify, and the alien voices. He had noticed how well sound carried down here in this deep slash at the edge of the plain. He surmised that it bounced off the canyon wall. The bellowing of a buffalo bull would repeat itself in echoes that sometimes made it difficult to judge the distance from which it came.

He gave up the deer as lost and drew back into some low shrubs. He flattened himself, trying not to acknowledge that he was frightened. The soldiers came from the direction of his hidden camp, where White Deer and the children waited in a tepee small enough that its short poles could not be seen above the trees. He had heard no shooting, so he hoped they had not been discovered. But perhaps the soldiers had captured them without having to fire a shot. He raised up, his eyes barely above the tops of the shrubs, and anxiously studied the soldiers.

He was relieved to see that they had no prisoners. It was only a patrol that had chanced upon this canyon and was searching it, watching for sign of holdout Comanches or Kiowas. Crow Feather was certain there were none. He had ridden out this gradually widening canyon all the way to its mouth, where the walls fell away toward the rolling plains east and south. He wondered that they did not see the tracks of his horse. Evidently the bluecoats were not observant, and they had none of the cannibal Tonkawas along to serve as their wolves.

The deer he had stalked took fright and plunged across the open grass toward timber farther down the creek. Several soldiers shouted with glee and began shooting at it. The first shots missed, but the buck finally turned a somersault and lay kicking. The riders lost any pretense at holding formation, racing jubilantly toward the fallen deer, making enough racket to stampede buffalo.

They would enjoy venison over a campfire tonight, venison Crow Feather had intended for his own family. But there was plenty of game in the canyon if the soldiers and all their noise did not frighten it away.

White Deer and Squirrel would have heard the shooting and be fearful that he had fallen to the soldier guns. He wanted to go back and put their minds at ease, but he could not risk being seen. He waited for the soldiers to finish gutting their deer and disappear southward. He retrieved his horse and rode to where the animal had died. He found that the bluecoats had left some of the best parts, the liver and the sweetbreads. He ate what he wanted, raw, and made a sack from the paunch to carry the rest back to camp.

He could hunt again tomorrow. For today, this would be enough. He wished he had a gun like the soldiers used. Using bow and arrow, he had to stalk his game much more carefully.

Winter was showing signs of giving way to spring when a buffalo hunter came up from the southern end of the valley with two wagons, his skinners and his cook. Crow Feather knew the sound of the big rifle. He had heard it the previous winter and spring when the first of the hunters had come down from the north. He had heard it many times last summer during the big fight at the wagon village where the buffalo hides were stacked so high, and so many warriors were killed or wounded throwing themselves futilely against the walls of the *teibo* houses. The hunters' rifles had a fearful range.

Some buffalo had come down into the canyon, seeking protection against the high-plains winter, though the numbers were far fewer than this refuge had sheltered in the past. The broad scattering of bones showed that earlier hunters had done a heavy slaughter here. This new hunter would soon kill all that remained if he was as sharp a marksman as those Crow Feather had watched last year.

Still, so long as he stayed he presented a high risk of discovery for the family hidden beside the tiny spring. Careful not to leave the protection of the timber, Crow Feather spied him out. He watched as the hunter shot into a small herd. In a short time he had dropped five times four. The pitiable remnants broke into a run and escaped southward down the canyon. They stood scant chance of survival. The hunter would almost certainly follow them in his own good time and dispatch them as he had brought down the others.

Crow Feather considered killing him. It would not be difficult to stalk the hair-face the next time his attention was concentrated upon shooting the buffalo. But such an action, satisfying though it might be, would only serve to alert the other *teibos* to Crow Feather's presence in the canyon and bring about his death or capture at the hands either of the hunter's crew or the soldiers. Whether or not it led to discovery of his family, it would leave White Deer and the children without his protection and support. At best, they would have to give themselves up and go to the reservation. At worst, they might starve.

No, it seemed wisest that he let the hunter be and hope he would soon become discouraged enough over his meager results to abandon the canyon.

He watched two men approach the killing ground in a mule-drawn wagon. These, he knew from other observations, would rob the buffalo of their skins and leave their pink-and-white bodies naked to the wind and the wolves. He watched the hunter ride out to meet the wagon. He could see that the man was angry, for he shook his fist and waved his arms in an agitated manner. The wind carried fragments of the sound to Crow Feather. The words meant nothing to him, but their delivery was harsh. The hunter was a man of hot temper. He rode away, shouting back over his shoulder. The manner of the skinners was sullen.

Perhaps, Crow Feather thought hopefully, *they will kill one another.*

He had to consider it unlikely, though he had heard that white men often killed their own kind when their brains burned from drinking too much whiskey or when greed led them to try to take that which belonged to others.

The hunters might leave the buffalo to the wolves, but Crow Feather had no such intention. That night, while the wagon men's campfire flickered farther south, he brought Squirrel. They cut up as much of the meat as they could pack on his horse and Squirrel's pony, walking to camp and leading the animals. He thought it unlikely that the hunters would notice, for they would have no interest in buffalo already skinned.

Two days after the first hunter appeared, another party found its way into the canyon. Crow Feather watched them as he had watched the first, fearing discovery of his hidden camp. He could see that these *teibos* were poorer than the first. They had only one wagon, an old one by the look of it, and the two mules which drew it were thin and of indifferent quality. They might do to eat if one were desperate, he thought, but they would have to struggle to pull that wagon under a heavy load.

The men seemed excited when they found where the other hunter had killed his first buffalo. They were moving south from the site of the stand when the first hunter intercepted them. Though the distance was great and he could hear nothing, Crow Feather could tell that the meeting was not pleasant. He saw a great deal of angry gesturing and waving of arms. One of the men climbed down from the wagon as the hunter stepped from his horse. They fought vigorously with their fists.

Crow Feather thought it possible that the fight might end with the death of one or both, but after a short time the two separated. The hunter climbed back upon his horse and shook his fist. The wagon men made gestures which Crow Feather sensed were an invitation for the hunter to come back and fight some more.

The use of fists was foreign to him. It seemed degrading to both participants, for it was a poor test of a man's bravery. The People fought their enemies with better weapons.

The reason for the fight was clear. The hunter did not wish to share the canyon and its meager harvest of skins. The People were more generous than that, at least between bands of their own. If they found their hunting grounds despoiled by enemies such as the Apaches, of course, they would fight and if possible annihilate the usurpers. The Apaches were not true human beings. Neither were the hair-faces.

It would have been justice had the two white men killed one another. He was disappointed that this had not come about. He would have considered it a great pleasure to have helped them, had such an opportunity arisen.

The more he pondered that idea, the more it intrigued him. It was obvious he could not kill any of the white men himself, lest retribution be visited not only upon him but, more than likely, upon his family. But if he could fan the flames of discord between the hunters, they might do themselves what he could not.

The question was, what?

He considered taking the horses and mules from one camp and leaving them at the other. Those who had lost them would almost surely blame those who had possession. He surveyed the possibilities and weighed the risks. He found no major flaws in the plan, though there was a minor one or two. He could not assume the *teibos* to be stupid. The boots they wore left a different print than his moccasins. It was reasonable that one of the first things they would do upon discovering their loss was to look for footprints. Moccasin tracks would be a giveaway. Instead of fighting, it seemed probable that the white men would join forces to search the canyon. Whatever he did, then, he had to manage to do it on horseback.

He told White Deer of his plan. Squirrel listened and, naturally, wanted to go. The only white men he had seen had been soldiers, and those, mercifully, had been at some distance. Crow Feather explained that one horseman might slip into a hunter camp unnoticed if he moved slowly and stealthily enough. The difficulty would be far greater for two. He left unstated the possibility of his being captured or killed. He said only, "You stay and protect your mother and the children."

By not including Squirrel among the children, he hoped he gave the boy a stronger sense of pride and responsibility.

The nearest camp was that of the bad-tempered hunter who had been first into the canyon. Crow Feather directed his attention to that one, for logic told him this man was the most likely to set off violence.

From boyhood he had trained himself against eagerness. Stalking a meat animal or an enemy, one had to have infinite patience. Before dark he made his way as near to the camp as he could without moving from the timber and risking discovery. He waited until the campfire had burned down to no more than a faint glow before he made his first tentative move. He had watched the skinners picket the hunter's two horses and the mule teams on grass near the creek, so he knew where the animals were. He had hoped the men would place them a little farther from camp, in the better grass, but their degree of caution disappointed him.

No, these *teibos* were not stupid.

He held his horse to a very slow walk, keeping him as much as possible to the sandier ground which would muffle the sound of his hooves. Crow Feather leaned low on the horse's side so that if it were seen it would appear to be a riderless stray.

He paused several times, listening for any sound from camp. One of the risks he had taken into account was that there might be a guard. He had noted that white men seemed inclined to post sentries, though it was not a custom among the People. More than once a Comanche camp had been taken by surprise for this lack of precaution. From what he had heard from the refugee Comanches he had encountered, this had happened to the great winter encampment. The bluecoats had descended a canyon wall and were among them before the People awakened to the fact that they had been invaded.

To the People, posting sentries could be taken as a sign of weakness, of anxiety and lack of confidence. It was seldom done except under recognized conditions of imminent danger.

He doubted that these white men felt much sense of danger. After all, had the soldiers not driven virtually all the People out of this country and to the reservation? That was why they could afford now to fight one another; they had no mutual enemy against whom they must band together. At least, he hoped that was the case.

He had more hope than confidence. He had to fight down a temptation to dismount and lead his dun the final short distance to the area where the horses and mules were tied. But there was that business about the moccasin tracks . . .

He had his knife in his hand, ready to cut the line by which the first mule was picketed, when one of the horses snorted and began pulling at its rope. It must have caught his scent and had sensed that he did not belong. The contagion spread among the mules. They began to squeal and thrash about.

Crow Feather heard a voice from the camp.

"Hey, boys, some varmint's disturbin' the stock. Git up quick, before we lose them."

He had no understanding of the words, but he understood one thing: he had to melt out of sight quickly. He drew away to the cover of timber along the creek, disappointment bitter in his mouth. He listened to the white men walking among the picketed animals, talking soothingly, trying to calm them down.

"Reckon what it was?"

"Could've been a bear. Maybe a painter. Them cats do like horseflesh."

He thought it unlikely he would have another chance tonight. If the men in camp had not posted a sentry before, they probably would now to protect their animals.

At least they had not seen him. He would wait awhile, until they had settled back into their blankets, then ease along the creek until he was well beyond their sight and hearing. Waiting, he wondered if he might have handled the mission in a different manner and achieved a better outcome. Probably not, he tried to tell himself.

He became aware of an unpleasant scent carried on the night wind. It was the smell of death.

He puzzled over it until he remembered other buffalo hunter camps he had seen last spring and summer. Always there had been a drying ground where they stretched and staked the freshly taken hides to the ground and let them dry. These developed a stench from the rancid fat and decaying bits of flesh that clung to them.

Indians had long been natural traders. Many times Crow Feather had traveled with others of his band far to the east to trade buffalo skins and meat and captured horses to tribes who lived there. Those tribes scratched the face of their mother the earth to plant crops, something the People would never do. But the produce which came from these efforts was good to the taste, a welcome change from a steady diet of meat. Trading brought the People such delights as pumpkins and squash and beans, delicacies they would never raise for themselves because their pride did not allow them to scratch in the ground like birds or like the white man's chickens.

Crow Feather knew little about white men's way of trading. He surmised that they set a considerable value on coins of silver because he had found these in the pockets of *teibos* who had fallen to warriors' arrows and guns. To him such things were of value only for decoration, but it seemed the white men had some other reason for wanting them. He had heard it said they would trade a buffalo hide for one or two such pieces of metal. Perhaps that was why this hunter was so bent on killing the buffalo out of the canyon. He wanted to trade their skins so he could have more of the shiny coins.

Women and magpies and crows were attracted to shiny things, but a man should have more dignity, he thought.

Dwelling upon the puzzle, he angered. The People's lives had revolved around the buffalo, ever since the first man. It was a sacred animal. One asked its permission before killing it and apologized to it afterward for the necessity. It was a bitter thing that the white man killed for such a trivial reason.

With his anger came another idea. It was less dramatic than his original thought of taking the horses and mules to create a fight between the two camps, but it satisfied his sense of irony. The hunter had killed the buffalo so he could trade their skins. But what if Crow Feather rendered those skins worthless? It would be more rewarding simply to kill the man, but this at least would thwart him in his greed.

He rode the horse carefully up out of the creek and onto the flat flood plain where the hides were staked. The animal did not like the odor any better than his rider did, but Crow Feather urged him up to the nearest of the skins. He swung his leg over the horse's neck and jumped so that he landed upon the hide and not on the ground where his footprints might give him away. He drove the point of his knifeblade through the drying skin, then slashed diagonally across it, from one corner stake to its opposite. He made a second slash that almost cut the hide into four pieces.

He hopped from one skin to another, careful not to touch the ground, slashing each in its turn. He had to leave a few that were too far apart, but he ruined most of them. He made his way back to his horse by stepping or jumping from hide to hide.

It occurred to him in retrospect that this might be an even better idea than the first. Had he driven away the horses and mules, the hunter would have recovered them the next day provided he did not die in a fight with his rivals. And he would still have the skins to trade.

Crow Feather tried to put himself in the hunter's place when morning's light revealed the destruction of his hides. It seemed natural that he would assume it was a gesture of vengeance by the other hunting party.

He decided to wait and watch. He spent the rest of the night in a timbered spot. At daybreak he saw smoke rising from camp as the cook prepared the morning meal. After a time, men came out to hitch the mules to the two wagons, and the hunter saddled one of his horses. They passed by the hide-drying ground as they started to leave camp. The hunter hauled up short, then jumped to the ground. He strode quickly among the ruined hides, making jerky motions with his arms and stamping his feet. He remounted and motioned for the men with the wagons to follow him. They moved off in the direction where Crow Feather, last night, had seen the red flicker of the other camp's fire.

In a while he heard a distant flurry of shooting. In his imagination he saw what was happening, though the sounds came from far away.

Much later the wagons returned. One of them had but a single man on the seat, where before there had been two. The hunter's horse was tied behind. Crow Feather could see a couple of forms lying in the beds of the wagons.

He watched solemnly as the survivors dug a grave and dumped two bodies into it. They broke camp and went southward. Crow Feather followed at a discreet distance to the point where the other *teibo* camp had been. It was deserted.

That was the last he saw of buffalo hunters that winter and spring.

FIFTEEN

Jeff Layne felt a stirring of excitement when Cap Doolittle pointed out the swelling of buds on the mesquite trees. Cap leaned his considerable bulk dangerously far out of his saddle to pull down a branch and examine it with the tip of a stubby finger. If his horse had moved even a little, Cap would have landed on the ground amid the rotted beans from last year's growth. "Leaves are fixin' to bust out. Spring is just over the hill."

Jeff had worn a jacket when he had left headquarters at daylight, but now it was rolled and tied behind his saddle, for the morning sun had warmed him enough to bring a little sweat. He knew it was as easy to become sick from getting too hot as from getting cold. "I'll be glad to bid the winter goodbye."

Actually, it had been mild compared to the many he had spent in states to the north. This southern part of Texas usually was spared frost until near Christmas, and even then had relatively few freezing nights. It paid for its mild winters with excessively hot and humid summers. Jeff did not intend to spend the coming summer here.

Cap asked, "When we goin' to start?"

Warmer days had brought Jeff a prickling impatience to be gathering the cattle. "Bad as I hate to, we'll have to be patient. The cows aren't ready to move." He pointed to a dozen or so moving slowly toward water. All but three were trailed by calves. One's brown-and-white sides bulged with a calf likely to be born within days, judging by her udder. The other two were simply too fat for this time of year. They were obviously barren. He would sell them to a butcher along the way or let them provide beef for the ranch's own hands.

Winter, gentle though it was, had left most animals at low ebb in flesh and vitality. Producing milk for their new-born put cows under physical stress. They and their calves needed a few weeks of green grazing to gain strength for the long walk. He knew, too, that spring was several weeks later in reaching the Texas plains to the north. "We wouldn't want to get the herd up yonder and find the grass ain't ready."

He had itched all winter to be leaving this place. His years-old dream of returning to his home country had soured under the cruel intrusions of reality. He realized he should not have expected everything to remain as in the mental images he carried from his boyhood. True, the land was not appreciably changed, but land alone did not make a home. The people on that land were vital to his memo-ries, and the people were no longer the same. None of his family was left. Most of the neighbors he remembered were gone. The disillusionment he had felt in his early visit to the lost Layne home place and the family burial plot had intensified during the winter.

The outlawing of Kelly Booth had been particularly painful. From their first meeting in Wichita, he had sensed in the cowboy a recklessness, a tendency to quick action without regard to consequences, yet he had instinctively liked him. He had hoped that somehow Booth would find his way past the ghosts of past injustices and take to higher ground. Instead, Booth had allowed his hatred for Vesper Freed to draw him into violent incidents that seemed to build an insurmountable fence between him and that higher ground. They left him wandering about with no clear aim beyond revenge.

Jeff stared southward toward the river, lost in his thoughts until Cap's voice jarred him. "What you lookin' at?"

"Just thinkin', is all."

"The way you stared, I thought maybe you could see somethin' I can't. Thinkin' about Kelly Booth, wasn't you?"

"I can't help wonderin' where he's at and what he's up to."

"Bad as I hate to say it, I've given him up for dead. He'll let himself get in somebody's gunsights one of these days. With the reward Vesper posted, there's more than enough of them huntin' for him."

"It's reached a point that I'm beginnin' to understand how they feel."

"You ain't startin' to sympathize with Vesper, are you?"

"I never thought I would, but I'm edgin' in that direction."

"It'll pass, like indigestion."

The burning of Freed's barn had been but the first in a series of retaliations. Jeff could not attribute them all to Booth, for the old bandit raids continued from across the Rio Grande, and there was no way to know how many involved him. Over the winter the much-harried Vesper Freed had lost enough cattle to have made up a couple of herds for a trail drive to the railroad in Kansas.

At least two attempts were made to set off wildfires on the Freed ranges, but these failed. There was not enough grass to sustain a consistent blaze. There would be by summer, however, if he kept losing cattle. Not enough livestock would be left to keep the grass grazed down.

Cap squinted, looking southward. "Well, I'll swun. There *is* somethin' down there."

Half a dozen horsemen moved slowly in Jeff and Cap's direction. Jeff reached down for the rifle beneath his leg, then left it in the scabbard. "Speak of the devil . . ."

Vesper Freed rode slump-shouldered, carrying a heavy burden of defeat and fatigue. The men with him were weary and dejected. Freed reined up facing Jeff, their horses almost nose to nose. His eyes had a hollow look, his face haggard. He had lost weight running futilely after those who preyed on whatever belonged to him. Worse, his arm had never quite healed. Booth's bullet had left the limb stiffened and of limited use.

For his many sins, Freed was paying a heavy price. He said to Jeff, "I don't suppose you seen them?"

Jeff could only surmise that Freed had been chasing after raiders. It was obvious he had failed, again. "What did they get this time?"

"Most of my horses. Bolder than brass, they was. About all they left me was what I had penned at headquarters."

"Did you get close enough to see any of them?"

"If you're askin' did I see your friend Booth, no. But I'd bet you he was behind it, him and the Ramírez boys. Their tracks was everywhere."

"You don't *know* it was them. There's other bunches raidin' over here." Though Booth and the Ramírezes had left Jeff and his partners alone, some others had not. Jeff figured he and the Smithwicks had lost a couple of hundred cows. That was another good reason for leaving here.

Freed said, "I'll have to go to San Antonio or someplace and buy me a new remuda. A cowboy ain't worth his wages afoot."

Cap was without sympathy. "Maybe you ought to find you some horses that're crossed with homin' pigeons."

Freed shrugged off the remark. "Tell me straight, Jeff. Do you ever see Booth?"

Jeff could honestly say that he did not.

Freed had the appearance of a man cut down from a whipping post after twenty lashes. "If you do . . . if you *can* . . . tell him I'm willin' to make some kind of a deal. Ask him what he wants to let me alone."

"What he wants, I doubt that you'd be willin' to give."

"Maybe, maybe not. At least we can talk about it."

"Last time I saw him was the day you shot old Santiago, and Booth shot you."

"I didn't shoot Santiago. One of the boys done that. Eva said she told you."

"She did. But I figured all she knew was what you told her."

"I told her the truth, same as I'm tellin' you. Anyhow, he was an old man and couldn't've had much time left. How much do they want me to pay?"

"It's not just Santiago. It's years of other things you're payin' for. I'd guess they're a long ways from figurin' the account is square."

Freed's face twisted in misery. "If you've got any way to get word to Booth . . ." He jerked his head, and the men followed him northward.

Cap brooded. "You don't believe he just wants to talk to Booth, do you? Vesper would give what's left of his arm to get him up close enough for a clean shot."

Bleakly Jeff watched the disappearing riders. "I don't know what to believe anymore, or who. I just wish the grass would hurry up and grow so we can put this damned country behind us."

Arletta's pregnancy was far advanced, but she seemed to handle it well. Mornings, Smithwick came over to the bunkhouse for breakfast so Arletta would feel free to remain in bed a while longer. This evening, as usual when they returned from a day's work, Jeff waited until Arletta and Smithwick had a few moments together, then he went down to the little rock house to satisfy himself that Arletta was all right.

She anticipated his question, for it varied little from one day to another. "I'm doin' fine. There's been women havin' babies ever since the Garden of Eden. If I could kill and skin a buffalo, I ought to be able to handle a little old baby."

"They ain't quite the same thing."

Jeff could only guess how much discomfort Arletta might be suffering, for she was careful not to let anyone see it except perhaps her husband, and English turned away questions that might have led to a straight answer.

He tried to calculate when her delivery time might be, for it could affect the timing of their move north. He tried to remember when he had first become aware of her condition, then count the months forward. The flaw was that he did not know exactly when the pregnancy had begun. It was not the sort of thing a man would ask.

He had better luck judging cows.

Arletta said, "You needn't think you're goin' to be leavin' me behind when you start north. I'll be in my wagon whether the baby is here or not."

"We could leave you with that Mexican *curandera*." She had obtained some kind of herbal medicine from a healing woman who lived on a ranch nearby. "Or we could take you to a regular doctor in San Antonio, and you and English could follow us later, after you've dominoed . . ." He corrected himself. ". . . after you've finished what you have to do."

To that, English demurred. "She's a stronger woman than you credit her for. And besides, I have invested a fall and winter in learning to be at least a bit of a cowboy. That would be wasted if I am not with you on the trail."

"You've got a whole lifetime to be a cowboy. It ain't all that sunny an occupation."

As always, it was more a discussion than an argument, and it came to a standoff. Arletta said she had been overcoming obstacles all of her life. She was not to be undone by such a fundamental human challenge as childbirth. She abruptly changed the subject. "Nigel tells me you and Cap came across Vesper Freed today."

"We did. He'd just lost a bunch of horses."

"And he was blamin' it on Kelly Booth?"

"Everything these days gets blamed on Booth. Him and Vicente and Manuel."

"Do you really think Kelly is guilty of all the things they say?"

"Nobody could travel around that much. But I'd have to figure he's done his share."

Her eyes pinched with concern. "Sooner or later, they'll kill him."

"Not if they don't catch him."

Afterward, Cap tried to ease his worry about Arletta. "There's been a many a young'un born in a wagon train. My mama birthed me halfway between Georgia and Texas. Got right up and climbed back into the wagon for another half a day's travelin'. Had to. She was drivin' the team, you know."

Occasionally Jeff suspected Cap might be a little reckless with the truth. "You remember that, do you?"

"Well, not all of it. I was sleepin' a lot at that age."

Losing Booth, Santiago and Vicente all at one time had left Jeff shorthanded, even though the winter work was light. He had hired two Mexican brothers out of Piedras, Gabino and Luis Enríquez, on Sheriff Golightly's recommendation. The lawman said, "I don't know it for a fact, but I think they may be cousins to the Ramírez boys. I hope that don't worry you none."

It had been Jeff's observation that a substantial percentage of Mexicans around Piedras were interrelated. It was an old if small community, dating back to the period of Spanish colonialism. "It might worry Vesper, but it won't worry me."

Both spoke English, a relief to Jeff. His Spanish had been slower than expected in coming back to him. He understood it well enough when someone was talking to him, but he often stumbled in his search for the right words and the proper order when he tried to answer. The brothers were competent hands, too, both on the range and at the bunkhouse dinner table.

Cap, who took pride in his cooking, became a little irked at the pair, especially Gabino, for adding a lot of chili pepper to whatever was on their plates. "It kills all the flavor. The way they load it down, beefsteak and *frijole* beans taste all the same. Don't seem like there's any point in me tryin' to cook them a decent meal."

The two brothers took a special interest in Smithwick because he had come originally from England. Luis pointed out that one of their distant ancestors had emigrated from Spain, but that had been a terribly long time ago. The brothers had never met anyone who had actually sailed across an ocean, so they asked a lot of questions about a body of water so huge that it took many days to traverse it. The biggest they had seen was the Rio Grande in full flood. Gabino was disappointed that Smithwick had not seen a whale. He found it difficult to picture an animal larger than a full-grown bull or a Percheron stallion.

In the process of teaching the Enríquez brothers about other parts of the world, Smithwick picked up a better working knowledge of Spanish as well as some help with his cowboy skills. Jeff thought this was of much more importance than Gabino's using too much pepper on his beef and beans. And the pair were elaborately deferential to Arletta, demonstrating a great respect for the mother-to-be. Luis, in particular, would bow and make a broad sweep with his big hat, bringing a delighted smile from her each time.

Sheriff Golightly showed up late one afternoon, looking tired enough to fall from his horse. He gratefully accepted Jeff's invitation to eat supper and spend the night. Watching Luis show Smithwick how to shoe a horse, the sheriff asked Jeff, "How're the Enríquezes workin' out for you?"

Jeff was glad the question had been asked of him instead of Cap. "They're good boys. They do all I ask them for, and more."

"I may need you to ask them for somethin' a lot different." The sheriff's face creased. "Do you ever see Kelly Booth or the Ramírezes?"

"Nothin' but their tracks, goin' to and from Vesper Freed's."

"I had a long visit with Vesper today. He's gettin' desperate. He made a proposition I think will interest you."

"We'll be leavin' this place soon as the grass is ready. I can't think of any proposition he could interest me with."

"It's not for you, it's for Booth and the Ramírezes.

But he figures maybe you'd have a way to get in touch with them." Golightly looked in Luis's direction.

"Through Luis and Gabino? I don't know that they're really kin. I've never thought it was my business to ask."

"You might want to make it your business. Vesper says he'll lift all charges if Booth and the Ramírezes will quit raidin' him."

"It'll take more than that. There's been blood spilled on both sides."

"Maybe enough that they're all ready to put a stop to it. Vesper claims that he is."

Jeff pondered. His doubts kept rising to the top, stronger than his hope for an end to the troubles. "I never knew Vesper to give up on a grudge. I've seen Indians send out a small party to lure somebody into chasin' after them, then run a big bunch in behind to close the trap. How do we know Vesper ain't just tryin' to lure Booth and the others to where he can get his hands on them?"

"I suspicioned the same thing. Vesper promised me he's on the square. Says he'll meet the boys on neutral ground, like your place here. Just him and them, and me and you to keep everybody honest."

"Do you believe him?"

"I want to. I'd like to see an end to this."

"There's other raiders besides Kelly and Vicente and Manuel."

"But just gettin' them three to quit would cut down a right smart on my ridin'. This job has gotten to be hell for a fat man. Come election time, I may not even run again."

Jeff smiled. Cap had the same problem. Much of the time he was finding reasons to remain at headquarters, declaring that being a cowboy *and* a cook was too much for a man of his age and physical condition. Besides, he argued, somebody ought to be around in case Arletta suddenly needed help.

"I'm not sure Luis and Gabino would know how to find the Ramírezes, if they *are* cousins. And if they did, I don't know that Booth and them would come to parley.

I'm not even sure I'd advise them to. Vesper's as slippery as a greased pig."

"At least go with me tomorrow and talk to him." Golightly glanced away, not looking Jeff in the eye. "I know Mrs. Freed would want you to say yes. She's scared of harm comin' to that boy of hers."

Jeff cursed Golightly in his mind. A man that devious had no business being a sheriff. But he had to say, "All right, I'll go and talk. But I'm makin' no promises beyond that."

He admitted to himself that Golightly's mention of Eva had been the turning point. The galling thing was that the lawman had known it, and had used it for leverage. Eva had been much on his mind, but he had hoped it didn't show. Years ago, he had thought he had locked her memory away where it would never bother him again. Returning to South Texas and seeing her had broken that lock.

He did not sleep much. He wanted to blame it on the sheriff's loud snoring, but he knew better. Old memories and new fantasies kept his mind astir while his body begged for rest. He was not ready for the sound of Cap Doolittle rustling around in the bunkhouse kitchen. Cap had a touch of the sadist about him. Rising earlier than everyone else, he always seemed to find a reason for banging all the pots and pans against each other and singing in a voice not meant for the choir.

Giving up, Jeff arose, dressed and haunted the coffeepot until it came to a boil. He hung a bucket of water by its bail over coals on the hearth and finished shaving by the time Golightly and the two Enríquez brothers tromped into the kitchen for breakfast. Smithwick came up from his house and gave a positive answer to Jeff's usual query about Arletta's condition. He gazed quizzically at Jeff's freshly shaved face, which until this morning had not felt a razor in a week. Jeff detected a fleeting smile of understanding, but Smithwick said nothing.

After breakfast, Jeff started out the bunkhouse door,

heading for the corral to saddle the sorrel horse. Cap followed him, drying his hands on a piece of cotton sack. "Don't you feel a little like a fly goin' into the spider's web? Say the word and I'll ride with you."

"Vesper won't risk doin' anything when the sheriff's with me. You and English keep an eye on Arletta. If she shows any sign that she's havin' trouble, you fetch that *curandera* over here quick."

"English could do that."

"And leave her here alone? Don't you know anything except biscuits, beans and cows?"

"I know about skunks. And you're fixin' to ride into their den."

On the way over to the Freed place, Sheriff Golightly talked about everything that came into his mind except the trouble at hand. He did not mention Freed or Booth or the Ramírezes, at least by name. He talked about horses and cattle and old times before the war, when he had been a younger, thinner man and had ridden with the Rangers. "Seems to me like things was simpler then. You always knew who your friends were. There wasn't all this worry about who was right and who was wrong. You just knew. Times, I get to thinkin' I ought to let the next election go by without me. I might decide to ride north with you."

"You'd be welcome."

"If I wasn't too old I'd turn my back on all this."

"It's not your age that'll stop you. You know you're needed where you're at. You're as apt to sprout wings and fly as to leave here."

"I suppose I've got no choice. When I was a young man it seemed like there was a dozen forks in every road, and I could take whichever one I wanted to. Nowadays the road is narrow, and I don't find any forks in it."

Jeff's pulse quickened as they neared the frame house with the gingerbread trim. He heard hammering. A couple of carpenters were building a new barn where the original had burned down. He saw a man sitting in a chair on the porch, a boy seated on the steps beneath him.

"It ain't like Vesper to be at the house in the middle of the mornin'," Golightly remarked. "He's expectin' us."

"He's takin' a lot for granted. For a nickel I'd've broken my promise and not come at all."

"I doubt as you ever broke a promise in your life."

Freed did not arise until Jeff and the sheriff had tied their horses and walked to the house. Courtesy would have brought him at least as far as the bottom step, but courtesy had never caused Vesper a moment's concern. *Showing his independence,* Jeff thought.

Freed did not address Jeff directly. Standing at the top of the porch, he looked confidently down upon the sheriff. "I see you talked him into it."

Stiffly Jeff said, "He didn't talk me into anything. I came here to listen. Then I'll decide what to do . . . or not do."

Freed motioned to his son. "Danny, you run along." The boy hesitated a moment at the door, staring at the visitors with unabashed curiosity. Jeff looked beyond the boy into the dim interior of the house, hoping he might see Eva there. He was disappointed.

Freed motioned toward a wooden bench on the porch. "You-all have a seat." He could easily have brought out a couple more chairs. They would have been more comfortable. Jeff suspected the bench was Freed's subtle way of establishing the superiority of his bargaining position. He had a chair, and they did not.

Freed seated himself, then turned to Jeff. "The sheriff told you my proposition?" He did not give Jeff time to answer. "Both sides would be better off with a brand-new deck of cards on the table. I'm willin' to erase all the charges I've made against them boys. They can come back and live on this side of the river without lookin' over their shoulders all the time."

"And in return?"

"They put a stop to their devilment."

"Sounds good, as far as it goes. But every deck of cards I ever played had a joker in it. Where's the joker in yours?"

"There ain't none. It's an honest, straight-out swap. Everybody wins."

Vesper Freed had never been one to give an opponent an even deal. "I don't know that they'd trust you. *I* don't trust you."

"At least help me meet with them and lay out the proposition. Let *them* decide if they trust me."

"Hell'll have ice on it two feet thick before they'll ever come here to parley with you."

"I figured that. What say I meet them at your place? I'll come by myself, unarmed. They'll come by theirselves. You and the sheriff'll be there to see that everything stays on the up-and-up."

"If things didn't work out, they'd be a long ways from the river. You could cut them off."

"What harm could I do them, just me by myself, and no gun?"

"Your ranch crew could do them a right smart of harm."

"I'll have my cowboys busy workin' cattle. I promise you, they won't interfere."

For the sake of Booth and the Ramírezes, Jeff wanted to believe. He wanted them free of their outlaw status. But he knew Vesper. Doubt outweighed his wish.

He became aware of a shadow just inside the door. Though he could not see her clearly, he sensed that Eva stood there, listening. His skin prickled with anticipation. He wished she would come out into the light.

Freed said, "I'll sweeten the pot. This all started over that piddlin' little piece of land the Ramírezes used to have. It won't run enough cows to amount to anything, and it's already cost me a lot more than it's worth. If they want it so damned bad, they can have it back."

Surprised, Jeff felt a moment of elation. But his doubts quickly pushed it aside. Vesper was giving up too easily.

Freed seemed to read his thought. "I promise you again: not one of my cowboys'll lift a hand in this. I'll come alone."

Jeff tried to read what lay behind the sheriff's eyes. He could see there the same wish that must be in his own.

Eva stepped out onto the porch. "He won't be alone. I'll come with him."

Freed's eyes flashed with surprise, then impatience. "What good do you think you can do?"

"I'll serve as a gesture of good faith. I can be their hostage, if they need one."

Jeff saw that this had not been part of Freed's plan. He stood up and took off his hat. He could only stare at her at first, fumbling for the words. "Thanks for the gesture, Eva, but if things went wrong, you could get hurt."

"My being there might help keep things from going wrong."

He saw a strength in her eyes that he had never seen before, certainly not when he had courted her long ago. In those days she had been easily swayed by whatever wind was blowing hardest.

Freed sputtered, "Woman, you don't make any sense at all."

"I want an end to this fighting. There's been enough hurt on both sides. If it goes on any longer, I'm afraid for Daniel."

The boy appeared around the corner of the house, riding a paint pony. He was smiling, showing the pony off in front of the visitors.

Just like a kid, Jeff thought. He remembered a pony he had had at that age. His father had been forced to sell it so he could buy beans and flour and salt for the family.

Freed's face furrowed. "I don't see what my son has got to do with this."

She corrected him. "*Our* son. He's been riding with you, and you've dragged him into trouble too many times." She looked back at Jeff. "Do you want to know who fired the shot that brought down Booth's horse after Vesper was wounded? It was Daniel."

Jeff found that hard to believe. "He's just a boy."

"A boy with a rifle in his hands can kill you as dead as

a grown man could." She looked back at her husband. "You've shown him all about fighting. Now let's show him how to make peace."

"You ain't goin' with me. You'd just be in the way."

Jeff suspected that if trouble did come, Freed would not hold back on his wife's account. "Eva, I don't often find myself agreein' with Vesper, but this time I do. You'd best stay out of it."

"I'll be there."

Jeff watched with wonder the contest of wills, as husband and wife stared at one another with hard eyes. It was Freed who finally turned away, back to Jeff. "Tell them I'll meet them at your place. By myself."

Eva's stern look told Jeff that this fight was not over.

He said, "I'm not sure I can get word to them. If I do, I'll let you know when they'll meet with you. *If* they'll meet with you."

"You just tell them it'll be worth their while to come."

Jeff found his gaze fastening again on Eva. The quiet, pliant girl of his memory was nowhere to be seen in the firm set of her jaw, the fierceness in her eyes. "Eva, I'd sure rather you stayed home."

"I'll be there."

Riding away, Golightly looked back at the couple facing one another on the porch. "You reckon she'll stand her ground?"

Jeff replied with admiration, "I wish she wouldn't, but I believe she will."

He wondered again why she had married Vesper instead of waiting for Jeff to come home. "Where was all that strength years ago when she really needed it?"

"It was there. She just hadn't found it yet."

SIXTEEN

The Enríquez brothers did not admit to any kinship, but they said they would see what they could do about getting word to the Ramírezes. They disappeared for two days. Just before sundown on the third day, as Jeff was nailing a new shoe on Socks's right forefoot, Nigel Smithwick pointed. "I believe your messengers have returned."

Jeff tried to read their faces as they rode up. On one level he was eager to hear the answer they brought. On another he was not sure what he wanted that answer to be.

Gabino nodded first at Smithwick. *"Inglés."*

Jeff asked impatiently, "Did you see them?"

Luis said, "We saw them. They are very nervous. They do not trust."

"Neither do I. But I wanted them to know about Freed's proposition."

"Even so, they say they will come. For their family's land, they will take the chance."

The news was not what Jeff had expected. But the Ramírezes and Booth must certainly have calculated the risks. "When'll they be here?"

"Saturday. They said tell the Freed he is to bring no one. He is to come alone."

"Did you tell them Mrs. Freed said she would come to be sure Vesper keeps his word?"

"They do honor to the Freed's woman but hope she does not come. They wish her no harm." Luis turned to Nigel Smithwick. "The Booth, he asks many questions about the *Señora Inglés*. We tell him she is well, but the baby does not choose yet to show himself."

"I appreciate his concern."

Jeff thought Smithwick might not appreciate that concern quite so much if he knew what Booth had revealed after rescuing him from the stampede. There was no reason for Smithwick ever to know. Certainly Jeff would never tell him. He looked toward the setting sun and calculated how long it would take him to ride over to Freed's. It was too late today.

Next morning he left his cot as soon as he heard Cap rustling around in the kitchen. Cap eyed him suspiciously while he pinched bread dough off into biscuit-size lumps and rubbed them against the greased bottom of a black Dutch oven. "A man can get himself shot, showin' interest in another feller's wife."

"I'm just goin' over to carry the news to Vesper."

"By the time you get there Vesper's liable to be miles away from his house. Cuss him all you want to, but you've got to admit that he's a hard-workin' son of a bitch."

"Then I'll leave the message."

"With his wife?"

"She may be the only one there."

"I stand by what I said."

Jeff would not admit it for a jug of Kentucky's finest, but he hoped he *would* find that Vesper was not at home. He would have an excuse to talk with Eva, if only for a few minutes.

He was nearing the Freed headquarters when he heard cattle bawling and saw a rising of dust a mile or so away. Squinting, he discerned that five or six riders had pushed a small bunch together into what appeared to be a rough corral of brush. His first thought was of border jumpers, but after watching for a minute he decided these were some of Freed's cowboys, branding new calves

they had gathered. More than likely Freed was with them.
Jeff could take him the message without riding any farther.

Pretending that he had not seen, he rode on to the
two-story house.

Eva appeared startled as she answered his knock on
the door. "Jeff!" She looked past him to see if he was
alone.

"I came to tell Vesper the boys are willin' to meet."

"He's working cattle south of here. You must've
passed him."

He could truthfully say, "I must have."

She stared as if she had never seen him before. "Come
on in, then. I'll fix you some coffee."

"I'd be much obliged." He followed her into the
house, into a hallway from which a set of steep stairs led
to the second floor. The kitchen was down the hall, past a
sparsely furnished parlor. Jeff was not used to parlors. He
felt more comfortable in kitchens or on porches.

She motioned for him to pull out a chair and sit at the
table. She opened the fire-box door of a large cast-iron
range and shoved into it several sticks of dried mesquite,
their ends jagged from the bite of an axe. She looked into a
pot that had been left on the cold end of the stove. "I'll
make it up fresh. Vesper didn't leave much."

Under other circumstances he would have told her
simply to reheat what was left; he would not be particular.
But he enjoyed watching her move about the kitchen,
grinding brown coffee beans, pouring water from a bucket
into the pot, setting the pot directly over the fire box
where the mesquite was beginning to burn vigorously. She
stirred a wanting he had long since forced aside. In her
maturity she seemed as desirable as when they had been
young. He fantasized about standing up and taking her in
his arms.

Their eyes met and held. She studied him with an
unflinching gaze that seemed to reach into a hidden corner
of his soul. For one wild moment he wondered how she
would react if he swept her from her feet and carried her
up those stairs. He looked away lest she read the thought

in his eyes. He felt a renewal of the old sense of loss she had once caused him. But over the years acceptance had blunted the bitterness that had been so much a part of it.

He said, "It's been a long time." He realized what an empty thing that was to say.

Her answer was just as empty. "Yes, it has."

He sensed that she was evading, just as he was, the burden both of them carried. "You've got a nice house here. Vesper has provided pretty good for you."

"He's made a lot of money." Her pained tone told him much that she left unspoken.

"A lot more money than I ever would."

"Money." She spoke the word as if it were a curse. "If you knew what that money has cost . . ." Her voice broke, and she turned away. "I've wished a thousand times . . ."

He stood up and pushed the chair aside. He thought he knew without her having to say it. He placed his hands gently upon her shoulders. She turned back to him, tears glistening. She put her arms around him and laid her head against his cheek. He smelled the fragrance of her hair and kissed her on the forehead. She raised her head and pressed her lips firmly against his. He answered with a fierceness that surprised him.

The coffee boiled over and sizzled on the stove top.

She pulled back from him and tried to shove the pot away from the hottest part of the stove, burning her hand.

"I'll get it," he said, then jerked his hand back from the blistering heat.

She tried to smile, but it was an awkward gesture that she quickly abandoned. "I'm afraid we've both gotten burned."

He licked a rising red welt on his forefinger to ease the fire. "I've been burned a lot worse than this."

"I'm not talking about now. I mean before."

"*That* was a bad one."

"What can we do about it, Jeff?"

"Nothin', I suppose. Nothin' we wouldn't both be ashamed of afterward." He wanted to take her in his arms again, even take her upstairs, but he forced himself to go to the window and look out. "I've always wondered. Why did you do it? Why did you marry Vesper instead of waitin' for me?"

"I was young. I didn't have a mind of my own. At least, I wasn't strong enough to stand up to other people. My father was deep in debt. It looked like we were about to lose our place. Vesper wanted to marry me, and Papa knew Vesper had money. There had already been a couple of our neighbor boys killed in the war. Papa said there wasn't a chance in a hundred that you'd ever come home. It got to a point that I couldn't stand my ground against him and Vesper both."

She moved up close behind him. "It doesn't sound like much of an excuse, but I was just a girl then. I'm a stronger woman now."

"Strong enough to leave Vesper?"

She was silent for a minute. "I've thought about it many a time, but I couldn't leave our son. Daniel's the only good thing that's ever come out of this marriage."

"You could take him with you."

"No. If there's anything in this world that Vesper loves more than money and land, it's our boy. He wouldn't lose much sleep if I left him. But he'd turn heaven and earth upside down if I took Daniel with me. He'd kill to get him back."

"He's killed for a lot less."

"So you see, I'm stuck with a bad bargain. If I could turn time back I'd do things differently. But we don't get all the choices we want in life, and the ones we make, we have to live with. I hope you understand."

"I wish things could be different for you."

"I wish things could be different for both of us."

He settled for touching his lips to her forehead. "Tell Vesper the boys'll meet him Saturday at my place. And it'd be safer for you if you didn't come. There's no tellin' what might happen if things go wrong." He left unspoken his suspicion that Vesper Freed had something up his sleeve.

He walked down the hall and out the door. As he

descended the steps she came out onto the porch. She called after him, "You never did get that cup of coffee."

"Maybe there'll be another time."

The melancholy look in her eyes told him she doubted it.

He rode on to Piedras to notify Sheriff Golightly and to be certain what day it was. He tried always to mark off the days on a calendar in the bunkhouse kitchen, but occasionally he forgot and had to remain in doubt until he was able to confirm or correct his assumption. He looked at the X marks on Golightly's calendar. "Is today already Thursday?"

Reared back in his chair, his hands clasped behind his head, Golightly chuckled. "I always figured a man is in bad trouble when he gets to where he doesn't know what day it is."

"Sundays don't mean much way off out in the country. But this Saturday could be damned important."

"You still don't trust Vesper?"

"I haven't trusted him since we were ten-eleven years old."

"I'll be out there to try and keep him honest."

"I'm afraid you're a way too late to change his ways. But I'll be obliged for your help."

Years ago, Elijah Layne had declared that Morris Golightly was dependable; nothing short of sudden death would cause him to go back on his word. Golightly showed up Friday evening, blankets rolled and tied behind the cantle of his saddle. "I wanted to be sure I got here ahead of Vesper."

"And just ahead of supper." Jeff was glad to see him. "Cap'll be hollerin' pretty quick now."

They had almost finished eating when Nigel Smithwick came into the bunkhouse kitchen, his eyes worried. "Jeff, would you come down and look in on Arletta? She says she is all right, but I believe she is suffering some pain."

Golightly set down his knife and fork. "I've had some

experience in this line. My wife birthed five young'uns in her time."

They found Arletta lying on her bed, embarrassed by the attention. "I told Nigel I'm all right. Just havin' a little gas, that's all. You've got more important things to be frettin' about."

Jeff said, "There's nothin' more important right now than you and your son."

Golightly gave her a critical look. "Young lady, I know the signs. You ain't far from deliverin'."

English was moving beyond worry toward panic. "Don't you think I had better get the midwife?"

She said, "I think it's a lot of fuss over nothin'. But it might not hurt if she was here." She grasped her husband's hand. "Nigel, I don't want you goin' nowhere."

"*Any*where," he corrected her. "But we need the *curandera.*"

She squeezed his hand. "*Any*where . . . *no*where . . . it don't matter a particle. I just want you to stay with me."

Jeff said, "I'll send Gabino."

It was somewhere close to midnight when the midwife arrived. Jeff stayed in the little house's kitchen, drinking coffee with Cap and Nigel Smithwick, watching the bedroom door which the Mexican woman had closed. In a while she came out. "She sleeps now," she said in Spanish. "I think nothing will happen, not for a while. You men go." She looked at Smithwick. "Not you. You stay."

Jeff had to translate part of it for him. Smithwick blurted, "You're damned right I'm stayin'."

There were times when he forgot where he came from and sounded almost like a Texan. Jeff smiled. "Holler if you need us. I'm fixin' to try and get some sleep."

He did poorly at it. Between concern over Arletta and worry over bringing Vesper Freed, Booth and the Ramírezes together, he spent most of the night staring into darkness. About the time he finally dropped off, he heard the door open. It was still dark outside. All he could see

was the dim form of a man. His first thought was of
Arletta.

"English? Is that you?"

The voice was Kelly Booth's. "No, it's me and Vicente."

Jeff rolled over on his cot and reached for his hat. It
was the first thing he put on of a morning, before shirt,
britches and boots, a habit born of long years sleeping
outdoors. "Kind of early, ain't you?"

"We camped out yonder a ways where we could keep
a watch on things. We suspicioned that Vesper might try to
get here ahead of us and set up some nasty little surprise."

"I wouldn't put it past him. Where's Manuel?"

"Still out there keepin' watch. What'll it take to get
Cap up? We're starved half to death."

They were in the middle of breakfast when Jeff heard
the clopping of horses' hooves out front. Through the
open door he could see that dawn was just starting to push
away the darkness. "Vesper's up damned early too," he
said.

Booth reached for the pistol he usually carried high
on his hip, but his hand came away empty. Sheriff Golightly had taken charge of his and Vicente's firearms and
stowed them in a cabinet.

Jeff went to the door and stopped, stunned. Eva Freed
sat with one leg crooked over a sidesaddle. Her son Daniel
was on the pony Jeff had seen him ride at the Freed place.
When his initial surprise passed, Jeff hurried out to lift Eva
down. "I'd hoped you wouldn't come. And for God's
sake, why did you bring the boy?"

"Vesper wouldn't shed a tear if something happened
to me. But he'd give up anything he owns to protect Daniel."

"Where *is* Vesper?"

"Somewhere behind us, I would expect. He was deep
in a whiskey sleep when we left."

The boy appeared bewildered. He looked with misgivings at the men who came out of the bunkhouse, and he

stared toward the rock house where the Smithwicks lived as if he might break and run in that direction.

Jeff said, "Come on in, son. You look like you need a good breakfast."

The boy eyed him warily. He knew hard feelings existed between his father and Jeff. It was natural that he would side with his father. "Where's the lady? The one that fed me here."

Jeff did not know how much the boy had been told about such ticklish matters as pregnancy. "She's a little sick this mornin', but you'll find aplenty to eat in the bunkhouse. You like biscuits?"

The boy nodded, hunger overriding mistrust, but not erasing it. Cap placed a huge, red-speckled hand on Daniel's shoulder. "Nobody's goin' to bite you, cowboy." He led the youngster to the door. "You can swab them biscuits with some of the best lick you ever sweetened your tongue on. Pure-dee blackstrap molasses. I know the man that raised the cane."

Eva said with some urgency, "I'm not certain what Vesper plans to do, but half a dozen toughs came in yesterday. They carried two or three guns apiece and looked like they knew how to use them."

Jeff scowled. "He said he wouldn't bring his cowboys, but he didn't say he wouldn't bring somebody else." He cut his gaze to Booth. "I knew he wasn't to be trusted. You and Vicente better hightail it south."

Eva protested, "Those men rode this way yesterday evening. They're probably out there somewhere, waiting."

Jeff searched the southern horizon as early sunlight began to root out the lingering shadows. His skin prickled with apprehension. The brush could hide a hundred men. No matter which way Booth and Vicente rode, Freed's gun-toters were likely to head them off. "You said Manuel is out there someplace. I hope he keeps his head down."

Booth nodded grimly. "He's not by himself."

"You brought men with you?"

"We knew Vesper wouldn't keep his word. We didn't see any reason to keep ours." He looked at Eva. "Lady, we didn't plan on you comin', but I'm glad you're here, you and your boy. I think Vesper'll be a right smart easier to handle."

Jeff looked worriedly at her. "There's no tellin' what Vesper may do to you when this is over."

"He won't do anything. He knows I'd shoot him." She made a bitter smile. "I did it once. Did you ever notice that little nick in his left ear?"

Jeff hadn't.

"I told him I'd place the next one three inches to the right. He's never put a blue mark on me since."

Jeff marveled. The Eva he had known long ago would never have considered such a thing. "You'd better come in and have some breakfast."

He sent the Enríquez brothers out to watch for Freed and whoever else might show up. He thought it best that Booth and Vicente remain indoors, out of sight.

Eva said, "I met the Englishman's wife at the Ramírez cemetery. Has she had her baby yet?"

"She's tryin', but things are goin' kind of slow. We've got a *curandera* with her."

"I might be of some help."

"We'd take it kindly."

The boy declared, "Mama, I'm goin' with you." He gave Jeff a look that said he did not want to remain with these strangers, even the big friendly bear of a man who had fed him.

Eva said, "Come on, then, but you'll have to stay out of the way. The lady in that house is sick."

"They said she's havin' a baby. I've seen cows havin' babies. They don't get sick."

The twinkle in Eva's eyes eased some of Jeff's tension. He had always thought she was pretty. Now he thought she was beautiful. She said, "Just the same, you stay out of the way."

Watching them walk toward the Smithwick house, Kelly Booth let his anxiety show. "You sure Arletta's all right?"

Jeff frowned at him. "She's another man's worry, not yours."

"I've got no notion of breakin' up a good family. But that don't mean I can't worry about her."

"Just so you know what your place is."

Gabino Enríquez called out. Walking around the bunkhouse, Jeff saw a rider approaching in a lope. He recognized Vesper Freed by the way he sat in the saddle. "Kelly, you'd better go inside till we see what kind of a temper he's in. And tell the sheriff. The sight of him may cool Vesper's innards a little."

Freed slowed, then stopped to give the place a cautious looking-over before riding in. Jeff walked out farther so Freed could see him plainly. He raised his arms to show that he packed no pistol. Sheriff Golightly stepped into view, and Freed came on, holding the sweat-lathered horse to a walk. Obviously he had run the animal much of the way.

"Damn a man who would abuse a horse," Jeff muttered. But he could understand that Freed was anxious about his son.

Freed leaned in his saddle to look over into a corral. Eva's and Daniel's were among the several horses penned there. He stopped a few paces short of Jeff and the sheriff. "Where are they at?"

Jeff said, "They're all right. There was no call for you to sweat your horse that way."

"I never would've thought you and them bandits would kidnap my family right out from under my nose."

The sheriff said, "Nobody's been kidnapped. Your wife came of her own free will to guarantee that you'd live up to your promises."

"You ain't seen me break any of them yet."

Jeff demanded, "What about that bunch of toughs you hired? They're waitin' out there now to catch the boys when they start south."

Freed's face flushed, betraying his guilt.

Golightly said, "You'd just as well get down and give that horse a rest. Booth and one of the Ramírez boys are in the bunkhouse, waitin' to talk business." As Freed dismounted, the sheriff held out his hand. "I'll take that iron, if you please. Nobody here is packin' except me." Freed reluctantly yielded his pistol.

Jeff signaled for Gabino to take the animal. As Freed handed him the reins, Gabino led it toward a water trough. Freed's eyes crackled, but he kept his anger under control. "I want to see Danny before I talk to anybody."

Jeff said, "He's down at the Smithwick house with his mother. She's tryin' to help Arletta."

Freed showed concern at mention of Arletta. "The Englishman's wife? What's wrong with her?"

"Looks like she's about to bring a young'un into the world."

"I'd hate for anything to go wrong with her. She's one of the few women ever treated me decent without I was payin' them to."

Booth stepped out of the bunkhouse. It occurred to Jeff that Booth and Freed had one thing in common beyond their mutual hatred: both had kindly feelings toward Arletta Smithwick. But it would take a lot more than that to build any lasting peace.

Luis went to the rock house and fetched Daniel. Jeff watched the desperate way Freed hugged the boy. It seemed a contradiction in the man's character. He muttered to Golightly, "They say every man has got a weakness."

"Been a many a wanted man caught because he couldn't stay away from his family."

Daniel said to his father, "Mama's helpin' that lady bring a baby."

"So they told me. But that's not a thing for a boy to be watchin'."

"I wasn't. They shut the door and wouldn't let me in. That Englishman was tellin' me stories about the place where he came from. He told me about London bridge and the tower where they chopped the queen's head off. There must've been some real bad people back in them days."

"I expect there was." Freed squeezed the boy's shoulder. "Now, you go back down yonder and talk some more to the Englishman. I've got business with these men." He did not take his eyes from Daniel until the boy was in the house. He turned then, the softness quickly gone from his eyes. "Let's be about it. I want to take Danny and be gone from this place."

With brittleness Jeff said, "You've got a wife here too."

"She came on her own. She can go on her own or she can stay. I don't much give a damn."

Jeff started for the door. "Let's go in the bunkhouse."

Freed did not offer to shake hands with anyone. He gave Booth and Vicente a disturbed look. "There's supposed to be another one. Where's Manuel?"

Vicente said, "I speak for Manuel."

Jeff thought it was plain why Freed was distressed. Both brothers and Booth were supposed to fall into an ambush when they left here. Now Manuel was a wild card. If he survived, the vendetta would go on, probably fiercer than before.

Freed said, "I ain't makin' no deals without everybody bein' here."

Jeff heard a disturbance outdoors. Luis Enríquez stepped inside, beckoning. "Mr. Jeff, you better come see."

Jeff guessed there must have been twenty horsemen. By far the majority were Mexicans, Manuel Ramírez among them. In the center, half a dozen gringos were being herded along like cattle. In contrast to the heavily armed Mexicans, their holsters were empty.

Freed followed Jeff outside. He looked as if a mule had kicked him in the belly.

Jeff gave full vent to the irony he saw. "You asked for Manuel. There he is. And there's the jolly gentlemen you sent to see that he never got home."

Freed's jaw clenched. He did not speak.

"I thought you were bein' damned generous, offerin' to give the Ramírez boys their land back. You'd've said yes

to anything because you figured on them bein' killed as
soon as they left this place."

Freed said something under his breath.

The sheriff jerked his thumb toward Freed's six men.
"Do you owe these fellers any money, Vesper?"

One of the riders said crisply, "He owes us for our
guns, unless these Meskins figure on givin' them back to
us."

That, Jeff thought, was about as likely as for the sun
to turn around and head back east.

The sheriff said, "I think you'd better forget about
them guns. Figure them as a cost of doin' business." He
turned to Jeff. "I'll escort these fine gentlemen as far as the
county line. Can I depend on you to see that Vesper leaves
here with all his vitals undamaged?"

"I'll want to see him make some promises first, with
witnesses."

The sheriff beckoned Jeff to one side. "You know,
don't you, that if he agrees to anything under duress he
can back out of it later?"

Jeff's spirits fell. "You're sayin' that whatever we do
here is a waste of time?"

"Under the law, yes."

"So I'd just as well send Booth and the Ramírez boys
back to Mexico. It's all been for nothin'."

"Sorry. The best I could do would be to charge Vesper with hirin' these thugs to try and do murder. But I'd
need at least one of them to testify, and there ain't a snow-
ball's chance in hell."

Jeff glared in Freed's direction. "So everything is back
where it started."

"Vesper got his hand called, and nobody got killed.
Look at it like that and it's been a pretty good day." The
sheriff walked to the corral and saddled his horse. He
mounted, faced Freed's six gunmen and made a sweeping
motion with his arm. "Come on, fun's over." He pointed
them toward Piedras and fell in behind them at a distance
that would make it difficult for them to turn suddenly and
overwhelm him. It was unlikely they would try, for they

were unarmed, and the job they had been hired for had
sunk like a rock in a mud hole.

Jeff watched them leave. "Vesper, you're the one who
asked for a parley. We can still do it."

Freed's angry gaze was fastened on Booth and Vicente. "Not in a hundred years."

Jeff studied the Mexicans clustered around Manuel.
Most appeared to be the same men he had seen that day
on the south bank of the Rio Grande. Some probably justified their raiding as Manuel did, taking what they regarded as their due from those who had dispossessed
them. But others looked as hard as the gringo gunmen the
sheriff had just taken away. They would do what they
wanted and take what they wanted whether they had an
excuse or not. Jeff would not trust them out of his sight.

"Vesper, I'll get Cap to fix these men somethin' to eat.
You'd better slip away while they're busy. Otherwise I'm
afraid they may do to you what you'd figured on doin' to
Booth and Vicente and Manuel."

Freed showed no reaction. Evidently he had already
considered that possibility. "I'm not leavin' without
Danny."

"What about Eva?"

"For all I care, she can stay here till horses grow
horns."

Daniel met them halfway between the bunkhouse and
the Smithwicks'. His eyes were wide with excitement.
"Can you hear that?"

Jeff stopped and listened. At first he heard nothing.
Then, faintly, he made out the thin cry of a baby. Nigel
Smithwick came out of the house, grinning broadly, and
motioned vigorously with his hand.

The boy said, "She sounds like a little calf, don't
she?"

"She?" Jeff stood slack-jawed, absorbing the disappointment. "We all figured it was goin' to be a boy."

"Mama said it's a girl. You reckon it makes any difference?"

"We looked forward to trainin' a new cowboy for this

outfit." A smile grew slowly across Jeff's face. "But I doubt that anybody'll want to send it back." At the house, Smithwick shook his hand so violently that Jeff almost lost his hat. "No, I expect she's a keeper."

Eva was washing her hands in a basin of water. To Jeff's silent query she said, "Arletta's all right now. Being the first one, it was a little tough on her."

Smithwick looked at Freed, then back at Jeff. "Did things go all right over there?"

"No, everything sort of went to hell." Jeff handed a towel to Eva. Her eyes told him she had a sense of what had happened though she had not seen it. He said, "You-all had better get away from here as quick as you can."

She glanced at her husband, who pointedly turned away from her. Freed said, "You'd just as well stay. You can look after the Englishman's wife."

"The *curandera* knows her business. I don't think Arletta will need me. But my son does."

Jeff sensed that she spoke more to him than to her husband.

While Freed set off for the corral to saddle Eva's and Daniel's horses, Jeff went into the bunkhouse to retrieve Freed's pistol from the cabinet where the sheriff had asked Gabino to put it. He also got his own pistol, strapping the cartridge belt around his waist.

Booth blocked the door. "Do you mean to just let Freed ride out of here?"

"I promised Sheriff Golightly."

"He deserves to get what he was fixin' to give us."

"Maybe so, but it won't happen here, not today." Jeff took another step toward the door. Booth did not yield. Jeff let his hand settle upon the butt of the pistol. "I don't approve of everything you've done, Kelly, but I still consider you my friend."

"A friend of mine wouldn't let Vesper just ride away."

"A friend won't let you kill him and have a noose hangin' over your head the rest of your life. I asked you to move aside. Now I'm *tellin'* you."

Grudgingly Booth took a step back. Jeff paused in the doorway. "You might want to go down to the Smithwick house. Arletta's just had her baby."

Most of Booth's anger seemed to flow away. "How's Arletta? She all right? And her boy?"

"They tell me she's fine. And it's not a boy."

At the corral the two Ramírez brothers watched Freed finish saddling up. Jeff did not like what he saw in their eyes. Nor did he like the look that a pair of *bandidos* beside them were giving to Eva Freed.

"Hold on, Vesper. I'm goin' with you."

"What the hell for?"

"Look at Vicente and Manuel, and you'll know what for." He quickly saddled the sorrel Socks. "They'll think about it for only so long, then they'll come after you. Let's move."

Riding out, he gave the Ramírez brothers a look that said *Stay here!* But he would not have given a busted cinch ring for the chance. He kept looking back.

Freed tried not to, but he could not help himself. At length he said, "Eva, you take Danny and go on ahead of us."

Her eyes met Jeff's, silently asking. He nodded at her. "If they come, it's better you and the boy aren't with us."

Daniel started to protest. His father quickly squelched him. "You go on now and do what I told you. I won't be far behind." To Eva he said, "If anything happens, make a run for the house. Pick up any of our cowboys that you see. Keep them with you."

Watching his family ride on while he and Jeff stopped, Freed asked anxiously, "You don't think they'd really hurt my boy?"

"Not unless he got in the way. But Eva . . ."

Both men kept watching behind them. Jeff saw no sign of pursuit, but the tension stayed.

Freed said, "You never got over her, did you?"

"I don't know what you mean."

"A blind man could see you still want her. You never was one to keep a poker face."

"She's your wife, so what I might want don't matter much."

"If it wasn't for Danny I'd tell you to take her and be welcome. But he needs her, and I need him, so me and her are stuck with one another. Unless you see some way out."

"One." Jeff made a grim smile. "I could shoot you and say the bandits did it."

"That's somethin' I might do, but you never would. You're not hard enough. That's one reason you'll be shovin' your boots under a poor man's table all of your life."

They rode in silence until they met several of Freed's cowboys, riding toward them in a hard lope. The riders circled around them excitedly. One demanded, "Where are they at, Vesper? Mrs. Freed said there's bandits chasin' after you."

"I told her if she came upon any of you to keep you with her."

"That's not what she told us. She said you and Mr. Layne might be needin' help."

Freed turned to Jeff. "I wonder which of us she was the most worried about?"

Jeff attempted no answer. "You've got help enough, looks like. I'll be goin' back."

"I've got one word to say, and it'll be the last time you ever hear it from me. Thanks."

"*Por nada*. I just didn't want your blood on my hands."

"Don't let yourself get the notion that anything has changed. What's mine is mine, and it stays mine. I still intend to see that Booth and those Ramírezes are buried so deep even the coyotes can't dig them up."

"I didn't figure it any other way." Jeff watched Freed and the cowboys ride northward. Turning, he headed for home. Halfway there he met Manuel and Vicente and four men from across the river. He raised his hand, and they stopped.

"You'd best go back. Freed's got a bunch of his cowboys with him."

In Spanish Manuel said, "The Freed is no friend of yours. Why did you go to protect him?"

"I went to protect those who *are* my friends."

"So the Freed has won for this day. But there will be other days."

Jeff looked back over his shoulder. He could not see the Freeds or the boy or the cowhands. Bleakly he said, "Yes, I suppose there will." Other days, and days beyond those until one side or the other was defeated, possibly even annihilated.

He wondered how long it takes a newborn to be ready to travel.

SEVENTEEN

At least twice a day, and sometimes more, Jeff went to the Smithwicks' house to look at Arletta's baby. After she got past the red and wrinkled look of the first days, he thought her about the prettiest child he had ever seen. Any disappointment over her not being a boy quickly melted away and would forever afterward be denied.

"She's got your hair," he told Arletta. "Brown with a touch of red in it. Goin' to be strong-minded like her mama. Nobody'll tell her what to do."

"You can't go by the color of a newborn baby's hair. It'll probably change."

"Red hair means a fighter. That won't change."

If early assertiveness meant anything, she would always be one who stood up for herself. She soon acquired strong opinions about feeding time and protested sternly if it was delayed. Arletta would shoo away any men other than her husband before she unbuttoned the front of her dress.

The parents named the child Margaret Rebecca Smithwick, using one name from English's mother and one from Arletta's. Cap was not sure he liked the choice. "Sure as hell everybody'll start callin' her Maggie. There ain't no baby deserves to be saddled with a name like Maggie."

Smithwick assured him that they would circumvent that problem by calling her Becky for short.

Cap liked that better. "The most sensible woman I ever knew was called Becky. I proposed to her, and she had the good sense to turn me down."

Seeing the youngster so often, Jeff could not judge the rate at which she gained weight. It seemed to him that she was growing much too slowly, though when English brought the *curandera* out to see about mother and daughter, the verdict was that they were progressing nicely. If anything, the Mexican woman assured everyone, they were doing better than most.

But when Jeff asked how soon the baby would be large enough that she could safely make a long trip in a wagon, the answer was noncommittal. *"Quién sabe? Maybe soon. Maybe not so soon. The mother will know when it is time."*

Cap reiterated his assurance that babies had been born along the immigrant trails without holding up a wagon train. Badly as he wanted to get started, Jeff had no intention of putting the baby in any jeopardy by exposing her too quickly to the rigors of the trail.

"Cap, that canyon has been there for thousands of years. It ain't goin' anywhere."

"You're the one that's a-faunchin' around, rarin' to go, not me. Right now I've got a hearth to cook on and a solid roof over my head. All the way up yonder I'll be cookin' out of a wagon, over a campfire, fightin' to keep the sand out of the biscuits and beans. It don't matter to me if we wait till the baby's ready for school. Of course you know there'll be some more by that time."

Cap was merely venting a little steam. The old cowboy cook was as eager as anybody to be getting started. He soaked the wheels of the wagon they had brought down from Kansas, making the wood swell tightly against the iron rims. Then he greased the vehicle thoroughly and bolted the chuck box upon it. Smithwick would help him awhile, then one or the other of the Enríquez brothers. Nobody would stay with him long because he was constantly rushing, pushing, calling upon his helper to hurry. "We got to have everything ready. We're liable to be leavin' just any day."

It had been many years since Jeff had last gone up the trail with a herd, but the memories were as fresh as spring dew on the greening grass. These were to be cows and calves. They would move slower than the steer herds with which he had ridden before. Small calves would be a complication. Newborns might have to be carried in a wagon their first few days. The alternative was to kill them at birth, which to Jeff was not only inhumane but wasteful as well. The bull calves would be turned into steers and eventually be a salable commodity at a Kansas railroad shipping point. The better heifer calves would become cows and increase the herd.

One positive side to a cow-calf herd was that it would usually not stampede as fast or as far as steers. Maternal instincts would soon overcome the instinct for flight.

Jeff knew they would have to haul a lot of equipment and supplies because the canyon was a long way from any town where they could restock. He bought two more wagons from the liveryman, who again offered to sell him the wagon yard, cheaper this time.

"Why would a man want to travel all the way up to the plains, where it's a hundred, maybe two hundred miles to a barrel of flour or a slab of bacon? He could stay right here and get fat layin' in the lap of luxury."

The liveryman was a long way from being fat. He looked as if he might be skimping on groceries to avoid bankruptcy. Jeff thanked him for his kind consideration but assured him that his partners had their hearts set on going to the plains.

He would hook these two wagons in tandem, one behind the other, so they could be handled by one driver and one team. He would defer buying most of the supplies until they reached San Antonio. Goods would be cheaper and the selection broader than in a small town like Piedras.

The two Enríquez brothers agreed to make the trip

but did not guarantee to stay on afterward. Gabino said, "*Los indios!* What of the Indians? That is a wild country."

"The army claims it's moved the Indians to the reservation. They say the plains are safe now."

"Is the army always right?"

Jeff remembered his years in the service of the Confederacy. The armies of both sides had predicted a short war and easy victory. "I've known it to miss a time or two."

"We had an uncle who tried to take his sheep far west on the Rio Nueces. The Apaches, they killed him and ate his sheep."

"But they're west. We're travelin' north."

Luis said, "The north is where the cold winds come from. I do not like the cold."

Gabino pointed out that at least they might finally have a chance to see snow. Living on the border, he and his brother had never seen it snow enough to cover the ground and turn the world white. "Our father saw snow once. But that was north of San Antonio."

Though Cap professed to be in no hurry to start, he admitted to the same worry that kept plaguing Jeff. "I keep wonderin' how long it'll be till war breaks out here again. There ain't nobody forgot their grudges, not Vesper Freed, and sure not Kelly Booth or the Ramírezes."

"We want to be sure the grass is ready for these cattle. And we wouldn't want to run into a late winter storm with Arletta's baby." But Jeff itched to get under way, to leave this contentious border country before someone reopened full-scale hostilities.

They began working the fringes of the Jones range and beyond, separating TE cattle from those of their neighbors and pushing them toward the ranch headquarters. This way when they were ready to start on the trail, the roundup would be relatively short.

In Piedras and a couple more settlements Jeff recruited extra cowboys to help with the drive. Some were Anglo, some Mexican. The Enríquez boys brought in three of their cousins, all named Gallegos and not one of them brothers. Jeff found bald-headed George Newby, who as a young man had helped Elijah Layne build the house in which Jeff had spent much of his youth. George had been to Kansas several times and knew the routine of the trail. He was one of those quietly competent people who knew what he could do and felt no need to prove anything to anyone, least of all to himself. He was the kind to whom a boss could give instructions and leave for six months, without concern for what would happen in his absence.

As a cowboy, Owen Palmer was a capable hand, but he was not inclined to look ahead much farther than sundown. He had never been north of San Antonio and had always regretted that being too young for the war had robbed him of a chance at adventure. Going up to the plains should offer him a chance for some excitement, he said.

Jeff told him, "I've had enough excitement in my life for both of us. I hope this trip bores you to death."

He rounded out his team with a solemn Herman Wurtz, who spoke with a heavy accent when he spoke at all. As a boy he had been among a party of immigrant Germans who had settled in the Texas hill country and had tried to re-create their homeland to whatever extent a new environment would allow. That had included some old-country ideas about absolute authority and patriarchy. Having a strong mind of his own, and American notions about life that clashed with his father's, he had rebelled in his late teens and drifted off to San Antonio, then farther south toward the border.

Arletta volunteered to cook for the outfit and free Cap for cowboy work, but her husband objected, and Jeff would not hear of it. "You've got a baby to take care of, and just travelin' is all the exertion you need. Countin' me and not countin' Cap, we've got ten men. That's aplenty."

Actually, it was probably more than he needed. But he suspected that some would drop out as the drive moved toward the caprock at the edge of the plains and away from the settled country. Once they passed the last town it would be difficult, probably even impossible, to find replacements.

He feared all along that hostilities would break out anew before he could get under way, and his fears materialized as they were finishing the roundup, throwing the herd together. They were cutting out strays that bore Vesper Freed's and other neighbors' brands when Eva Freed came loping up to the gather. Her horse gleamed with sweat though passing showers had left the spring day relatively cool. She was so nearly exhausted that he thought she might fall from the sidesaddle before he could help her to the ground.

"Jeff," she gasped, struggling for control, "I need your help. It's Vesper."

"What's he done now?" Jeff thought nothing would surprise him, but Eva's news did.

"He's on his way to Mexico. He found out somehow where the Ramírezes and Booth stay. He's hired the same group of toughs he had before, and another dozen or so. He's determined to hunt down those men and settle the feud for once and for all."

Jeff gritted his teeth. "I figured he'd come to somethin' like that, or *they* would. But those boys are slippery. Chances are he'll never find them."

"He swore he'd keep on their trail this time until they're all dead. Those men he has with him aren't just cowboys. They're as rough-looking a set as I ever saw."

"He's already got a head start. Even if I caught up with him, I don't know what I could do."

"You could bring Daniel back."

"Daniel?" Jeff felt his stomach go cold. "He took the boy with him?"

"No, but Daniel followed him. I'm afraid he'll hang back until it's too late for Vesper to send him home."

Jeff chewed on his lip. He could trail Freed, but it was unlikely he could catch up to him before dark. If Freed and his men rode through the night, Jeff would probably lose them. He saw Gabino Enríquez looking toward him from halfway around the herd. He waved his hat over his head, then beckoned. Gabino hesitated until Jeff repeated the gesture, then set his horse into an easy lope far enough out from the herd that he would not disturb the cattle.

Jeff said to him, "You know where your Ramírez cousins are. You've got to take me to them."

Gabino stalled. "They may be many places."

Jeff had no time or inclination for sparring with him. "Mrs. Freed says Vesper is on his way there with a small army. Now, if we ride like hell maybe we can get there in time to warn them and let them get away. Otherwise . . ." He let Gabino consider the consequences.

Gabino required only a moment. "I think I may know where to find them. When do we go?"

"Right now." Jeff took Eva's hand. It was trembling and cold. "We'll do the best we can. Why don't you stay with Arletta? If we can get Daniel back, you'll see him sooner there."

She looked pale and frightened. "Thank you. Now, please hurry."

By not having to follow tracks they were able to travel faster, limited only by the endurance of their horses. They pushed the animals to what Jeff considered their limit, but it was long after dark before they plunged into the river. They hauled up on the other side, giving the horses a chance to rest a few minutes after the exertion of swimming.

Gabino pointed. "They stay at a little *ranchito* owned by my cousin Felipe Rocha. It is perhaps twenty miles more."

Jeff looked up at the stars. The horses were almost exhausted. Daylight would catch them before they could travel another twenty miles. A sinking feeling began to take hold. The years at war and on the buffalo range had sharpened his instincts. Those instincts told him they were going to be too late. But after giving the horses a rest he said, "We'd better spur up."

They were still some distance away when the cool early-morning air brought them the crisp rattle of gunfire. Jeff reined up to listen, trying to fix the location.

Gabino's eyes reflected his sense of defeat. "I traveled as straight as I could."

"It's not your fault. We gave it all we had."

"I will ride ahead. Perhaps there is still time to help my cousins."

"It sounds like a siege. We'd have no chance of breakin' through Vesper's bunch." Gabino started to ride on anyway. Jeff grabbed the reins. He thought for a minute he might have to restrain Gabino with force. "One or two guns won't make much difference now."

Gabino wept, partly from helplessness, partly from rage.

"Come on," Jeff urged patiently. "Let's go in slow. Don't give them any excuse to kill us."

The shooting trailed off, then went at a furious pace for a few moments. Jeff could tell by the movement of the reports that the conflict had changed from a siege to a running fight. Shortly, that too was over, and the firing stopped.

Jeff shuddered. A coldness swept over him. The silence was more ominous than the gunfire.

They came to an opening in the chaparral. Across a newly plowed small field he saw an adobe house, shed and corrals behind it. He saw eight or ten men walking around. Several others lay on the ground. He tried to pick out Vesper Freed but could not.

Gabino looked like a man gazing upon his own death. Jeff cautioned, "You'd better stay here. They'd shoot you on sight just for bein' a Mexican."

"What if they shoot you?"

"Then get away fast. They'll want no witnesses."

Jeff raised his hands to show that he was coming in peacefully. He saw a gringo lower his pistol to within inches of a man's head and squeeze the trigger. It took much of Jeff's will to keep from drawing his own pistol and charging down upon the murderer. The face burned itself into his brain.

It was unlikely he would ever be called upon to testify as a witness to this crime, for what had been done here was beyond Texas jurisdiction. Mexican law as practiced along the border often did not allow such culprits to reach trial. Should the man fall into the hands of authorities on this side of the river, he was likely to be introduced to *ley fuga*: told to run, then be shot trying to escape. From such a sentence there was no appeal.

Jeff wished he knew some way to assure such an outcome.

Several men walked out to meet him, their faces belligerent. He recognized some of them from Freed's aborted ambush attempt. "What do you want here, Layne?" one of them demanded.

"I'm lookin' for Vesper Freed and his boy."

The man pointed his thumb toward the adobe house. "They're inside." When Jeff started in that direction the man said, "You'd best be careful how you go in there. Vesper's as liable to kill you as to look at you. He ain't thinkin' straight."

"Is the boy all right?"

The grim look on the gunman's face was answer enough. Jeff dismounted and dropped the reins, knowing Socks would stand as if he were tied. He paused at the door. "Vesper? Vesper, it's me, Jeff Layne. I'm comin' in."

He heard no answer. Cautiously he pushed the door open, waited a moment, then stepped inside. In the gloom he saw Freed kneeling on the floor. Danny Freed lay on a goat hide atop a straw mattress.

Jeff did not have to move closer to see that the boy was dead. He thought of Eva, and his throat clamped tight.

Freed turned only far enough to recognize Jeff, then dropped his head. He said nothing, but Jeff saw his shoulders heaving.

It seemed inconceivable that Vesper Freed was crying. His son was the only person who could bring tears to those hardened eyes.

"I'm sorry, Vesper. I tried to get here in time."

"*She* sent you?"

"She came as soon as she realized Danny had followed you."

"I never once thought he'd do such a thing."

"You set the pattern. You've taken him with you before when you chased border jumpers."

Freed's voice was husky, the words slow and painful. "He must've known I'd send him away, so he stayed back till the shootin' started. I had no idea in God's world that he was there till I saw him come spurrin' in. He never made it."

"They couldn't've known he was just a boy. At any distance he would've looked like a man."

Freed cried a little more. Jeff felt his sorrow and, for the moment, knew pity for his old adversary. His thoughts turned again to Eva. This would devastate her.

God, why couldn't we have gotten here in time?

Freed arose and walked slowly to a window, its glass broken into shards. He looked out, clearing his throat.

Jeff asked, "What about the Ramírezes, and Kelly Booth?"

Freed's voice strengthened as bitterness began to edge into his grief. "You'll find the Ramírezes layin' out in the yard. They tried to shoot their way out of here and make a break. My boys brought them down."

"And Booth?"

"If he was here, he got away." Freed turned, his face darkening. "But I'll get him. I'd make a pact with the devil himself to get him."

This was hardly a time to say that Freed had been in league with the devil for years. "We'd best be gettin' Danny across the river. If soldiers show up they'll likely stand everybody against the wall and ask no questions." On the north side of the river, raiders like the Ramírezes were considered bandits. On the south side, they were considered patriots and had the support of the Mexican army's border units.

Freed seemed at first to be in no mood for retreat. Jeff suspected he was in a suicidal mood, ready to charge into hell with a bucket of water. But presently Vesper got a grip on himself. "I saw a wagon out yonder by one of the sheds, and a couple of mules in a corral. Would you get some of the boys to help you hitch them up? I want you to take Danny home."

"Ain't you comin' with us?"

Freed's eyes were fierce. "I got things to do."

"Booth won't be easy to catch."

"There ain't been nothin' easy in this life. I'll trail him from here to the gates of hell if I have to."

"What'll I tell Eva?"

"What's to tell her? The only thing we ever had together is gone now. There won't nothin' bring Danny back." His mouth curved downward, his face deeply creased. He looked like an old, desperate man.

Jeff was about to ask him if it would be all right to take the Ramírez brothers too. It was proper that they be buried in their family cemetery. He decided against asking. He would simply do it.

Freed said, "You see that my boy is buried proper."

"You ought to be there yourself."

That was a forlorn hope. Freed's eyes crackled with fury. "I'll go back when I've sent Kelly Booth to hell!"

EIGHTEEN

Its mother's milk warm in its stomach, the baby dropped off to sleep while Arletta Smithwick cradled it in her arms and rocked slowly in a chair Jeff had thoughtfully brought to her when he had bought the two wagons in Piedras. Arletta's gaze went to Eva Freed as the older woman stood at the window, nervously searching southward for any sign of movement. The shadows were lengthening rapidly. Daylight would soon be gone.

Jeff ought to be back soon, Arletta thought. *If he is coming back at all.* She tried not to dwell on the grim possibility that he might not come back, that Freed or some of his gunmen might have killed him.

Nigel Smithwick was outside, pacing back and forth, making no attempt to hide his growing anxiety. He disappeared a few minutes, then returned with Luis Enríquez. Both led saddled horses. Nigel came into the house. "We are not waiting any longer. We are going to see if we can find Jeff."

Arletta protested, "It'll be dark before long."

"Luis knows the way." Smithwick kissed her, took a moment's loving look at his daughter, then went outside. Arletta rose from the chair gently, lest she awaken the baby, and placed the infant in a cradle Cap and the Enríquez brothers had fashioned out of raw pine lumber. She joined Eva at the window, watching her husband and Luis move southward in a long trot.

She tried to sound cheerful. "You can depend on Jeff. We always did, and he never let us down."

Eva was slow to reply. Arletta knew she was trying to control the fear that had her by the throat. "This may be beyond Jeff's control. I lost so much time in finding him . . ."

It was dusk when they heard the hoofbeats and the squeaking of wagon wheels that had gone too long ungreased. Eva jumped to her feet from the table where she had been sitting. Halfway to the door she stopped, her eyes stricken with dread. "Arletta, I have the most terrible feeling . . ."

Arletta glanced at the baby, still asleep in the cradle. "Maybe it'll be good news. If it isn't, puttin' it off won't make it any better." She took Eva's arm as they walked outside together.

Jeff rode alongside a rickety old wagon. Gabino sat on its plank seat, his horse tied behind. Arletta knew immediately that the news was bad; she could see it in Jeff's haggard face as he dismounted slowly. Eva made a small scream and broke free of Arletta's grip, rushing to the wagon. Jeff stepped toward her as she looked over the sideboard at the three blanket-wrapped forms lying side by side in the wagon bed. She turned to him, her eyes brimming.

"Daniel?"

Jeff could only nod, then grab her as she started to slump to the ground. Arletta looked up into her husband's face and read it all in his eyes.

"The other two?"

"Vicente and Manuel."

Arletta gripped the wagon's side board to brace herself. "What about Kelly Booth?"

"He escaped."

She sighed in relief, then felt guilty for it because there was so much tragedy around her.

Eva found the strength to stand on her own feet, but Jeff continued to hold her. In a small voice that threatened to crack she said, "I'll be all right now."

Arletta put an arm around Eva as Jeff released her. "Come back into the house. You need to lie down."

Eva kept looking at the wagon. "I want to see my son."

Jeff pulled back the blanket that covered the boy. Danny's face was peaceful, as if he had dropped off to sleep. His face had been washed, his hair combed. Arletta gave Jeff a silent look that said *Thank you*. Some men would not have been so mindful of a grieving mother's feelings.

Jeff said, "If it's any consolation to you, Vesper didn't know Danny was there till it was too late. And the men on the other side couldn't've known he was just a boy. It's a terrible thing, but I don't know who you can fault for it."

"Daniel thought the sun rose and set with his father. We should both have thought he might follow after him."

"Vesper's takin' it mighty hard."

"Not hard enough, or he would be here."

Eva walked beside her son as Jeff and Gabino and Luis carried him into the bunkhouse. Arletta felt the comfort of her husband's arm around her waist as they followed a few steps behind. She leaned her head against his shoulder. He stopped at the door. "You had best go inside. Eva will need you. I'll unsaddle my horse, and Jeff's."

"What about Vicente and Manuel? They have no women here to weep for them. I don't count Gabino and Luis. They're men."

"I guess it will be up to you."

"Then I'll weep for them, and pray a little too."

Inside, the men had placed Danny upon a cot. Eva had her arms around him, her face hidden against his cheek. Jeff left her alone with her mourning and spoke quietly to Arletta. "While you're prayin', you might pray some for Eva. And even for Vesper Freed."

They buried the Ramírez brothers first because their family cemetery was nearest. Luis had ridden all night to fetch the priest from Piedras. Arletta looked regretfully upon the grave of Santiago Ramírez. New grass had barely begun a tentative rise over the mound, and now two of his sons were being buried beside him. The service done, Gabino headed south on a fresh horse. Somewhere below the Rio Grande, Manuel had left a widow and children. They had to be told. The telling should be done by a blood relative.

Vesper Freed's father and mother lay in a small cemetery south of the gingerbread house. There being no Protestant minister in Piedras, the priest stayed to offer what comfort he could. Whatever the differences in their religions, his God was the same as Eva's. Before he began the graveside service the padre took a long look southward. Arletta sensed that he hoped for Vesper Freed to appear, but Freed was not in sight.

Eva appeared emotionally drained. She had cried all the tears that were in her. Jeff stood beside her during the service, and he continued standing there after the prayers were done. The sheriff had brought the priest in a buckboard. While Father Valentín said his goodbyes to Eva, Nigel Smithwick asked the lawman, "Is anything to be done about all this?"

"There's nothin' I can do about things that take place across the river. In this case, I can't say what I'd *want* to do. Both sides've taken an awful loss."

The baby was beginning to fret. It would soon be feeding time. Arletta rocked her gently in her arms while she watched Eva struggling to keep her composure. "Vesper Freed should've been here."

Sheriff Golightly shook his head. "It wouldn't've helped Eva much. Might even've hurt her more, because she feels like Vesper brought all this violence on himself."

"He did, didn't he?"

"It's all in how you look at it. It takes two sides to make a fight."

Smithwick asked, "Do you include Kelly Booth?"

"He's helped keep the fire fanned. If he gets away from Vesper and I find him in my jurisdiction, I'll have to jail him for the mischief he's done on this side of the river."

Arletta said, "But you can understand why he did it."

"Yes. That's what makes my job so hard."

When the sheriff and the priest had gone, Arletta told Eva, "You've got no business bein' by yourself. Why don't you come back with me and Nigel . . . Nigel and me?"

"You have little enough room in that house just for yourselves. Besides, I'd rather go home. I have a lot of thinking to do, and some packing."

"Packin'?"

"I'm not staying any longer than I have to." Eva turned to Jeff. "When will you be starting north with your cattle?"

"Four or five days. Depends on the work."

"Could I travel along with you as far as San Antonio?"

Jeff was taken aback. "Are you sure that's what you want?"

"I'd have gone a long time ago, but I knew Vesper would come after Daniel. Now he'll not want me any more than I want him."

"But what's in San Antonio?"

"I have an aunt and uncle there. I can stay with them until I decide what to do. All I am sure of now is that I have to get away from this place."

Jeff took her hands. Arletta felt she was intruding where no outsider was needed, so she turned away. But she heard Jeff say, "Anything you want. If we've got it, you can have it."

Nigel Smithwick opened the blanket and peered in at the baby. Regretfully he said, "You had better stay with Mrs. Freed for a day or two, to make certain she will be all right."

"I don't like bein' away from you."

"We'll be busy gathering the cattle. Just tell me what you may need from the house and I'll fetch it to you at Mrs. Freed's." He kissed the baby, which stirred restlessly and began whimpering for nourishment. He kissed Arletta and turned quickly toward his horse.

Arletta stared after him, knowing she would do as Nigel suggested but knowing also that she would not like even one night's separation from him. She sensed Eva coming up beside her.

Eva said, "I'll be all right. I know you'd rather go home. Why don't you?"

Arletta hugged the baby against her breasts. "Because right now you need a friend."

Eva touched Arletta's arm. "You're the best one I'll ever have."

"Not quite." Arletta nodded toward Jeff, who was swinging up onto his horse. "There's a better one."

Several of the Freed cowboys had brought Eva's buggy to the cemetery. Arletta drew it to a stop in front of the Freed house. Eva stared at the gingerbread-decorated structure, summoning courage. A cowboy helped her step down, then held the baby while Arletta followed. She sensed Eva's dread about climbing those front steps. The cowboy handed Arletta the little bundle of diapers she had brought along for the day, then took charge of the buggy and team. The rest of the hands had ridden to the barn to unsaddle their horses.

Eva said, "I don't want to go inside. It'll be so big and empty in there."

"We'd still have time to go back to our place before dark."

"No, I have to face it sometime." Eva clenched her fists, then opened the front door.

Arletta was surprised by the coldness of the house. The wealth of gingerbread trim outside had led her to expect the interior to be richly furnished. It was not. It was almost Spartan in its plainness. She sensed that it was a house which had not known love, except for that lavished upon the boy. Eva looked up the stairs but made no move to climb them. She proceeded instead to the kitchen.

"I'll fix some supper. I'm sure you're hungry."

"You'd do better to rest."

"No, I need to keep my hands and my mind busy."

Eva seemed to try to submerge her sorrow in a torrent of talk about every possible subject except the one foremost on her mind. She avoided mention of Danny or of Vesper Freed. Arletta listened patiently, speaking only when Eva asked a question or appeared about to run out of things to talk about. She feared that if Eva stopped talking for long she might collapse.

When it was time to go to bed Eva reluctantly climbed the stairs, carrying a lighted lamp. She stood for a minute at the door of the room that had been Danny's. She did not go inside. She carried the lamp into another room. "You and the baby can have this bed. It's Vesper's."

The room smelled of tobacco and spilled whiskey that had soaked into the soft pine flooring.

It was the first time Arletta knew that Eva and Vesper did not sleep together, though she had suspected it from fragments she had heard. She nursed the baby and got it to sleep. Though Eva had closed the door, Arletta could hear her quiet sobbing across the hall. It stopped after a while. Eva had not slept the night before. Exhaustion had finally caught up with her.

Arletta was a long time in going to sleep. The bed was strange, and it felt strange also to share it with the baby instead of her husband. She hoped she would not have to remain here long.

Eva slept late. Arletta was in the kitchen, nursing the baby, when the smell of coffee brought Eva down the stairs. She looked fresher than yesterday, though it would be a while before her eyes laughed again. She made up a batch of biscuit dough and put it into the oven, already hot because Arletta had built a fire in the stove. She sliced bacon from a flat slab and dropped it into a pan. She broke and scrambled three eggs. Arletta had seen chickens pecking around the yard. There was hardly a ranch that did not keep some chickens if the coyotes would allow them to live.

Eva talked with a false cheerfulness that deserted her once they had finished their breakfast. She looked around the kitchen, her eyes heavy with sadness. "I suppose I had as well begin packing. I'll take most of the cooking utensils. Vesper will probably eat with the cowboys anyway.

He would starve to death if he had to cook for himself."
Her voice took on a bitter edge. "More than likely he'll
find himself a saloon woman to move in with him. He
knows them all from here to San Antonio."

She avoided going into Danny's room until far into
the afternoon. She blinked back tears as she stood in the
doorway, surveying it. "The Walker family in town has
several boys. They can use the clothes in here." She pulled
out a bureau drawer and rummaged through it, coming up
with a flannel baby dress and a pair of knitted booties. "I
made these while I was carrying him. I'll want to keep
them for remembrance."

From deep within the drawer she withdrew a small
wooden horse with one leg broken off. "We had an old
cowboy who carved this for him. He and Daniel wor-
shipped each other. Daniel cried for two days when the
old fellow died." She tucked the horse into the folds of the
dress and backed out of the room, clutching the small bundle as if it were sacred. "If there's anything in there you'd
like to have for the baby . . ."

Arletta wanted nothing that would remind her of this
sadness. "I've already got more than I need."

She had no idea of the time when she awakened to the
sound of boots on the wooden stairs. The room was pitch
dark. She heard rather than saw the door swing open,
squeaking slightly on its hinges. She pulled the blanket up
over her shoulders as a match was struck and the white
spark flared into a red flame.

"What in the hell?" blurted Vesper Freed, several
days' whiskers blackening his face. "Who are you?" Then
he recognized her. "Mrs. Smithwick!" Mouth hanging
open, he lighted a second match and rolled the first one
under the sole of his boot. "I had no idea there was anybody in here. I hope I didn't scare you none."

"Startled me a little, is all. Eva didn't expect you back
so soon."

"I doubt she was anxious for me to come back at all."

As the match went out and the room fell into darkness, Arletta saw light flicker beneath Eva's door across the hall. The door opened, and Eva stood with a lamp in her hand. "Vesper?"

Freed was a dark figure against the yellow light. "I came to catch a few hours' sleep. I'll go down to the bunkhouse."

Arletta was almost afraid to ask. Her throat tightened and nearly choked off the question. "Kelly Booth. What about Kelly Booth?"

Freed did not answer her. He was looking at his wife. "You've buried Danny?"

"Beside your folks. That seemed the right thing to do."

"It was what I'd've done. I'll ride over there in the mornin'." He started down the stairs and stopped, looking back. "I saw there was some stuff stacked in the parlor."

"Mine," Eva said. "I'll be gone from here in a day or two."

Freed pondered, staring at her. It was hard to read what was in his face, but his voice seemed to carry a touch of regret. "I'd kind of expected that." He walked on down the stairs and toward the door.

Arletta shouted after him. "What about Kelly Booth?"

Freed turned. "You better grab ahold of somethin', Mrs. Smithwick. I know he was a friend of yours."

"Was?"

"He's dead. We caught him tryin' to swim back across the Rio Grande. He didn't swim very good with my bullet in him."

Arletta had her hand on the stair railing, and she gripped it tightly as she felt herself losing her balance. Her throat seemed to close. She had a dozen questions to hurl at Freed, but no sound came except a short cry. Freed was gone anyway, slamming the door behind him.

Eva's arm went around Arletta's shoulder. Arletta had shared Eva's grief. Now it was time for comfort to flow the other way.

* * *

Arletta slept no more that night, giving way to tears as she remembered pleasant incidents from better days. She knew she had to go home. Jeff and Nigel should be told about Kelly Booth.

Eva gave her no argument. "With Vesper back now, I've got to get away sooner than I intended. I'll go home with you if that invitation still stands."

"It does."

After breakfast the two women loaded into Arletta's wagon and Eva's buggy the things Eva had packed to take with her. They saw Freed ride off in the direction of the family cemetery. Eva said, "Let's hurry. I'd as soon be gone when he comes back."

But the dim wagon road passed near the burying ground. Freed saw them coming and rode out to intercept them. Arletta braced herself and tried not to look at him as he drew his horse in close to Eva's buggy, just ahead of Arletta's wagon. He eyed the goods in the two vehicles. "Ain't you takin' more than that?"

Eva's voice was strained. "It's all I need. I'll tell the Walkers to come and get any of Daniel's clothes they can use."

Freed did not remove his gaze from her. "Where was it that we went wrong?"

"Wrong? We never were right, not from the first. You didn't win me. You *bought* me."

"Didn't turn out to be much of a bargain for either one of us. But at least we had Danny." He looked away, toward the cemetery. "Where'll you go?"

"I'd as soon you didn't know."

"I guess it don't make much difference." He cleared his throat. "Well, take care of yourself."

Eva flipped the lines, and the buggy pulled forward. As Arletta came up to Freed he touched his fingers to the brim of his hat. He said, "It was kind of you to come over and stay with her." He looked at the baby who lay in her lap. "Seein' that young'un takes me back. I wish . . ."

She was surprised to see a tear start down his whiskered cheek. It would have been easy, for a moment, to overlook the fact that Freed had shot Kelly Booth and let him drown.

Freed said, "You hang tight to that Englishman for the young'un's sake. Then you'll never find yourself wishin' . . ."

Breaking off, he turned away and rode toward the house.

Arletta started the wagon moving, following Eva's buggy. She looked back, puzzled. She had thought she knew all she needed to know about Vesper Freed. But the more she knew, the less she understood.

NINETEEN

———

C row Feather had not seen anyone in the canyon
since the buffalo hunters had left. Once, however,
he saw a dozen horsemen silhouetted along the high
rim to the west. He felt certain they were soldiers. Evidently they did not see him or his sequestered camp, for
they made no attempt to find a way down the steep wall.
The sight of them was a reminder, if he needed one, that
he must remain vigilant.

Protected from the bitter winds which swept the open
plains above, the grass began greening earliest near the
wall. As the greenness spread across the canyon, some of
the buffalo began to migrate up the old game trails and
out onto the huge, open prairie above. The tonic effect of
spring's green grass started them to shedding their dense
winter hair. Wherever a tuft of it fell on bare ground it
carried with it an accumulation of grass seeds picked up
from the winds and from the bed grounds. The buffalo
dung added nutrients to the soil so that the grass grew
taller and richer. The People recognized this circle of life.
They witnessed at close hand its constant perpetuation,
each element in its own time, its own natural order.

Crow Feather saw some good in the buffalo's moving
up to the higher ground. The fewer that remained, the less
temptation there was to lure white hide hunters back into
the canyon. He could not depend upon them to kill one
another every time, as they had done before. He could

only hope that at least a few buffalo would remain to provide meat for his family.

Since they had taken sanctuary at the hidden spring beneath the overhanging canyon wall, he and the boy Squirrel had found game enough to keep everyone well fed. White Deer's breasts provided sufficient milk for two, though the oldest of the babies was beginning to eat solid food after White Deer softened it by chewing it first.

Squirrel was big enough now to look after himself, for the most part. White Deer had more than enough to do, mothering the babies and the older girl. That only one of the three was her own seemed never to enter her mind.

Crow Feather's grief over Rabbit's death had eased. Now and again he found himself thinking it would be good if he found a second wife to share White Deer's burdens. But he saw little likelihood so long as they remained here, isolated from all others of their kind.

Often a dark loneliness swept over him. He had spent his life surrounded by others of the People, sometimes in small groups of several families, other times in grand encampments which offered pleasant socializing and game playing, much smoking and singing and recounting of old stories. Even on the war trail he had never been alone for any length of time. Always he had been with or near other warriors. The solitary life he and his family led now was unnatural to them. The Comanches were a gregarious people.

He could almost wish he had gone to the reservation with the others. Though it might be a miserable life, at least it would be a shared misery.

He chided himself for allowing such a thought even a moment's consideration. He had often found white men's horses imprisoned in a corral and had gloried in being able to liberate them from such confinement. The reservation must be like a huge corral, he thought, where a man was kept penned up like the horses, robbed of his freedom to move as the mood struck him, as the wind called him. It might be tolerable for women, used to being tied to the village, to the tepee, to their many labors. But a man should be free.

He tried to dwell upon the positive side. Here, he was living in what many would consider an idyllic situation: game, grass and water plentiful, his family close beside him. In recent times, many in his band had thrust upon him a leadership that carried onerous responsibilities. He disliked trying to settle quarrels between other men's wives over the proper distribution of meat. He disliked having to select a campsite, knowing full well that some would find fault with it and complain until in his vexation he was tempted to do violence. Here, he did not have to endure the camp noise that sometimes drove him to distraction, though it carried with it the opportunity for pleasant fellowship.

On balance, he knew he was better off in the canyon —even with its sometimes deadening loneliness—than on the reservation. There, for all intents and purposes, he would be a prisoner, almost a slave—like the captured Mexican and *tejano* women and children enslaved by the People.

He was no child, and he was certainly not a woman.

Late in the afternoon he rode into the west wall's dark shadow that slowly stretched across the canyon. Squirrel was at his side. Squirrel had loosed the arrow that had brought down the deer which lay across Crow Feather's lap. The boy was learning to be a hunter. During the winter months Crow Feather had fashioned him a longer, stronger bow that challenged the boy's muscles and made them tough. He knew few boys of comparable age who could drive an arrow so far with accuracy. Squirrel was a son to make a man proud.

The girl came skipping out to meet them. He had to admonish her not to come directly at the horses that way; they spooked too easily. She begged Squirrel to let her ride his pony, but he refused. Such a noble animal was too good for a woman, he said. Crow Feather did not interfere. A good hunter had a right either to offer or refuse the use of his horse.

White Deer was pleased to see the young buck Crow Feather was bringing in, and doubly pleased when she learned that her son had killed it. She watched as Crow Feather lifted the carcass from his horse and carried it into the trees, where she would take over the butchering. He noticed, however, that her cheerful mood seemed to fall away. The trouble in her eyes made him look quickly to the two babies, asleep together on a deerhide mat in the cramped little tepee that served in lieu of a full-sized one. So far as he could see, neither appeared ill.

"What is it?" he asked her.

"Probably nothing." Her forehead creased with worry. "Did you see anything today?"

"I saw our son kill a deer. What did you see?"

"I heard something. I did not see it." She pointed straight up the overhanging wall. "It was there, along the edge. Horses, I think."

"Buffalo, more likely. Most of them have gone out of the canyon. They graze on top."

"Perhaps." She shuddered. "But I had a feeling it was something else. The sun was shining and warm, but I was cold. I am still cold."

"Then hurry and cook the fresh meat. It will make you warm again."

It did not. After the children had gone to sleep that night, he could feel the little bumps that arose on her skin as she crawled beneath the blanket to join him. He folded his arms about her, hoping to share his own warmth. He felt her shiver.

"I am fearful," White Deer told him. "Each time you ride out, I wonder if you will come back."

"What would prevent me from coming back?"

"The soldiers. The rifles of the buffalo hunters, which shoot so far. What would become of us if they took you away or killed you?"

"They will not."

"I am sure others have thought as you do, but where are they now?"

"Nothing will happen to me. But if it did, Squirrel is

good with the bow, better than I was at his age. He would keep you in meat."

"A boy. It is a man we need. A man *I* need." Beneath the skin blanket, she pressed her body against him, her hands searching over his shoulder, down his arm. She was beginning to feel warmer now. Her breath upon his face set his blood to racing.

Crow Feather had been concerned that she not become pregnant again and add to her labor, though he had observed that so long as a woman continued to nurse a baby she seemed less likely to find herself with child. White Deer was nursing two.

Sensing her hunger and responding with his own, he pushed such thoughts aside. He raised up, and she slid beneath him.

It was not good to mention the name of one who was dead. Before sleep carried him away she said, "The one who was my sister has been gone now for a long time. Do you ever think of finding another wife?"

"Never." He rubbed his hand lovingly along her thigh. "What need have I for another woman?"

He came wide awake long before daybreak, disturbed by a dream and a shout which he realized had been his own. He tried to remember what the dream had been about, but it was without solid form and drew quickly away from him. It left just enough vague images to taunt him. He remembered being in a dark place, perhaps a deep hole in the ground, struggling in vain to climb walls that offered no hold for his hands. He remembered falling back in a blind panic and shouting out to the bear spirit to help him. And he saw the woman with the red hair, reaching toward him. He did not know if she was trying to help him or to drag him down.

Before, she had shot him.

His own shout had awakened him. He turned to White Deer, wondering if it had awakened her also. He could barely make out her dark shape, but he could see the gentle rise and fall of her bosom as she slept.

He thought he knew what the trouble was. He had given little conscious thought to what she had told him about hearing something up on the canyon rim, but at a subconscious level it had insinuated itself into his dreams. Past visions from the bear spirit had always remained clear and sharp in his mind afterward. This had been no vision, for reach as he might, he had been unable to grasp it, to bring it back for conscious review. It was like a wisp of a cloud that passes before the moon and is gone.

Sleep was gone, too. He lay awake, staring up at the few stars he could see through the smoke hole until they began to fade in a brightening sky. He left the tepee and walked eastward past the spring, greeting the rising sun with a prayer for this to be a good day. The canyon looked peaceful as first morning sunlight bathed it in gentle hues. But the dream still haunted him. The feeling of fear that had awakened him lingered insistently.

It was unlike any vision he had known, but he sensed that the bear spirit was trying to tell him something. He wished it could be clearer in its purpose.

He had avoided riding up on top, above the canyon. There had been no need. All he could want, other than the company of his own band, was available to him between the high walls. Beyond that, he had recognized the risk of being seen and pursued. Much of the prairie was wide open, without trees or brush, nothing but its occasional shallow depressions to hide a man and a horse from view. And even if he avoided being seen, he could not avoid leaving tracks wherever the ground was bare. Soldiers had overlooked them before, but he could not depend upon all being so blind.

They ate of the venison, then he said, "I have thought upon what you heard. I will go up and see what it was."

Much of yesterday's anxiety returned to her eyes. "What if it was the *teibos*?"

"Then we should know."

Squirrel caught some of his mother's fear. "It might be the cannibal owl."

Crow Feather smiled. The cannibal owl was a story

used mainly to frighten mischievous children into submission. But there were adults who believed in it as well. It was one of the darker legends that had passed from generation to generation since the grandfathers of his grandfathers. "If it was the owl it could have flown down here. No, it probably was only buffalo, and they do not have wings."

Squirrel was not satisfied by the easy dismissal of the cannibal owl. "I will go with you, *Powva*," he offered, though his voice sounded tentative.

Crow Feather tried not to smile again. "No, I go alone. If it is the owl, my horse is fast enough to outrun it. You must stay here so that you can fight it away from the little ones."

Squirrel looked at his mother. Straight-faced, she said, "You and I can fight it together. It may require us both."

She followed Crow Feather out to where he had his dun horse tethered on a long rawhide rope, giving it a wide range to graze upon. Her expression revealed the depth of her worry. "There are many things more dangerous than any cannibal owl."

He tried to laugh away her concern. "They would have to fly like the owl to catch me." He squeezed her hand, then swung upon the horse. "I will return before the sun goes down."

He looked back several times. Always, she was watching him.

It took a while to reach the zigzag game trail where the buffalo climbed up out of the canyon, well north of the spring. Crow Feather remained close to the western wall on the slim chance that enemies might be looking down into the canyon. They would have to walk to the very edge to see him. He had never liked to do that. His stomach always became queasy at the thought that malevolent spirits might cause the rocks to give way treacherously beneath him and send him plunging helplessly from a great height.

The ancient trail was wide enough in most places for two horses to have walked side by side, though it narrowed in spots. He held to the inside, which seemed prudent. Far down the steep slope he saw the rotting carcass of a buffalo cow which had slipped or been butted over the edge, breaking her legs. He could imagine her lying there, dying slowly and in agony, unable to arise. It was a sobering thought.

From old stories he knew that in a long-ago time, before the spirits had given the People the first horse, they had driven whole herds over bluffs and washouts. To obtain meat they clubbed or speared to death those not killed by the fall. It was almost beyond his powers of imagination to visualize the People without the horse.

He paused just before he reached the top. He tethered the dun and finished the climb afoot, peering cautiously over the rim, not exposing more than his head. Seeing nothing that offered danger, he went back for the horse.

On top, he looked at the place where the game trail ended. The ground there was beaten out a bit, as was the trail itself from the passage of cloven hooves. But that small piece of bare ground could easily be overlooked by anyone riding at what he would consider a safe distance from the edge of the chasm. He had developed a certain contempt for the soldiers' powers of observation. He suspected most were more interested in stopping to eat whatever they carried in their saddle bags than in finding stray Indians.

The plains appeared endless, the new grass plainly visible when he looked down but mostly hidden by the brown residue of last year's growth when he lifted his gaze toward the horizon. The buffalo were not fooled. They were grazing the new grass, though instinct told them to eat some of the old as well, so the new would not rush through their digestive tracts like water. They were dotted brown and black across the prairie, not nearly so many as he had seen in the past, yet enough that it was difficult to imagine the white man ever killing them all. But he knew they could. He too had doubted, until he had traveled far north into the land of the Cheyennes and had seen the heavy slaughter for himself.

For now the plains appeared free of the hunters. They had retreated north after the big fight at the wagon village where the shaman's medicine had gone bad and many good warriors had been slain. He had not yet seen sign that many had returned. But they would. He had never understood greed like that of the white men, greed that made them keep coming no matter how many died at the hands of the People's warriors. They were not true human beings. They would be back, and sooner or later they would invade the canyon again.

He did not know how long he could keep his family hidden. He could only hope that the People would rise up in wrath and flee the reservation, coming back onto the plains which for generations they had held against all comers, such as the Apaches and the Utes, and would eventually hold against the white man. They would still be there now had not the soldier chief surprised them in their winter encampment and stolen most of the horse herd before the warriors could get mounted. He felt confident that when they had horses enough they would come back. Horses had always been easy to come by in the white man's settlements and on ranches of the Mexicans far to the south.

He followed the canyon rim back, paralleling the path he had taken from camp but far above it now. He rode among the buffalo, which moved aside at his approach but did not interrupt their grazing for long. From memory he knew when he reached a point directly above the family's hiding place. He had been watching the ground, intermittently looking up at the horizon as a precaution. The only tracks he had seen had been those of the buffalo.

Yes, it was as he had told White Deer. What she had heard must have been merely the passing of buffalo, their sound perhaps distorted on its way down the steep wall.

Then he stopped, a tingle of apprehension racing along the skin of his back. He saw a hoofprint that was not split. It was solid . . . the print of a horse, shod with iron. He let his gaze sweep the horizon. He saw only buffalo. But as he examined the ground more closely he saw other horse tracks. The riders were definitely not of the People. They had been traveling along the rim of the canyon, perhaps watching for a way down. It was probably only by the intercession of the bear spirit that they had not found the game trail he had used.

Hunters? If they were hunters, why had they not killed buffalo? They must have been soldiers. Who else would venture so far from the white-man settlements?

His first inclination was to hurry back to the game trail and down to his camp, to move it to a safer location. But where? Sooner or later it seemed the white man would appear no matter where he took his family. He knew of no better hiding place than the one they had now, secreted beneath the great caprock. A person would have to ride almost into its center before he saw it, for the poles were short and the small tepee masked by the trees.

Even if he knew a safer place, traveling would carry too much risk. It seemed inevitable that the reservation people would sooner or later rebel. If he remained patient long enough, others of the tribe would join him and they would drive the white man away.

The soldiers swarmed at him suddenly, like a pack of wolves descending upon a crippled buffalo. He did not see where they came from. The plains were never quite so flat as they appeared, and they had probably been riding in a depression that the grass had hidden. In his surprise, his heart seemed to swell almost to bursting. Reflex took over. By instinct more than by conscious thought, he reined the horse southward, away from the game trail that might lead them down into the canyon. He applied his quirt to bring out all the speed the dun could muster.

It was not enough to outrun a bullet. He felt the animal falter beneath him, then plunge headlong, hind end flipping over its head. Crow Feather's forward momentum carried him beyond the horse. He slid in the grass, losing his bow and most of his breath. He jumped shakily to his feet, addled by the brutal impact.

He searched desperately for the fallen bow. The fall had flung most of the arrows out of their quiver. He grabbed at a couple of those, knowing even as he did that the move was futile. One of the soldiers raced by him, swinging the butt of a rifle, striking a glancing blow across the side of Crow Feather's head. Crow Feather staggered, managing to bring a knife out of its scabbard on his waist.

He never got to use it, for a soldier raced up behind him, his leg extended, and struck the back of Crow Feather's head with the iron stirrup. Crow Feather was knocked forward onto his face. Stunned, he felt rough hands taking hold of his arms, crossing his wrists and tying them behind his back. Crying in rage, he worked free and managed to rise to his knees before a heavy boot struck him squarely in the back and knocked him down again. Something else, probably a rifle butt, clubbed the back of his head. Fire flashed before his eyes.

He heard sharp voices and exultant shouting, the soldiers talking excitedly. The words were as meaningless as the grunting and squealing of hogs he had found penned beside a white man's barn in the *tejano* settlements. He threshed and fought against the rope that bound him, tearing his flesh until he felt the blood begin to run warm down his wrists. Through a crimson haze he turned from one knot of soldiers to another, glaring fiercely as he had seen a cornered animal glare at its captors before it made its final, fatal break for freedom.

For Crow Feather there was to be no break. Someone tossed a rope over his head and tightened it around his neck. Any attempt to run would choke him. He cried out to the bear spirit. He heard no reply, only the elated voices of those who had taken him. He tried to count. There were three times four, perhaps four times four. Dirt burned his eyes. He could barely see.

One of the men had stripes on the sleeves of his blue coat. He spoke out in an authoritative voice and pointed northward. The soldier at the end of the rope gave it a jerk that choked Crow Feather and burned his neck. He saw that they were going to make him walk. He managed a quick glimpse at his dun horse, enough to know that it was dead.

As the soldiers began moving he saw one pick up his bow and gather some fallen arrows. Trophies of war.

They skirted the edge of the canyon, remaining a safe distance from the edge, though now and then one or two soldiers would ride to the rim and look over. Approaching the point where the game trail came out onto the top, Crow Feather feared they would find it and decide to follow it down. He had to exercise a strong will not to look in that direction and perhaps direct their attention to it.

After what seemed an eternity they passed the trail without the soldiers noticing it. Crow Feather felt some of the weight pass from his shoulders, and he whispered thanks to the bear spirit. It had heard him after all. For the moment, at least, his family was safe.

As evening shadows stretched long across the bottom of the canyon, White Deer stationed herself at the edge of the timber that ringed the little spring. She watched the north, where Crow Feather would be coming from. Darkness overtook her, and Squirrel went out, calling in a small voice. She answered, "Here."

"The babies are crying. They are hungry."

"I have been watching for your father. He should be here."

Squirrel knew, for he had heard Crow Feather say he would return before the sun went down. He tried to think of the many small things that might have delayed his father. The horse might have lamed itself so that Crow Feather was having to walk and lead it home. He might have decided to stalk a deer or kill a buffalo for fresh meat.

Squirrel refused to think about the larger and more ominous possibilities.

But a sleepless night passed, and he was forced to consider them. He could see by the weariness in his mother's eyes that she had not slept either. He said, "I must go and see what has happened. He may be hurt. He may need my help."

White Deer was adamant. "He told you to stay here. If your father is alive, he will find his way back."

If he was alive! That told him his mother had considered the grimmest of possibilities, one Squirrel had refused to allow himself to contemplate, that his father might be dead. It was a staggering thought.

While his mother was busy nursing the babies, Squirrel stole out where his pony was tethered. Riding away, he heard her calling, but he pretended the wind was in his ears.

He knew where the game trail began, but his father had never allowed him to use it since the day they had carefully picked their way across its narrow places and descended into the canyon. He hesitated at the foot of it, studying the tracks left by his father's horse. They went up, but he saw no tracks coming down. Whatever had happened to Crow Feather, he was still on top.

It occurred to Squirrel that the cannibal owl might have taken his father. It might be up there still, waiting. He took a while, gathering his courage, then started up.

The north wind struck him hard as he finished the climb. Its spring freshness brought bumps to his skin, though the bitter cold of winter was past. Once he was out in the open, he realized his father would have admonished him to move slowly and carefully, being sure there was no danger before he finished the ascent. He would remember next time, but at this moment his fear for his father outweighed the fears he had for himself.

Almost immediately he found the horse tracks. There were many, and for a while he lost those of his father's mount. It came to him that all the others were of shod hooves. That meant white men, probably soldiers.

His father's tracks led southward near the edge of the canyon. Cautiously looking around him, Squirrel started south. He had ridden awhile before he saw buzzards circling, then dropping down out of sight.

His courage almost deserted him. He had to fight against a strong urge to put his pony into a run toward the game trail and the comparative safety of the canyon. But he forced himself to move forward, struggling with a fear that where the buzzards circled he would find his father.

Instead, he found his father's horse. The buzzards reluctantly gave ground as he approached, fear clutching at his stomach. Two coyotes slunk away, one dragging a strip of horseflesh in the grass. The scavenging birds had already pecked away the eyes and were beginning to rip at the cold skin. Squirrel dismounted, holding firmly to the rein because his pony was uneasy at the smell and kept trying to pull away. The dried blood led Squirrel to the bullet hole in the horse's side. He walked around, searching among the many tracks. He found a couple of arrows lying in the grass. They were his father's. The stone tips showed no sign of blood; they had not been dug out of an adversary.

At length he came upon signs of a scuffle, of old grass stems broken down, of many boots that had left marks in the sand. Bending, he discovered moccasin prints among those of the boots. Finally the tracks indicated a general movement northward. The boot prints stopped. Only horse tracks remained . . . horse tracks and the prints of a single pair of moccasins.

It was clear to him now. His father had been overtaken by soldiers, and they had led him away. The full import struck him with the force of an enemy war club.

Tears burned Squirrel's eyes, and he gave in to a strong feeling of helplessness. But he did not accept it for long. He could not. All his father's responsibilities fell upon his shoulders now. In the eyes of others he might still be a boy, but in his own he was at this moment a man, for he carried a man's burden. It was up to him now to protect and preserve the family.

Sitting straighter than he had sat before, he urged the pony back toward the game trail.

TWENTY

The beginning of the drive brought several visitors to watch or to participate. The rancher Matthews, who had sold Jeff three hundred cows, came with his son, camping in the yard with other hands who could not find room in the small bunkhouse. The rancher Jones and his wife, who owned the land Jeff had leased, walked down from their big house to wish them well. Jones stopped at the corrals to saddle a horse.

The short, sturdy Mrs. Jones brought an old doll for the baby. Its head was of china, with cheeks red as apples and big brown eyes and black eyelashes painted on. "This was our daughter's," she told Arletta. "I made up some new clothes for it out of quilting scraps. You can put it away till your Becky is big enough to play with it."

Arletta clutched the doll with a delight that made Jeff wonder if she had ever had one of her own. He knew that during her childhood her well-meaning but inept father had kept the family balanced precariously on the brink of hunger. He watched with concern as Mrs. Jones hugged the baby against her generous bosom. There appeared an outside chance she might smother it.

Jones, on days when his rheumatism did not bother him too much, had helped Jeff and the others ride the perimeter and throw back TE cattle that strayed too far from home. He delighted in doing, if only in a limited way, the work that had built the ranch for him when he was younger. "If it's all right with you, Jeff, I'll help you throw them off of the bed grounds and ride along with you a ways. It'll take me back to old times."

Jeff gladly accepted the help. Getting a herd strung out the first time was always a challenge. The old rancher's friendship was one thing he would miss.

The herd had been gathered loosely just east of the ranch headquarters and bedded down on a grass flat where the brush was small and scattered. Jeff and Smithwick and Jones stood in the yard, looking into the breaking dawn toward the cattle and the men who had served the last shift of night guard. Jeff asked, "English, what do you think of your investment now?"

"More properly, yours and Arletta's. My own cash input was minor."

"You put in blood and sweat. Without that, all the cash in the world don't mean nothin'."

Two hundred cows in the herd had been bought from a rancher named Sharkey, east of Piedras. He and one of his brothers had come to help get the cattle moving.

Jones looked behind him before he spoke. "Them Sharkey boys are likable enough, but they'll bear watchin'. Once you get three or four days up the trail, they're apt to slip in one night and stampede the herd."

Smithwick demanded, "Why? How would that profit them?"

"Because a lot of the cattle would strike out for home. The Sharkeys'd count on you-all bein' in a hurry about goin' on, so you'd leave the ones you couldn't find right away. They'd get some of their cattle back at no cost to theirselves."

Jeff said, "It's a trick some outfits used to play against the drovers puttin' herds together for Kansas. They'd sell some of the same cattle three or four times."

"Reprehensible."

Jones nodded. "There's been killin' done over less."

Jeff said, "Been more than enough killin' around here. But we'll give those boys a watchin'."

Eva Freed's buggy was drawn up next to the chuck

wagon, which Arletta would be driving. Eva and Arletta stood talking with Mrs. Jones, Arletta rocking the baby in her arms. Jeff watched Eva until she turned to face him. He quickly covered by pointing northeastward. "Arletta, you and Eva'll want to stay on the upwind side, out of the dust. You can make a head start when you're ready."

Smithwick took the baby from Arletta and placed it in its cradle, wedged firmly between the seat and the front of the wagon bed.

Arletta hugged Mrs. Jones. The ranchwoman was near tears. "You keep a sharp lookout for Indians. And if you decide you don't like it up there, you'll be welcome to come back here and stay with me."

"I don't think Nigel would approve of that." Arletta tried to smile, wiping a finger across one eye. "But I'll write you a letter somewhere along the way."

A year ago she would have had to get someone to write for her. But with Nigel Smithwick's patient teaching she had learned to do well enough for herself. In one of the other wagons she had packed a boxful of books.

Smithwick helped her climb into the wagon. Jeff took Eva's arm, boosting her up into the buggy. He held her longer than was necessary. He said nothing; nor did she. Her gaze touched him for just a moment, then she looked toward the chuck wagon.

Arletta spoke to her team, and the animals strained into the traces. The wagon began to move, the baby crying out in surprise, then going quiet. The motion of the wagon should quickly rock her to sleep. Eva turned the buggy in behind the wagon. Cap Doolittle followed with the two other wagons, the rear one coupled to the lead vehicle by a short tongue. His belly bounced as a front wheel banged into a sizable rut. He would do the principal cooking on this trip, with some help from Arletta. He was his own best customer.

Jeff glanced at the rising sun, then turned toward the herd, where several cows and calves had become separated and bawled for one another. The horsemen were ready.

Nigel Smithwick raised his reins in anticipation. Jeff took off his hat and waved it over his head.

The nearby riders pressed in upon the loose herd, shouting, slapping quirts or coiled ropes against their leather chaps, pressuring the cattle into movement. The effect was somewhat like putting them through a funnel, so that they left the bed ground in a long, narrow file. The bawling intensified as nervous mothers and anxious calves lost each other.

To Jeff the sound was pleasant, taking him back to other times, other herds. With these thousand or so cows and their calves strung out alongside and behind him, with more than a dozen riders beside and behind them, he was back in the element for which his boyhood had prepared him. He had strayed away from it for many years, but now those long years fell away and he felt as if he had never done anything else. It was, in a peculiar way, a homecoming.

He might have ridden the point himself, setting the course and the rate of movement, but he preferred to remain in a swing position where he could see all of the herd. He had assigned the point to veteran drover George Newby, not by ordering him as boss to employee but by asking him politely if he would like to do it. He had known Newby would accept without question, for riding the point was a position of trust. To be offered it was a tribute.

The rancher Jones drew up beside Jeff, his smile like a second rising of the sun. "They can have all their cities and their four-story buildin's, their big bridges and such. There ain't a prettier sight in the world than a herd of cattle takin' the trail."

"Yes, and it's a special glory when they're your own."

Jeff thought back to a day up on the high plains when he had ridden to the edge of a chasm and looked down into the autumn-brown floor of a broad canyon. There, as far as he could see, buffalo grazed by the hundreds, probably the thousands. It had hurt to tear himself away. It had hurt even more to lead a wagon train of buffalo hunters and skinners there, knowing they would soon lay waste to that great herd. But it had been his job. It was his line of work. If he had not, someone else would have.

That canyon had remained in his mind long after he had left it, and a sour guilt had persisted like a boil that never heals. To that canyon he intended to take this herd. Where the buffalo had been, his cattle would graze . . . his cattle and English's and Arletta's.

He had been instrumental in killing life out of the canyon. God willing, he would bring new life to it.

Jones stayed with him until mid-afternoon, as did Matthews and his son. They shook hands all around, then rode southward together, back toward their homes. Jeff's throat tightened as he watched them go. It was unlikely he would ever see these people again.

A little later the Sharkey brothers took their leave. For them, Jeff felt no sorrow. There was a chance he might be seeing them once more, or at least their handiwork. It paid to guard a herd extra well the first few nights on the trail, for until cattle were trail-broken they seemed to watch for an excuse to run. If Jones was right, the Sharkeys intended to furnish that excuse.

Jeff left his swing position and loped up past Cap's wagons and Eva's buggy. He pulled in beside Arletta and looked down at the cradle by her feet. Arletta had rigged a diaper between the seat and the corner of the wagon bed to shade the baby's eyes. They were open.

"Looks contented, don't she?" Jeff said.

"She's a good traveler. You don't need to fret on our account. Me and her . . . her and me, we're doin' fine."

"I never doubted it for a minute."

He dropped back to Eva's buggy. There was much he wanted to say to her, but whatever he said always sounded idle and empty of emotion. "You doin' all right up here?"

Her replies always seemed an evasion of what her eyes hinted. "Just fine. And you?"

"Just fine." He rode beside her an awkward minute or so, then stopped and let her pull ahead. Cap came along with his two wagons. "If I was you, Jeff . . ." He broke off.

"You'd do what?"

"Hell, I don't know. But I'd do *somethin'*. I'd be lettin' her know the way I feel."

"I'm not sure how I feel."

"Everybody else knows. It couldn't be plainer if you painted it across your shirt."

"For a man who's been a bachelor all his life, you're full of advice."

"I don't charge extra for it."

A mile or so from the bed ground a brindle cow made a break from just behind Smithwick's position and set a course back toward the ranch in the hardest run she could muster. The Englishman spurred after her, shaking down his rope and building a loop. He swung it over his head and sailed it across her long horns as if it were something he had done all his life. Kelly Booth would have slid his horse to a stop and delighted in bringing the cow over backward, but Smithwick slowed her gently without making her hit the ground. She was heavy with calf, so that a hard fall could have had serious consequences. One of the Gallegos cousins moved in behind the cow to help Smithwick coax her back to the herd. He rode up close and removed the rope from her horns so she would not have to be thrown down to retrieve it.

Jeff smiled in appreciation. Old Santiago's roping lessons had served well, and Smithwick had the right instincts about not being unnecessarily rough with the stock.

That, Jeff thought, was the difference between a cow-*boy* and a cow*man*.

The cattle had not gone two miles before a brown-spotted cow of mature years laid claim to the privilege of leading the rest. Followed by her long-legged steer calf, she worked her way forward, the sharp tips of her horns enforcing her dominance over any animals that blocked her way to the head of the line. Jeff watched her with amusement, wondering if she would be able to maintain that position or if she would sooner or later meet her match in another domineering matron. A few challenged her, but none stood long against her fearsome determination.

Though it sometimes took a few days, Jeff had observed on other drives that each animal established its own place in the hierarchy and thereafter could be found in about the same relative position in the line of march day after day. It was highly probable that from here to the end of the drive the spotted cow would hold the lead against all comers. He noted with satisfaction that she carried the Matthews brand as well as the more recent TE. It seemed appropriate that she was a Matthews cow and not a Sharkey.

She suffered no nonsense, not even from her own rambunctious calf which in its exuberance moved ahead of her a couple of times. Tossing her head threateningly and making a false rush with those sharp horns lowered, she quickly taught the adolescent a lesson in obedience.

Jeff was not given to naming his cattle, but he gave a name to this one. "Give 'em hell, Queenie."

It was common practice for drovers to push a steer herd extra hard the first two or three days, hoping they would be too tired to run during the night. But the high percentage of small calves in this herd made Jeff reluctant. Newby held a pace that allowed most of them to keep up with their mothers. Inevitably, some dropped to the rear, to the dusty drags where Owen Palmer rode with one of the Gallegos cousins. Anxious mothers would turn back, bawling until they found their offspring. Before long the same calves would drop behind again, and the cows would repeat the noisy process.

The drive skirted Vesper Freed's range. Jeff wondered uneasily if Vesper might intercept it and ask his wife to come back. He wondered if Eva might even hold out such a hope. If so, she was disappointed, for Vesper never showed himself.

Jeff had not seen Freed since the day Danny and the Ramírez brothers had died in Mexico. It was just as well, for the report of Kelly Booth's death had only intensified the old bitterness that towered like a granite mountain between them. It would not take much, Jeff thought, to bring them to a shooting if they met.

The outfit camped its first night on a creek seven or eight miles from the starting place. For a cow-calf herd on the initial day, Jeff considered it a good day's work. Cap and the women had moved well ahead to set up camp. With a little help from Arletta, Cap had supper cooking by the time the cattle and the cowboys caught up. The cows and calves were given plenty of time to drink, then were loosely bunched on the north side of the creek. Jeff knew within reason that it would not rain tonight—there had not been a cloud worth the name in two or three weeks— but he had never shed his old habit of crossing a creek or river before camping so he would not confront a flood at daybreak.

Among the supplies Jeff had bought in Piedras had been an old army tent large enough to shelter the Smithwicks and their baby on the trail and at their destination until there was time enough to build something more substantial. The smaller tent they had used on the trip from Kansas was turned over to Eva to provide privacy so long as she remained with the herd. Cap and the women had raised both tents by the time Jeff rode into camp.

Cap pointed his thumb toward the fire. "Coffee's already boiled. Got a bottle in the chuckbox if you want to sweeten it up a little. You look like you need some sweetenin'."

"I wouldn't want to be a bad influence on the younger boys." But Jeff poured a little whiskey into his coffee. It had been a long day, and he was not likely to get much sleep tonight, listening, waiting for the cattle to run. He saw Eva watching him. He started to hide the bottle, then realized she had already seen it. It shouldn't be any surprise to her, he thought. He was not a schoolboy; he was a man sliding rapidly toward his middle age.

She gave him a tentative smile. "Don't back away on my account. Put enough in there to do you some good."

He added half again as much as the first time. The

whiskey helped moderate the strength of Cap's coffee. "I didn't know if you had feelin's against such as this. I heard there was a bunch of wives marched into a saloon somewhere a while back and took choppin' axes to every keg and barrel and bottle in the place."

"They must not have much tolerance for human nature. If drinking a little whiskey is the worst sin you have to answer for, I don't see that anyone has cause to criticize you. Least of all me."

"I've done worse. But you don't want to hear about it."

"I doubt that you could shock me."

He could, but he would not. "If a dog's asleep, you'd best not kick him."

To Jeff's relief, the cattle showed no inclination to run that night, and in the morning hours long after midnight he managed to get a little sleep. It was not enough, but his recollections of drover life included a lot of sleepless nights and sleepy days on the trail. At one point, he caught himself dozing off in the saddle. The sorrel horse had enough cow sense not to take him into the middle of the herd. He would wake up startled and find the cattle moving along peaceably at their slow, deliberate pace. He hoped the other men had not noticed. Probably some of them were doing the same thing.

A coyote howled the second night, and a few of the cows got to their feet, nervous about the safety of their calves. Jeff crawled out of his blankets and unhitched his night horse from the picket line. He had not taken off his clothes, not even his boots. He rode out to the herd and made a slow circle. Most of the cattle seemed peaceful. He heard the coyote send up another cry and moved out toward the sound.

The call of a coyote was not unpleasant to the ear under most circumstances, but it could be troublesome if it made a herd jumpy. Jeff purposely talked and sang so the coyote would hear him coming and retreat. The next time it howled, it was somewhat farther away. Jeff turned back toward camp, satisfied.

The third night, coyotes were not what concerned him. He had thought often of Jones's warning about the Sharkeys. As evening approached, just before time for the herd to bed down, he asked Gabino Enríquez to move up and take his place in the swing position. "Tell Cap I may be late comin' in for supper. Tell him to save me a biscuit."

Gabino asked suspiciously, "Do you need help, *patrón?*"

"I think I can handle it."

Smithwick had taken up a position farther back on the side of the herd. He pulled out and met Jeff. "I suspect I know where you are going. I'm going with you."

"You've got a wife and baby up yonder."

"I also have an interest in this herd, and in you. If something happened to you, Arletta and I would be in a bad way."

Nigel Smithwick was not ordinarily one to push himself upon other people, but Jeff had learned on the buffalo range that once English set his mind to something, he did not let go. Besides that, he was a damned good shot. "Suit yourself." He did not want English to see how grateful he was for the company. He did not want to encourage him to take unnecessary chances. The last thing Jeff needed was a young widow and a baby on his hands.

They rode in an easy trot along the backtrail until darkness overtook them. They could have followed it farther by the lingering faint scent of milk slobber and fresh droppings, but Jeff decided they had gone far enough. If the Sharkeys were coming, they would probably do the easy thing and simply trail the cattle. He dismounted and loosened the girth to let the horse breathe more easily.

"It's liable to turn into a long wait."

Smithwick followed his example, stamping his legs to ease the saddle stiffness.

After a while Jeff began to wish he had waited to eat supper, for his stomach reminded him how little he had eaten since breakfast. One of Cap's biscuits—or several of them—would taste almighty good. He had not taken a nip from Cap's hidden bottle since that first night, when he had been so tired. He could use one now, for the night turned cool enough to make him shiver. He had not thought to tie a jacket behind his saddle. Neither had Smithwick, but the Englishman showed no discomfort. He had always been more tolerant of cold on the buffalo range. Jeff guessed England must develop thicker blood than Texas.

He was about to decide they had made this ride for nothing when Smithwick gently nudged him. Smithwick's hearing was better than Jeff's. He had not fired as many shots with army rifles and buffalo guns over the years. Now Jeff heard voices and the muffled sound of horses' hooves. He put his hand on his horse's nose so he could quickly shut off any attempt to nicker at the others. Two riders passed just to the west. Jeff thought he recognized the voice of the younger Sharkey brother, loud in complaint.

"I don't see why we can't stop and at least make us some coffee. My belly's wonderin' if my throat is cut."

"We got a job of work to do. Tomorrow you can eat half of a steer if you want to."

Jeff waited until they were well past him, then tightened the cinch and swung into the saddle. He and Smithwick followed the pair, hanging back far enough that he did not think they would notice, yet close enough that he could see their vague shapes in the dim light of a rising quarter moon. He did not want to overtake them prematurely.

After a time he could see firelight where the wagons were camped. The herd seemed to have settled down for the night, though he could hear a calf bawling for the mother it had not yet found. A cow responded several times, then the bawling stopped.

He and Smithwick almost rode upon the Sharkeys. They stopped when the younger one spoke just ahead. "That fire sure does look good. I'll bet they're eatin' supper."

"Forget it. Late as it is, they've done et."

Jeff slipped the saddlegun from its scabbard and laid it across his lap. Smithwick drew a pistol. Moving up, Jeff said loudly, "There's probably some left. Let's go in and see."

The younger Sharkey was too startled to move. The older brother let his right hand drop toward his hip, then caught himself and raised it. He was looking into the muzzle of Jeff's rifle.

Irony edged into Jeff's voice. "There's no need for you boys to be bashful. Cap generally fixes more than enough. There's always some left in case of company."

The older brother regained his composure. "We're on our way to San Antonio."

"So are we. If you'd told us, you'd've been welcome to ride along with the herd."

"We're in kind of a hurry."

"Not too big a hurry to eat supper with us and stay the night, I hope." Jeff had not lowered the rifle.

Sharkey looked from Jeff to Smithwick, whose pistol rested across the horn of his saddle. "No, I reckon not."

"We'd be tickled to have you stay in camp with the rest of us tonight. In fact, we'll feel put out if you don't."

The brothers seemed to cave in. The older one said, "That's plumb hospitable."

Jeff and Smithwick rode just behind them toward the campfire. They passed the herd, most of it bedded down, a few calves taking a late supper, a few cows still roaming around restlessly. The brothers looked at the cattle, then at each other.

Jeff said, "No need tyin' your horses to the picket line. Just turn them loose in the remuda. We can catch them for you in the mornin'."

The younger brother suggested, "We could take our turn on night guard."

"You're company. We wouldn't think of askin' company to work. Anyway, we've been suspicious that somebody might try to stampede the herd, so we've told the men to shoot first if there's any trouble. You wouldn't want to get caught up in anything that dangerous."

"No," said the older brother. "I reckon we wouldn't." He sounded beaten.

Jeff called out, "Cap, looky who's here. I hope you've got aplenty left, because we want to treat these boys right."

Jeff had discussed Jones's suspicions with Cap, who declared, "Bring them on in." The area around the wagon was lighted not only by the cooking fire but by a lantern Cap had placed on top of the chuckbox so the night guards could easily find the camp. "After supper they can roll out their blankets right here by me, next to the fire."

Jeff grinned. The Sharkeys would play hell sneaking away.

He filled his tin plate and sat on his rolled blankets to eat a belated supper. Smithwick sat beside him. Arletta stood behind her husband, her hands rested upon his shoulders. The Sharkeys squatted on their heels, the younger brother eating eagerly, the older one looking as if he found flies in his beans.

Cap watched them in satisfaction. "Sure is a good thing Jeff and English happened to come across you-all. Otherwise you never would've gotten anything to eat tonight."

The older Sharkey mumbled, "I don't know how come us to be so lucky."

"Ain't nothin' much ever gets past Jeff Layne. Or English either."

The Sharkeys left after a daylight breakfast. They headed off in a northerly direction, maintaining the fiction that they were going to San Antonio. Jeff suspected that once they were out of sight they would swing around toward home.

Smithwick dropped his plate into Cap's wreck pan, a large washtub full of hot water. "They do not strike me as the bravest pair who ever came down the road. Do you think they may return tonight?"

"Not likely. They know we're onto them. They know if they try again they might get their tailfeathers shot off."

Arletta sounded concerned. "And would they?"

"If we caught them at it." He addressed her misgivings. "But you don't need to worry. It ain't fixin' to happen."

It didn't. The outfit reached the southern edge of San Antonio and found several steer herds gathered along the river, ready to start up the trail for Kansas. A few stray steers had joined Jeff's cattle along the way, and he had made only a halfhearted effort to drive off those whose brands he could not easily read. It was not uncommon for drovers to eat beef all the way from South Texas to the railroad and never once butcher an animal that belonged to their herd's owner. Though some might regard this as bordering on theft, it was so widely practiced that most people in the trade accepted it as normal. Many a man who carried a rope for catching strays balanced it with a Bible in his saddle bag.

The strays would keep the TE outfit fed, along with a few fat barren cows Jeff had acquired despite his best efforts to avoid buying them. He decided to buy a few more steers, for they would be cheap here at the southern end of the trail. He did not want to have to butcher producing cows for beef.

They found a place on the river large enough to accommodate their herd without encroaching on others. The animals were allowed to spread out to rest and graze, the calves to find their mothers if they had lost them. This area had once been a grazing ground for the Spanish mission herds, watched over by native Indian converts and by early Canary Islanders imported by the Spanish government to settle the region and hold it for the king. Animals straying from these herds and from early Spanish ranches along the Rio Grande had formed the nucleus of the wild-roaming cattle later found in such great numbers. Their crossbreeding with early American colonists' cattle had produced the hardy, self-reliant Longhorn.

"This'll be our best chance to buy whatever supplies

we'll need to get us up to the plains and see us settled," Jeff told Cap and the Smithwicks. They would probably skirt a few smaller towns, but these could not be depended upon to furnish all their needs. "We'll take all the wagons in."

He turned reluctantly to Eva Freed. During the days and nights on the trail he had often been aware of her gaze following him, and when he could steal a look at her he took advantage of it. He knew she grieved for her son, but she held the sorrow inside and tried not to impose it on anyone else. He had not once heard her mention either the boy or Vesper Freed, though he knew both must have been heavy on her mind.

He said, "I suppose you'll want to go in when we do."

She nodded. "It'll be hard to say goodbye to these good friends."

"You don't have to. You could go on north with us."

"And do what? I have no part in what you and the Smithwicks are doing."

"We could find somethin' for you to do. Arletta'll have more work than one woman ought to say grace over."

"You're skirting around the real issue, Jeff. Sooner or later, the two of us living so close together . . . I may not be living with Vesper anymore, but I am still married to him."

"You could fix that." He hated to say the word, but he saw no way around it. "You could get a divorce."

"I wasn't raised that way. Neither were you. I made a vow, 'Till death do us part.' You're a man of your word. You can understand why I can't break mine."

Jeff had no argument that he felt would stand up. Divorce was uncommon and widely condemned. He could not think of more than two or three people he had ever known who had been divorced, and they had subjected their families to so much scandal that they had regretted the decision. Perhaps the time might come when it would seem an acceptable way out of marital difficulty, but Jeff doubted he would live that long.

"At least let me ride along with you to where you're goin'. I'll feel better, knowin' where you're at."

"It won't be any easier to say goodbye there than here."

"But it'll put it off a little longer."

He left Cap and the Smithwicks downtown, trusting them to decide what was needed. He rode alongside Eva's buggy up St. Mary's to where her relatives lived. "I don't know how long I may stay with them," she said. "I don't want to impose any longer than I must. I may find a school here that needs a teacher, or a store that needs a book-keeper."

"Just so I can find you."

"It would be better for both of us if you never do . . . if you just ride away from here and don't look back."

"Could you let me ride away and not watch me go?"

She clasped her hands tightly in her lap. "You know I can't. So go, Jeff. Go now, while I still have the strength to send you away." She turned her face from him.

He looked over his shoulder as long as he could see her. She was watching him all the way.

TWENTY-ONE

Arletta had never considered Jeff Layne much of a talker, certainly not like Cap Doolittle or even her husband Nigel. But for the first few days after the herd set out northward from San Antonio he talked even less than usual. Times, she saw him looking back toward the south, his expression that of a man in mourning. She knew what was on his mind. Everyone knew. But no one spoke of Eva.

The cattle had settled down to the trail routine. They had run a couple of times early in the drive and seemed to have worked that rebellion out of their systems. Each morning as the drovers rode into the edge of the herd, hollering the animals up from their bed ground, a spotted cow would rise to her feet, allow her calf a brief time to nurse, then strike off behind the point rider. Of all the cattle in the herd, she alone had a name, Queenie. She had the haughty air, the impatience with her inferiors, that befitted the title. Her crown was a pair of sharp-tipped horns that pointed forward, ready for battle with anything that challenged her authority. After the first days, nothing did.

Arletta admired Queenie's independence, a trait on which she had prided herself. She had drawn heavily upon this strength after her father's death, because for a time she had no one to lean upon, no one to share her responsibilities. It was different now. Nigel could help her carry whatever burdens might present themselves. But she found security in the knowledge that she had taken care of herself before and could do it again.

She never looked at Queenie without feeling a glow of spiritual kinship. *Me and you together, we can whip anything,* she thought.

The baby Becky had adapted quickly to daily travel. Arletta kept the cradle wedged firmly at her feet in the front of the wagon. The child seemed soothed by the steady motion and sometimes complained when the wagon stopped. *You're going to have a mind of your own too,* Arletta thought.

That was the way she wanted it. She would raise Becky not to be dependent upon other people. As Arletta saw it, that had been Eva's principal problem in her youth, allowing herself to be manipulated by her father and Vesper Freed. By the time she acquired the strength and maturity to stand her ground, she had no ground to stand on. She was mired in a situation that gave her little but grief.

"We'll see to it that you never get your foot in that kind of a trap," she told her daughter.

It would be a challenge to keep the child from becoming spoiled, however, if she continued to receive the kind of attention the drovers had been giving her. All of them tickled her under the chin at any opportunity and baby-talked to her in English or Spanish, or in the case of Herman Wurtz, German. She would often respond with a gurgling noise that each of them took as a personal message, though Arletta thought most of the time it was simply gas.

From San Antonio northward, Jeff set a course that skirted west of the more traveled cattle trails whose eventual destination was Wichita. Most of the herds being driven to Kansas were pointed by way of Austin, Waco and Fort Worth. Arletta remembered those towns from the trip southward last summer and fall. But because this drive was aimed toward the Texas high plains, most of the Chisholm lay too far east. Jeff had mapped a route that would follow military roads as far as possible up through old Fort Mason, Fort McKavett and Fort Concho, then beyond onto the lower plains.

Arletta found this a pleasant country of tall limestone hills and long, broad valleys, most of them watered by bubbling springs and sparkling creeks, their water as cool and pure as she had ever tasted. She would have been content to stop and unload the wagons almost anywhere. But Jeff's vision was of a high and distant land, a faraway canyon.

A few days out of San Antonio they came into a German-immigrant village known as Fredericksburg, which centered on an odd-shaped wooden church with six sides. She had never seen one like it. Because they had bought a full load of supplies in San Antonio they needed to add but little here. Earlier, the town had been home to immigrant Herman Wurtz. The sight of it now made him ill at ease, calling up violent arguments with his father and other elders who clung to old-world ideas while Herman had embraced the new world and its freedoms. Nevertheless, he willingly served as interpreter for Arletta and Cap when they went into a store to purchase some extra coffee and bacon, more out of precaution than need.

Arletta had heard several foreign languages spoken on the buffalo range, but she was having trouble enough at times with her husband's brand of English. She had no ambition at this point to learn another tongue. She was fascinated, nevertheless, at the ability of people to converse with each other in words that had no meaning to her but which seemed perfectly clear to them. In South Texas they had been Mexicans. Here they were Germans. Listening to them lent a sense of reality to the much broader world she had been reading about in books Nigel had found for her.

She picked up a volume she found lying in a chair where the proprietor had been sitting. Not only were the words foreign, but the letters were shaped differently than those Nigel had helped her learn to read. The storekeeper chuckled over her consternation. Wurtz showed no emotion. Arletta had never seen him smile much except at the baby.

While they were putting the supplies together, an elderly man entered the store. He and Herman nodded in recognition of one another but did not speak. The old man went about his business, and Herman continued with his own. Leaving the store, Arletta asked him, "Who was that?"

"My father," Wurtz said matter-of-factly.

"Your father? But you two didn't even speak."

"We had nothing to talk about."

"How long since you last saw one another?"

"Five years."

Jeff and Nigel sat on their horses, waiting. Nigel's rope was looped around the short black horns of a young milk cow shaped considerably differently than the beef cattle in the TE brand.

Nigel asked Arletta, "What do you think of her?"

"We've already got a whole herd of cows out yonder. What did we need another one for?"

Jeff said, "You'd have to rope and tie those range cows down every time you went to milk, and you'd be lucky if you got enough to color a cup of coffee. This is a springin' heifer . . . first calf comin' pretty soon. Then you'll have all the milk you need for the baby."

Arletta thought the baby was getting all she needed now, but she realized that situation would not continue indefinitely. "I'll bet you ain't never milked a cow, Nigel."

His well-to-do upbringing in England had not included tasks of such a nature. "I always fancied that as a woman's chore."

"Looks like I'll have to teach *you* a few lessons."

Nigel tied the heifer up short behind the wagon. She set back on four stiff legs and resisted the tug of the rope as long as she could, then moved in short sidewise jumps, fighting against the restraint.

Cap said, "Too bad she ain't givin' milk already. She'd be churnin' butter for us."

Arletta smiled. "Looks like we'll have two cows with names. I'm goin' to call her Rebel."

Northwest of Fredericksburg and short of Fort Mason, Arletta was startled one day to hear a pistol shot. Her first thought was of Indians, though everybody had been saying the Indian troubles were over. She stood up in the wagon and looked back with some apprehension, drawing on the lines to halt the team. She could easily reach a rifle laid against the side board if she needed it.

The shot had startled some of the nearby cattle, but most of the herd continued to plod along unconcerned. At night, it might have stampeded them. Arletta saw Jeff and Nigel and a couple more riders come together for a short discussion. Then Nigel rode toward her. Her tension subsided, for he showed no sign of excitement.

"It was merely a skunk, but Jeff thinks it might have been rabid. He said it was acting peculiarly."

"Rabid? You mean hydrophobia?"

"Jeff says they incubate it while they are denned during the winter, then disperse in the spring and spread it. We have to be watchful that none of our cows are bitten."

Arletta had always watched out for skunks, but for a different reason.

River crossings were a challenge. Before Fredericksburg there had been the Pedernales. South of Fort Mason they came to the Llano. It was broad, but fortunately it was low because no rain had fallen in a while. The road crossed over on a mostly rocky bottom, which eased the task for the wagons.

She was disappointed to find that Fort Mason no longer lived up to its name. There had once been a fort, but most of its buildings had been dismantled, the cut stones reused for constructing stores and homes. Activity, what there was of it, centered around a courthouse square. The names on the storefronts were a mixture of English and German. At least here she did not have to rely upon Herman Wurtz as interpreter when she bought a couple of dozen fresh eggs from a housewife to provide a breakfast treat for the men.

A squad of black cavalrymen and a white lieutenant circled the cattle and drew up beside Arletta's wagon after the outfit left Mason, heading toward Fort McKavett. They paused briefly, the lieutenant paying respects to Arletta and dutifully admiring the baby in the wagon bed. "Are you folks taking these cows to Fort Concho?"

"Yep, and then on north. A long ways north."

His air became one of slight condescension. She knew her language was not that of a schoolteacher, but she was learning as rapidly as she could.

"Why so far? There is still good grazing land to be had around Concho. It may be a bit expensive for your taste, some of it as much as fifty cents to a dollar an acre. But the grass is strong."

"Up on the plains it's free. At first, anyway. Time the state finds out where it's at and starts askin' money for it, we ought to've saved enough to buy whatever part we want."

"You know, of course, that most of it was still in Indian hands as recently as last fall? There may be a few of the beggars skulking around up there yet."

"There were border-jumpin' bandits where we just come from. I reckon if there was any place perfect, everybody'd be crowdin' in on top of one another."

"For me, they can have this endless, dusty West. I plan to resign my commission shortly and go back to Illinois where I won't have to ride a hundred miles for a conversation with civilized people."

Arletta wondered if he considered her *civilized people*. She suspected he did not. She was tempted to call Nigel up and show this officer what *really* civilized people sounded like.

She said, "Illinois used to be a frontier like this, didn't it?"

"God forbid that Illinois was ever like this." He touched his hat brim. "A promising-looking little girl you have here, ma'am. It's too bad she'll grow up in this God-forsaken part of the country. She'll probably have to settle for being some cowboy's wife."

"She'll be whatever she *wants* to be," Arletta replied stiffly. Watching the officer and the black soldiers ride on, she decided if the lieutenant represented civilized people, she had as soon not be considered one of them.

Arletta had little fear of wolves and none of coyotes. Having spent as many of her years living outdoors as beneath one roof or another, she had developed a good working knowledge of animals wild and domestic. Despite having heard stories about incidents which always seemed to have taken place somewhere far away, she had never known a person who had ever been attacked by a wolf or even a pack of wolves. She knew the Indians had coexisted with them for ages and for the most part considered them brothers. To her, the coyote was simply a smaller cousin to the wolf, sneakier, perhaps smarter, but not to be feared unless one owned a flock of chickens. She had heard them yipping and howling every night on this drive and had not let them cost her a minute's sleep.

She paid little attention, therefore, to the dirty-brown animal she saw a couple of hundred yards away, crossing an open flat between two live-oak mottes. She and Cap had moved out ahead of the herd to set up camp for the night. She had lifted the baby's cradle out of the wagon and had set it on the ground nearby. Now she sat on a bedroll picking rocks out of the dry beans Cap would put on the coals to cook through the night for tomorrow's meals. Cap was working up biscuit dough for supper.

Later she would remember the skunk that had been shot back down the trail, but it had seemed a trivial incident, easily dismissed from mind.

She did not know exactly what caught her attention . . . a gurgling sound from the baby, or perhaps a fleeting glimpse of color from the corner of her eye. Glancing around, she saw the coyote not twenty feet away, approaching the cradle.

Her skin prickled with sudden terror as she imagined the animal grabbing the baby and dragging it away like a rabbit. She jumped to her feet, spilling the pan of beans.

She ran toward the baby, shouting at the coyote in a panicked voice. "Git! Git!" She grabbed Cap's iron pot hook, the nearest weapon she could see, and made a wild swing.

Ordinarily a coyote would not have ventured into camp, certainly not when it could plainly see two humans there. Even if it had, a sudden movement and a shout like Arletta's would have sent it running desperately. But this coyote made no such retreat. It kept coming, its amber eyes fixed on Arletta. They were savage, raging eyes. She saw a trickle of foam that fell away from its bared teeth. She swung the iron bar again. It glanced off the coyote's hip as the animal leaped at her.

Her skin went cold as ice, and she seemed unable to move her feet. Defensively she thrust out her arms to shield her body. She felt the sharp bite of the coyote's teeth as it clamped down upon her left wrist. She heard a scream and knew it was her own. She swung the bar again and brought it down across the animal's hindquarters. The blow had no effect.

She heard Cap shout and saw him grab his pistol from its resting place in his chuckbox. She could hear herself screaming but had no control over her voice.

Cap brought the muzzle of the pistol down within inches of the coyote's head and fired. She felt the animal jerk, its teeth ripping her skin. Cap fired again, and the coyote fell on its side, jerking, kicking. In its death agony it lunged at him, clamping its teeth upon the leg of his trousers. He kept firing into its body until the pistol was empty and black smoke from the gunpowder set him to choking.

He turned to her, his eyes frenzied, his mouth hanging open. "My God, hon! My God!"

The shots had frightened the baby. It began wailing. Arletta heard herself crying. Cap kept shouting, "My God!" as he grabbed her bleeding arm.

Regaining composure, he led her quickly to the chuckbox. He uncorked a bottle and poured whiskey over the wound. The torn flesh was already burning, and the alcohol intensified the blaze. Cap did not stop pouring until most of the whiskey was gone, spilling over her arm and dripping red on the ground from the blood it washed away. More blood kept coming.

Her instinct was to try to stop it, but Cap caught her right hand and held it. "Let it bleed. Let it carry away all the poison that it can."

She had never seen Cap really frightened. Once they had stood side by side behind a wagon, fighting off an attack by a Comanche war party. He had shown only a grim determination. Now, however, a dark, primordial fear was in his eyes. His huge, red-spotted hands trembled. "Hon, you been bit by a hydrophoby coyote!"

She seemed unable to move, absorbing the full import. He kicked aside the pan that had held the dry beans and helped her seat herself on the bedroll.

"Cap, what'll I do?" She looked toward the crying baby. "Please, do somethin' for Becky."

"Becky ain't the one that's hurt." Tears filled Cap's eyes. She imagined he was already seeing her dead. A bite from a rabid animal was almost always fatal. No one knew a cure for rabies.

Cap squeezed her hands so hard she thought he would break her bones. "That madstone! Where's it at?"

The fear, the burning pain . . . she could not quite fathom what he was saying. "The what? What madstone?"

He shook her violently. "Last year, in the Territory. That old Indian gave you a madstone. Don't you remember?"

She tried, but nausea and shock were beginning to set in.

"Think, girl! Think! Where'd you put it?" He shook her again.

It came back to her. "In the trunk, in your second wagon."

"Don't you move." For a man of such bulk, he strode swiftly, almost vaulting up into the wagon, throwing off bedrolls and a folded tent.

She heard horses running and saw several riders hurrying in from the herd. Nigel was in the lead, Jeff not far behind. Nigel slid his horse to a stop and dismounted so abruptly that he went to his knees. He jumped up and came running. "That shooting! What was it?" He saw the blood, and his face went the color of skim milk.

Arletta could not answer. She could only point at the dead coyote.

Jeff was there then. He took in the situation without asking questions. He picked up the iron rod and stuck it into the fire. "We've got to cauterize those wounds."

Nigel's arms were around Arletta. He held her desperately. "Will that kill the poison?"

"I don't know. If it's already got into her blood . . ."

Cap came trotting from the wagon, holding a leather pouch. "Wait! I found it. The madstone."

Jeff and Nigel stared until Cap reminded them of the old Indian's gift. "Boys, we got to boil it in milk before it'll work."

Jeff said, "That heifer ain't freshened yet. We'll have to get it from one of the beef cows." He jerked his head at Gabino Enríquez and one of the Gallegos cousins, who had ridden up just behind him. "Let's go."

As Jeff swung into the saddle, Cap handed him a tin bucket. "The longer it takes you, the less chance she's got."

The baby seemed to have cried itself out. Nigel dragged up their bedroll and spread it out on the ground. "You'd best lie down," he told Arletta. "The less you move around, the slower the poison will circulate."

Cap stood over her, flexing his big hands and looking impatiently toward the herd. "Why the hell don't they hurry up? How long does it take to rope and stretch a cow?" The men had barely had time even to reach the cattle.

Arletta turned her head. She could see the stirring dust. She caught a glimpse of a man swinging a rope and in a moment heard a cow bawling in anger and fright. She heard the baby whimpering again. "Nigel, won't you go see about Becky?"

"Becky is all right. You are the one we are concerned about at the moment."

Cap said, "You ought to've seen her, the way she rushed in there. I heard her scream, and there she was beatin' that coyote away from the baby with a pot hook. Saved that young'un, she did. Bravest thing I ever seen a woman do."

Choking, Nigel laid his head against Arletta's shoulder.

Jeff came loping up, holding the bucket at arm's length in an effort to keep its contents from splashing out. "Pour this up and give the bucket back to me."

Cap frowned into the container. "Is this the best you can do?"

"We're goin' to have to milk some more cows."

"It's a start anyway." Cap emptied the milk into a pan and handed the bucket back. Jeff spurred away. Cap raked glowing red coals out of the fire onto flat ground and set the pan on top of them. As the milk began to boil, he dropped the madstone into it. In a few minutes he brought it, dripping milk between his fingers. He placed it atop the most savage-looking tooth mark. He held it against the skin until, to Arletta's surprise, the stone adhered.

"It's drawin'," Cap declared. A little of hope began coming into his eyes.

Nigel's jaw quivered. "Do you think it will really work?"

"Worked on me one time. They carried me ten miles to where there was a feller had a madstone. I was bit near as bad as Arletta is, but it saved me. Sucked the poison right out of there."

Nigel remained dubious. "It sounds like an old wives' tale to me."

Jeff came with more milk. After a time Cap removed the stone, boiled it again, then reapplied it. As it released itself from one puncture wound he would place it against another. The process continued far into the night. The cowboys dragged off the coyote and rustled their own meager supper, for Cap was occupied.

For once Jeff stood back, letting the cook take the lead. Arletta managed to put most of her fear aside and place her faith in Cap's quiet confidence. Again and again, Cap boiled the stone in fresh milk to restore it. Finally it no longer adhered to any of the wounds.

Cap said solemnly, "It's done all it can do. Now, Arletta, there's one more thing. It'll take all the guts you've got."

She had seen Jeff place the iron bar back into the fire. It glowed now. A cold chill ran through all of her body. "Let's be gettin' it over with."

She closed her eyes as Cap lifted the bar from among the coals. Nigel and Jeff took a firm hold on her arm. She felt the heat as Cap brought the bar down toward her skin. She stiffened herself and gritted her teeth. "Go on. Do it."

She heard herself cry out and smelled the burning of the hair on her arm, of her flesh. She dropped away into a faint. When she came back, Nigel was applying wagon grease to the burn. His hands were shaking as if he were suffering fever and chills. He looked up at Cap. "What do we do next?"

"Just pray. Pray that we got it all."

Behind Cap, Gabino Enríquez made a sign of the cross.

TWENTY-TWO

Fort Concho stood on high ground along the south side of the river from which it had derived its name. A stone hospital building no more than a couple of years old was its most imposing structure, its cupola easily the tallest thing on the post except for the flagpole. Jeff and Nigel Smithwick had rushed Arletta there the day after her fight with the rabid coyote, leaving Cap and the rest of the crew to bring along the cattle in their own good time. She had been running a low-grade fever from the effects of the bite and the burning of her arm. The post surgeon had looked her over, listening with undisguised doubt to Jeff's account about the madstone.

The doctor said, "I suppose to whatever extent faith heals, such remedies have their value. I think the more important thing was washing the wound with whiskey and cauterizing it. I could not have done much more than you did."

Jeff could see that Arletta and English were reaching out for whatever hope the surgeon might offer. "Then you think she'll be all right?"

"If quick action means anything. But there are no guarantees."

"Is there anything you can do to help her?"

"I can provide something better than wagon grease for that wound, and dress it properly. Beyond that . . ." He looked at Arletta, holding the baby in her lap, and jerked his head at Jeff. "Would you come with me a minute, sir? I could use your help in lifting a patient."

Jeff followed him and quickly saw that the move was a ruse to get beyond Arletta's and English's hearing. The doctor looked out a window upon the dusty parade ground, where black soldiers of the Tenth Cavalry practiced horseback drill. "I would strongly suggest that you arrange for the young lady to remain in Saint Angela, across the river. I should like to keep her under observation."

Jeff thought of the herd, of the need to press northward. "How long?"

"Two weeks should tell the tale. If she is to be all right, we will know it by then. If not . . . well, sir, I do not think any woman should be out on the prairie when she comes to such a terrible end. At least here there are things I could give her to ease her passing."

Jeff clenched his fists and leaned his forehead against the wall. "God, doctor, what have I brought these people to?"

"It could have happened to her anywhere. I have seen wild animals cross the parade ground right here. At night sometimes it sounds as if the wolves are almost under the windows. There is no reason to blame yourself."

"I could've stayed in South Texas with them."

"Rabies is hardly unknown there either. Now, I know of a small cabin which she and her husband can use. It is not very comfortable, but it is better than a campsite on the trail. Will you leave her?"

"Of course. I'm obliged about the cabin."

While the doctor treated and bandaged the wound, he outlined his proposal that Arletta remain for observation. "Just until we see you satisfactorily on the road to recovery, of course. A couple of weeks should be enough." He did not mention the bleak possibility he had presented to Jeff.

Arletta recognized Jeff's concern for the herd. "I hate to hold up the drive."

Jeff said, "They're still a good day behind us. Won't

be here till tomorrow night at the earliest. We'll rest them a few days, then start grazin' them north real slow. You and English can catch up to us easy." He tried to shrug it away as if it meant little.

Smithwick said, "We will feel as if we are slacking off on our share of the work."

"You'll have more work than you can see around when we get to where we're goin'. There'll be aplenty of buildin' to do before winter catches us."

The doctor said, "One more thing, Mrs. Smithwick. You had better wean your baby onto cow's milk. If the fever lingers, your own might be harmful to the child."

Jeff felt a cold lump in his stomach. He hoped Arletta did not realize what was left unspoken: that if she did not survive, it would be well for the baby to be weaned as quickly as possible.

The next afternoon he set out on the Fort McKavett mail road to intercept the herd. He came upon Cap first, driving the chuck wagon. The trail wagon had been hitched to its rear so Jeff and Smithwick could use the lead wagon of the pair to hurry Arletta and the baby into town.

"She goin' to be all right?" Cap demanded.

Jeff explained that they might not know for a couple of weeks. Cap's face twisted, and he scratched his leg. "These cows can graze off a right smart of country in two weeks."

"We'll loose-herd them east of town a few days, then move on slow. It's the best I know to do."

Cap nodded and scratched his leg again.

"What's the matter?" Jeff asked. "You got the itch?" On the buffalo range Cap could easily have had buffalo lice. On this trail, bugs of several kinds seemed attracted to bedding. Some of them were biters.

"Scraped my leg climbin' up into the wagon. I poured a little whiskey on it, but I hate to waste that stuff on the outside."

"You can buy some more in Saint Angela. Looked to me like they had enough of it to put the river on a rise."

They spread the herd out to graze along the north side

of the Concho River, a comfortable distance east of the military post. Jeff did not know if the land belonged to anybody. If someone complained he would simply move the cattle. Cap was eager to see about Arletta and the baby, so he took the cook to their cabin after the men had eaten supper.

He found Arletta in good spirits. Her arm was sore, but her fever was gone. Her blue eyes were bright as she sat in a rocking chair, holding the baby in her arms and trying to get it interested in a bottle of warmed milk. She let Cap gently pinch the infant's cheek and indulge in some baby talk that made no sense to anyone except him.

She said, "I feel foolish sittin' here rockin' when I ought to be out there helpin' you with the cookin' and all."

Cap snorted. "Truth is, I only let you do a few things around the wagon to keep you from gettin' lazy. A woman without enough to do will nag a man till he turns to drink. And speakin' of drink, I'm fixin' to go and get me one before them soldiers soak it all up. Comin', Jeff?"

Jeff lingered another moment, looking at Arletta, finding comfort in the freshness that had returned to her eyes. He fingered the baby's tiny hand and told Nigel Smithwick, "No use you comin' out to the herd. The boys are handlin' everything."

"I don't wish to shirk my share."

"Right now your job is takin' care of Arletta and the girl."

Jeff and Cap found a rude saloon built of pickets, the gaps chinked with mud. The owner's investment, beyond the stock, appeared to be about a dollar and forty cents. The bar inside was a couple of rough boards propped between two stacks of wooden beer barrels. A dingy piece of canvas was tacked over them to keep customers from getting splinters in their arms. The place reminded him of a couple of dives he had seen in Dodge City the first months after the town opened for business, receiving buffalo hides.

Cap's face contorted as he swallowed his first drink.

"Damn! If I ever tasted worse, I've forgotten where it was. It's goin' to take another one to wash away the leavin's."

Jeff never quite finished his glass. "It's got me out-matched. Drink up and let's go."

Cap raised his pants leg and poured some of the whiskey on an angry streak below his knee. He winced from the burn. "That ought to heal the scratch or take off the leg."

The leg looked worse than Jeff expected. "Maybe you'd better let that post doctor take a look at it."

"Just a scrape. There's a rough edge on one of my wagon rims. I been wounded worse than this by a South Texas horsefly." Cap drank the little that was left in the glass. "I'm ready."

Jeff turned, then stiffened in shock.

"Kelly Booth!"

The cowboy stood in the open doorway, his teeth shining white through many days' dark growth of whiskers. In no way did he resemble a ghost. "Howdy, Jeff . . . Cap. You-all are sure a sight."

Jeff felt paralyzed. Booth gripped Jeff's hand with a strength that brought pain, then clapped his hands against Cap's broad shoulders, raising a puff of dust. "You stayin' sober, you old belly robber?"

Cap's eyes were as large as hen's eggs. "I must be drunk. You're dead. And yet I'm lookin' at you."

"I've got more lives than a cat. You ever try to kill a cat?"

Jeff found voice, though not a strong one. "Vesper Freed said he saw you die."

"Vesper saw what I wanted him to see."

"He told Arletta that he shot you, and you drowned in the Rio Grande."

"He creased me, but I'm a better swimmer than he figured. Since he thinks I'm dead, he's not huntin' for me anymore." He extended his arm. "Here, feel. You'll see that I'm not a ghost."

Jeff managed, "How'd you find us?"

"It ain't hard to track a thousand cows. Come on, I'll buy the two of you a drink."

Jeff said, "Let's find a better place." He felt a profound relief at the cowboy's reappearance, the familiar broad smile, but reservations immediately began to trouble him. They walked out the door and down the dirt street that was Concho Avenue, looking for a more likely place to buy a drink. "If I was you I'd head north or west, plumb out of this country. Freed won't stay fooled forever."

"You're goin' north, ain't you? I thought I'd string along if you'll have me."

Cap looked expectantly at Jeff. Jeff was reluctant to give an answer. As glad as he was to see Booth alive, he had rather he be alive in Montana or Wyoming or California . . . anywhere but Texas. Wherever Booth went, trouble followed like horn flies follow a bull.

Jeff lost any taste for more whiskey. "You-all can drink one for me. I'm goin' back to the herd. The boys'll want to know that you're alive after all."

It was a lame excuse, and he knew it sounded that way. As he walked toward the post where his horse was tied he heard Booth asking about Arletta and the baby and English. Cap was telling him about the coyote and the madstone. "Looks like she'll be all right. She'll be tickled to see you're alive and kickin'. I want to show you that baby. Knows me, she does. Reaches for my hand when I talk to her."

Jeff mounted and rode on, thinking about Vesper . . . weighing the chance that Vesper would never find out.

It didn't weigh much.

The third day, a man came to the herd in a buggy and claimed that he owned the land the cattle were grazing. He demanded a hundred dollars for the grass they had consumed. Jeff gave him fifty, and he left as happy as if he had gotten it all. Reluctantly Jeff rode into town to tell the Smithwicks he would have to resume the trek north.

Cap went with him for a parting visit with the baby. "Soon as she's old enough, I'm goin' to teach her how to make biscuits. Bein' pretty is helpful, but bein' a good cook . . . she'll have her pick of boys from a hundred miles around."

Jeff told Smithwick, "You won't have any trouble catchin' up. We'll follow the North Concho, then push on up to a big spring a day or so's drive past the head of the river. I figure we'll be ten-twelve days gettin' there, travelin' slow. An officer from the fort made me a sketch off of Colonel Mackenzie's map. It shows some places we can expect to find water from there on. The rest of it we'll work out for ourselves as we go."

Arletta said, "I'm feelin' fine. I don't know why we can't leave with you."

Jeff saw silent disagreement in English's face. "You know what the doctor said. You'll catch up to us at the big spring or a little ways past."

English thanked him with his eyes.

Jeff said, "This is the last town we're apt to see, so enjoy it while you can." He leaned over the baby and stroked its cheek with his rough hand. He kissed Arletta on the forehead and walked out.

Cap remained inside, trying to play with the baby. She was too young to give him much response, but he talked to her as if she understood it all. "You'll be back with your old Uncle Cap in a few days. I'll make you a sugar teat."

Smithwick followed Jeff to where the horses were tied. "Jeff, what about Kelly Booth?"

"What about him?"

"He's been to visit us a couple of times. He seems unsure of your welcome."

"I can't say I'm sure of it myself."

"He's been a good friend to Arletta and me. And you should have seen him carry on over the baby."

Jeff still had his suspicions about Booth's feelings toward Arletta. "I haven't told him he can't go with us."

"But have you told him he *can*?"

"I guess not. I will, soon's we get back to camp."

"Up on the plains he should be out of the law's reach."

"By the time the law finds us there, the paper on him ought to be cold and forgotten." He did not speak the rest of his thought: *or somebody will have killed him.*

Arletta followed Cap to the door, gripping his thick arm. "You take care of yourself. Me and the baby, we owe our lives to you."

"You're makin' a lot out of a little, hon. I just happened to be there, that's all."

"Well, I'm awful glad you were." She kissed him on the cheek. Grinning broadly as he walked out to the horses, Cap turned once to wave at her. He slapped a big hand against Smithwick's shoulder. "You're the luckiest man I know, English. I don't know what any of us would do without Arletta."

"Thanks to you, Cap, it appears we will not have to."

Riding out toward the herd, Jeff said, "You know, that's twice you've saved that girl." The other time had been during a Comanche raid on the buffalo-hunting camp, when a warrior had tried to make off with her. Cap had brought him down with a rifle shot.

"What else is an old fart like me good for?"

The leisurely movement up the North Concho was pleasant. The water ran clear and cool between high banks lined by tall pecan trees. A small remnant of last winter's nut crop still clung amid the new foliage, dropping as wind whipped the long branches. Though much of the fallen crop had rotted amid old leaves on the ground, Jeff found some still oily and sweet to the taste. The only problem was that they were small. It took longer to peel them out with a knife blade than to eat them.

The river valley was wide, with a row of tall, rough hills on its west side, a gentler stretch of prairie and smaller hills to its east. If it were not that he had already set his mind on the far canyon, Jeff thought he might have been content to find a place here. He occasionally had to ride out ahead of the herd and drive away cattle that otherwise might mix with the TEs, but as yet the country did not appear to be overstocked. Very little land, even on the deep-soil flats, had felt the bite of a plow.

One day Cap stopped the wagon, stood up and hailed Jeff by waving his hat over his head. He pointed as Jeff spurred to him. "I wisht you'd look at that!"

Ahead, buffalo grazed. Jeff rough-counted at least three hundred spread across the green flood plain. They would have to be chased away lest they spook the cattle. Cap declared, "Just like old times up north. Makes a man want to oil up his rifle."

Jeff enjoyed the sight of the buffalo for their own sake. He had no desire to kill another unless it became necessary for meat.

Cap made a grab at his lower leg and sat down heavily on the wagon seat, wincing, hurting.

Jeff eyed him critically. "That leg's gettin' worse, ain't it?"

"I just stood up on it wrong." But there was no mistaking the pain in Cap's eyes. And something else. Uneasiness, even a touch of fear.

Jeff felt a chill, though the wind was soft and warm. "Are you sure you scratched that leg on the wagon wheel?"

Cap looked away. "That was what I figured."

"When you were fightin' the coyote off of Arletta, is there a chance that it bit you too?"

"If it did, I didn't notice it. I was too excited, tryin' to get it loose from her."

A cold dread came upon Jeff. "Let me see your leg."

Reluctantly Cap raised the cuff most of the way to the knee. A discolored rag was wrapped around the wound. It smelled of kerosene. Cap undid it carefully, the leg painful to the touch. "I been washin' it with whiskey, then wrappin' it with a coal-oiled rag. The coal oil has raised a blister."

It was as bad as Jeff expected. Perhaps worse. Critically he said, "I wish you'd gone to see that post doctor."

"It didn't amount to much at the time. It still don't. I've weathered worse than this."

"We could make it back to Fort Concho in a hard day's horseback ride."

"And who would cook for the boys? I ain't spent ten dollars on doctors in my whole life, and I don't figure I need to start now. I ain't no baby."

Jeff felt numb with fear for his old friend. If the problem was rabies, it was too late to do anything that might cure it. He remembered what the doctor had said about Arletta: that at least he could give her medication to ease her passing. "That leg is infected. If it gets worse, you could lose it. I want to take you back to the fort."

Cap seemed to shrink before his eyes, slumping on the wagon seat, his head down. "Hell, what're we talkin' about? We both know it ain't no use." His voice dropped so low that Jeff had to strain to hear him. "I'm already runnin' a fever. That doctor can't save my leg. He can't save *me*. I been bit by a hydrophoby coyote."

Jeff reached desperately for hope. "Maybe it ain't really rabies. Maybe it's just the infection that's causin' your fever."

"No, I know what it is. I can feel it comin' on me like a pack of hungry wolves. I got it, and there ain't no shakin' it."

"For God's sake, Cap, why didn't you . . ." He broke off. He had intended to ask why Cap had not used the madstone on himself as well as on Arletta. The question was futile now.

Cap answered what Jeff had not asked. "I didn't realize I was bit. Wasn't much of a scratch when I first noticed it. I figured it came from the wagon wheel." He shook his head. "Ain't no use talkin' about what I ought to've done. Ain't nothin' to do but keep plowin' ahead." He flipped the reins and shouted at the team.

Jeff could only stare after him, dread spreading through his veins like poison. Dread and, unaccountably, a touch of anger at his old friend for his carelessness.

By the time they reached the place Jeff had chosen for

the night's camp, Cap's fever was high enough for anyone to see it. He started to climb down from the wagon but stopped, shaking. Jeff reached up to give him support. On the ground, Cap held on to a wheel for support. He tried to make light of his situation. "Better keep your distance, Jeff. You don't want me to bite you."

Jeff climbed into the wagon and threw down Cap's tarp-wrapped blanket roll. "There'll be no cookin' for you tonight. You're goin' to bed."

"It ain't even dark yet."

Jeff did not argue. He sought a smooth place on the ground, pushed up some dry leaves with his foot and rolled out the blankets. "Now, lay yourself down."

"What about supper?"

"You think you're the only one around here who can burn up a pot of beans? Lay down."

As the cowboys rode in, he tried not to look as grim as he felt. "Cap's sick. Who knows how to cook?"

Kelly Booth walked over to the bed and looked down at Cap. "You been eatin' too much of your own cookin'." But his voice betrayed an edge of concern. He came back to Jeff. "He looks bad. What's wrong with him?"

"His leg's infected." Jeff knew by the shocked realization in Booth's eyes that the cowboy was not fooled.

"That coyote bit him."

"It looks that way."

Booth turned away, choking off a curse. "How long has he got?"

"I don't know. Never was around anybody before who was in this shape."

"I seen a feller once. It's a miserable way to die." Booth stole a glance at Cap, who lay with his eyes closed. "I wouldn't even wish it off onto a snake like Vesper Freed. Why a good man like Cap?"

"Because he *is* a good man. He was thinkin' of Arletta and the baby. He never thought about himself."

Two Gallegos cousins set in to preparing supper. They made flat Mexican-style bread in a Dutch oven and heated up a pot of beans Cap had let cook the night before. They fried steaks from a hindquarter of beef in the wagon, what was left of a stray steer that had foolishly attached itself to the herd and refused to be chased away. Jeff forced himself to eat a little, but food lay heavily on his stomach. Cap took only some coffee and a pinched-off bit of hot bread.

"Damned poor substitutes for biscuits. I ought to be up doin' the cookin'."

Booth tried to cover his anxiety. "You never was half the cook you thought you were."

"How would you know? You've got no taste. You couldn't tell liver from rice puddin'."

Jeff knew both men were attempting to deny the awful reality that lay before them. He could not. He walked off into the darkness, holding a cup of coffee that had gone cold.

He never spread out his blankets. He dragged his roll close to Cap's bed and sat on it. George Newby and Herman Wurtz came up to him. Quietly Newby said, "You'll want to stay by Cap tonight. Me and Herman'll split your turn on night guard."

Jeff nodded his thanks and watched Cap fall into a feverish sleep. After a time Cap awakened, throwing off blankets. "Damned hot night," he complained.

Actually, the air had taken on enough of a chill that Jeff had draped a jacket over his shoulders. "Mighty hot," he agreed.

Cap lay in silence, lying on one side awhile, then the other, wiping sweat from his face onto his sleeve. He had on all of his clothes except his boots. At length he asked, "You awake, Jeff?"

"I'm awake."

"You reckon I'll be like that coyote, foamin' at the mouth and tryin' to bite everybody?"

"I don't know. I hope not."

"If I show signs, I want you to shoot me."

"Cap . . ."

"I want you to shoot me like I shot that coyote. Put me out of my misery before I can hurt somebody, before I can give one of them what I've got. Promise me, Jeff."

Jeff tried to swallow but could not. "I can't promise a thing like that."

"Then let's go over yonder to one of them pecan trees. Tie me to it so if I go out of my head I can't hurt anybody."

"For God's sake, Cap . . ."

"I've heard stories. There was a Mexican freighter got bit one time down between San Antonio and Helena. They said they had to chain him to an ox cart, he got so wild. Raged out of his head, tried to bite and scratch like an animal. All they could do was stand there and watch him thrash around. Taken him all night to die."

"Maybe it ain't the same with everybody."

"I wouldn't want to go through that. I wouldn't want to put my friends through it."

"Maybe you're wrong about the rabies. Maybe it's just an infection, like you thought at first. Try and go to sleep."

Cap became quiet. Lying on his back, he drifted away. Jeff pulled a blanket up over Cap's broad shoulders against the night chill. He sat then, determined to stay awake, to keep watch all night. But fatigue overcame his will, and after a time he drowsed.

He awakened with a start. It was still dark. The cook's lantern atop the chuckbox was the only light. He realized that Cap's blanket had been laid back. Cap was gone.

His first thought was that Cap had awakened and had walked off into the darkness to relieve himself. He felt the blanket. It was cold and dry. Cap had been gone for a while.

He called, "Cap!" He cupped his hands around his mouth and shouted again. He heard nothing except the stirring of men he had awakened.

Kelly Booth raised up in his blankets. "What's the matter?"

"Cap's gone."

Jeff fetched the lantern from the wagon and looked around, but he realized he would find no tracks to indicate which direction Cap had taken. He roused the rest of the men. "Let's scatter and see if we can find him. He may be out of his head, so be careful how you approach him."

He caught his own night horse from the picket line and made a wide circle. It was too dark. He could have passed within ten feet of Cap without seeing him. He gave up and returned to the wagon. The rest of the men began coming in. Nobody had found a trace.

Jeff looked toward the eastern sky for the first sign of daybreak. "We'll go out again soon's we have any light at all."

It was custom to keep the coffeepot on coals for the night guards. Booth went to the chuckbox for a cup. He never got it. He shouted, "Cap's six-shooter is gone!"

Cap always kept his pistol, its holster and belt in the chuckbox when he was not wearing it. Jeff went to see for himself, his eyes meeting Booth's in dismay.

As soon as first daylight began to break through the darkness, the men silently mounted their horses and began to scatter for another search. Jeff had barely left camp when he heard a shot. One distant pistol shot, echoing back from the hills.

He touched spurs to his night horse. Kelly Booth pulled up beside him and took hold of Jeff's reins. "No! You don't want to go."

Jeff fought Booth for the reins. "Turn aloose!"

"You know what he's done. You don't want to see him, not like this. Let us go fetch him in."

Jeff gave up the fight. Cap had walked away far enough that the shot would not stampede the herd, then had spared himself the agony of a long and frightful dying. And he had spared his friends the agony of watching.

Jeff dismounted and leaned against the horse. He had held back his tears at the time of his father's death. Now, for Cap, he held back nothing.

TWENTY-THREE

The rope and leather thongs had seared blisters around Crow Feather's neck and wrists. The binding of his arms behind his back had forced him to walk in an unnatural position that brought cramping between his shoulder blades and a general stiffness in all of his upper body. In breaking a horse, it was customary to cause the animal to feel pain when it made a move the breaker did not intend. He supposed the soldiers were trying to break him like a horse.

They had jerked him down several times, the rope choking him and burning into his flesh. He had soon realized that resistance was useless and certain to cause suffering. It might even anger the soldiers enough that they would murder him. Comanches had often killed prisoners who resisted to the point of antagonizing their captors. He expected no less at the hands of the bluecoats.

Somewhere, sometime, surely the bear spirit would give him a chance to escape. But each step took him farther from the canyon, farther from his hidden family.

Before nightfall the patrol came into a large camp where many more soldiers were gathered, their canvas tents set in military order, their horses picketed in long, straight lines. Crow Feather felt most of the white men's eyes turned on him. Some laughed and made remarks which he supposed were disparaging. Anger and shame warmed his face. He felt the fool, letting himself be brought to such a sorry state.

He was led to the far edge of the camp, where he saw several others like himself, most of them Comanche, including two women. There were a couple of Kiowas and a Cheyenne. All were breakaways, he assumed, or holdouts like himself who had finally been rooted from their hiding places. They acknowledged him with their eyes but made no other sign of recognition in the soldiers' presence. He gritted his teeth hard as a trooper removed the rope from around his neck. A warrior of pride would rather die than humiliate himself by letting his enemies see that they were causing him pain.

The soldier spoke while he untied the leather string that bound Crow Feather's hands. Crow Feather assumed he was issuing an admonition, but only the tone had any meaning; the words were like the growling of a surly dog. Crow Feather waited until the soldier no longer was watching before he gingerly rubbed the wrists to try to restore circulation. The flesh was raw and torn, stained with dried blood. The wrists burned as if he held them to a fire.

None of the other prisoners were of his band. He did not know whether to regard that as a good omen or bad. He feared his own were confined to the reservation, or were dead.

One of the prisoners recognized him. "I cannot say your name, but I remember you. I am of Three Bears' people. You once made us welcome to join you in the buffalo hunt. Later you went with Three Bears to the Cheyenne land to see for yourself how the *teibos* were slaughtering the buffalo."

Crow Feather admitted that he could not remember the man, but he remembered Three Bears very well. He assumed Three Bears must still live, for if he were dead this warrior would not be speaking his name. He would refer to him obliquely, if at all.

"Three Bears is a wise man," Crow Feather said. "He

saw while the rest of us covered our eyes. We waited too long before we heeded his counsel."

He recognized that he was not the only one who had been treated like a captured animal. Others' wrists and necks showed the bruises and abrasions of ropes and leather thongs, though few appeared as severe as his own. In particular he concentrated on the two women, who sat together a little apart from the men, their heads down. One had mutilated herself and cut her hair short, an indication of mourning. She made him think of White Deer, and his thoughts turned to escape.

He studied the soldier camp and counted four soldiers stationed around the little knot of prisoners. "We are three times their number. If we all acted together we could overwhelm them." He nodded toward the picket line where the army horses were tied. "We could each take a horse and be away."

"But each of the sentries could kill one of us before we could reach them," the warrior responded bleakly. "And the rest of the soldiers would be on us before we could reach the horses." He made a rubbing motion with his hand. "They would rub us all out and be glad. Look at their faces. They hate us."

That was only fair, Crow Feather thought, for he hated the soldiers. He hated what they had done to take away the freedom of his people. He hated the way they had dragged him from his family. He had done much thinking on the fate of White Deer and the children. Without him, they might well starve.

"What do you think they intend to do with us?"

"Take us back to the reservation, if they do not kill us on the way."

"Back? You have been on the reservation?"

"Yes. We were in the winter encampment when the soldiers came. They made us walk all the way. In the rain the one who was my wife became ill and died. In the winter I stole a soldier horse and escaped. Two days ago, they found me."

"How is it on the reservation?"

"They give us tents and blankets. They give us beef, though it is not enough, and it is not good like the buffalo. We have no freedom. They herd us as they herd their cattle and horses, and count us often to see if any are gone. They put over us one of their holy men. They call him Quaker. He is not a bad man, but he does not control the soldiers. Many among the bluecoats want to kill us. Only their chiefs hold them back."

Crow Feather considered the army's forbearance a weakness. Were the circumstances reversed, he would kill the soldiers. They had no business here. This was not their country.

He gave his attention for a while to the horses tied on the nearest picket line, trying to decide which was likely to be the fastest and have the most endurance.

The man from Three Bears' band said, "I know what is in your mind, for it was in mine. They wait for you to try so they can beat you with the butts of their rifles. Or shoot you, if you do not easily give up."

Crow Feather saw that the warrior's body bore many bruises, and his jaw was swollen. "You tried?"

"Last night. I never reached the horses."

"I cannot stay here. My family is hidden back there. Of what use am I to them as a prisoner?"

"Of what use would you be to them if you were dead?"

As darkness fell, soldiers came among the prisoners, giving them hard bread that was difficult to bite and chew, and boiled meat of an uncertain kind. Crow Feather suspected it might be dog, a mark of the soldiers' contempt. They knew Comanches did not eat dog, though Cheyennes would. The man of Three Bears' band assured him it was horse meat. He had seen them butcher a captured Indian horse before Crow Feather had been brought in. That was better. Crow Feather ate his fill, for he would need strength if he was to get away from here tonight.

The soldiers did not offer him a blanket. Being on a scouting expedition, they had little more in the way of provisions than the minimum they needed for themselves.

He tried to get some sleep early, knowing he would need stamina later if he managed to slip away. But after the setting of the sun came a spring night's chill, and he shivered. He probably would not have slept anyway, for the burns on his neck and hands and the knot that had lodged between his shoulder blades gave him no peace. He lay with his eyes open. He avoided looking at the soldiers' small campfire, for it would hamper his ability to see in the darkness. Besides, it teased him with its unattainable warmth.

He had made but little talk with the other captives except for the one from Three Bears' people. He considered inviting them all to join him in making a break. During the confusion it seemed likely that at least a few might get away in the darkness. He had no doubt that he would be one of those. But most would probably be sacrificed. He decided it would be selfish to cause others to die so that he might escape. He would make his break alone. With a little help from the bear spirit he might do it so quietly that the soldiers would not even know until daylight.

The guards changed at dark. There were still but four, though the rest of the camp was no more than a stone's throw away. Any alarm would bring many guns into play.

Though Crow Feather could not sleep, he thought it likely that the sentries sooner or later would feel the weight of fatigue. More than once he had bided his time at the edge of a *tejano* settlement until the stars had traveled half of their nighttime course, then had slipped in and escaped with horses beneath a sleeping settler's window.

Lying flat on his stomach, his head barely off the ground, he crawled as slowly as the hard-shelled terrapin, testing the nearest sentry's alertness. He had moved no more than the length of his arm when he heard the soldier cough and saw that the man was moving toward him. He went still, pretending that he had merely turned in his sleep. Eyes closed, he could sense the trooper standing so close that Crow Feather could smell the grease and the dried horse manure on the man's boots. After a time the sentry seemed satisfied and retreated. But he had shown that he was awake.

Crow Feather would have to wait.

He had had no experience with army sentries and did not realize they worked in shifts during the night. Disappointment came as bitter medicine when new guards came to relieve those who had done their tour of duty. By the stars he judged that the night was half over. His skin prickled with impatience, for now he must wait out a fresh set of sentries who might or might not ever relax their vigilance.

He waited until he was sure the eastern sky must soon yield up its stars to the first false light of dawn. He could wait no longer if he was to make his break this night. He had not seen any of the sentries move in some time. He could only hope they had dropped off to sleep. He began to crawl, as slowly and carefully at first as he had done earlier. When he detected no response, he moved faster, imitating the snake's silent gliding, his belly barely clear of the ground. He kept watching back over his shoulder.

When he had gone halfway to the picket line he pushed himself up into a low crouch and moved on noiselessly. Earlier, before dark, he had decided he liked the looks of a brown horse tied third from the end on the nearest line. He laid his hand on its tether and felt for the knot.

Something struck him on the back of the head, and he fell against the horse. Startled, it began to rear back on the rein, pulling the whole line taut and stirring up the rest of the horses. All of them were stamping, threatening to break the line in their sudden excitement.

He heard a loud voice, more triumphant than angry, and felt rough hands grabbing him. He fought free, only to be grabbed again, this time by more hands. He cried out in frustration and rage. Something struck him again, once between the shoulder blades, then across his temple. He fell amid a blinding shower of lights, as if he had been caught in the wind that carries the first sparks of a prairie fire. He felt a horse's hoof strike the middle of his back as the animal struggled to break free.

The rough hands began dragging him back toward the other prisoners. He could not see the soldiers, for a thousand tiny fires blazed before his eyes.

"Smart son of a bitch, ain't you?" a soldier snarled, though Crow Feather did not understand the words. "We were onto your little game. Mess around with us and next time we'll beat your brains out."

Another soldier said, "These bronco Indians, they're hard to convince."

"He'll be a good Indian time he's walked to the reservation with a rope around his neck. Or he'll be a dead one!"

Lieutenant John Gladwell, five years out of the Point and four years on the Indian-fighting frontier, walked from the Fort Sill guardhouse as he heard the horses approach. He buttoned his coat, which he had worn open for comfort so long as he could not be seen by officers of higher rank or by the enlisted men who seemed always to seek an excuse for slovenliness. He saw a squad of blue-clad troopers with a handful of Indian prisoners. All appeared gaunt and trail-weary, most especially the Indians, who had walked for days while the soldiers at least had traveled on horseback.

A sergeant saluted. "We rooted out a few more, sir. Most of them appear chastened enough. But there's this one Comanch . . . he's a hardcase. Kept tryin' to escape. Clubbin' wouldn't stop him. We finally had to tie him down every night."

Gladwell approached the Indian, careful to remain a little past arm's reach. One never knew what these savages might do. "The man has been injured rather severely. Has a doctor seen him?"

"Nobody's seen him but us, and we've seen him a way too much. I'd stand off a little farther was I you, sir. He's liable to jump you."

Gladwell held his ground. He did not want to give

any appearance of fear. "Has he actually attacked any-one?"

"No, he just kept tryin' to sneak off. But he'd fight like a catamount when we'd catch him. Some of the men've been sorely tempted to kill him."

Gladwell squinted thoughtfully, studying the battered warrior as if he were a horse up for auction. "An imposing specimen, all in all. I see an old scar on his side. Bullet wound, would you say?"

"I'd say so, sir. It healed ugly, but these Indians fancy their scars. They're like campaign ribbons."

The Comanche's eyes were swollen from the beatings, but through the narrow slits that remained open, Gladwell saw raw defiance glowing like banked coals. This one, he thought, would merit considerable observation. He studied Indians with the same detached scientific curiosity he devoted to the other wild flora and fauna of this isolated outpost.

"It's interesting to speculate on what motivates some of these people. Why would he keep trying when he must have known he would never succeed?"

"You can't judge them like regular human bein's, sir. They're more like wild animals. You ever try to tie up a wolf, or pen an antelope?"

"It is not as if we will tie him up. Once we feel he can be trusted, he'll have the run of the Comanche reservation."

"I don't know that this one can ever be trusted. I'm afraid he's a wild horse that nobody can ever break. He's liable to have to stay in the guardhouse till the day we carry him out to bury him."

"I hope he's not one of those who wills himself to die rather than accept the inevitable. Perhaps a few weeks inside the walls will convince him that the sun has set on the free-roaming Indian."

The sergeant had wearied of the discussion. "Trust him all you want to, sir. Just don't turn your back on him."

Gladwell saw dread in the Comanche's face as the

sergeant motioned for him to enter the guardhouse. The
sergeant spoke harshly and gave the man a push. The Indian spread his arms and braced himself against the door
facing, resisting until two more soldiers came to the sergeant's aid. One jabbed his rifle butt against the warrior's
kidneys. The reluctant Indian fell inside, and they grabbed
him by the arms, dragging him.

This one, Gladwell thought, *should make a fascinat-
ing study.*

TWENTY-FOUR

J eff found the crudely copied military map accurate in its delineation of the North Concho River and its description of the large spring north of the Concho headwaters. Around the spring he found empty tins and bottles and boxes, ample sign that the military had used it often in recent times. Old tepee rings and burned-out campfire pits indicated that it had been an Indian gathering place for ages. Fresh tracks told him buffalo were in the habit of watering there, and wild horses. He decided to rest the cattle again, scattering them on grass within easy reach of the water. He did not want to stress the cows so much that it seriously affected the milk flow to their calves.

There was more to it than the welfare of the cattle. The loss of Cap Doolittle made it difficult to muster the will for riding on. Jeff awoke each morning expecting to see Cap standing in the chuck wagon's lantern light, preparing breakfast for the crew. He listened for the big man's voice and thought a hundred times what Cap would say about this or that or some other thing. It was as if someone had cut off his right arm.

There were times when he considered driving the cattle back down to Fort Concho and seeking a buyer. The heart had gone out of him.

The third day at the spring he heard the wagon approaching before he saw it. He had a hunch it carried

Arletta and English, catching up. He braced himself for the difficult duty of telling them about Cap.

Their grim faces indicated that they already knew. They must have passed the new grave and the crude headboard for which he had used a tail gate out of the trail wagon. He had carved Cap Doolittle's name, the date and a single word: *Friend*. Inevitably, wind or animals or simply the ravages of time would tip the board and leave it to rot on the ground. The grave would grass over, and in the future no one would know that a good man lay buried there.

Arletta spoke first, her voice on the point of breaking. "What happened to Cap?"

Jeff knew no easy way, so he told her the straight of it, neither withholding nor embellishing anything.

She looked down at her hands, then at the baby in its cradle at her feet. "He did it for us . . . for me and the baby. I feel so guilty . . ."

Smithwick put his arm around his wife's shoulder. Jeff reached out to take her hands in one of his own. "You've got nothin' to feel guilty about. You didn't call that coyote into camp. Your first thought was to keep it away from the baby, and you did right. Cap's first thought was to save you, and he was right. He was unlucky, that's all, and a little careless. He should've looked himself over to see if that coyote might've nicked him too. He just didn't think of it."

He saw that she did not totally accept what he said. He asked, "What about you? Are you sure you're all right?"

"I was till I saw Cap's grave. Looks like the madstone must've worked, else I'd be where he is." She cleared her throat and sat up straight. "Who's been doin' the cookin'?"

"First one and then another, mostly one of the Gallegos boys. We ain't been where we could find a new cook."

"I haven't felt like I was totin' my weight up to now. I'll take over the chuck wagon."

It would be good for Arletta to have work enough to keep her hands and her mind occupied. Smithwick nodded his approval. Jeff said, "Fine. The Gallegos boy don't pick the rocks out of his beans."

That night Arletta fixed biscuits in one of Cap's big black Dutch ovens, using sourdough starter Cap had kept alive for years. The aroma as she lifted the coal-covered lid, then the flavor as Jeff bit into his first hot, brown-crusted one, was the same as it had always been when Cap had made them.

Arletta said, "He was a good teacher." She turned away so Jeff could not see her tears. He probably could not have seen them anyhow, for his own were in the way.

She asked, "When're we goin' on?"

"On? I don't know if I even want to. Without Cap . . ."

She turned back to face him. "You're quittin'?"

"I've done some studyin' on it."

"What do you think Cap would say?"

"There's no way to know."

"You're wrong. When did you ever see Cap back away from somethin' just because it looked tough? Once he made up his mind to do it, he whipped up the mules and let the devil take the hindmost. If he was here he'd tell you to do the same thing. And he'd probably cuss you for even thinkin' otherwise."

"He'd cuss, all right."

"Then don't even think about quittin'. He'd be mad at you, mad as hell that you'd come this far and thought about turnin' back." She put her hands on her hips. "I think I'm a little mad at you myself. I've never seen you give up on anything before."

Chagrined, Jeff considered his response. "Cap always got up and started fixin' breakfast about four. Will that be too early for you?"

The heifer they had bought for a milk cow birthed her calf one night on the bed ground. She had never been broken to the milking procedure, so the cowboys had to rope and tie her to something steady, like a bush if one was nearby, a wagon if nothing else was available. Jeff delegated Owen Palmer to do the milking, which subjected him to bruises even though the heifer's hind feet were tied, and a lot of tail-switching which struck him in the face or across the back of the neck.

"You wanted adventure," Jeff reminded him.

Arletta's baby took eagerly to the milk, which even to Palmer seemed to make the effort worthwhile.

From the big spring northward, the military map was sketchy. It showed a great many canyons, though Jeff could not discern from it which was the one he sought. Places on the map bore notations about good grass or no grass, good water, bad water or no water. But much of the plains region remained a mystery. Only recently had the military begun systematic explorations that would result in accurate mapping. Not yet were all the Indian trails followed to their ends, nor all the hidden watering places found and noted. That would require time, patience and pain for many unlucky soldiers from Concho and other posts.

He knew he would have to pick his own way northward, filling in for himself the missing parts. From here it seemed likely that the canyon he wanted lay northward with possibly a slight deviation to the east. The trip up the North Concho had carried him a little farther west than he had intended, but the extra distance had been justified by the grass and dependable water. From here the herd would cross the upper end of the Colorado River and pass west of the Double Mountains. It would swim at least two branches of the Brazos and almost surely the Red. But between these rivers and streams he had to scout out unmapped watering places for the cattle.

Few white men, other than soldiers—and not any great number even of those—had traversed much of this terrain. Its grazing potential was tremendous, and after the graziers would come the farmers. But until the Comanches and the Kiowas had been driven to the reservation it would have been foolhardy trying to settle there. Maps and deeds on file in Austin had been worthless pieces of paper, for actual possession was all that counted, and the Indians had that.

Moving away from the spring toward the Mucha Que peak to the north, Jeff was struck by the large number of buffalo he had to chase aside to clear a path for the cattle. It would not be long, he knew, before hide hunters would filter southward from the railroad, killing every buffalo they could roust out of the draws and headers. Given the speed at which they had decimated the herd in Kansas, he thought it likely that four or five years would see the end of the buffalo in Texas, at least in practical terms. A dozen times he wanted to lope over to the chuck wagon and tell Cap to come with him and look. Each time, the pain of the loss would strike him anew.

The buffalo, often a thousand or more within view at one time, were a sight few people would ever enjoy again. He knew that, and he took advantage of it every time he could. He pointed it out to Arletta, who now drove the chuck wagon. "I want you to look and remember so you can tell Becky someday. By the time she's old enough to remember, it'll all be gone."

Arletta said, "I've seen them in Kansas, bigger herds than this. I hate to think that I had a part in wipin' them out."

"We'll have no part in killin' off these. We'll be buildin' somethin' instead of tearin' down."

He realized that what they had done in Kansas had not been entirely negative. In helping bring the buffalo and Indian era to an end they had set the stage for a new era, that of the settler, the farmer, the prairie town.

In taking this herd up onto the plains, they were opening a new doorway for Texas. They would not themselves eliminate the buffalo, but their enterprise depended to a substantial degree upon others doing just that. Once the buffalo were gone the Indians could never return, and the Texas plains would open for settlement as those in Kansas had.

It would be for future generations to argue the right

and the wrong of it. For Jeff's generation, few except the Indians themselves would even debate the point.

He explored the rim of the caprock where the plains broke away abruptly on the south and the east. It would be unnecessarily arduous to drive a herd through the ragged canyons that fingered off in a rainbow of colors beneath. It would be far simpler to keep the cattle up on top, where the terrain was flat or rolled gently, where trees and brush were too scant to obscure his view of the distant horizon. He would skirt along the fractured edge of the plain, watching for the vague landmarks that would lead him to the specific canyon burned into his memory. He could only guess how far north that would be from here. Many days . . . many, many days. And though the numerous canyons he saw stretching off eastward and southeastward looked much alike, he was sure that when he came to his own he would know it.

Nigel Smithwick looked weary when they bedded down the cattle for the night, several days north of the big spring. It was hard for Jeff to imagine how different this wild country must be from the staid and settled England Smithwick had known most of his life.

Jeff said, "You're weakenin', partner. We could stop awhile and throw them down into any one of these canyons. There's grass enough, and water."

"You would not be satisfied. And if you were dissatisfied, Arletta and I would be dissatisfied too. So lead on, partner. We are with you all the way."

One day George Newby, riding point, turned his horse around and began waving his hat. Jeff thought he could hear the old cowboy shouting, though the wind and several thousand plodding hooves fragmented the sound of Newby's voice. Loping up, Jeff saw perhaps fifteen riders approaching from the northwest. He thought first of Indians and felt vulnerable. He had been assured at Fort Concho that few Indians remained at large on the plains, but it would not be the first time he had found the military to be mistaken.

"It's soldiers," Newby said, which made Jeff wonder

how the man's eyes could be so much better than his own. Newby was probably ten years older. But Nature was not always evenhanded in passing out her blessings. "You don't reckon they're goin' to make us turn back?"

"I don't see that they've got any such right. They don't own this country, though I've known a few who thought they did."

Heading up the patrol was a first lieutenant of about Jeff's age or perhaps a bit older, his thick moustache salted with gray strands and brown dust. He raised a gloved hand and pointed to the herd, stretched out for a quarter mile. "What in the name of Joseph and Mary is that?"

Jeff turned as if to see. "Last time I looked, it was cows." No Confederate officer would ever have asked such a foolish question.

"I can see that. But what are you doing with them up here? The cattle trails to Kansas are a hundred miles to the east."

"We're not headed for Kansas. We're takin' them a little ways north of here."

"This is buffalo country, not cattle range."

"Where we're goin', it'll be cattle range when we get there."

The officer stared at the oncoming herd as if he still found it difficult to believe. "You know, don't you, that we've barely cleared the Indians out of this country? We can't guarantee that we've found them all, or that some we've driven away won't come back. We're scouting now for a few who have broken out of the reservation."

"Indians are your job, not ours. We're just lookin' for grass. We won't bother any Indians if they don't bother us."

"We can't guarantee your safety. By all rights, I should turn you back."

"Except that you've got no right to do it. We're all freeborn American citizens here. Exceptin' for an Englishman and a Mexican or two I'm not sure of. So I don't see that we're any concern of yours."

"You will be. At the first sign of trouble you'll be crying for our help."

"I'll make you the same deal I make the Indians, Lieutenant. You don't bother us and we won't bother you."

The man's moustache twitched. "Is that a promise?"

"I've never called on the government for help. I don't figure to start now."

"Very well. You may proceed."

Like if you had any authority to stop us, Jeff thought. "We'll be makin' camp in a couple of hours. We killed a beef yesterday, so there's plenty of meat. We'd be glad to share if you'd like to camp with us tonight."

The chuck wagon was approaching. The lieutenant's eyes widened. "Is that a woman I see?"

"Sure is. She's got a baby with her, and a husband back with the herd."

"Holy Mary and Joseph! I thought it might be ten years before I saw a white woman up on these plains. The age of miracles has not passed." He broke into a smile. "Yes sir, I believe we will camp with you. I want to learn what manner of people you Texans really are."

"We're just like everybody else." Jeff winked at the silent but amused Newby. "Only a little different."

The appearance of the open plains changed but little from one day to the next. Most of the time the land appeared generally flat, and one could see for miles, all the way to a level horizon that at times seemed to blend with the sky so that it gave the impression of extending into the clouds. The Enríquez brothers complained that it made them nervous to see so far. They were used to the South Texas brush that limited their view, that put close limits on the world with which they had to contend.

Luis said, "I feel like somebody is watching me from a long way off and seeing me naked. There is no place to hide."

"What is there to hide from?" Nigel Smithwick asked him.

"From all my sins, and all the sins I have thought of."

* * *

Jeff was not sure at first, but something in the roll of the prairie gave him pause. Then he found a place where the constant wind had scoured out two parallel gullies in the soft earth, about as far apart as the right and left wheels of a wagon. He rode eastward a little way to a point where the plain broke away. There he looked down into a broad valley which stretched before him for miles. Far to the east he could see a broken line of hills that marked the other side of the valley. Small timber delineated the meandering path of a creek. Well to the north he noted a freestanding peak isolated in the western part of the valley, an erosion-resistant remnant that reminded him of a wide stone chimney standing in lonesome isolation after a cabin has burned.

His heartbeat quickened with excitement. He rode back to the herd, waving at Arletta as he passed the chuck wagon. He pulled in beside Nigel Smithwick. "How's your memory for landmarks?"

"I've given it very little test since we ascended the caprock. All this open prairie looks much the same."

"How about comin' with me? I want you to see somethin'."

They loped back to the place where Jeff had looked down into the valley. He pointed to the distant freestanding formation. "I think we're at the bottom end of the canyon, where it opens out onto the broken country to the south and east."

He began riding northward along the edge, eagerly pushing the sorrel horse into a trot. He came to a place where the wall broke back and a benign slope led down to the valley floor. "Ain't this where we brought up the wagons after we got them loaded with hides?"

He could see gullying where there had not been grass enough to hold the soil together against wind and rain after the wheels' heavy pressure had cut deep ruts into the earth.

Smithwick nodded vigorously. "You're right. We had to double the teams and pull the wagons up one at a time. This is the place."

It would be many miles up to the head of the canyon where the walls were higher and narrowed on both sides. Jeff had found the upper end first while scouting for fresh hunting range. Standing on the rim, he had stared down in fascination at the canyon floor, where big shaggies grazed in peaceful indifference to the slaughter that awaited them. He had discovered a zigzag game trail beaten out by buffalo and other animals in their migrations back and forth between the sheltered canyon floor and the high prairie above. It had been too narrow for wagons, so another place had to be found farther down the canyon for their descent.

This slope was much gentler, but still a little steep for comfort. Jeff said, "To be safe, we'll take the wagons down one at a time." He grinned. "Arletta'll be pleased. I know she's been lookin' forward to the end of this trip."

"The baby seems to have thrived on it, though. I am afraid she'll grow up with restless feet and be difficult to keep at home."

They rode back and signaled for the cowboys to hold up the herd. Taking the wagons down into the valley would be the first priority. Jeff and Smithwick rode to Arletta. Jubilantly, Jeff told her, "We're almost there."

"Praise the Lord. I was beginnin' to watch for railroad tracks. It looked like we was goin' all the way to Dodge City." She corrected herself. "*Were* goin'."

"I figure we're a couple hundred miles south of Dodge. Maybe more. But it's about as close as any town we could go to in Texas."

This was the Panhandle region of the state. Somewhere to the north lay whatever was left of Adobe Walls, the hide-trading post where the big Indian fight had taken place. To the northeast, in Indian Territory, would be the military's Camp Supply. East or a bit southeast would be Fort Sill, headquarters for the Indian reservation to which the Comanches, the Kiowas and the Cheyennes had been pushed. By the map he calculated that it was more than two hundred miles back southward to Cap Doolittle's lonely grave, and three hundred or a bit more to Fort Concho.

Arletta's chuck wagon was first to descend the steep slope. As she started to put the team into motion, Kelly Booth rode up and cut her off. "You walk and carry the baby. I'll take the wagon down."

"I've driven down worse than this," she protested.

"You wasn't motherin' a child then." He dismounted from his horse and reached up to help her down from the wagon seat.

"I've never called on others to do somethin' for me that I could do for myself." But she gave up the argument. She lifted the baby from its cradle and stepped back out of the way.

Jeff had reservations about Booth because of his penchant for recklessness, but he said nothing. He and three cowboys tied ropes to the wagon to hold it in check for the descent. Booth seemed to take delight in speed and did not use the foot brake until it appeared the wagon was about to get loose from him and overrun the team.

Jeff was much relieved when the wagon reached the valley floor. He was glad Arletta had not chosen to ride down with Booth. She walked behind the wagon, carrying the baby.

"We could've carried a basket of eggs and not broken a one, if we'd had any eggs," Booth told Arletta as she walked up to examine the wagon.

"We *will* have eggs one of these days. First thing I'm goin' to send for once we get settled is a crate of layin' hens."

"The wolves and the coyotes'll be pleased."

"And I'll nail their hides to the barn door."

They brought the other wagons down in the same manner as the first. Booth let the hoodlum wagon drop both wheels on its left side into a washout and spill part of its load of bedrolls. Jeff decided that henceforth the cowboy should not be trusted with any vehicle larger than a wheelbarrow, and they did not have one of those. It took a considerable amount of pushing, pulling, heavy lifting and blistering profanity to get it righted and moved the rest of the way down the slope.

Jeff was glad Arletta was out of earshot, though he suspected she had heard it all before. It was almost impossible for a woman to avoid overhearing such language from time to time. If she wanted to be ladylike she pretended deafness or, at the least, pretended she did not know what the words meant.

Once the wagons were in the valley and moved back out of the way, the cowboys started bringing the cattle down, narrowing the file to lessen the chance of animals being crowded into the gullies and risking broken legs. Queenie led the way. Jeff sat on his sorrel horse at the bottom and gloried in the sight of the herd spilling down over the rim, dust boiling upward over a swirling mass of horns. Cows and calves lost one another in the slipping and sliding descent, so that the gathering below was a boiling aggregation of walking, searching, bawling mothers and young.

He wondered if he had ever seen a spectacle more pleasing to his eyes.

Nigel Smithwick pulled his horse in beside Jeff's. "Shall we disperse them along the creek? The grass looks good."

"They'll be wantin' to drift south, down into that rough country. Let's push them up toward the head of the canyon before we turn them loose. It'll take them longer to work their way back down here."

Hemmed in by the canyon walls, the cattle would be able to drift in only one direction. From now on it would be a regular job for the hands to ride the southern end of the valley and keep the animals pushed back, lest they lose themselves in the rugged little canyons and cedarbrakes far below.

The sun dropped down over the western wall, and shadows spread eastward like a dark blanket. The herd was still a few miles short of the head of the canyon, but it had a lifetime to do that.

"Turn them a-loose!" Jeff shouted.

The cowboys pulled back, and the cattle stopped walking as realization slowly spread that they were no longer being pushed. Cows and calves mated up, and a slow drift began toward the creek. Jeff sat contentedly, his hands braced atop the saddle horn. He watched them drink their fill, then begin scattering to graze. Some of the cows warily eyed a handful of buffalo, giving them room enough. The buffalo, their eyesight weak, seemed to be made nervous by the unaccustomed scent of the cattle. They sniffed the wind, then edged away, switching their tails in agitation.

Jeff had mixed feelings. On the one hand he was gratified that at least some buffalo had found their way into the canyon despite last year's heavy slaughter. On the other he knew that if there were many buffalo he would have to drive them away lest they present too much competition for the grass. He had a gut feeling that cattle and buffalo would not be a peaceful mix. One or the other had to give. Inevitably, that would be the buffalo. For this plains country to develop large cattle ranches in the style of southern Texas, the buffalo would have to yield. And they would; the price of hides would guarantee that.

Smithwick asked, "What about camp?"

"Tell Arletta to stop wherever she wants to. Tomorrow we'll start lookin' for the best place to set up permanent." He felt a warm glow of contentment as he looked over the cattle, the riders, the wagons. "Tell her we're home."

Smithwick trotted toward the chuck wagon. Jeff settled back in the saddle, smiling to himself. He had gone to South Texas seeking peace and finding none. Now a profound sense of peace settled over him, a calm he could not remember that he had ever felt before.

Only one element was missing. He wished Cap were here to share it.

Little Squirrel had never seen the white man's cattle before. The sight of them was unsettling to say the least. He had heard talk of them, but he had imagined they were much like the buffalo. These creatures were unlike anything he had ever seen, in reality or in his dreams. Smaller than the buffalo, they were of all colors, whereas the buffalo ran to brown and black, though buffalo calves had a reddish coat. The cattle's horns were long, twisting or curling toward the ends, and their legs were longer than those of the buffalo. When they ran their gait was even, without the buffalo's awkward rocking motion.

What bothered him most was not the cattle themselves but what they represented. White men had moved into the canyon. He had seen them a-horseback, close enough that he knew they were not soldiers. They did not wear blue uniforms or ride in single or double file as troopers often did.

He considered putting an arrow through one of them so he could examine him closely, for he had never been near enough to a white man to touch him, to see if the skin was really that pale or if it was made so by some sort of medicine paint. It seemed probable to him that the white man served a different set of spirits than the People, and the requirements of those spirits would not be the same. He hid in the brush and watched one of the *teibos* approach, near enough that Squirrel could see the dark hair on his face, above and below his mouth like the beard beneath the chin of a buffalo. He wore a hat with a very wide brim that threw a shadow not only across his face but over his shoulders as well.

Curious, Squirrel thought.

Squirrel might have been able to put an arrow into him, but he decided against it. There were other white men in the canyon. He had counted as many, almost, as the fingers on his two hands. If this one were killed he would surely be missed, and the others' search for him might result in their finding the family's hiding place.

When the man rode away, Squirrel arose from hiding. He had been stalking a deer, but it was gone now, frightened by the rider. He feared that might be the start of a pattern. The deer might not stay in the canyon now that the white man was here. Nor might the buffalo, for it was well known that wherever the white man went, the buffalo were rapidly killed off.

If this came to pass, what would his family eat? Since his father's disappearance, Squirrel had managed to keep enough meat in camp that no one went hungry. He had killed rabbits and squirrels. He had killed deer. He had even killed a couple of buffalo.

Now hunting would be more difficult, for not only might the game disappear, but he would be in constant danger of discovery by the white men. He wished his father were here. *Powva* would know what to do.

Several cows and their calves drifted by him. He wondered how their meat would taste compared to that of the buffalo. Probably not nearly so good, he thought, for the spirits which protected the People had created the buffalo. He had no idea what spirits, if any, had created cattle.

At least the cattle were not as difficult to stalk as deer. Staying downwind, he moved close and fitted an arrow to the string. He considered a cow but knew her carcass would be much too heavy for him to carry back to the hiding place in one trip. The white men might discover whatever he had to leave behind. He drew back the string and drove his arrow behind the last rib of a brindle calf. The little animal gave a surprised snort and went down on its hind legs, as he had seen buffalo drop. It flopped onto its side and kicked a few times while its mother anxiously nosed around it. Catching the blood scent, she gave a deep-throated bawl such as he had never heard. A chill ran along his back at the sound of it.

He summoned his courage and went out to claim his kill. For a moment he thought the cow was about to charge him, as she lowered her head and threatened with her sharp horns. But she lost heart and ran a few steps, stopping to turn and face him, slinging her head in futile bluster.

He cut the calf's throat and watched its lifeblood pump out into the sand.

Perhaps it was not a bad thing that the white men had come. Their cattle were easy to hunt.

TWENTY-FIVE

J eff knew as soon as he saw it that this was the place. He found it some five miles below the head of the canyon, where the valley was about a mile wide. A large spring bubbled forth near the base of the hundred-foot wall and started a narrow tributary snaking its way toward the creek that ran more or less down the valley's center. The headquarters would be built far enough out from the overhanging cliff that it would not be endangered by falling rocks or sloughing-off, yet near enough to gain protection from cold winter winds scouring the plain above. Cottonwood trees along the creek would provide summer shade.

He showed the site first to Nigel Smithwick, then the two of them took Arletta there in the wagon. Jeff said eagerly, "Now, the final choice is up to you, and if you see a better place you're welcome to it. I wouldn't want to influence you one way or the other. But this is the prettiest spot in the canyon. There ain't no need in lookin' for a better one."

Holding the baby, she pointed to marks in the earth, lines he had made with a long stick. "Looks like you've already laid out your plans."

"Don't let that sway you if you'd rather go someplace else. But right here is where we can build you and English a dugout to live in till we can afford to haul in lumber and build you a real house. Yonder's where we'll put *that,* when the time comes, under the biggest cottonwood. And over there'll be the bunkhouse, and out yonder the barn and the corrals. I've got it all figured. But you make up your own mind."

She smiled at his enthusiasm and touched her husband's arm. "Whatever you and Nigel want to do, I'll be tickled with it."

Jeff said, "It'll be a great place to raise Becky and her brothers and sisters. All the room in the world for them to run and play in."

She lifted the baby, touching her cheek to its forehead. "And fall into the creek and get all wet and muddy, and run off to where I can't find them when I need them. It'll be just fine."

They had brought no plow, but one of the first things Arletta did was to mark off a large garden plot and laboriously begin breaking it into rows with a hoe.

Jeff told her, "We intended this to be a ranch, not a farm."

"We're goin' to have some tomatoes and some okra and some squash and stuff." She pushed back her slat bonnet and wiped sweat from her brow. "We can't live on beef and buffalo and venison alone. I want somebody to start puttin' up a fence so we can keep the cattle and horses out of my garden. And first time anybody goes to a town for supplies, I want a garden plow."

"And a crate of chickens. What else?"

"I'll think of some more. We'll make this place look like a home."

Her labor in the garden soon shamed her husband and Kelly Booth into taking over the job for her.

Jeff had known that all the hands would not stay. He had seen the increasing uneasiness of the Enríquez brothers as they had ridden for days across the featureless plains. He was not surprised one afternoon when he found Gabino leaning on a shovel, talking earnestly to Luis at the site where they were digging into a slope for the Smithwick dugout. He could read the message in their faces before Gabino even spoke.

"Mr. Jeff, pretty soon now my brother and me, we are going home."

"Maybe this country'll grow on you if you give it a chance."

"My brother grows sick for home. And me . . . well, there is a girl . . ."

Jeff smiled. "You don't have to explain. I'm much obliged you've stayed with us this long. I'll pay you when you're ready to go."

They stayed long enough to finish excavating for the dugout, then left. One of the Gallegos cousins went with them, but two decided to stay. Jeff watched the other hands, wondering if some of them might take it into their minds to drift south too.

George Newby, the old trail driver, seemed from the first to like the canyon. "I expect that I've rode fifty thousand miles on horseback in my life, and all the time this place was waitin' for me not five hundred miles away."

Owen Palmer, who had joined the drive expecting adventure, was disappointed that he had not seen one Indian anywhere along the way. Jeff told him, "If you'd been here a year ago you'd've seen enough to last you till you're a hundred and six."

"You told me you figure it's maybe two hundred miles north to Dodge City. I think I'll take me a *pasear* up thataway and see it. They tell me a man can get himself plenty of action up there."

"More than enough sometimes." Jeff had seen about all he wanted of it. "Are you figurin' on comin' back?"

"If I don't have to milk that damned cow anymore."

"Deal. How about takin' a wagon and fetchin' back some stuff for Arletta?"

"Fine, if you ain't in no hurry."

"Take your own good time." With the money Palmer had in his pockets, it would not take long for Dodge to clean him out. "Just be sure you buy the supplies first, before you do anything else."

He had thought the silent Herman Wurtz was the most likely to decide to leave, other than the Enríquez brothers. Occasionally, when Wurtz spoke at all, he forgot himself and started talking in his native language. Jeff had thought he would want to return to one of the German settlements where he would be among his own kind. But from the first he accepted the solitude of the canyon. "At Fredericksburg they talk too much of the old country," Wurtz said. "This is a new country, and a new life."

Jeff thought he had enough cowboy help to take care of starting a new ranch. Besides himself there were Nigel Smithwick, Kelly Booth, George Newby, Owen Palmer, Herman Wurtz and two Gallegos cousins. Even if a couple of these decided sooner or later to leave, the operation would be manageable. He just hoped he could finish the summer's essential construction work before he lost any more.

The Smithwicks would be using their tent until the dugout was ready. Jeff and the other men could continue to live outdoors as they had lived on the trail, sleeping in their bedrolls, eating from the chuck wagon. But before snow fell, they should have better shelter. Even under the canyon wall, winter could be punishingly cold.

Kelly Booth rode in one day with troubled eyes. "Jeff, have you seen any varmint tracks?"

"What kind of varmint?"

"I don't know, but it looks like we must be sharin' this canyon with some kind of critter that likes beef. Bear, maybe, or a painter. I found a cow this mornin' toward the head of the canyon. Her bag was fit to bust. I remember that cow from the trail. She had a heifer calf. She ain't got it now."

"Maybe it just died."

"I didn't find any trace. That's the second cow I've seen lately that's lost a calf up in that part of the canyon."

Jeff looked up at the high wall. The sun had dropped behind it an hour ago. "Me and you'll go up there in the mornin' and hunt around. More'n likely there's a den with a she-wolf and a bunch of hungry pups."

After breakfast he left Nigel Smithwick to supervise the construction and rode north with Booth toward the

narrowest part of the canyon. It was not difficult to find
the cow. Her udder was full, the teats strutted. They roped
her head and heels, stretched her on the ground and
milked her enough to relieve the pressure. Nature would
take care of the rest, drying her up until the next calf
came. The cow arose looking for someone to fight. The
two men gave her room to let her temper settle.

Jeff said, "I'll ride on this side of the creek. You take
the west side. Maybe we'll see somethin', tracks at least."

They moved slowly, in a walk. Jeff searched the
ground for paw prints and looked out across the valley for
any likely-looking place that might contain a den. He was
aware that he could ride within rock-throwing distance of
one and miss it. Wolves and coyotes were canny enough to
keep their holes inconspicuous, and they rarely killed
nearby lest they give their hiding place away. All he saw,
besides cattle, was a startled doe that bounded out of her
hiding place in the creek's scrub timber and dashed across
to Booth's side. Seeing Booth, she cut back, disappearing
in the brush.

Jeff had gone a mile or so when he heard two pistol
shots in quick succession. Whirling, he saw Booth spurring
a fast retreat. Jeff put the sorrel into a lope, barely slowing
as he splashed across the creek. He reined up beside the
wide-eyed cowboy. "By the looks of you, you jumped a
grizzly bear."

"It was a wolf. A two-legged one. He shot an arrow
at me out of that brush yonder." Booth brought his hands
to within inches of each other. "Just missed me by that
far."

Jeff was dubious. "Did you see him?"

"A wink was all. But I damned sure saw the arrow."

"Maybe you hit him."

"You know how poor a shot I am with a pistol. Probably scared him about as bad as he scared me, but I doubt
I drawed any blood on him."

Jeff pondered what to do. The lieutenant had warned
him there might still be some Indians about, but he had
chosen not to let that possibility deter him. Now here it

was, a reality. He had had all the Indian fighting he ever wanted. He had come here seeking a peace that had eluded him elsewhere. He had no wish for trouble. Still, the knowledge that one or more Indians were hiding in the canyon would keep everybody uneasy.

"Maybe if you scared him as bad as he scared you, he'll leave." But that was by no means assured. "We'd best go see if we can pick up his tracks. Maybe we can find where he's holed up. But let's don't crowd him. I don't want no flint arrowhead lodged amongst my vitals."

Booth retraced his path, leaning far out of his saddle to pick up an arrow stuck at an angle in the sand. "It wasn't no four-legged wolf shot this at me." He handed it to Jeff.

Jeff fingered it with curiosity. "Looks a little shorter than the ones I've had sent my way." He had never made a study of arrows, but he knew that various tribes had their own individual ways of marking them. This one was utilitarian, without any decoration beyond the trimmed feathers set in the end to make it fly straight.

They moved cautiously toward the brush that lined this portion of the creek. Jeff carried his saddle gun across his lap. He trusted it far more than the pistol on his hip. Booth had the hammer of his pistol cocked back, though in Jeff's opinion he could not hit a barn with it from the inside.

From the corner of his eye Jeff caught a glimpse of movement far ahead. It could have been anything . . . a wolf, a rabbit, a calf, or simply imagination. But he had a hunch about it. "I think your Indian just went yonder."

Booth was about to spur off in pursuit, but Jeff cautioned him to hold back. "Been many a man lured into a trap that way, better shots than you are."

Shortly, he found tracks in the sand. He dismounted and dropped to one knee. "Moccasins. And little ones, like they was made by a woman, or a kid."

"You think it was a woman shot that arrow at me?"

"If so, you and her could both stand some marksmanship practice. Let's see if these tracks take us anywhere."

Following them was a slow process, for they were frequently lost in the grass. Jeff made no claim to being an expert tracker. He and Booth would zigzag until they cut across the footprints again, leading toward the west wall. Jeff remembered the game trail that had first brought him down into this canyon. As he recalled, it was a bit farther north. Perhaps the fugitive was making for it. That seemed odd, for once on top he would be in the open, easy to see and follow. It was Jeff's guess that the Indian had left a horse tied somewhere and had been stalking a deer or a calf afoot. Once he—or she—reached the top, the chase would become simply a horse race. Depending upon the speed of his horse, he might very well get away.

That suited Jeff. Let the army worry about it. He had not lost any Indians.

He saw something he had not noticed before, a modest header which seemed to reach back beneath the canyon wall. A stand of timber had obscured it. The tracks led to a point where a narrow creek—actually only a rivulet—ended in a pool of water not more than eight or ten feet across. There the ground swallowed up the flow. The seep or spring which fed it was hidden behind the foliage near the overhanging cliff.

"Kelly, you've ridden out this canyon several times. Did you know this was here?"

"I don't reckon I ever got this close before."

"And I ain't sure I want to get any closer now." Jeff studied the small water hole. He found deer and cattle tracks and paw prints of several varieties of small animals. He also saw moccasin tracks, none of them man-size. "I think we'd best get down and walk. Keep our horses between us and whatever's in that timber."

His chest was tight with apprehension. It would have been easy to ride away and not disturb whoever or whatever was hidden in the trees. But he had come too far to turn back. "You still with me?"

"Yeah, but I'm kind of wishin' I was in San Antonio."

He saw the faces then . . . a woman in buckskin dress, a small girl and standing in front of them a boy he would guess to be no more than seven or eight. Wearing a breechclout, the boy held a bow, an arrow fitted to the string. All the faces were filled with fear.

"Whoa up. He's little, but he could kill one of us." Jeff stood still, studying the group with surprise. Behind them, hard to see beneath the foliage, was a tepee, smaller than most he had seen. The lodgepoles of a conventional-sized one would have extended above most of the trees, making the camp much more visible. On the ground he saw many moccasin tracks, none of them large.

"It's a family without menfolks, just a woman and two kids." He heard a sound from within the tepee, a sound like many he had heard from Arletta's baby. "There's another young'un inside."

Booth's expression turned to sympathy. "The daddy probably went and got himself killed. I'll bet these folks are hungry."

"I see what's left of a calf's leg hangin' by the tent. That boy's the only hunter they've got. He's been doin' the easiest thing, killin' our calves."

"Everybody has to eat. What're we goin' to do about them?"

"Notify the army, I guess."

"You sure the soldiers wouldn't just kill them?"

"Not a woman and kids, for God's sake."

"It's been done. Reckon how long they been here?"

"A lot longer than us, judgin' by the way the ground's packed. Probably wintered right where they're at."

"Then they've got more claim on this place than we have."

"That's not for me and you to decide. The government says they've got to go."

Booth's face twisted. "The same government told Santiago Ramírez and his family that *they* had to go."

"That was different."

"Not much, when you come down to it. What do we do now?"

"Nothin', except ease back out of here the same way we came. Next time we see any soldiers, we'll tell them."

"These folks might be gone by then."

That would suit Jeff. "No tellin' when we may see soldiers." He walked, leading his horse a little way before he mounted. He did not want to cause the Indian family more fright than he already had.

Booth said, "That doe you flushed across the creek a while ago, she ought not to be hard to find again."

"You got a taste for venison?"

"I was thinkin' that family could use the meat. They might go a little easier on your calves."

Jeff grinned. "There's times, Kelly Booth, when you act almost civilized."

"I remember how it was to be a hungry kid. And I expect it's what Cap would've done."

Being the better shot, Jeff brought down the doe with his saddle gun but stood back and allowed Booth the pleasure of gutting it. Booth laid it in front of him on the saddle, though his horse did not appreciate the smell of fresh blood and threatened for a moment to dump both rider and load. The two men returned to the header. They could not see the family now, for they had hidden somewhere back in the timber. But Jeff could feel their eyes upon him, and a chill ran down his back.

Booth shouted, "We've fetched you-all some meat." He allowed the doe to slip from the saddle. The horse made a sidewise jump as the carcass struck the ground at its feet. Booth grabbed at the saddle horn to keep from following the deer.

Jeff said, "I doubt that they savvy English."

"I'll bet they savvy meat."

Arletta was scandalized. "You mean you'd leave that poor woman out there in a tepee with all them young'uns?"

Jeff said defensively, "That's the way Indians live, in tepees."

"They could die."

"They won't starve. We'll keep them in meat as long as they're there. Venison . . . buffalo . . . anything so they'll leave our beef alone till the army shows up."

"No tellin' when that might be. I want you to take me there, Jeff. We're goin' to bring them in."

"Bring them here?"

"It's the Christian thing. We can't leave a woman and those little ones out there, helpless."

"They've got their own way of livin', different from ours. They won't want to come."

"Just let me talk to the woman."

"She won't understand what you're sayin'." Jeff looked to Nigel Smithwick for support, but the Englishman remained silent. He had lost arguments to his wife as Jeff was losing this one. Somebody—Jeff forgot who—had warned him long ago about arguing with a redheaded woman.

She said, "I learned to talk with my hands to Mexican women in Piedras. Women can always make theirselves understood to one another if menfolks will just leave them alone."

Next morning Jeff and Kelly Booth rode ahead of Arletta and her husband, who traveled in a wagon. He grumbled, "We'll be damned lucky if that Indian boy don't put an arrow in somebody."

Booth took up for Arletta. He always did. "She's got a good heart."

Jeff reined up at the small pool of water and pointed toward the trees. He saw no sign of life, but a little of the tepee was dimly visible through the foliage, now that he knew to look for it. "I'll go first. They've already seen me once. Maybe the boy won't shoot at me."

Arletta was already on the ground. She lifted her baby from the cradle. "No, I'll go. They'll know that a woman and a baby don't mean them no harm."

Nigel Smithwick joined her. "You'll not go alone. We'll walk together."

Jeff knew that arguing with Arletta when her mind was made up was like trying to hold back a storm. At any sign of danger Smithwick would quickly step in front of his wife. The Englishman had that kind of nerve. Jeff said,

"Go slow, then, and don't just stand there if they show fight."

He could almost feel angry at Booth for finding that cow without her calf. They could have remained in blissful ignorance until the Indians simply went away.

Arletta called softly, "Hello. We're here to help you."

Nobody appeared until she moved closer and called a second time. The Indian woman materialized from somewhere in the trees. Then came the boy and the girl. The boy was without his bow. Jeff breathed a little easier, but he and Booth did not crowd the Smithwicks.

Arletta began talking. She told the woman about the new ranch they were building, that there would be a nice place for them to camp at the headquarters, that they had a milk cow and there would be plenty for everybody to eat. The Indian woman could not possibly understand a word of it, but Arletta handed the baby to her husband so she had both hands free and supplemented her words with a lot of what might have passed for sign language.

Jeff could only guess what the woman was thinking, though he had a hunch she understood the gist of Arletta's argument, at least about going with her. And he could see that the woman was refusing.

After a long and futile session Arletta gave up. She returned to where Jeff and Booth waited. "The best I can tell, she wants to stay here till her man comes back."

"How long do you reckon he's been gone?"

"By the looks of the place, a long time."

"Then the best thing for us to do is to leave these folks alone . . . bring them meat to keep them fed till they leave or the soldiers come."

"No!" Arletta had a look in her eye that Jeff had seen on the buffalo range. It meant she would stand her ground till hell froze over six feet solid. "I looked inside that tepee. There's two babies in there. We won't leave her out here with those young'uns, all by herself."

She looked over her shoulder toward the hidden camp. "I'm comin' back tomorrow, and the next day and

the day after that, till I've convinced her. I think I'm a
stubborner woman than she is."

And she was. The third day, the Indian woman gave
in. They loaded her camp goods into the wagon. It had no
tail gate because that had been used for Cap's grave
marker. She rode sitting backward, holding the two babies, her legs hanging off the open end of the wagon bed.
The boy rode his pony behind, leading a mare with the
little girl sitting on its back.

TWENTY-SIX

Arletta moved her family into the dugout as soon as it was ready, but spent little of the daytime in its dark interior. She was usually at the chuck wagon preparing meals for the men or in her garden, hoeing out the weeds, breaking more ground. At first she saw little of the Indian woman, who had set up her small tepee beneath the cottonwoods and kept out of sight most of the time. But gradually the woman overcame most of her distrust and began to accept the new surroundings, the comings and goings of the ranch's men. She ventured out to watch in curiosity as Arletta worked her garden or kneaded up dough on the chuckbox lid.

Arletta wished they could converse, for she perceived that they had some things in common. Each was sustaining a family in a difficult situation. There were things each could offer the other if they could only communicate more readily. Through much of her life Arletta had been denied the company of other women. Now she had another woman living within a stone's throw, yet the best she could manage was a little awkward sign language. She offered to share the cow's milk for the two Comanche babies, but the woman declined. Arletta guessed she knew nothing about milk beyond the human kind. The woman did her own cooking on an outdoor fire despite Arletta's invitation for the family to eat at the chuck wagon with the cowboys.

The boy and girl overcame their shyness much quicker, their large brown eyes alive with interest in so many strange new things. The boy picked up Arletta's hoe when she laid it down. He chopped at vegetables as well as weeds until she showed him the difference. He began picking up and speaking a few English words: *hoe, garden, weeds, cow, baby* . . . He stumbled over *vegetables*. That one he could never get right.

He pointed to himself and spoke a word over and over. She surmised that it was his Comanche name, but she could not duplicate the sound of it. She called him what the cowboys had begun calling him: Dogie, the name for an orphaned calf. He accepted that, having no idea what it meant.

He seemed to like the cowhands instinctively, once he got past his initial fear. They catered to him, feeding him biscuits stuffed with strips of bacon or swabbed in canned molasses. In particular, he attached himself to Kelly Booth, following him around the headquarters, sometimes tagging along on his pony when Booth rode out on horseback. "Just like a little pup," Booth said, enjoying the attention. He carved a wooden whistle for the youngster.

Arletta supposed the boy favored Booth because the cowboy had taken the family a freshly killed deer the day he first discovered them.

One day as she was kneading up dough for biscuits, she heard the boy cry out and drag his small sister away from a patch of weeds. She wailed in fright.

"*Noo-be-er!*" he shouted at Arletta. "*Noo-be-er!*"

Cap's old six-shooter and cartridge belt were stowed where he had usually kept them, in the chuckbox behind a sourdough keg. She grabbed the pistol and went running. The Indian woman was just behind her. Arletta heard the singing of the rattles before she saw the snake, coiled and ready to strike, its forked tongue darting. Gripping the pistol in both hands, she drew back the hammer and blew the reptile's head off. The long body continued to convulse after the brain was shattered.

The Indian woman was talking excitedly to the two

children and anxiously searching the girl's body for a possible snake bite. She found none. Her voice went stern.
Arletta assumed she was giving the youngsters a lecture
about venturing into weedy areas where they could not see
what was on the ground.

When Arletta's own baby grew large enough to
wander around, it would have to submit to the same lecture, probably many times.

The boy stared in fascination at the smoking pistol,
then lifted an admiring gaze to Arletta's face. His eyes said
thank you in a way that words could not have expressed.
He reached up, wanting to touch the pistol, but Arletta
shook her head. Firearms were not for little boys. She
wished they were not for grown men, either.

Owen Palmer came back from Dodge City earlier
than expected. His money had melted much faster than he
had earned it. Fortunately, he had followed Jeff's instructions about buying the supplies before he began his cele-
bration, so the wagon was loaded with a variety of goods
including a garden plow, wire, and two crates of laying
hens as well as a couple of roosters. The Indians were
particularly intrigued by the poultry. Arletta supposed
they regarded them as a domestic version of the wild prairie chickens which abounded on the plains.

She enlisted the help of her husband and Kelly Booth
in building a crude enclosure that would serve as a chicken
roost and protect her new acquisitions from nocturnal
prowlers.

"I've got just about everything I need now. A milk
cow, chickens and a garden. Reminds me of the farm we
had in Ohio when I was little."

Jeff said, "But that garden is as much farmin' as we're
goin' to do. We don't want a bunch of grangers findin' out
this soil will grow crops. They'll plow up everything from
here to the Union Pacific railroad."

"Ain't nothin' wrong with farmin'. It's a good life."

"Only if your hands fit a plow handle. Mine don't."

The young milk cow had finally gentled down so that
Arletta could handle her and take over the milking chore,

which first one and then another of the cowboys had accepted only with highly vocal reluctance. Nigel Smithwick had built a special pen with a stall. The calf had to be kept away from its mother except at milking time, when it would be turned in for a minute or so to encourage the cow to let down her milk. Then it would be tied off until Arletta had obtained all she needed. The calf would be untied to finish what was left, keeping both it and the cow reasonably content.

Arletta was finishing the late afternoon milking when the Indian boy came to her, pointing southward and speaking excitedly. She saw a horsebacker approaching. She assumed he was one of the cowboys and paid little attention while she untied the calf to let it suck. Giving the rider a second look, she realized he was leading a packhorse. The boy's keen eyesight had told him this was not one of the hands.

"It's all right, Dogie. Nobody's goin' to hurt you."

The even tone of her voice seemed to ease his concern, though his mother quickly ducked back into her tepee and out of sight, taking the little girl with her. Carrying the bucket, Arletta walked out of the milking pen to the chuck wagon.

"Whoever he is, looks like it's up to me and you to greet him." She felt no apprehension. This would be the first company to show up since the TE outfit had come into the valley. He would be welcome.

Recognition did not come until he was twenty feet away. He gave the tepee a moment's keen attention, though the Indian woman was not in sight. Riding up almost to the wagon, he brought his hand to the brim of a badly worn hat. "How do, Mrs. Smithwick?"

Her mouth dropped open. "Vesper Freed!"

He acknowledged her apparent shock. "I didn't go to scare you. I know I must look like a bandit. It's been a mighty long trail." He looked around carefully. "Where's your menfolks?"

"Out workin' cattle, most of them."

From the site of a bunkhouse under construction

came the sound of an ax. Freed's hand dropped near the butt of the pistol he wore high on his hip. "Who's that?"

"Just Herman Wurtz. He's trimmin' logs."

Freed gave the half-finished bunkhouse a moment's cautious study before he dismounted, tying the two horses to a tree. He was gaunt and weary-looking. His whiskers had been allowed to grow into a dark and tangled beard. Only his eyes seemed still the same . . . and the commanding voice. His attention shifted to the boy, who had moved into Arletta's protective shadow. "Have you-all made treaty with the Comanches?"

"One family, is all. A woman and her kids."

"I'd never trust an Indian. They're worse than Mexicans. They're liable to sneak in some night and slit your throat. That boy looks old enough to use a knife."

She felt apprehension beginning to build. Freed wore a six-shooter high on his hip. That was not unusual in itself, for every man on the place carried a pistol whenever he rode out. Still, her mind raced as she pondered the significance of Freed's traveling such a distance. She was glad Kelly Booth was out in the canyon somewhere.

Or Freed might be here for Jeff.

"You lookin' for somebody in particular?"

"You shouldn't have to ask me that. Where are you hidin' Kelly Booth?"

"We're not hidin' anybody."

"I know he's with this outfit. Won't do no good to lie about it."

"Findin' him won't bring your boy back."

"But maybe I'll be able to sleep again. I ain't had a good night's rest since them Enríquez brothers got home and let it slip that Booth is here."

"You rode all this far just for revenge?"

"To settle with Kelly Booth I'd go halfway around the world. And it feels like I have. I must've ridden out a hundred canyons, huntin' this outfit."

"What about afterward? You think Jeff and the others'll just let you up and ride out of here?"

"I think they will, if I take somebody with me."

Arletta chilled. She sensed who Freed had in mind. "They'd never let you get away with it."

"You're a good woman, Mrs. Smithwick, and I wouldn't hurt you. I'd let you go soon's I knew I was in the clear."

"And where would that be? Fort Concho? San Antonio? I've got a baby here, Mr. Freed. I couldn't leave her. I *wouldn't* leave her, and nothin' you did could make me."

Freed's gaze returned to Dogie. "I got a hunch this outfit sets some store in that boy, else they wouldn't tolerate him stayin' here." He let the suggestion hang there like the rattles on a snake.

Dogie had ventured forward for a better look at the visitor, but he seemed to realize he was the subject of discussion. He pulled back behind Arletta again.

Freed beckoned to him. "I used to have a boy a lot like you. Come here, son, and talk to me."

Arletta placed a protective hand on Dogie's shoulder. "He doesn't understand you, Mr. Freed." She thought, *I don't either.* Freed's eyes looked strange to her, even a little crazy. He had drowned himself in grief and bitterness until reason had slipped away. "Before you touch this boy you're goin' to have to come past me."

Freed made no move toward them. "I shouldn't've needed him or you either one. Had a bunch of men with me when I started. But the trail got too long for them, and they started droppin' away. Time I left Fort Concho I was by myself."

"You should've gone back with them. You've got all that land down there, and a home. You'll find nothin' up here but misery, and like as not a grave."

"A grave can't be no colder than that empty house. And land . . . that land was for my boy as much as for me. Without him it don't amount to a bucket of cold spit."

Herman Wurtz stopped his chopping and, curious about the visitor, ventured toward the wagon. He carried his ax. Freed drew his pistol and motioned with it. "You! You come on up here." As Wurtz neared, Freed demanded, "Drop that ax and step away from it."

Wurtz gave Arletta a worried study before he complied. "This man, does he hurt you, Arletta?"

"No, but he might hurt *you* if you don't do as he says."

Wurtz eased the ax to the ground and moved protectively toward Arletta. His eyes asked the question.

Arletta said, "You've heard us talk about Vesper Freed. This here is him."

Freed squinted at Wurtz. "Dutchman, ain't you? Damned if the country ain't gettin' all settled up with foreigners."

"*Ausländer?* Yes, all of us are foreigners, and you also. All but this boy."

"Him and his don't count. They're more kin to the wolf than they are to people." Freed motioned with the pistol. "Set yourself down on the ground, Dutchman, and keep your hands where I can see them. We're liable to have to wait awhile."

From the corner of her eye Arletta caught a movement. She tried to keep her expression unchanged, hoping the men riding in from the range would come close enough to see what was happening and to act before Freed was able to counter them. But the sound of their horses alerted him.

His eyes lighted. "Dutchman, I want you to go out yonder and stop them. Tell Kelly Booth to come in by himself. If the rest of them stay out there I won't need to hurt Mrs. Smithwick or this boy."

Wurtz arose but stood his ground. "Let Arletta go to them. You need somebody to stay, *I* stay."

Freed shook his head. "For all I know they might be happy to get rid of you anyway. But they'll think more of Mrs. Smithwick." He made a circular motion with the barrel of the pistol. "Now git!"

Arletta nodded at Wurtz. "I'll be all right, Herman."

Wurtz struck out in a trot toward the riders, looking back a couple of times for reassurance about Arletta. The horsemen reined up, circling around as he reached them and pointed toward the wagon. Arletta could see that the ensuing discussion was brisk and probably heated. But soon Kelly Booth pulled away from the others and edged his horse forward in a walk.

The Indian boy looked up at Arletta with big, frightened eyes. Though he could not understand the reasons for the trouble, he understood well enough the threat in Vesper Freed's manner. He seemed to realize it was directed primarily toward his friend Booth. He tugged at Arletta's skirt and said something she could not understand. He pointed toward the chuckbox.

Freed shouted, "That's close enough, Booth. Get off of that horse."

Booth did not obey immediately. "Arletta, are you all right?"

"He won't hurt me, Kelly. Run!"

Freed pointed his pistol toward the boy. "But I might hurt *him*. Git down, I said!"

Booth complied, keeping his hand high enough above his pistol to indicate that he did not intend to reach for it.

Freed swung the six-shooter back toward him. "I already killed you once. Why ain't you dead?"

"You're better at killin' horses than killin' men." Booth signaled Arletta with his eyes to move farther from the line of fire. He was not going to stand helpless and let Freed kill him without making a try at defending himself. Arletta eased closer to the wagon, pulling the boy with her.

Freed said, "You and your people didn't give my Danny a chance, but I'm fixin' to give you one. See if you can reach that pistol before I kill you."

Booth crouched and jumped to one side as he whipped the pistol from its holster. He never got to fire it. Freed's shot sent Booth spinning half around, the pistol falling from his fingers.

The Indian boy darted to the chuckbox and reached behind the sourdough keg. Swift as a rabbit he was back, bringing Cap's old pistol, thrusting it into Arletta's hands.

Freed was aware of the movement and spun around, bringing the weapon to bear on her. But he hesitated, and in that moment she sighted down the barrel and fired. Recoil almost wrested the pistol from her hands. She managed to hold it and level it again, trying to sight through the burned powder's black smoke.

She realized she had not hit Freed, but she had distracted him. A rifle cracked. Freed's body snapped as old Santiago's had snapped in the river. Arletta saw her husband on one knee, weapon in his hands, smoke curling from its barrel.

Freed stared at Arletta in disbelief. He sank forward on one knee, then the other, and finally onto his side. He lay gasping, blood trickling from his mouth. He attempted to speak, but only a rasping sound came from his throat.

Arletta ran to Kelly Booth. He was on his knees, pressing both hands against his side and struggling for breath. The horsemen spurred toward the wagon, Nigel and Herman Wurtz running behind them in the dust.

Arletta knelt beside Booth, grasping his shoulders to stop his swaying. "How bad are you hit?"

Booth's breath came painfully hard. "Son of a bitch . . . he shot me in the side again."

Nigel dropped his rifle and tore at Booth's shirt, exposing the wound. Jeff gave Booth a glance, then trotted to Vesper Freed. Freed remained on his side, the fallen pistol inches from his trembling hand. Jeff tossed it out of reach and dropped to one knee. "For God's sake, Vesper . . . why couldn't you have left it alone?"

Freed's hand moved to the hole in his chest. Blood pumped between his fingers with each rapidly fading heartbeat. "Did I . . . did I get him?"

Jeff lied. "You got him."

A crooked smile came to the bewhiskered face. The Indian boy moved closer to Freed, drawn by curiosity. Freed tried to focus his gaze. "Son . . . Danny . . . come here to me."

The boy went no farther, but Freed did not know. The eyes remained open after their light was gone.

Jeff rolled his old adversary onto his back and closed his eyelids. His voice was bitter. "A hundred times I wished to see Vesper dead. Now he is, and all I can feel is sad. Damn it, there wasn't no sense in it comin' to this."

He rose and walked back to Kelly Booth.

Smithwick had the shirt pulled up so he could see the wound. "Cracked a rib or two, I should say. An inch or two farther in, and Kelly Booth would be but a pleasant memory."

Booth had regained most of his breath. "I never even got a shot at him."

Jeff declared, "You couldn't have hit him anyway. For a man who causes so damned much trouble, you're a pitiful shot."

Arletta still held Cap's six-shooter in both hands. Jeff reached for it, and she gladly gave it up. She could feel tears beginning to burn her eyes. In a minute, she knew, she would burst into crying.

Jeff put an arm around her shoulders. "You did what you had to do. You saved a man's life."

"And caused another to lose his."

Jeff shook his head. "That man died months ago, down in Mexico. The bullet that killed his son killed Vesper, too." He jerked his chin, beckoning Smithwick. "English, you'd better take Arletta to the dugout. Right now she needs you a lot more than Kelly does."

Leaning heavily on Smithwick, Kelly Booth told her, "He'd've killed me if you and English hadn't done what you done. I thank you, Arletta."

"Maybe this just squares us up. Me and Nigel, we've owed you ever since you saved him from that stampede."

She wondered later about the strange look that came into Jeff's eyes.

TWENTY-SEVEN

Crow Feather sat on the rickety canvas cot, which had one leg shorter than the rest, and stared dejectedly at the stone wall of the guardhouse. The old wound in his side ached, and he suspected the soldiers had rebroken his ribs—cracked them, anyway—the last time he had tried to escape. It was by no means his first attempt, or even the second or third. This time he had managed to grab a horse tied just outside the building and had gotten as far as the perimeter of the post before they had ridden him down and knocked him from the saddle with the butt of a rifle.

He blamed himself, mostly. He had grabbed the nearest horse he saw after flattening the guard who came to bring him his dinner. He did not take into account that the horse had already been ridden for half a day and was tired. And he had found the soldier saddle more hindrance than help, its iron stirrups beating against his bare shins as he urged the horse to run faster. Once he was on the ground the soldiers had punished him more than was necessary to bring him into submission. He was convinced they were trying to break one of his legs so he could not run again. Had one of their chiefs not followed the chase and ordered them to stop, they might have killed him.

He supposed they were tired of his constant efforts to break out.

He heard the iron door groan on its hinges and

looked up at the soldier chief who seemed to be in charge of the guardhouse. He had a man with him. The man was dressed like a civilian for the most part, though he wore soldier boots and blue trousers. The darkness of his face told Crow Feather he was probably a Mexican.

Lieutenant John Gladwell said, "This is the man. He is one of the most unrepentant Indians we have ever had in here. Perhaps you can find out what it is that makes him keep trying to break out when he must know by now that it is useless."

The dark-skinned man studied Crow Feather for a minute. When he spoke, Crow Feather was surprised to hear him talking in the People's tongue.

"My name is Terrazas. When I was a boy, some of your warriors took me prisoner in Mexico. I lived for a while with the Quahadies until I was sold to some Comanchero traders. The lieutenant has brought me here to try to help you."

He was the first man except for other Comanches that Crow Feather had been able to understand since he had been captured. Even if some of the pronunciation was wrong, typical of captives, Crow Feather felt uplifted by hearing the words.

"I am known as Crow Feather. I am a Quahadie."

"The soldier chief is called Gladwell. He is a good man, even though he is white. He truly wants to help you."

"No one can help me, unless they set me free."

"They are afraid to set you free. They are afraid you will leave the reservation."

"I *would*. That is why I keep trying to escape."

"But it is hopeless. Your people are all here now. The few who remain out are being hunted like wolves and captured or killed. Soon there will be none left except on the reservation. There is nothing out there for you anymore."

"My family is still out there."

The Mexican paused, then spoke to the soldier chief in the language the white men used. The chief nodded and said some words to the Mexican.

Terrazas reverted to the Comanche tongue. "The soldier chief says he had begun to suspect it was such a thing. But it is possible your family is already somewhere on the reservation."

Crow Feather was sure they were not. Goes His Own Way had discovered that Crow Feather was imprisoned and had come to see him. He had searched diligently among the People but had not found anyone who knew of White Deer and the children.

Crow Feather explained that. "They are still where I left them. Or they are with the spirits. I must go and find them, or find where they have died."

The Mexican spoke again to the soldier chief, and the soldier chief talked to him at some length. The lieutenant left. Terrazas sat down in a chair and pulled an odd-looking white-man pipe from his pocket. He filled it with tobacco and lighted it with one of the strange fire sticks Crow Feather had seen the soldiers use. There were many marvels in the white man's world.

The smoke smelled good. The Mexican noted that Crow Feather liked the aroma and offered him the pipe. Crow Feather took much pleasure from the man's generosity.

The lieutenant returned in a few minutes with a large piece of paper that had some sort of drawings on it. The Mexican explained that this was a map.

"If you can show us where you left your family, we can find them and bring them here to you."

Crow Feather tried, but he made little sense of the ink marks. There were lines which he took to be rivers and canyons, but it was impossible to find anything which would identify the specific canyon he sought. Even when the lieutenant showed him how much of the map signified a day's travel, he could not differentiate. There were too many lines, too many scratchings.

He could see exasperation in the soldier chief's face and decided the man could do nothing to help him. He had no choice but to continue trying to get away. Sooner

or later, with the help of the bear spirit, he would manage.
Or he would die.

The lieutenant talked briefly with the Mexican, then
walked away. Terrazas said, "The soldier chief goes to talk
to those who are chiefs above him. He does not know if
they will allow him to do more to help you."

Crow Feather did not fully understand. The People
followed a chief by their own choice. If ever they decided
the chief was wrong, or they simply preferred to go another way, they went as they chose. A man of the People
could not be forced to do something against his will, nor
was he prohibited from doing something of his own
choosing, short of murdering his own kind. That one
white man could command another and impose punishment was a notion alien to his experience.

He lay back upon the cot after the Mexican left and
stared up at the ceiling. He had whiled away many days
staring at its patterns and those of the walls, imagining the
shapes of horses, of buffalo, of warriors. Across the ceiling
he had often envisioned a great battle in which the People
were always the victors, unlike the fight at the buffalo
hunters' wagon village. In his imaginary battles the spirits
were always favorable. The bear spirit always smiled.

Now and again another being intruded on his imagin-
ings, unbidden, ambiguous. She was the white-woman
spirit, the one with the long red hair. He could not decide
whether she was benevolent or malicious, in league with
the bear spirit or against it.

The early morning sun was barely clear of the eastern
sky when the Mexican returned, the soldier chief two steps
behind him. Terrazas said, "The lieutenant wants to talk
to you. He will make good talk. If I were you, I would
listen."

"I hear."

"He has talked to those who are chiefs above him.
They have much doubt but have said he may do this thing
if he can make a treaty with you."

"What is this treaty?"

"We will take you to seek your family if you will

promise that you will not break away, that you will return with us whether we find your family or not. That you will not try again to escape but will stay where your people stay."

Crow Feather swallowed hard. This was not a thing he would have expected from the soldier chief. He was a man of heart, even if he was white. "Have you still the pipe? We will smoke and make this treaty."

The horse they gave him to ride had a rough gait which aggravated the ache in his ribs, but that was a small matter against the importance of the mission. Though he was accompanied by twice four pony soldiers as well as the soldier chief and the Mexican, Crow Feather felt liberated. The open sky had never seemed bluer, the trees and grass greener, the air fresher, after such a long time within the dreary walls of the guardhouse. Leaving Fort Sill, they traveled toward the place where the sun would set. He was not sure how long the trip would require . . . three days, perhaps four. It was different going back on a horse. He had come here on foot, with a rough rope searing his neck like a heated iron.

The Mexican informed him that though it was not usual to take Comanches out to find other Comanches, it was not unknown. Those who had been on the reservation for a while could testify to the others that life there was less terrible than they might have heard. The government's requirements were confining and, to a people used to total freedom, sometimes galling. But in the main the soldier chiefs and the Quaker holy man tried to keep most of their promises. There were ration days, beef days. There were times of hunger, but there had been times of hunger in the earlier days, too, when the buffalo were not to be found.

It was not a life the People would have chosen, the Mexican said, but it was better than dying, and in the final analysis that was the choice: the reservation or death.

"The soldier chief says to tell you that your family will have a lodge, and there will be food. And when your children are big enough they will go to the white man's school and learn to follow the white man's road."

"The white man's road is not my road."

"It is the only road that is open. The old ways are gone. They were not good ways all the time. Because of the old ways, my mother and father were killed by Quahadie warriors and I was made a prisoner. I was starved and beaten and forced to do hard labor. I was then what you are now, a captive. For me, those were not good ways."

Crow Feather had never spent time trying to see through another man's eyes. He had seen many captives, mostly women and children, in various camps of the People. He had given little thought to their feelings, any more than he gave much thought to the feelings of the camp dogs. He had regarded those not of the People to be something less than true human beings.

Now he was in their place, and his old thoughts were being challenged.

Through the guardhouse window he had watched the comings and goings of the soldiers and of white people who did not wear the soldier clothes. He had not realized before that there were so many. There were too many for the People to defeat. Even if each warrior killed ten of the *teibos*, there would still be so many that the ones killed would not be missed.

He had to give weight to what Terrazas said. The old roads had been closed. Only the white man's road was left. Crow Feather would never travel comfortably on that road; he was too old to change so much. But Squirrel and the other young ones would grow up knowing that road. It would seem less strange to them. Losing the traditional ways would not seem so sad to the young because they did not know them as the older ones did. The loss would not scar their souls so deeply.

The fourth day, he knew they were nearing the canyon. He recognized the place where the soldiers had come together after they had captured him, throwing him among other prisoners. He told Terrazas, who relayed the information to the lieutenant.

They came around the head of the canyon, and he pointed them southward along its rim until they came to the game trail that led down to the floor. Descending, he expected to see buffalo, but he was disappointed. He saw other animals in their place . . . white man's cattle, like those he had often seen while raiding in the *tejano* settlements.

The lieutenant appeared as disoriented as Crow Feather felt. "Cattle? There should be no cattle within two hundred miles."

They moved down the switchback trail in single file, three soldiers ahead of Crow Feather, the rest following as if they expected him to make a break for freedom down the steep side of the canyon. At the foot of the trail Crow Feather pointed southward. The men rode in silence, looking in disbelief at the long-horned cattle which grazed along the narrow part of the canyon floor.

Crow Feather's pulse began to race as they approached the place where he had left his family encamped. He told Terrazas it was just ahead. He could not wait. He put the horse into a long trot, then a lope. He knew the soldier chief would not approve, but he could not help himself. Instead of trying to stop him, the soldiers spurred to stay up. He thought it likely they were eager to finish so they could turn back to the comforts of the fort.

Passing the pool of water below the spring, he shouted White Deer's name, and Squirrel's. No answer came. He drew rein at the edge of the trees where the small tepee had been erected. The tepee was gone. The place was deserted.

He turned in dismay to Terrazas. "This is the place, but they are not here."

Terrazas repeated in English. Crow Feather saw doubt in the soldier chief's face. Probably he thought the whole trip had been a hoax, that Crow Feather had simply hoped to escape somewhere along the way.

Crow Feather pointed out to Terrazas where the tepee

had stood. The ground was still packed. A rock-ringed fire pit harbored cold gray ashes and blackened remnants of firewood. Bones and pieces of animal hide were scattered some distance from the campsite. "They were here," Crow Feather insisted.

The lieutenant showed signs that he believed. Then one of the soldiers shouted from near the small water hole. "Lieutenant, here's some wagon tracks."

Crow Feather did not understand the words, but he understood the import of the parallel lines solidified in dried mud. He read the unspoken thought in Terrazas' eyes: *they have hauled your family away.*

The question was, were they dead, or were they alive?

The lieutenant said, "Where there are cattle, there must be people. Let's follow this valley south and see where it leads us."

Terrazas translated for Crow Feather, who eagerly nodded agreement. For him there was no longer any thought of escape, or thought for his own future. All that mattered was finding his family, or finding out what had happened to them.

He was the first to observe the wagon camp beneath the tall cottonwood trees. He pointed it out to Terrazas, who squinted, trying to see. Terrazas spoke to the soldier chief.

The lieutenant ordered, "Close up, men, and be ready. We don't know what manner of men we may find here. This far from civilization, it could be a den of outlaws."

Crow Feather saw the wagon. Wind tugged at a long skirt, telling him a woman stood there. He could not see her clearly. Then he saw the tepee beneath the trees, and his heart leaped. He shouted for joy and pushed the horse into a run.

The lieutenant was caught by surprise and drew his pistol, but Terrazas stopped him as Crow Feather rushed by.

A boy stepped out from behind the wagon, paused for

only a moment, then came running. *"Powva!"* he cried. *"Powva!"*

Crow Feather jumped from the horse's back before the animal came to a full stop. He swept the boy into his arms and came near crushing him.

The woman shouted, and White Deer came out of the tepee with the small girl. They too came running, and Crow Feather opened his arms to receive them.

He turned, after a minute, to see the white woman. She was smiling, and tears glistened on her cheeks.

He saw that the touch of the late afternoon sun lent a sheen of red to her hair.

Jeff Layne had not talked much since the death of Vesper Freed. He supervised the finishing of a dugout bunkhouse, large enough to shelter the men during the coming winter, and a third dugout adjacent to it where Arletta could cook and feed the crew. He assured her that if she could get by for the time being, cooking in the fireplace and on the stone hearth, he would see that they freighted in an iron cook stove at the first opportunity.

Most of the time he drew inward, absorbed in his own thoughts.

Kelly Booth decided to leave after his ribs had knitted. "It's not the same between me and Jeff anymore. I know he puts part of the blame on me for the feud gettin' so far out of hand."

Arletta said, "We'll miss you."

"No you won't. You've got English, and you've got that little girl. By the time I'm three days gone you'll forget you ever knowed me."

"Where'll you go?"

"Up to Dodge City, maybe. Anywhere but Wichita. That judge has probably got a long memory."

Arletta hugged him. "You're wrong about one thing. We won't forget you."

She saw sadness in Jeff's eyes when Booth rode off to the north, toward the game trail that led up onto the top. But she saw relief there, too.

Jeff said, "You've got to like him. But you've always got to be a little afraid too, because you never know what he's fixin' to do next. He brings trouble to everybody around him."

Nigel Smithwick said, "It appears he has decided to go north to Dodge City. There is no telling what difficulty he may fall into there."

Jeff shrugged. "Whatever it is, he'll get out of it all right. Like he said, he's harder to kill than a stray cat." He surveyed the new construction they had done. "Looks like we're pretty well fixed to go into the winter. Reckon you folks can do without me for a few weeks?"

Arletta felt a glow. She had sensed this coming on. "San Antonio?"

"I've got to let Eva know what happened to Vesper. She's bound to be wonderin'."

Watching Jeff disappear southward, toward the wide part of the canyon, Arletta told her husband, "We'd better start buildin' another dugout. I'll bet you he don't come back alone."

"*Doesn't,*" he corrected her. "A dugout will be a terrible letdown after that big house she had before."

"I've been in that house. It was cold. A dugout is snug and warm."

They put their arms around one another and walked toward their home.

ABOUT THE AUTHOR

ELMER KELTON was raised on a West Texas ranch and spent his formative years among cowboys and old-timers. The author of more than thirty novels, Mr. Kelton won his sixth Spur Award from the Western Writers of America in 1994 for *The Far Canyon*. He has won four Western Heritage Awards from the National Cowboy Hall of Fame, the Levi Strauss Golden Saddleman Award for lifetime achievement in Western literature, as well as honors from the Texas Institute of Letters and the Western Literature Association. Mr. Kelton lives in San Angelo, Texas.